Praise for

Tu-Shonda L. Whitaker,

Essence bestselling author of *Game Over*

"All hail to the Queen of urban fiction writing. If you are an author in the game you better watch your back because Tu-Shonda Whitaker has arrived on the scene!"
—KEISHA ERVIN, bestselling author of *Me and My Boyfriend*

Praise for

Flip Side of the Game

"A riveting story that captures your attention from the very first page!"   —DANITA CARTER, bestselling author of *Success Is the Best Revenge* and *Revenge Is Best Served Cold*

"Tu-Shonda L. Whitaker stands and delivers with this debut novel. *Flip Side of the Game* is filled with gut-wrenching emotions, drama, and authentic conflict. Every woman of color in America should read this book. I know 95 percent of them can relate to Vera Wright-Turner."
—DANIELLE SANTIAGO, *Essence* bestselling author of *Little Ghetto Girl: A Harlem Story*

"Urban literature with a romantic twist . . . raw and uncensored."   —SHELIA M. GOSS, bestselling author of *Roses Are Thorns, Violets Are True* and *My Invisible Husband*

Also by Tu-Shonda L. Whitaker

Flip Side of the Game

Game Over

Cream
(contributor)

Kiss the Year Goodbye
(contributor)

THE

EX

A NOVEL

FACTOR

Tu-Shonda L. Whitaker

One World Ballantine Books New York

The Ex Factor is a work of fiction. Names, characters, places, and incidents are the products of the author's imagination or are used fictitiously. Any resemblance to actual events, locales, or persons, living or dead, is entirely coincidental.

A One World Books Trade Paperback Original

Published in the United States by One World Books,
an imprint of The Random House Publishing Group, a division
of Random House, Inc., New York.

ONE WORLD is a registered trademark
and the One World colophon is a trademark
of Random House, Inc.
READER'S CIRCLE and colophon are
trademarks of Random House, Inc.

LIBRARY OF CONGRESS CATALOGING-IN-PUBLICATION DATA
Whitaker, Tu-Shonda L.
The ex-factor : a novel / by Tu-Shonda Whitaker.
p. cm.
ISBN 978-0-345-48666-0
1. Sisters—Fiction. 2. African American women—Fiction.
3. Domestic fiction. I. Title.

PS3623.H563E9 2007
813'.54—dc22
2006048267

Printed in the United States of America

www.oneworldbooks.net

2   4   6   8   9   7   5   3   1

Book design by Laurie Jewell

To my daughters Taylor and Sydney,

I pray to teach you what dreams are made of!

•   •   •

Acknowledgments

In my Father's house there are many mansions,
if it were not so I would've told you. . . .

—ST. JOHN 12:2

My Father God, my solid rock on which I stand, I come before You as humbly as I know how, thanking You for Your grace, Your mercy, and for Your Son, Jesus Christ, who saw to it that I would have life and have it more abundantly.

To my husband, Kevin, and my children Taylor and Sydney, no words could ever describe the joy you bring me. I thank you for your love and neverending support.

To my mother and father, Barbara and Melvin, thank you for always being in my corner and for always believing that even my wildest dreams would come true.

To my family in America and Trinidad, who are there to support me no matter what, I couldn't ask for a better family. And to my aunties, who ask everyone they meet, "Did you read my niece's book?"

To my dear friends, who laugh at my corny jokes, listen to me read page after page, and dare me to dream bigger, thank you for your love, support, and for always keeping it real.

To Kenya Williams—no matter how long we're apart, when we have an opportunity to talk, I am reminded of what a true friend is.

To Keisha Ervin and Danielle Santiago, my little sisters, I want soooo much for the two of you, because I *know* that you are able to capture the world! Forever be blessed!

To my dear friend, Valerie Hall-Moore. Why'd you move to Atlanta? Dang, Val, Jersey just isn't the same. I miss you!

To Nakea Murry, my homegurl! Girlfriend, nobody makes me laugh more than you. You are such an inspiration to me. Thank you for always believing that I could write anything, even when I had my doubts.

To Lisa Scofield-Ham, thanks so much for your love and support and thanks even more for being my friend.

To Treasure E. Blue, K'wan, and K. Elliot, you are three of the baddest authors in the game!

To Vickie Stringer, you are one in a million!

To Melody Guy, what a wonderful editor you are. I can't thank you enough for believing in my writing. The opportunities you have presented me with are endless, and I hope to make you proud.

Danielle Durkin, thanks for assisting with this project, and I look forward to working with you again.

To Selena James, working with you was such a treat that I had to thank you again. Be Blessed.

To my church family and co-workers, thanks for all the love and support.

To the fans, readers, bookstores, book clubs, and message boards, your support is endless and I thank you so much for the e-mails and the words of encouragement. I will forever be grateful for people like you. I encourage you to e-mail me at info@tushonda.com. I would love to know what you think of *The Ex Factor*.

And to all of those who nodded their heads and understood when Lauryn Hill said, "When I try to walk away you do your best to make me stay . . . this is crazy . . . ," I wrote this novel for you.

Be blessed and enjoy!

THE

EX

FACTOR

Since arithmetic
is the Universal language
then you should understand
that one plus one
has recently begun
to equal two . . .

And that I am no longer
diggin' being multiplied by you
simply to be equivalent
to just one . . .

And when I told you about
the light bill
and the phone bill
and the rent that was due
you had *me* take it to the power of three . . .

And when it seemed that the Universal language
had begun to vibe wit' you
you became a wiz at this mathematical quiz
and suggested that we remove your fraction by way
of an unnatural subtraction

And I was feeling that
so I agreed
'cause there was no way I wanted you and me . . .
to equal three . . .

And when you asked me to add
just one more chance to your simple-ass list of things to do
I explained to you that one plus one
now equaled two
and that you really needed to understand
that I had subtracted me from you
in order to get two . . .

And I had to explain that there was no rhythmatic flow
and that you and me could never be
and to consider me to be
like one of those Colored Girls
who has had enuf of your rainbow . . .

And to know that I will not be added to you,
or vibe'n wit' you,
'cause I'm not feel'n you
and that's why I'm speak'n to you
in this Universal language
for you to see
that the soulmatic equation
that used to be
you and me
is now a constant flow . . . of zero.

{ Imani }

"I'MA SLICE HIS fuckin' throat," Imani hissed as she watched the pregnant Shante board the prison's shuttle bus in front of her.

For two years Imani had been asking Walik if he was still fucking with Shante and he swore to her that he wasn't. He said that Shante had the type of pussy a niggah just wanted to hit it and quit it—nothing more than that. He swore on their son, Jamal, and on every block he had locked in the street that Shante was no longer a factor.

"On some real shit," Walik constantly assured Imani, "fuck that dusty bitch. She's just a used-up jump-off! Why you even sweatin' that shit? You know she hate you 'cause she ain't you. On the real, she like a stray dog around here, any niggah that feed her can keep her!"

"Whatever."

"Come on, Imani, I made you, why would I play you?"

"Then why is she calling me, Walik?" Imani would ask.

"I don't know, her ass is crazy."

"Then you better handle her crazy ass." Imani would hand him the phone. "Call and check that bitch!"

Walik would take the phone and cuss Shante out, time and time again. And that was always enough to psych Imani up as if nothing had ever happened, returning their relationship to full-pledge "wifey and my boo" mode . . . but not this time. Imani was convinced that forgiveness was a big piece of shit found underneath a CURB YOUR DOG street sign.

Imani reached for her six-year-old son's hand as he leaned against her thigh and began to fall asleep. "And to think I spent my last dime and got my wig tightened 'cause I was comin' to visit this niggah." Imani mumbled as low as she could, trying her best to keep her bottom lip from trembling. She wanted to cry, but instead she tucked in her bottom lip and began to rock slightly from side to side. "I ain't got on no drawls underneath this skirt and shit. My ass all hangin' out. I gave my son a double dose of nighttime Tylenol so this niggah could get some visiting-hall pussy in peace, and I won't have to stop bucking the dick to say, *Turn around, Jamal.*" She pushed her burgundy-tipped wavy micro braids behind her ears and turned to board the rickety old prison bus.

Stepping onto the platform, she took a deep breath. Already the stale air and the condemned look of the bus had started to get to her. The faded, cracked leather seats, the smells of fried chicken, baby formula, and hair products, and the rough feel of octagon-shaped wire window bars that usually left imprints on Jamal's cheeks when he pressed his face against them were enough to make her feel as if she had boarded the bus to Oz.

For a moment she thought about turning around and going home, but the more she stared at Shante, the more determined she was to see Walik's face, so she could look at him and say, *See why I ain't fuckin' wit' yo' ass?*

Imani sucked on the inside of her cheek as her eyes started to burn. *Sorry, triflin' no-good motherfucker! I swear to God,* she thought, *all this hold-a-niggah-down-ride-or-the-fuck-die-shit is a wrap. No more paying for your collect-call promises, no more splitting my welfare check with your commissary account, and no more playing in my pussy while you listen to me nut over the phone. Fuck you! What's good for the thug is better for the thugette. If you can get yo' cleanup woman on then it's time for the maintenance man to get in check. Besides,* she started sucking on her bottom lip, *I'm tired of yo' eight and a half inches of overrated, cheating-ass dick!*

Imani found a seat in the third row, directly across from Shante. *I'ma kill him,* she thought, trying not to focus on the sticky foam rising through the cracked leather seat. Instead, while Jamal drifted back to sleep, she crossed her legs and leaned her head back. She turned her neck to the right, moved her eyes up and down, curled her lips, and cleared her throat loudly.

Shante looked up and spotted Imani. A snide grin spread across her face. Shante rubbed her nine-month-pregnant belly. "When your son wakes up," she spat at Imani, "ask him if he wants a li'l brother or sister."

Imani lifted her head. "Unless you want me to crack your shit open, you'll keep any mention of my son outta ya mouth."

"Oh, what, *my stepson* was created from the scraps of a golden nut? Paleeze, humph, maybe the next time you'll spend less time watching your son so nobody else'll have to marry ya man." She flashed her left hand, showing off a thin gold band with a matching solitaire. "Get a good look, 'cause it's blingin'!"

A few of the other women who were settled on the bus started to hiss and buzz. They knew something was about to jump off. "Don't get nothing started," yelled one of the passengers. "Hurry up and settle that shit, please. 'Cause I'ma go off if I lose some time from my visit."

For a split second Imani felt as if the pit of her stomach had died; she blinked and somehow it came back alive. "You fat-ass, rotten-pussy bitch! Shrek wouldn't even marry yo' crazy-lookin' wack ass, let alone Walik. Why don't you try divorcing your second baby daddy first? Or do you have to remember who he is? Oh, that's right," she snapped her fingers and twisted her neck, "you were a dyke back then! Stupid ass, you look like a walkin' STD talkin' about somebody wanna marry you and live with yo' crab-infested-ringworm-leaky-eye kids! I don't even know why you're pregnant again, don't them three baboons you already got prove you can't do nothin' with retarded-ass nuts?"

"What you say?" Shante couldn't believe that Imani was taking it there. "You talkin' about *my kids*?"

"Yeah, and what?" Imani looked Shante up and down, and spat out as if she were making a mix tape, "Niggah-niggah ask about me. I cusses 'em all out, from eight to eighty, if they try to play me crazy! Trust and believe you don't want it with me, you tired-ass dusty bitch! Fuckin' used-up jump-off. For real, for real, you like a stray dog around here, any niggah that feed you can keep you. Do ya'self a favor: clean up ya house and get ya kids' beds off the floor!" Imani shot Shante the gas face. She swallowed hard while trying to stop the aching tears sneaking up in the back of her throat. "Better learn to play your position, bitch!"

"Dusty bitch? A stray dog? Get my kids' beds off the floor?" Shante stood up. "You dumb-ass trick. Don't you see me here, pregnant as hell by Walik? The niggah been locked up for *two years*. What you think we've been doing, holding hands? You're the stupid ass! You gon' call me a *used-up jump-off*?" Shante squinted tight. "As a matter of fact this isn't even your day. Aren't you assigned to *Saturdays*? Today is uhmm, *Sunday*? Seems to me that you better play yo' position, *bitch*!"

Before Shante could blink Imani walked over and caught her in the face with a mean left hook. Instantly her lower lip popped open and blood spat out. By the time the guards, who were helping the last of the women onto the bus, looked toward the fight, they saw Shante reaching for Imani's throat. Imani balled up her fist and pounded Shante in the head, over and over again. Short of punching her in the stomach, Imani took her foot and kicked Shante in the knee, causing her to fall forward. Before she hit the floor, Imani yanked Shante's shoulder-length hair, twirled it around her fist, and pulled it so hard that the whiteness of Shante's hair follicles was rising from the root. It took three male guards and a bottle of pepper spray to break them up. As Imani wiped her eyes, trying to free herself of the stinging spray, she felt an officer grab both of her arms, placing them behind her back. "You're under arrest." Another guard wiped her eyes with a cold compress. "You have the right to remain silent. Anything you say can and will be used against you . . ." Once Imani's eyes were clear she saw the police had boarded the bus and were arresting her and Shante. Shante was hollering and screaming, desperately trying to reach for Imani. But Imani stood there, shooting her a look that said *Do it, bitch, I dare you.* Imani didn't care that Shante was five foot three and she was five foot seven. Or that Shante was high yellow and would wear the evidence of a slap for a week. Fuck the dumb shit, if Shante could give it, Shante could get it.

"Do you have someone that can pick up your son?" the officer asked Imani. She shook her head wildly, feeling as if she were waking up from a trance. Her heart started racing and her palms began to sweat. "Oh my God!" she cried, "My baby! My baby." She looked toward the seat where Jamal was waking up and rubbing his eyes. "I need to call my sister." Tears raced down Imani's cheeks and slid toward her neck. "She ain't gon' believe this shit."

"**EVERY FUCKIN' TIME** I turn around he's gone! Where the hell is he?" Celeste screamed at the top of her lungs while licking the salty tears that ran from her eyes and slid into the corners of her mouth. "You ain't workin' that much. Humph as much as you liked your big dick sucked. Believe me, I know you ain't the type to not be getting fucked . . . so tell me, who is she?" Celeste continued to cry hysterically as she slammed her fingers against the telephone pad, attempting to break the voice-mail code on her husband, Sharief's, cell phone. "So when did it start, huh, Sharief, when did you start to cheat? What, my pussy wasn't tight enough? What, I didn't fuck you long enough? In case you haven't noticed, I stay occupied with three kids every day, I'm tired when you come home . . . I'm not in the mood for a freak session. What the hell is wrong with missionary position? I still wanna be touched, Sharief, I wanna make love to my husband, but instead you fuckin' some bitch in the street . . . and when I find her, I'ma kill her!" Finally, Celeste broke the code: "Bingo." She grabbed a pen and wrote his code down. "Zero . . . four . . . one . . . one . . ." Celeste chuckled as she read the numbers out loud. "Stupid ass! How the hell can you hide the bitch you cheating with so well, but you're dumb enough to have oh-four-one-one as your code. Niggahs, I swear."

Celeste began to listen attentively as the message started to play . . . *"Hey Sharief, this is Monica. I'm whispering because I'm in Negrils and Chauncey is hinting at popping the question. Don't worry, though, I'll be saying no. Anyway call me. Oh, be sure you remind Celeste to start early with cooking the food for the party, I couldn't reach her."* Monica giggled. *"Another thing, if you can tell me what UTFO stands for then I'll give you the other ticket for the Audio Two, MC Lyte, and EPMD concert. Peace out . . . wit' yo' big-ass head . . . sucker punk. Okay, let me call Listra and tell her this shit. She is going to laugh."* Is it me, Celeste thought, *or was my sister just a little too damn playful?*

Celeste hung up, lit a cigarette, and started pacing the floor. *I'm buggin'.* She placed the phone back on the base as the cigarette hung from the corner of her mouth. "All of these years I've put into you, Sharief." She folded one arm under her breasts and took a drag with the other. "What else could I have done besides stand on my head and suck ya dick backward? Some kinda way you gon' have to explain this shit to me, motherfucker! Tell me, do you ever think about someone else besides yourself? What about the kids, Sharief? Kayla, Kai, and Kori. They need you, we need you." Tears were flooding Celeste's face as she continued to take neurotic puffs off her cigarette. "You're the only daddy Kayla knows. And yes, it was my idea that we play pretend. But you seemed to love her so much and you swore to me that it didn't bother you when she started calling you daddy. In fact you said you liked the sound of it. So I trusted you, because you promised to be the first daddy I knew that wouldn't leave . . . and I believed you . . . and me believing you somehow meant you were perfect. Which is why when the doctor said I had high blood pressure I still took a chance and became pregnant with your child. Because you wanted a son named Jeremiah, after your grandfather. You were so proud when you thought we were having a boy. You had it all planned out, his first haircut, his first football game, your first father-and-son talk. It was a perfect plan until I found out you were the dog." Celeste sucked the butt of her cigarette and pointed to her chest. "But what I'm trying to figure out is when you changed. I'm not sure." She ran her hand across her chin. "But I think it may have been when the little boy you wanted turned out to be twin girls. But then again, maybe it was when we moved to Jersey . . . and you wanted to stay in Brooklyn . . . Damn I can't remember . . ." Celeste took a drag and paced from one end of the bedroom to the next. "But what I do remember is putting up with the smell of your stankin'-ass feet. And I remember how you would burp and never say excuse me. Oh, and I remember how you would take a shit and leave the door cracked. And I remember forcing myself to listen to that goddamn reggae music and that fuckin' DJ Dahved Levy and his nerve-wrecking 'Rocking you—rocking you—rocking you . . .' I wanted so bad to say, *Shut . . . the . . . fuck up,* but I didn't . . . I listened.

"My mother always said that a woman had to be her man's whore, confidante, and a li'l bit of his mother all rolled into one. But didn't I cook, Sharief? Didn't I wash your clothes? I never denied you pussy, I just didn't want to be twisted around like a contortionist . . . and I didn't want yo' dick in my ass, but that was my choice. But I did everything else. I thought moving away from Brooklyn would bring us closer together . . . ha! Wasn't that a joke?" Celeste mashed the cigarette butt in the ashtray and nervously lit up another one. Taking a pull, she sobbed, "All I'm saying is for you to give me back my shit. And I don't mean the material things, you can keep that. Just give me back what I like to do before I met you. Give me back my independence. Give me back my moves and my grooves. Please un-ass the Anita Baker song I like to sing, my wide smile, the switch in my voluptuous hips, and my nonsaggy tits. It's quite simple, just give me back my shit. Please, take my soul off the abortion table. I'll proudly go back to being a statistic: a black, struggling single mother with a triflin' baby daddy."

"Mommy! Mommmmyyyyy!" Celeste's ranting was interrupted by the older twin, Kai, yelling her name. *Goddamn,* she thought, *I can't get my misery on for five minutes.* She wiped her eyes and mashed her cigarette in the ashtray. "What is it, Kai?"

"I sleep with you?"

"It's *can* I sleep with you—"

"Why come? You scared, Mommy?" Kai asked, misunderstanding her mother's statement.

Celeste wanted to say yes she was scared but she knew four-year-old Kai would never understand. "Kai, it's not *why come,* it's *how come,* and no I'm not scared—and no you can't sleep with me."

"Peeeesssse."

"I said no." Celeste sucked her teeth. "Now go back to sleep!"

Kai started screaming and stormed back into her room. "Don't make me beat your ass up in here, now shut up!" Celeste really wanted to wring Kai's neck, but instead she took a quick shower, rubbed her body down with Victoria's Secret Body Butter, and threw on a lace camisole and matching bottom. She looked at herself in the mirror and pinched her full cheeks. She hated that her face was covered in freckles, mainly because she felt they killed the sparkle in her hazel eyes.

Celeste never felt beautiful but you would never know. She rocked the best gear, always seemed to have money, and most of the time, even on a Sunday morning, she was fly. She wore makeup to cover her freckles, clothes that complemented her big breasts and shapely thighs. After that she kept it movin'. Hell, wouldn't you?

Anything else would be too time consuming, and you're way too anxious to nurture the pain, you just want it to go away. So you float through life as if you are the ultimate Ms. It, secretly living from one Friday to the next. But you're fly and the gear you're draped in cost more than the amount of money in your bank account . . . But you were never taught any other way.

By the time you were seventeen, you were busting at the seams for some dick. So you started checking for niggahs and one thing about your mother is that she taught you how to woo a man and run his pockets. "Don't be a gold digger," she always said, "but don't be fuckin' with no broke niggah."

Never once did she go over her household budget or tell you how much money she made. Never once did she teach you about having a bank account or maintaining good credit.

Therefore, you went out into the world ill prepared. By the time you were eighteen you moved on your own, but you never knew what was more important: paying rent or buying clothes; needless to say, with priorities that fucked up, the rent killed you. Your mother tried to talk you into claiming three of your cousin's six kids so you could get Section 8, but you were embarrassed and wanted nothing more to do with a system where the caseworker was nasty and thought she was better than you.

So you were determined to do what you had to do, not to mention your new boo consistently fucked the shit out of you. Hell, the dick was so good that it was almost worth being broke. He would've helped out financially but he was on the come-up, trying to get his legal hustle on . . . and you understood . . . until late one night your phone rang and there was a chick on the other end screaming, "Tell this bitch something, tell her!"

"Who is this?" you yelled, with your heart racing and chest heaving. You felt empty because a part of you died the moment you heard your new boo in the background say, "Hang up the fuckin' phone." You were infuriated, you were hurt, you felt stoned and you didn't know what to do, so you cried . . . and you cried. Until he came back . . . a week later . . . and apologized with his tongue and his dick hitting all the right places. And by the time he'd fucked his way back in, he forced you to literally come to the conclusion that he lied because he loved you.

Life goes on until you find out about another chick he's cheating on you with but now you're six months' pregnant and he starts to disappear for weeks on in. Rent is more than late; it's not being paid. And new boo's dick is not hitting it anymore, no pun intended, not to mention that most of your meals are eaten at your mother's house. You can't stand this life because you swore you would never be nothing like your mother but nevertheless you're off to the same start.

You have the baby. It's a girl and he never comes to the hospital to see either one of you, but you give the baby his last name anyway . . . because that's what you were taught, that children were to have their father's last name whether he was in their life or not.

When you come home from the hospital, you find out you've been evicted, so you and the baby go live with your mother. And that's when it clicks: your situation is all fucked up.

So you're back home, three years go by, and new boo has turned out to be a no-good baby daddy. And you can't take it. Your mother is doing her own thing and your sisters are following suit, which handicaps you from living your life. And now you've officially gone from being grown to being a miserable playmate for your child. You hadn't seen your baby daddy since your daughter was born, until one afternoon you see him hugged up on some bitch and rubbing her pregnant belly. You get mad. The hurt, the anger, and the embarrassment floods back. So you take him to court for child support and when it's all done you walk away with thirty dollars a week. He looks at you as if he never loved you and on the way out he says, "Either go hard or go home." Instantly you feel like that's what you need to hear, those hateful, hurtful, yet magical words that force you to face reality. So you begin to get your shit together, you get a well-paying job doing customer service for an insurance company, your baby is now three years old, and you've saved enough money to move out on your own.

As you go to look for apartments, the first person you see is a honey-glazed and well-chiseled cop walking the beat. You can tell that he's a rookie by his uniform but he seems to be chillin' and the guys you think he'd be arresting, he's kicking it with. You can tell by the smoothness of his face that he's younger than you but he's grown and judging by the bulge in his pants he's been grown for a long time. You try to stop staring but you can't. He reminds you of some of the men your mother has dated: golden brown, nicely built, and strong. He notices you and after you look at the apartment, he's waiting for you outside. You exchange numbers with him and after dating for a month, you bring him home to meet your mother, Starr, and two sisters: Monica and Imani. They all seem to click instantly.

A year later he asks you to marry him and you feel good to be the first one in your family to actually get married and not just live with your *ole man.* So now you're the Mrs. and the real shit begins. He likes his dick sucked but you can't stand the smell of pubic hairs. He begs you to stick his dick in your ass, but last you remembered sodomy was a crime. He likes Victoria's Secret negligees but they don't sell your size. He's a neat freak; you throw your clothes around. He likes to save money; you depend on next week's paycheck. He's structured and he likes to eat at a certain time but you never cook. He loves your daughter as if she is his own, yet you keep your third eye open. He's strict and assigns her a bedtime, but if she cries loud enough you let her stay up. He doesn't tolerate her acting grown or being in adult conversations, but you try to convince him that she's intelligent and needs a playmate, which is your excuse to get pregnant.

When you have the baby, which turns out to be twin girls, you talk your husband into moving out of Brooklyn and you find a suburb in Jersey, an hour and a half away from everything.

At your insistence your husband buys a brand-new, six-bedroom Colonial that neither one of you can afford, but you promise to get a job and help out. Yet before you know it, the twins are four years old, you're still unemployed, Victoria's Secret still doesn't fit, you refuse to suck dick, and fucking you in the ass is out of the question. But now you're up shit's creek, because you feel your husband has found a freak. The possibility of this reality is kicking you in the spine, your knees starting to shake as you stand in the tri-fold mirror looking at three different dimensions of yourself, hating the dull freckles on your face, craving another cigarette, cussing at the air, all while trying to figure out what the fuck is really going on.

◦ • ◦

CELESTE STROKED HER short red and natural curls, which crowned her round freckled face to a T. She swallowed the rising lump in her throat. "To hell with Sharief." She walked out of the bathroom, peeked in Kai's room, and saw that she had fallen back to sleep, while Kori and Kayla, who were in their respective bedrooms, looked as if they'd been sleeping peacefully all night.

Celeste walked back into her bedroom, dimmed the lights, and turned on the radio. Marvin Gaye's "Let's Get It On" was playing softly. She started moving her shoulders from side to side. Sitting down on the bed, she leaned the back of her head against her wrought-iron headboard. As the song continued to play, she began rubbing her E-cup breasts, massaging her stiff nickel-sized nipples. Thoughts of Sharief sucking them and tittie fucking her raced through her mind as her pussy started to thump. Lifting her arms in the air, she took off her camisole. One breast fell slightly over her navel. Playing with her nipples again, she lifted the right tittie up and began to suck it, bending her neck as best she could. Seductively she pulled her nipple in and out of her mouth. After sucking the right one, she started sucking the left. Twirling her fingers in and out of her soaked pussy, she could feel the nut building. Knowing that she could cum at any minute, Celeste reached under the bed for her beaver dildo. Afterward she sat up, took her bottoms off, and opened her legs wide while letting the beaver lap between her thighs. "Uhmm," Celeste moaned, "tell me you love this pussy, work it! Do that shit! Uhmmmmmm-mmm . . . I'm cumin', oh yes, fuck me, fuck me, fuck me!" As Celeste exploded the phone rang.

Immediately she came back to reality and for a moment, she felt embarrassed. Reaching for the phone, the cum between her thighs felt like Elmer's glue. "Hel-hel-hello."

"Celeste!"

Celeste couldn't make out the person's voice; all she knew was they were crying hysterically. "Who is this?"

"Imani!"

"Why are you calling me screaming? And furthermore do you know what time it is?"

"Just shut the fuck up and listen. I'm locked up."

"Again?" Celeste snapped. "What did you do this time, Imani? And if you're locked up why aren't you calling collect?"

"First of all I didn't do shit, just like I didn't do shit the last time. And furthermore this bitch-ass pig let me use the phone at his desk."

Celeste could hear the officer snarl at Imani, "You need to be getting to the point."

"Don't call cops pigs," Celeste snapped. "I can't believe this, what are you locked up for? Oh don't tell me, it was Walik's shit again, right, and he asked you to take the fall because you would get less time?"

"Celeste—"

"No, shut up. Didn't you get enough of being locked up for the first six months of your pregnancy? Now you're back in jail? Well, if you think I'm coming to get you, you're in for a surprise. Call your mother, or better yet Monica. 'Cause this Cinderella, over here, ain't trying to hear it." Celeste paused for a minute. "Where the hell is my nephew?"

"I can't stand your fat miserable ass!" Imani's head felt as if it would explode. "You think I wanted to call you? If Monica had been home, I wouldn't be talking to you. Look, don't worry about me, I just need someone to come and get Jamal. I'm downtown Brooklyn."

Celeste sucked her teeth.

"You know what," Imani hissed, "never mind, fuck it! I'll call Monica back."

Celeste rolled her eyes as the phone clicked off. "Goddamn!" She flicked the light on. "Stupid ass! Let me try and find somebody to go and get this broad." She picked up the phone and called Sharief. Instead of hanging up when his voice mail came on, she pressed 2 and text messaged him, "9-1-1."

[Monica]

TIRED OF THE phone ringing nonstop, Monica knocked it off the hook. She was in the middle of bustin' a serious freak.

No longer having to taste, lick, and fuck herself with her fingertips, Monica cried into the pillow's edge stuffed into her mouth. Before she was seduced by her brother-in-law's dick, Monica was playing with herself on a regular. Flicking her clit, feeling it rise and fall was the only way she could make certain she obtained a nut. Otherwise she was up shit's creek. The square, Chauncey, just wasn't doin' it, and Monica grew tired of fucking him, so she prayed for a change. But God never seemed to hear her prayers for a rock-solid stiff one that she could grip between her pussy lips and ride into the sunset. He only seemed to hear the parts about the light bill, phone bill, car note, student loan, and mortgage being paid on time. Somehow, in between *Jesus' name we pray* and *Amen,* God ignored, *Please make him black like the stroke of midnight, with chocolate-glazed lips, and dreads. Okay scratch the dreads, maybe a bald head or a faded Caesar with a hook part.*

Thrusting her neck forward as best she could, Monica took the pillow out of her mouth and held her neck down as far as it would go, trying her best to get a bird's-eye view of Sharief drinking the fresh juice from her pussy, something they both got off on. While trying to see, Monica struggled to hold her pussy lips open as Sharief licked his way from the bottom of her pussy to the tip of her melting clit. For a brief moment she studied Sharief's face and imagined that her being in love with him was an open invitation for all hell to break loose.

I know this is fucked up, Monica thought as she watched Sharief lick between the slit of her dripping-wet pussy lips, causing her clit to go through convulsions. *But I can't help it.*

Sharief continued to suck Monica's clit while she studied what she could see of his face. His skin was the right mix between gingerbread and apple butter. He reminded her of the rapper Common with chestnut eyes and a strong, royal, and fierce stare that rested underneath perfectly arched eyebrows. His wide nose lay nicely between his chiseled cheekbones and was more than a perfect match for his beautiful face. He had a smooth bald head with lightly faded-in sideburns that connected to a well-groomed and perfectly lined beard and mustache. His entire stance commanded attention. The energy in his face told the story of a brother who didn't play or fuck around with life, but instead was a black man who handled his shit and was confident when doing it.

Monica closed her eyes; she could feel ecstasy building. Her hands started to shake as her chest began to heave up and down. She swore that Sharief must've taken a special class on how to suck a clit, because he was knocking all other niggahs outta the box. No man, unless he was born to do so, would be able to compete with Sharief. Slowly Sharief dipped his long fingers in and out of her welcoming slit, his manicured fingertips racing the swiftness of his warm tongue, playing in the thickness of her creamy cum.

Goddamn he got me goin'! Monica thought while feeling Sharief press his tongue against her clit and then watching it spring back for more. He licked it around the base, at times favoring one side more than the other, causing her legs to spread and flutter against the sides of his bald head like an erotic butterfly.

"Talk to me, Monica," Sharief said between licks.

"What?" she asked, surprised, failing at her attempt to stop panting. "Right now?"

"Tell me how it feels."

"Like heaven . . ."

"No, talk nasty!" he demanded, softly biting her clit. "Kick some shit to me."

"Ai'ight." She was trying not to wrap her legs around his head and bury it. "I want you to lap up the cum from my pussy." She grabbed the back of his smooth bald head and pushed it farther in. "Eat this pussy like you own it. Take your tongue and work it like a snake. In and out and slowly, hit me off with hard strokes. Eat me like I got the sweetest pussy in the world."

"It's a good pussy, Monica."

"How good?" she moaned. "Tell me how you like to eat it."

"I love to eat it." He licked her oozing juice as if it were melting butter. "Your cum is thick and sweet, ma. I can't wait to stick my dick into it and fuck the shit outta you." Continuously proving his ability to pâté a pussy, Sharief licked and flicked his tongue back and forth. "I swear I ain't never had no pussy like this. Never. This is a fat-ass pussy. Nice and soft with a juicy-ass clit. I'ma pop this cherry wide-the-fuck open."

"Oh, you got the skills for that?" Monica said, desperately trying not to tremble. Unable to stop trembling, she screamed, "Goddamn I'm cumin' . . ."

"You cumin', baby?" Sharief moaned, flicking his tongue faster.

"I'm cumin', baby."

"Who's is it, baby?"

"Oh Goddddd!"

"Not God, baby . . . Sharief . . ."

She wrapped her legs around his head. He took her clit into his mouth, placed it between his teeth, and pulled it softly until she exploded, her cum covering his lips and leaving a trail down his chin. He wiped his mouth with the back of his hand, took his head from between her legs, and lay on top of her. Caressing her nipples and licking her earlobes, he whispered, "You know we're wrong, right?"

"Wrong? I'm not Celeste's keeper."

"That's fucked up." Sharief moved his head down, slid his dick in, and simultaneously sucked both of her C-cup breasts. While sucking them, he felt as if he were French-kissing her nipples, his tongue going wild with both of them in his mouth. "Don't fuck nobody else," he snapped. Sharief stood on his knees and folded Monica's legs across his chest Indian-style. He pounded his dick in and out of her vaginal canal, determined to bury his dick in her wetness.

"Hmmm?" Monica moaned, her tone evident that she was caught off guard. "Where did that come from?"

"Don't play with me." He slapped her on the ass. "Don't fuck ole boy . . . again."

"Ole boy?" Monica said. Sharief's grinding was causing her head to lift off the bed.

"The square niggah." He slapped her on the ass again. "The janitor or whatever he is."

"He's a math teacher." Monica wiped the tears falling from the corners of her eyes. Sharief's grinding felt like it was ripping through her stomach and soaring its way toward her heart. His grinding was bittersweet, a callaloo of pain and pleasure, but a mixture she could live with.

"I don't give a fuck what he is." Sharief stopped for a moment and wiped the drizzling sweat from his brow. Grinding again, he said, "Don't fuck him . . . anymore."

"Don't worry about him, worry about us."

"Us? Humph, I'ma be fuckin' you *forever.*"

That was all Monica needed to hear. The *forever* part. Forget being caught up in the moment; this was the truth. Exactly what she'd been waiting for. Something to riddle this situation of the stinging guilt she'd had behind sleeping with her sister's husband for the past six months. Not to mention constantly having to hear Celeste's nags of Sharief never being home and most recently her cries about a recurring dream that he was cheating. "My dreams never lie. I know he's cheating on me," Celeste had confided in Monica just yesterday while they were on the phone.

"Celeste, please with the dreams. He's been working a lot of long hours," Monica had said, desperately trying to pacify Celeste, but as usual Celeste was working her last nerve. A few moments later Sharief came in from work and walked over to greet Monica. Monica's right shoulder was hunched, holding the phone to her ear while she stood at her bedroom window. Sharief kissed her lightly on the lips and she began to unbutton his shirt, his tie already hanging loose around his neck.

"Monica, are you there?" Celeste asked, getting agitated. "Are you listening?"

"Yes," Monica said, Sharief now standing behind her, unsnapping her bra and kissing from the nape of her neck to the small of her back.

"Well then, I'm telling you, it's not just my dreams but even in my gut I feel that he's cheating."

"Do you have any evidence of that?"

"No, but he doesn't make love to me anymore . . . and every time I turn around he's working. What do you think I should do?"

"I think you should chill," Monica said, now ass naked, lying on the bed spread-eagled, "he's faithful . . ."

But now, at this moment, with the *forever* word dangling in the air, mixing in with the sweat, pussy slurps, ball slapping, and grunts of *I love hittin' this shit,* Monica no longer gave a fuck about how Celeste felt. After all, all is fair in love and dick. *So fuck Celeste,* Monica thought, nearing an orgasm. *And fuck their marriage.*

Fuck the perfect house and fuck the perfect kids. The dish has been cheating on the spoon. Hell, if anything, Celeste should've never suggested that Sharief stay in Brooklyn with me. Big deal, if his shift didn't end until two sometimes three in the morning and his commute home would be riddled with darkness? Bitch, you knew how far Somerset, New Jersey, was when you insisted on taking your fat ass there! Nothing was wrong with Brooklyn. Nevertheless, ever since we were teenagers Church Ave. wasn't good enough for you. You had to be Miss Priss and move to the 'burbs.

Always fuckin' lecturing me about being a fifteen-year-old pregnant statistic who dropped out of high school. You never got enough of putting me down, did you? Which is why when my baby was stillborn you told me you had no remorse for me, that I didn't need to be a baby mama anyway. I never forgot that, Celeste, and so, I say touché! You better hope the baby mama shoe doesn't hurt your wide-ass foot too much. And as far as me dropping out of high school, I got my GED, graduated from college, and now I'ma fifty-five-thousand-dollar-a-year registered nurse, and what? Now it's your turn to grovel, bitch, and wonder about your man who was just sucking my clit. Remember you wanted to be a stay-at-home soccer mom, so get ta car-poolin'.

You knew your husband had just made detective . . . but did you care? Noooo, not Queen Bee. Well guess what? You left your fine-ass, bald-headed man with too much idle time. Eating too many dinners with me. Too many nights we were up late talking. I was the one waiting for him to come home. Bringing him late-night snacks and sitting with him during his breaks at the station. It was me, Monica, not you. All you did was sit home, get fat, and complain about the kids whining all the time. You stopped doing your hair and taking care of yourself. You slipped and I was there when you fucked up. So . . . from what I can see . . . you got what your hand called for.

Didn't you ever listen when Mommy said men will be men, and all men cheat? Well, if you didn't, you should've 'cause I'm fuckin' the proof.

Uncrossing her legs, Monica let the left one rest on the bed and threw the right one over Sharief's shoulder. "That's all you got?" she said, looking him dead in the eyes, trying not to scream at the hard-ass strokes he was rammin' into her.

"That's all I got?" Sharief asked, surprised. "Oh, you want more?"

"I thought you wanted to pop the cherry? You twirling it."

"Oh, so the dick ain't rough enough?" He grinned.

"If it ain't rough it ain't right."

A snide smile ran across Sharief's face as he looked at Monica and started pounding her with the deepest and most intense strokes that he could muster up from the pit of his shaft. The swift motions of his hips caused his dick to run like a marathon in and out of her pussy, pounding against her G-spot and lightly kissing her clit with its movement.

"That's it?" Monica snapped, trying not to stutter. "That was a li'l-boy stroke. I know this big dick got more back than that."

Motherfuck, Sharief thought, his dick ready to bust. *Ai'ight, ai'ight, I gotta stay still for a second otherwise I'ma 'bout to lose control.*

"Why you so quiet?" Monica said, throwing Sharief a hard hip. "What? You trying not to bust a nut?" She started flexing her inner walls.

"Oh, you playin' me?" Able to calm himself, Sharief started pounding Monica even harder than before. Flipping her over without ever causing his dick to fall out, he placed his hands at the small of her back and started bangin' her doggy-style. His dick wreaking havoc on her wetness, the friction causing her to squeeze her ass cheeks every time she felt his balls slapping against her skin. "I don't hear you talkin' shit now!" Sharief said. "What— what? Cat got your tongue?"

"No, I'm waitin' for you to fuck me," Monica said calmly.

"Just for that . . . I'ma punish you." Sharief laughed, trying not to focus on the nut he felt creeping up. He took his dick out, slid his right hand in between her ass, and collected her juices all over his fingers. He stuck two of them into her asshole. "Sharief," she moaned, "don't play."

"Nah, don't punk out now. You were brazen when you were talkin' that bullshit. *Oh, I'm waitin' for you to fuck me.* Remember that shit? *If it ain't rough it ain't right.*" He bent his head down underneath her ass and ran his tongue from the tip of her clit to her tailbone. Monica's heartbeat thumped its way down her spine. Her mind felt as if it had taken flight into the Twilight Zone.

Sharief got off the bed and stood on the floor. He pulled Monica to the edge of the bed, her ass greeting his shaft. He grabbed her by the waist, hunched her behind in the air, and moved his dick in between the slit. Her arms were tucked under her breasts as her head lay flat and turned to the side.

"Sharief, it's gon' hurt?" Monica sighed. He could feel her tensing up as he spread her ass cheeks.

"No, it's not." He ran his tongue in between her butt cheeks, tickling her asshole. "You trust me?"

"Yes."

"Well then, relax. I would never hurt you, Monica. I know what I'm doing." Sharief took Monica's juices and lubricated her asshole as he slowly worked his way in. The muscles in her ass contracted around the head of his dick. Sharief was sure when he started to cum he would be nuttin' for days. Getting into the mix of pounding into her sweet ass, he started slapping both sides, with one hand and then the other, trying his best not to call her name.

"How did you lose your teeth, Red?" came out of nowhere. Monica, who'd just swallowed a spiked fist in her throat from nine inches of a thick black dick taking refuge in her virgin asshole, was scared shitless. She never expected to hear her mother's voice while fucking her sister's husband. "Take it out, Sharief."

Instead of taking it out, he stroked.

"No, I'm serious," she said, agitated. "Didn't you just hear my mother's voice?"

"No, I didn't. So . . . can we get back," he massaged her ass cheek, "to handling this situation?"

"Awl Red." Starr's voice came across the air again. "You got a rip in the seat of yo' catsuit. And that thing was bad too."

"I heard that," Sharief said, looking around. "And my dick just went soft." He slid it out.

Monica turned her head from side to side and spotted her cell phone vibrating with the red light from the walkie-talkie beeping. "It's my phone," she laughed. "My mother is always hitting the walkie-talkie by accident."

"Well, you need to start cutting that off, baby." Sharief nervously grinned. "That shit has caused Tarzan to stop swinging. Look at this." He pointed to his dick. "My man done passed out."

Monica laughed. "Sharief, go take a shower." As he left, she grabbed her Nextel off the nightstand and hit the walkie-talkie button. "Excuse me, Ike and Tina."

"Ike?" Starr snapped. "Ain't no Ike over here, fuck around and get this niggah burned up. They be callin' his high-yellow ass Krispy Kreme. Humph, if you don't know, you better ask about me."

Monica rolled her eyes. "Ma, what's the problem? You're hitting the walkie by mistake again."

"Oh, I'm sorry, boo. I was trying to see if we could call 1-800-DENTURE and see about gettin' Red some more teeth, 'cause the ones he had he coughed out."

"What?"

"Yeah, girl, and them dentures was designer too. They was the gold-plated Flavor Flav teeth, equipped with an overbite. Red and Jimmy were special guest stars at a Where Are They Now concert, at the Roseland Ballroom. We had a good ole time except Red kept getting blindsided by the disco ball. Chile, my man know he a throwback."

"Ma, get to the point, how did Red lose his teeth?"

"Oh, he was doing a rendition of Michael Jackson's 'Bad' on stage, bust a split and coughed his teeth out. Wait a minute, baby, my phone is ringing." Starr looked at the caller ID. "It's Celeste. Monica, let me hit you back in a second." And she clicked the walkie off.

They are crazy as hell, Monica thought. She grabbed her robe and as Sharief walked out of the bathroom she walked in.

After a quick shower, Monica slipped on a short black satin spaghetti-strap nightgown. She slowly walked down the stairs, bracing herself for when the midsummer heat attacked her.

Sharief was lying back on the couch, dressed in army fatigue shorts and a wife beater. He was watching an ESPN Classic boxing match. It was a little after midnight, and the heat was sweltering. The air-conditioning unit on the first floor had conked out last week, forcing Monica to use four fans, one in each corner of the room.

Monica lived in a small two-story corner row house. Although the place was small, it was laid. The living room had an Afrocentric flare to it. A red suede couch rested against an exposed brick wall; hanging directly above was a South African mud-cloth throw with fringed edges. Cattycorner to the couch was a matching love seat filled with an abundance of mud-cloth pillows. Five-foot-tall candles were at both ends of the couch. An elephant-shaped coffee table with a glass top and a bowl of marbles complemented the hard wooden floors. There were African statues placed sporadically around the room. Directly across from the couch and above the fireplace was a forty-six-inch plasma TV, and on both sides were six-foot-tall glass shelves where Monica kept her collection of elephants and Annie Lee figurines. Down the hall from the living room was an L-shaped kitchen and a small bathroom. Upstairs was Monica's bedroom, her office, and a full master bath.

Monica went in the kitchen and took out two frosted bottles of Heineken. She handed one to Sharief. "You know I don't drink, ma," he said, tapping her on the ass. "Just give me some water." He handed her back the beer.

"Damn, baby. Loosen up," she said.

"I'm good, ma, I just choose not to drink."

"All right." Monica walked into the kitchen and placed the beer back in the refrigerator. She grabbed Sharief a bottle of spring water and came back into the living room.

"Monica." Sharief twisted the cap off the water bottle.

"Yes." She lay between his legs with her back against his chest.

"Let me ask you a question."

"Shoot." She took a sip and then ran the cold bottle across her forehead.

"You still wanna fuck ole boy?"

"What?" She was caught off guard. "Why?"

"Because I'm wondering, if the dick was bangin', would it make a difference with us?"

"Us? Oh, now there's an us? Besides, who said the dick *wasn't* bangin'? Men kill me. Just 'cause your dick game is decent, you swear all others fall behind you."

"I ain't saying all that."

"Well hell, you damn sure insinuated it. Let me inform you, a niggah with a big dick and a niggah you want for your man are two totally different things."

"Really." Sharief smirked, taking a sip. "I always thought that most women equated a big dick to wedding vows."

"Oh my God!" Monica rolled her eyes. "You are such an asshole."

Sharief laughed. "I'm an asshole? I'm not an asshole. It's not my fault that ole boy nut in under a minute," he said with confidence.

"Whatever."

"So tell me," Sharief took another sip, "is ole boy coming to your mother and Red's wedding?"

"I invited him." She took a sip of her beer. "Is your wife going to be there?"

"Don't play."

"That's what I thought."

"Anyway . . . why did you invite him?" Sharief asked.

"Because that's who I wanted to invite as a guest, problem?"

"Yeah it's a problem."

"Well, sweetie." She tapped the hand that he had placed on her stomach. "You'll live." Monica stood up and walked over to turn the radio on. Michael Jackson's "PYT" was playing. "This is my shit!" Monica started moving her shoulders and simultaneously turned the volume up. She started sliding from side to side. "Come on, dance with me." She placed her beer on a coaster and started doing the snake.

"You are so played." Sharief laughed, moving his head a little.

"Well, what you got?" She snapped her fingers and moonwalked across her freshly waxed wooden floor. "What—what?" She placed her hands on her knees, threw her ass in the air, and started breaking it down.

Michael Jackson's song continued to play: ". . . *Always wanted a girl just like you . . . where did you come from baby . . .*"

She tooted her lips up, swaying her hips from side to side. "Oh, I forgot you a li'l young niggah, you don't know nothin' about this." She snapped her fingers and twirled around.

"Young?" He frowned. "I'm twenty-eight and yo' ass is only twenty-nine."

"You still young!" She laughed. She snapped her fingers and tooted her ass in the air. "Woooo . . . what you know about that?"

As Sharief prepared to take on Monica's challenge, the DJ dropped another Michael Jackson hit and started playing "Bad."

"Oh hell yeah!" Monica dropped to the floor.

As if the music were speaking to him, Sharief got on the floor and broke out into a Michael Jackson kick, topping it off with a Michael Jackson scream while shaking his right knee and snapping his fingers. Monica danced around him as if he were a pole in a strippers' club. Afterward she started doing every Michael

Jackson dance she could think off including all the dances from the "Thriller" video. "Don't hate, boo." She laughed, pointing at Sharief. "Don't hate. Watch this!"

Despite the fans being on full blast, sweat dripped down the sides of Monica's face, curled over her neck, and dripped into her cleavage. She loved every bit of it. Seeing Sharief act silly completely turned her on, making the reality of him being her sister's man even harder to withstand.

(Starr)

"IS IT HER birthday or somethin'? She havin' a party?" Red asked Starr as she pressed her daughter's bell. The music from Monica's stereo slipped through the crack of the front door.

Starr pressed the bell again and tapped her foot. "No, it ain't her birthday. Must be a niggah over here." Starr was becoming more pissed by the moment. Then she remembered that Monica kept a spare key to her front door under the welcome mat.

As Monica went to bust a split she looked up and Starr, Red, and Jamal were standing in the doorway. "I rang the doorbell about four times but I guess this is why you didn't hear me." Starr pointed around the room. "I used the spare key under the mat."

"Ma, you scared me." Monica placed her hand on her chest while making a mental note to hide the spare key someplace else.

"Uhmm-hmm, now tell me what y'all got going on?" Starr pointed to Sharief.

"What are you talking about?" Monica nervously frowned, standing up.

Starr sucked her teeth as she noticed how short Monica's gown was. "You need to put some clothes on."

"I'm okay," Monica said as she diverted her eyes from Starr's. She prayed that her mother didn't see any guilt on her face.

"Now, I asked you a question," Starr repeated. "What is going on here?"

"Yeah, that's a good question," Red said, looking around and cocking his head to the side, facing the radio. "Usually I don't say nothing. But I don't appreciate this."

"Appreciate what?" Sharief asked, trying to erase the look of guilt on his face. "Huh?"

"Don't *huh* me. People who say *huh* can't hear. Now, I do enough old-school concerts to know when somebody is makin' fun of my gig." Red pouted his lips and started tapping his foot. He was five foot ten with a sprinkle of freckles across his cheeks, a beer belly, and a tired Afro that was thirty years old and contained a growing bald spot in the middle. Red reared back on his legs, his pearlized white cape covered the rip in his catsuit.

As Red tried to speak, his lips folded inside his mouth. He placed his hands on his sides, causing his pudgy stomach to protrude. "I'll have y'all to know that I am very upset."

"Don't worry 'bout it, baby," Starr said, still giving Monica the evil eye. "Some people can't appreciate a throwback. We gon' add a li'l rappin' to your gig and turn all these ma'fuckers out!"

"Just calm down," Sharief said while glancing over at Starr, who was standing with her lips twisted and her hazel eyes in *cut-a-niggah* mode. Her short and spiked platinum-blond hair enhanced her attitude. Usually when Starr walked into a room she exuded an aura that let people know she had arrived. She wore rings on every finger, including her thumb, two anklets on each leg, and a series of gold bangles that clapped together every time she moved. She was a five-foot-five, 245-pound butter-colored voluptuous black woman who knew that she was sexy, and tonight was no different. She was dressed in a black satin spaghetti-strap tee, and the waist of her purple spandex pants was decorated with a gold three-layer chain belt. Her wide feet were stuffed into metallic gold-and-lilac strappy stiletto sandals that tied around the ankle in a satin bow, showing off her French pedicure.

Starr cocked her neck to the side, trying to talk herself out of cussin'. She tapped her foot and took a deep breath; she was down to her last cigarette and needed a puff.

Red looked at her and wiped the bubbling sweat off her forehead. "You see my woman, Sharief, and you telling me to calm down?" Red snapped, his cape floating in the air as the fans blew his way, revealing the rip running up his ass. "You better hold ya roll, Sharief, fo' I been done cripped on a fool."

"What are y'all doing here?" Monica said, trying her best to ignore Red. "What's wrong? And why do you have Jamal out this time of the night? Where's Imani?"

Immediately Jamal started to cry. Monica looked at his red and puffy eyes and held her arms out. Jamal walked over to her while trying to hold his baggy jeans up.

"Aunty's baby," Monica whined, giving him a hug.

"Aunty Monica." Jamal sniffed, giving up the battle with his pants and hugging her around the knees, "I was crying and niggahs was laughin' at me, like they wanted beef or somethin'. I almost told them, you might see me sleep but you don't know me."

"Jamal, what did I tell you about that street language?" Monica rubbed the back of his head. "Now tell me what happened."

"My Imani," Jamal sniffed, "had to wreck shop."

"Wreck shop?" Monica was confused.

"Listen," Starr snapped, "your sister done got herself into some mo' bullshit, that's what. Had my grandbaby out there in the street with her and then she gets arrested."

"Arrested." Monica was in shock. "Oh no, for what?"

"Like the child said," Starr pointed to Jamal, "she done whipped somebody's ass."

"Oh no!"

"She'll be released tomorrow. But I have something I need to do with Buttah in the morning, so I need you to keep Jamal tonight. Now," she looked at Sharief, "don't you have a wife waiting on you?"

"I'm going home, Starr," Sharief said defensively.

"Does your wife know that?"

"Like I said," Sharief reiterated, "I'm going home. It's late and because Monica is close and home is farther away I usually stop here to rest."

"Impersonating Michael Jackson—" Starr said.

"They was impersonating me, baby," Red corrected her.

"Whoever or whatever," Starr said, "y'all was doin' didn't put me in the mind of you trying to rest. Now I suggest that you take a stretch, pull ya drawls outta ya ass, take a shit and do whatever you gotta do, but then you need to go home to the sister you're married to. Understand? Like Mama Byrd says, don't no chicken-coop cock need to be around stray chicks."

"Oh, Ma." Monica sucked her teeth. "That sounds ridiculous."

"Anywho," Starr continued. "Monica, let my grandbaby stay here for tonight, 'cause when I get with your sister Imani, I'ma hurt her."

"Why is it that I'm always keeping the kids?" Monica was pissed. "I'm the one who doesn't have any."

"And keep it that way." Starr kissed Jamal on the cheek. "We don't need no unclaimed egg in the chicken coop."

"Why do you keep talking about chickens?"

"Bye, Monica." Starr waved and Red simply grunted on his way out the door. As Starr and Red got into their yellow-and-white ragtop 1974 Deuce-and-a-Quarter, Starr glanced at Monica's door once more. In the pit of her stomach she felt sick and for some reason wished Monica were still a kid so she could beat her ass.

"Don't let them bother you, baby," Red said as he started to drive.

Starr looked at him and wondered if he thought the same thing. "Bother me about what?"

"About them making fun of me. They just jealous because they think I'm getting all your attention. They'll get over it."

"Yeah, baby." Starr turned the radio on. "I hope so."

{ Celeste }

"WHEN ARE YOU coming home, motherfuckah? I've been calling you all damn night!" Celeste screamed as Sharief groggily answered his cell phone. He'd fallen asleep on Monica's floor next to Jamal. Sharief wiped the corners of his mouth and looked at his watch. It was six AM. *Damn,* he thought as Celeste went on, *she just never shuts the fuck up.*

"See how you lie?" Celeste screamed.

"Do you ever shut the hell up?"

"Answer my question!" she demanded.

"I'll get there when I get there." Sharief rose from the living room floor and stepped into the bathroom.

"Where the fuck have you been?" Celeste screamed. "Do you know how long I've been calling you! Huh, motherfuckah?"

"Whoool, slow down." He sat down on the toilet lid. "I ain't gon' be too many more mafuckers. Ai'ight? And don't call me screamin' in my ears, carrying on around my girls."

"Oh, now you're concerned? Where've you been, Sharief? Huh, answer that, where have you been?"

"Celeste, I'm not in the mood to argue with you, okay? You know I'm at Monica's. I just got off work and I'm tired. Now, what you need to understand is, the last thing a black man who's been workin' for twelve hours needs to hear is you naggin' him."

"Well guess what . . ." Celeste lit her cigarette and took a drag. "Let me inform yo' black ass that I don't give a damn!"

"Celeste, kill it. You know my hours. And you know how far we live."

"And so do you!" she screamed.

"You want me to come home now? If you do, I'll leave here and come home. Never mind that I've had no sleep so I'm taking a chance of falling asleep at the wheel, I'll be there."

"Well, if you fall asleep at the wheel, just let Lil' Kim know that Faith was the wife and she got all the death benefits."

"I'm hanging up."

"Look, Sharief." Celeste didn't want him to hang up; she knew she wouldn't hear from him anytime soon if he did that. "There was an emergency last night with Imani. Her wannabe gangstress, ride-or-the-fuck-die ass is locked up again. She's downtown Brooklyn. I called my mother so she could get Jamal. Imani is such a selfish-ass bitch!"

"Damn, chill with the name-calling." Sharief frowned.

"Chill with the name-calling? My nephew was in that dingy-ass precinct where that crab-apple-bottom bitch receptionist must be suckin' yo' dick since you telling me to chill!"

"Yo, there you go again." Sharief placed his hand on the side of his neck and massaged the thumping vein that he felt would explode.

"Fuck you!" Celeste screamed. "Punk-ass fuckin' spook!"

"I gotta go," he hissed, "you on some crazy shit!" And he hung up.

Celeste sat on the edge of her bed. Her eyes burned and her chest hurt. She kept thinking that it may have been last week when she started to notice a change in Sharief . . . but then she thought, *Maybe not last week, maybe the week before* . . . or the week before that . . . Celeste sat back on the bed with her knees pulled to her chest. That's when she realized there was no specific time she could think of when all hell broke loose . . .

[Monica]

OR HOURS MONICA stared at the ceiling, drifting in and out of deep thought. She thought about her father, whom she didn't know. She thought about her mother, who barely knew her father or her sisters' fathers. And for a moment she thought about the father of her stillborn baby, and wondered where he was.

Monica placed her hand on her stomach and felt an unexplainable hardness in her abdomen. She squinted her eyes as she pressed on her stomach, wondering what the hardness could be. When she was seventeen she suffered from fibroids. Everyone told her that she had to be mistaken; "It only happens to women in their thirties." Well, they were wrong, she had two tumors pressing on her left fallopian tube. A week after the tumors were discovered, they, along with her left fallopian tube, had to be removed.

Monica prayed that the tumors had not returned; she couldn't take another ounce of her womanhood being siphoned out. Immediately she felt as if she were drowning and holding on to her femininity by a string.

"Monica," Sharief called, walking into her bedroom.

"Damn, you scared me." She let out a deep breath.

Sharief sat down on the edge of her bed. He placed her feet in his lap and wrapped his hands around them. "Monica, I wanna talk to you about us."

"I don't want to talk." She snatched her feet back and continued to look at the ceiling. "It's a wash. We're both outta line. Truth be told, I'm not tryna be my brother-in-law's booty call. That shit's a wrap."

"Monica—"

"Let me finish," she said sternly. "I'm not some li'l young, get-money chick from around-da-way, tryin' to get souped up over some Common-Sense-lookin' cop niggah. This ain't the free-pussy lounge, so let's keep it real. Go home to your wife and get some brain, maybe then y'all can get back together." She sat up in the bed. "Ya dig?"

"Have you lost your goddamn mind talking to me like that? You think this about pussy?" Sharief asked, taken aback and standing up.

"I don't know what it's about, but I do know that it's not every day your brother-in-law sucks your clit out the socket, okay?" Monica was saying all that she could to piss him off.

"Get the fuck outta here," Sharief was in disbelief, "let me keep it real for you, since you seem to be in La-La Land. You wanted your clit sucked out the socket. You wanted me to fuck you last night, the night before, months before, years before, you wanted to be fucked 'cause you been on my dick since I met you."

"Whatever, niggah," she yarned. "Beat it with the bullshit."

"Check this, ma." He pointed his finger, upset with himself that he was allowing her to take him there. "Let me put you down on some real shit. A niggah don't ever leave his wife for the side-line broad, so you're giving yourself too much credit. If and when I leave my wife it'll be because I want to, not because your pussy is that grand!"

"It's not that grand?" she questioned. "Well, I can't tell, as much as your face stays in it! So please, all of y'all niggahs are just alike."

"Don't compare me with anyone else!" he yelled, banging his fist on the dresser.

"Would you please, Jamal's downstairs."

"He's sleep."

"He can still hear you!"

Lowering his voice, Sharief pursed his lips tight. "Check it, learn keep your legs closed, since you so fuckin' stand-up." He turned toward the doorway, then turned back around and tossed the house keys she'd given him at the foot of the bed. "From this moment on you are my wife's sister!" And with that said, he slammed the door behind him.

{ Imani }

"YO, TASHA AND Quiana here?" Sabrena, Imani's friend and neighbor, asked her. " 'Cause Shante needs her ass cracked! Or should we get my .22 to do it?" Sabrena was standing at Imani's front door with her neck twisted and her heavy breasts resting on her stomach. Sabrena was always in whip-ass mode, and fucking up whoever was nothing but a word. "Yo," she chuckled, "you know how we roll. Blind, cripple, and crazy. From eight to eighty, I'll beat a bitch's ass! Straight duff a ho, pregnant and all." Sabrena placed her hands on her hips as she walked passed Imani and into the living room, where Lil' Kim's "Put Ya Lighters Up" was on full blast. Tasha and Quiana were sitting on the couch, smoking a blunt. Imani had been out of jail since this morning, and in an effort to clear her mind she'd called her friends over for their pre-club ritual.

Despite Tasha's, Quiana's, and Imani's eyes being half closed, they couldn't help but stretch them and give Sabrena a quick once-over. Tasha and Quiana cracked a sly, one-sided smile, while Imani placed her hand over her mouth, took a deep breath, and shook her head. God knows, they'd grown tired of telling Sabrena, *Just because Rainbow has it in your size doesn't mean you have to rock it.* Flopping down on the arm of Imani's white leather couch and throwing one thigh over the other, Sabrena wore a knockoff Louie V halter-scarf top with white-fringed denim shorts that fell just below her ass cheeks. Her size sixteen thighs were completely exposed and she didn't give a damn; as far as Sabrena was concerned she was that bitch. On her feet she wore white open-toed, three-inch riding boots that zipped on the side. And her French manicure consisted of neon pink for the base and bright white for the stripe.

Chewing gum, Sabrena blew a big bubble and popped it. " 'Sup niggahs?" She snapped her neck from side to side. "Y'all know we been dying to bust Shante's ass." She placed her gum on the back of her hand and reached for the blunt. "Just say the word and that bitch's days are numbered."

"How did y'all know I had a fight with Shante?" Imani asked, sitting down in the recliner and sipping on a cup of orange juice mixed with Banana Red Cisco.

"Please, chile," Sabrena took a pull, "er'body knows." She blew out the smoke. "Plus, Jamillah and Itief from the Parkway catch that same bus to see their kids' daddies and they saw the whole thing."

"I didn't see them on the bus." Imani arched her eyebrows.

"I guess not, since you were whippin' ass!"

Imani's face lit up. "Oh, that's what they said?"

"Yeah, girl." Quiana's eyes popped out as she received the blunt back. "They said you got wit' that ass and tore it up! They said the whole bus was rockin'. Word up." She laughed. She passed Imani the blunt back and gave her a high five. "They said all that bitch could do was cry."

"Humph." Imani took a pull and slowly blew out the smoke. "I did catch that bitch a few times."

"Yeah, and the next time it's gon' be a group effort," Sabrena snapped. "If she know like I know, she'll keep her ass off this side of Flatbush."

"That's wassup," Imani agreed, "but girl, I gotta get my shit together and get rid of this niggah. I'm straight done with his ass."

Before one of the girls could respond, the phone rang. Imani peeped at the caller ID: Monica. "Damn," she mumbled to herself, taking one last pull off the blunt and passing it. "This bitch don't give me a chance to breathe." Imani hadn't called Monica since she'd been home. Part of her felt embarrassed and the other part didn't feel like explaining how she'd ended up in jail fighting over Walik. She snatched the phone off the receiver. "Yeah."

"Yeah?" Monica said, obviously pissed off. "Yeah? Where the hell, besides jail, have you been all day?"

"Monica, please." Imani rolled her eyes. "I just need some time to clear my head."

"You have a six-year-old son over here. He has been worried about you all day. He keeps crying, and he's being fresh. I swear if he talks about farting and shitting one more time I'ma beat his ass!"

"Look, don't beat my son, he's expressing himself! And I'm sorry that he's been worried about me, but this shit with Walik has me fucked up right now and I just need to get it together."

"This shit with Walik? Fuck that broke-down can't-even-sell-weed ma'fuckah!"

"There you go, he ain't never sold weed no way, straight diesel. If you gon' cuss him out, then get it straight."

"Who you getting smart with, me? How do you spell *loser*, Imani? I'll tell you," Monica said, answering her own question, "It's spelled *W-a-l-i-k*! You just stuck on hustlin' yo' pussy the fuck backward! Where was he when you were in jail without a bail for six months, huh? Do you know how much of my money I spent getting you a lawyer? Where was he at then?"

"For your information, he was on the come-up. Anyway, what

difference does it make, I ain't fuckin' with his chicken-lickin' ass anyway."

"You know what, talk to your son, because I am so not feeling you right now."

Monica called for Jamal to come to the phone. Jamal stumbled into the room and frowned up his face. " 'Sup, Aunty . . ." He looked around and spotted a can of air freshener on Monica's dresser. "You just sprayed that?"

"Yeah, why? It smells like raspberries, doesn't it?"

"Naw, it smell like you been bustin' farts." Jamal pinched his nose together. "This place smell like a sewer."

"Imani," Monica spoke into the phone, "I'ma beat his li'l nasty fart-talkin' ass!" She pointed to the phone. "It's your mother on the phone, Jamal, she can hear you."

"Okay, Aunty, I'm sorry." He smiled at her and his dimples started to glow. "Maybe you didn't fart," he went on. "Maybe you just need to doo-doo, or did you try to doo-doo and strain too hard? One time I thought I had to fart and when I checked my Superman drawls I had a big ole dukey stain in 'em. My Imani was like, *Boy if you don't get yo' shitty ass outta here and change them funky drawls.* So," he said, taking his fingers from his nose and pointing between Monica's legs, "maybe you need to check your drawls, maybe they shitty."

"Jamal!" Monica squinted and held her hand up in the position of a backslap. "Don't get knocked out! Talk to your mama on the phone." She shoved the phone at him.

"This Mama-Starr or Imani?" he asked, excited.

"How many times do I have to tell you to stop calling your mother by her first name? Starr is Nana or Grandma and Imani is Mama or Mommy to you! Now talk to Imani, I mean your mommy!" Monica rolled her eyes at Jamal and walked out of the room.

He placed the phone to his ear and started smiling. "Imani, you home?"

"Yes, baby," she said, feeling the excitement in his voice. "I'm home." She thought about getting on him about his nasty mouth, but hearing his voice melted her and all she could say was, "I love you, boo-boo."

"I love you too, Imani, I missed you. Imani, I was crying."

"You were?"

"Yeah I was like this." He frowned up his face. "Boo-hoo-hoo."

"Oh baby, I'm sorry."

"And do you know niggahs was laughin' at me?"

"Who was laughing at you?" Instantly Imani caught an attitude. "What niggahs?"

"Them pigs. You know how they do!"

"Humph, don't I. Well, if anybody else laugh at you, you tell 'im that your Imani will beat their ass!"

"That's wassup . . . Imani?"

"Yeah, baby?"

Jamal started to whisper. "Uncle Rief told Aunty Monica he was gon' punch her in the face."

"What?" Imani couldn't believe it.

"Yeah," Jamal continued to whisper, "you should've heard him, he told her I can't even believe I was feeling you, trick. Then it was a lot of noise. Like this, crumble, crumble, crumble, raaaaahhhhh. Then Aunty Monica said, 'Boy, is you crazy, Jamal sleep in the other room.' Then Uncle Rief said, 'Hol' up, shawtie, you might see me in the streets but you 'on't know me.' Imani, he sound just like a rapper."

"Jamal, stop lyin'! I already told you about lyin' so much!"

"Imani, I ain't lyin', you shoulda heard him, she told him 'My Adidas'll walk all over your face, dawg. Punk, lazy-eye niggah! Then he said, 'Punk? Lazy-eye? You tryna flex? You booty-scratchin' fart face! Yo' breath smell like pissy eggs! And if you mess with me, I'll knock yo' teeth out and put 'em back in crooked!' Yo, that's a wild boy, Imani!"

Imani was trying her best not to laugh. She knew she couldn't condone Jamal telling lies, but what he'd just said sounded so ridiculous that she couldn't help it. She hit the mute button and fell out. Jamal continued to ramble on. Imani took a deep breath, unmuted the phone, and resumed her conversation. "Enough with the lies, Jamal! Stop it! You know what, you can't watch the *Chappelle's Show* no more!"

"I ain't lyin', Imani! They were!"

"I mean it, now I love you and good-bye," she said sternly. Imani pressed the end button on the phone but held the receiver in her hand. "I don't know what I'ma do with that boy." Placing the phone back on the base, she glanced at a picture of her and Walik sitting on top of her TV. "Y'all know when I got home earlier today, I reported that bitch, Shante, to welfare."

"Get the fuck outta here, who'd you call?" Sabrena asked.

"Welfare Fraud has a twenty-four-hour hotline, and I blew that bitch's spot up. I said, 'Hello this is an anonymous call, and I'd like to report Shante Smith of 1252 Church Avenue, apartment 13D. She's receiving state welfare and she's working full time at Citibank in Midtown.' I could tell that fuckin' operator felt like she'd won the lottery. She said, 'We will get on this right away. It's people like this that keep our taxes rising. Have a good evening, miss.'"

"Good for the bitch," Tasha said.

"Humph, you better be careful," Sabrena warned as she looked around the room. "She ain't the only one with a caseworker and j-o-b, all y'all niggahs in the same boat."

"Whatever, Sabrena." Quiana dismissed her.

"But yo' on some real shit," Sabrena continued, "maybe you need to walk away. Walik keeps doing the same shit over and over again."

"Walk away?" Imani snapped, getting defensive. "That's my son's father."

"Bitch." Quiana flicked her hand. "*You* was the one who said *you* needed to leave his ass alone and now you acting like Sabrena crazy. Leaving his ass is quite simple, all you have to say is *Bye ma'-fucker.*"

"For real," Tasha agreed. "Shit, all you doing is dismissing the dick, not the child support. Matter of fact, what you really need to do is call your Welfare caseworker and give her that niggah's real name and Social Security number. Hem his ass up in child-support court."

Imani sucked her teeth. "Please, so Welfare can take the money? Spare me. Plus, I ain't giving him away so that bitch can have him all the time, hell no!"

"What the fuck is you giving away?" Quiana countered. "Imani, Walik is a bum."

"Quiana, I know you ain't talkin'," Imani snapped, "not when you snuck and married Quinton on Family and Friends Day in the middle of the prison yard. And when he came home he still beat yo' ass and he wasn't even holdin' no paper." Imani pointed to Tasha. "Correct me if I'm wrong but weren't you and Shay, from Norstand, pregnant at the same time?"

"Oh no you didn't!" Tasha looked at Imani like she was crazy.

"Have you lost your mind, Imani?" Sabrena asked.

"Sabrena, you got nerve." Imani looked her up and down. "When Umar went to prison you ain't never hold him down, not even for one day."

"What the fuck I look like to you? A dumb bitch? That niggah was selling bootleg CDs. He couldn't at least catch a gun charge? Fuckin' CDs, come on now. I'm embarrassed. That's some real punk shit." Sabrena rolled her eyes. "Bitch, you know that's a soft spot with me."

"Whatever, I should've known y'all wouldn't understand me and Walik." Imani felt like she wanted to coldcock her friends in the face. "None of y'all have ever had a man like Walik. I've been with him since I was thirteen years old. I'm twenty-three now, that's ten years."

"Ten years?" Sabrena said. "Ain't you tired of that dick? The way he fuckin' you has got to be played."

"Don't you worry about it."

"But Imani," Quiana jumped in, "let's not forget you went to jail for six months fuckin' with his tired ass!"

"Yeah, remember?" Sabrena rolled her eyes. "And that wasn't even yo' shit. All you were doing was lying on the couch with morning sickness when the cops kicked the door in. And six months later you were the one in front of the judge copping a time-served and a year's probation plea."

"I got charged as a minor."

"You still went to jail," Quiana said.

Imani couldn't help but agree. "Yeah . . . and then he go and fuck that bum bitch." Tears started to stream down her face. "I got something for his ass, though. I'ma call crackhead Larry and give all his shit away."

"I'm wit' that." Sabrena rolled her eyes. "Since he wanna play you, let his ass come home naked."

"I was ride or die for his ass," Imani cried. "I was pregnant and I still held his ass down. Hell, ain't that love?"

"Hell yeah, that's love," Quiana snapped. "Shante ain't never did no time for his ass."

"All that bitch did was have him take care of her daughter and get pregnant. All I wanna ask him is, *When did she become your girl, and where the hell was I when the switch took place?*" Imani wiped the tears from her face.

"That's why we gon' fix his ass," Sabrena insisted, "and, Imani, don't be cryin' over no niggah; cry over his ass when you riding his enemy's dick."

"True story," Imani agreed. She got up, her friends following closely behind her into the bedroom. Imani opened the closet and Walik's shit almost fell on top of her. When he'd first asked her to hold his things for him, Imani had complained she didn't have the room. Her two-bedroom, Section 8, twelfth-floor Brooklyn flat was just enough for her and Jamal and nothing extra. But at the time she couldn't refuse Walik; after all, he was her man, and she was determined to hold him down no matter what. Well . . . today was a new day and Walik's shit had to go.

"And after this," Quiana said, "we going to the club and get our party on. Fuck these fake-ass get-money niggahs in the street."

"Yeah, I need to get outta here," Imani agreed.

Since they were now on a mission to give Walik's shit away and get to the club, the girls lined up. Imani had gone into the kitchen and grabbed the garbage bags. When she came back, the assembly line began: yank, yank, pass, and trash . . . Yank, yank, pass, and trash.

"It's a shame we gotta punish niggahs like this," Sabrena said. "Don't go back and start fuckin' with him again, Imani. And I mean it!"

" 'Cause if you do," Tasha said, "all you gon' be doing is buying this shit all over again."

"Fuck his ass." Imani rolled her eyes. "Let him go be with Shante, they got a family and all."

"And don't fall for no fake-ass apology," Sabrena said. " 'Cause even though a niggah says he's sorry, he still lyin' and you can tell by how he apologizes what the hell he really did."

"Word," Tasha countered. "I know for me, if a niggah says he's sorry and stays at my spot all day and night, that means he fucked a bitch. And all he's feeling is guilty."

"Yup, and if he says sorry," Quiana said, "then he gets mad and leaves, I know he's getting ready to fuck the bitch, and then he'll say I was always accusing him and always having an attitude, and that's why he fucked her."

"That's a niggah for you. But," Sabrena said, taking Walik's nickel-plated .38 and Desert Eagle out the closet and resting them on the bed, "if he says, 'Look, ma, I'm sorry, either you can believe me or not, but I love you and I ain't leaving you,' and he don't have no attitude or base in his throat, then all the bitch did was suck his dick."

"But," Tasha stressed, "if the niggah comes home and eats your pussy without saying a word, and he goes straight for the clit, best believe it's a bitch out in the street pregnant."

Imani's voice cracked. "That ain't always true, Tasha. Walik ain't never ate my pussy."

"Imani," Sabrena turned to her, "you fucking up my high and shit. Go get dressed. I'll call my li'l crackhead cousin over here to get this. We might not ever find Larry in time, and believe me my cousin'll have this shit sold in five minutes. Keep him from stealing my shit for a li'l while."

"Ai'ight, I'ma go get dressed," Imani sniffed.

Imani grabbed her gear before she left, then went in the bathroom to take a shower.

Once Imani stepped out of the shower, she slipped on a white terry-cloth strapless Juicy dress that came midway to her thick thighs. The tattoo in the middle of her right thigh, of two cherries with cream dripping on them, glistened from the shimmering lotion she rubbed over it. The top of Imani's dress was so tight that her C-cup breasts threatened to spill out. She stood in the mirror, glazed her lips with Oh Baby MAC Lipglass. She popped her lips together, slipped on her pearlized tinted Christian Dior shades, and stepped out the bathroom door. "Ready to roll?"

"Look at you, ho," Sabrena said, returning from setting Walik's bags of clothes outside the apartment door. "Turn around. That shit you got is fiyyah. I know you spent your whole check on that shit. Let me see them shoes."

Imani kicked one foot out, showing off her two-inch white patent-leather Marc Jacobs thongs.

"That shit is nice." Quiana grinned, grabbing her purse and popping an orange Tic Tac in her mouth. Quiana pushed her white round eye shades on top of her Pony hair micro braids. She ran her hand down the front of her blue-and-white diagonal-striped Baby Phat halter dress, to straighten the wrinkles out.

Tasha pulled the side of her Giants' football-jersey dress down, so that it would fall off her shoulders. She looked down at her feet to make sure her heels weren't dirty; she'd bought brand-new blue Chinese slippers and spray-painted numbers on them to match her football-jersey dress, and with this ensemble she knew she was the shit.

"Let's get it cracked," Tasha said. Tasha was the designated driver of the clique, since none of the other girls, including Imani, had her license.

"One minute, I almost forgot," Imani said, walking back into her bedroom and grabbing Walik's guns. She placed them in Jamal's backpack and walked out the door. By the time they got into Tasha's 1993 red CR-V and finished complaining about being cramped, Tasha'd pulled in front of the police station, where Imani turned in Walik's guns. Under the new "Ask No Questions" program, Imani handed the policemen the guns, and they never said a word.

"I am now officially through with that niggah!" Imani said. A few moments later her cell phone rang. When she peeped the caller ID she sucked her teeth. "I cannot stand answering a blocked number."

"Don't answer," Tasha said as she started to drive.

"Nah," Imani flipped her phone open, "it could be something wrong with my son." She placed the phone to her ear. "Who dis?"

"Imani."

"Yeah, this Imani."

"I know who this is, where you at?"

Imani was so hyped, pissed off, and hurt by hearing Walik's voice that she didn't even notice he hadn't called collect. "This niggah!" Imani said loudly.

"Who?" Sabrena frowned. "Walik?"

"Who the fuck else?" Imani said.

"Imani," Walik said calmly, "where are you?"

"I'm on my way to Club NV. Where the fuck are you? On the bottom bunk jawbreakin' a dick, mess hall, or the law library, workin' on that case tryin' to get out?"

"Imani—"

"Oh shit, I got it, you in the license-plate program."

The girls fell out laughing in the background.

"Yeah," Tasha said, peeking in the rearview mirror at Imani in the backseat, "tell that niggah to get a sock and gun his meat!"

"Imani," Walik laughed hesitantly, "y'all got jokes . . . real cute . . . and I tell you what." He was still calm, never raising his voice. "I'll see you in a minute, ma. I'ma let you get that off for now, 'cause I know you're hurt. My peoples told me what happened between you and Shante. But check this, tell big girl and them two li'l anorexic ma'fuckers to mind their business. Matter a fact, take yo' ass home. I don't even want you hangin' with them."

"Kiss my ass, niggah! I wish I would go in the house. My name ain't Shante. You's a no-good, sorry-ass liar that can lick the crack of my shitty ass!"

Imani's girls fell out laughing.

"If you don't like what she's saying then buck, niggah!" Tasha said, still laughing.

"Ahhh haa! Tell that niggah to find him a punk at roll call in the morning!" Sabrena screamed.

"Yo," Walik said calmly, "you see I'm being calm, right? You playin' me and I'm takin' it, but one thing you better do is tell that big-tittie, gold-tooth-wearin' ho that my size thirteen will make her lung collapse."

"Oh please," Imani snapped, "don't play yourself 'cause your feet about a size three. So hurry to the weight room and lay on the bench press and suck a dick. And furthermore, why you on my phone? You don't give a damn about nobody but yourself, you sorry good-for-nothin' rotten-dick bitch! I hate the day that I fell for yo' ass, but not to worry, 'cause the niggah that's runnin' yo' block that you once had locked, his cum slides down my throat with ease. Plus, he lets Jamal call him daddy."

"What you say to me, Imani?" Walik said, his voice rising. "Check it, in a minute I'ma see about you."

"In a minute, niggah please, you got years. Jailhouse ma'fuckers always about to see somebody in a minute. The only thing you gon' see in a minute is the fuckin' yard or the movie room. Go get a new jumpsuit and give it a rest. I can't help it if that niggah's dick bigger than yours!" And with that, Imani hung up.

"And turn that shit off!" Sabrena insisted. "Fuck that niggah, we at the club now!"

Once Tasha parked the car, everyone walked toward the front of the club. The bouncer lived in the same building as Sabrena and Imani, so the girls didn't have to wait long to get in.

"Oh hell yeah!" Sabrena yelled, waving her arms in the air as they stepped into the club. "I'm tryna leave with a big baller tonight!" The music was blasting and the club was jam-packed. Usually the middle of the floor was designated as the dance area but tonight people were dancing all over the place.

"This shit is fire!" Tasha said while ordering an apple martini.

"Look at Papi-chulo over there, Mami." Quiana grinned, waving at the guy.

The girls stood by the bar, watching the crowd, dancing slightly in their spots, and waiting on their favorite song to seduce them to the dance floor. As if on cue Mariah Carey's "It's Like That" started blasting.

"This is my fuckin' theme song!" Imani started getting her bounce on. Closing her eyes, she started working the hell outta the spot she was standing in. Tasha, Quiana, and Sabrena started dancing around her, clapping their hands and cheering her on. "Do that shit, Imani!" As if he'd floated in on cloud nine a sexy copper-toned Puerto Rican brother with wavy black hair corn-rowed to the back and falling to his shoulder blades danced his way over, parted the girls' circle, and started freaking Imani from behind. Imani could feel his hard dick pressed against her ass, but she didn't give a damn. All of her energy was going to the atmosphere and she was enjoying the hell outta being caught up in the moment. Sweat ran down the sides of her face, curved over her neck, and dripped between her breasts. Imani dropped it like it was hot and came back up in an instant. "Do that shit, girl!" Tasha yelled. "Freak his ass!"

Imani continued to do her thing and with each movement, she felt as if she were shedding pieces of her broken heart. She did a spin and was now face-to-face with the guy she was dancing with. She almost lost her balance as she saw how fine he was: six feet tall with a tight eight-pack, well-defined triceps and biceps, chiseled jaw, and a shadow goatee on his chin.

"Damyum . . . what's yo' name?" Imani asked, seemingly taken aback by his beauty.

He looked her up and down. "Kree. Now tell me, do you have another name besides Fine?"

"Imani." She blushed.

"You look sweet as hell, girl."

"Really?"

"Yes, really."

Imani couldn't control her wide smile, and when she attempted to stop showing all her teeth she couldn't control the blushing. Before Imani could speak the music took over and Teairra Mari's "Make Her Feel Good" started playing: *There any boys around that know how to make a girl feel? . . .* " Without saying a word Imani resumed dancing, and Kree followed suit.

Dancing with Kree was making Imani's panties wetter by the moment. The way he moved made her feel as if electric currents were running through her skin. She loved the fact that he wasn't afraid to dance and was still thugged out as hell: baggy jeans, the waist of his white Dolce & Gabbana boxers showing, and his tight and just-right wife beater caressing every curve on his chest.

This niggah gon' fuck around and make me cum, Imani thought as she continued dancing and swaying her hips. She dropped to the floor and popped back up as if her knees were made of springs. She did a spin to face Kree and as she placed her arms around his neck, she saw Walik taking slow sips of beer while eyeing her every move.

Oh shit, Imani thought, *what the fuck is this niggah doing out of jail?* She started counting the months in her head. For a moment she was confused. *Did his ass escape 'cause I told him to go suck a dick? Is it that serious? But I don't think he escaped, 'cause then he wouldn't be here, right? But then again,* she thought, *he is crazy. But maybe he maxed out. But I thought he maxed out next year, June. But I have to be wrong because this niggah is leaning against the bar, sipping a beer, and watching me work it out on the dance floor.* Instantly Imani felt as if Walik had fucked up her high, and the buzz she had before hitting the club had officially left.

She looked around for her girls in case she needed backup but they were scattered around the club. Sabrena had found her a baller, Tasha was kicking it with the bartender, and Quiana managed to get Papi-chulo's full attention.

Them bitches, Imani thought. In an effort to play off her surprise, she took her hands from around Kree's neck, turned around, and threw her ass directly into the pit of his shaft.

Walik walked over and stood in front of Imani. He took a sip of his drink and licked his lips. Imani was praying that she didn't piss on herself. Although she tried not to, she couldn't help but stare at Walik. He was six foot three, 245 pounds of well-put-together brown-sugar lovin'. He had a sexy-ass Gerald Levert beard, lined and trimmed to a T. His hair was freshly braided and styled with zigzag parts going different ways. Walik nodded and acknowledged Imani. She rolled her eyes, threw her hands in the air, dropped to the floor, and snaked her way back up, all while looking Walik directly in the face.

"A niggah outta jail," Walik smirked, looking Imani up and down. "What you gotta say now?"

Imani started singing. *"Are there any boys around that know how to make a girl feel . . ."*

"I'm ready to go," Walik said sternly, speaking to Imani but staring at Kree.

Immediately Kree stopped dancing and stared Walik down. "This you or something?" He pointed to Imani.

"All day long," Walik snapped.

"Don't seem that way to me," Kree responded.

Imani placed her hands on her hips. "I'm dancing, niggah, what?" she spat at Walik.

"You want me to slap the shit outta you?" Walik said to Imani.

"Yo, my man," Kree said, "don't trip. Please don't. My PO is in this ma'fucker and I don't need him witnessing me knockin' you the fuck out."

"Niggah," Walik pushed Imani to the side, "who the fuck are you?" He pushed his shirt open to reveal the butt of his gun.

"Wooo . . . I'm scared," Kree said sarcastically. "Niggah, is you fuckin' playin' cops and robbers with me? See that camera up there?" He pointed toward the ceiling. "It's a niggah with a TEC-9 pointed directly at your fuckin' head. Now, my advice to you is to take it the fuck down."

"Ma'fucker, please." Walik frowned. "Get the fuck out my face. Imani, get ya shit."

"Niggah," Imani spat, "I ain't going nowhere with an escaped convict."

"Escaped?" Walik laughed. "For your information, I was paroled."

"Paroled? Then go get your bracelet checked in and leave me alone." She looked at her watch. "Your curfew passed over an hour ago."

"Didn't I tell you to get your shit and let's bounce? Why you still popping off at the mouth?"

"I ain't moving," Imani insisted.

"If you wanna live you'll get yo' shit and get this niggah the fuck out my face," Walik said, "before I catch another case!"

"Whatever, yo' I ain't beat for this bullshit." Kree twisted his smooth lips. "Stay sweet, ma." And he walked away.

"I swear I feel like dragging you all over this fuckin' club!" Walik stared at Imani.

"Niggah, please." Imani sighed.

"You fuckin' that faggot-ass Rican?"

"What you think?" Imani snapped. "I ain't fuckin' yo' black ass."

"I asked you a question: Are you fuckin' him?"

"Did you fuck Shante?"

"I did . . . and I was wrong."

"Well then, ditto."

"You was wrong, or you fucked him?" The vein in Walik's neck started thumping.

"You know what," Imani could feel the tears clouding her eyes, "I don't even feel like arguing with you. No I'm not fuckin' him. I don't even know him."

"You look like you knew him to me."

"Whatever," she screamed. "I just met that niggah. Now either you believe it or not." She turned to walk away. "Fuck you!"

Walik grabbed Imani by the waist. "Where you goin'?" He pulled her close so that her back was against his chest. He kissed her on the back of the neck. "You know I love you and I trust you, right?"

"I've heard it all before, Walik."

"This time is different, baby. Being in prison made me see that I was fuckin' up my life and fuckin' up my relationship with you and my son. Y'all my world, ma. But let me explain something to you." Walik nuzzled his broad nose into Imani's neck. "If I catch you with another niggah, I'ma beat yo' ass. Now, I heard that shit you said on the phone, *Go suck a dick, go get a new jumpsuit,* your friends all snappin' on me and shit, it's cool. I can take it, 'cause I know you're hurt and it's some shit we gotta work through . . ."

"Niggah—" She tried to pull away from his embrace.

"Don't interrupt me." He pulled her back in. "I'm speaking. But if you ever in your life talk about my son calling another man daddy or how a niggah's cum slides down your throat, it's gon' be over for you."

"Who the hell you talking to—me?" Imani started to raise her voice.

"Don't do that, ma," Walik said calmly. "You see I'm talking to you right, all nice and calm. I really wanna choke the shit outta you, so it would be your best bet not to wild out on me in here."

"What you expect me to do, Walik? Look at what you did, she's pregnant, Walik." Tears filled Imani's eyes.

"I love you and I ain't goin' nowhere. I'm sorry. I really am. That bitch was coming to see me and shit. You know how it is when a niggah locked up. They mind be all fucked up, they can hardly think straight."

"What about me, Walik?"

"Imani, you my fuckin' wife. I ain't gon' have you in prison, fuckin' me like that, sitting on my lap, all out in the open."

"Please, we used to do it all the time."

"I know, baby, but come on, at least I wasn't on no downlow shit. I just wanna be honest. All she doing is having my baby. Fuck that bitch. You know she like a stray dog, any niggah that feed her can keep her. Hell, she can't ever get what you and Jamal got. I love you, and I ain't leavin'."

Imani turned around and buried her head in Walik's chest. His cologne was causing such a seduction in her nostrils that she felt like she had popped some Ecstasy and was just starting to trip. *Why do I let him do this to me?* "Walik, this is too much. I don't think I can swing with it, this time." Imani lifted her head so she could watch the reaction on his face.

He started sucking on his bottom lip, a habit he'd had since he was a kid when he would get mad. Trying to control his temper, Walik squinted at Imani. "Let's go, right now."

"Walik—"

"What the fuck did I just say, I'm not playin' no more. Now, you my wife . . . bottom line. I love you, I ain't leavin', and on top of that I wanna fuck you in our bed, understand?"

Imani's pussy melted on the spot. "Walik," she whined, "I wanted to hang with my girls for a while."

"Hang out tomorrow."

"My mother's bachelorette party is tomorrow."

"So what you saying?"

"Nothing." Imani turned her head, looking around for the girls. She spotted Tasha, placed her hand to her ear, and made a motion for Tasha to call her, then she pointed to Walik and waved bye.

Tasha shook her head.

Imani and Walik walked outside. Walik looked at Imani and pointed to a cab. "Since you can hang out in the club and shit, then you know you got to pay for this, right?"

{ Celeste }

SHARIEF HADN'T BEEN home in two nights. He called Celeste and told her he was working a double shift and would be home sometime this morning.

Anthony Hamilton's "Charlene" was on repeat, playing seductively through the kitchen's surround sound. It was eight o'clock in the morning and the kids were still sleeping. Celeste sat at her marbletop bar that doubled as a breakfast nook with her ankles crossed, sipping on a cup of instant café au lait.

She took a puff off her Virginia Slims Menthol Light. The music continued to play softly in the background as the aroma of cinnamon-and-spice potpourri filled the air. The house was completely clean, and all she had to do was wait on the freshly waxed kitchen floor to dry, go to the grocery store, come back, and begin setting up for Starr's bachelorette party this afternoon. If everything went according to plan, Starr's party was going to be the first exciting thing she'd done since fucking herself with the beaver dildo.

Celeste took one last drag off her cigarette and mashed it in the ashtray. Afterward she stretched her leg and touched the floor with the heel of her foot to see if the wax was dry, but it wasn't. As she lifted her cup to take a sip of coffee, the phone rang. "Hello?"

"Hey, Celeste," Monica said, faking excitement, "what time did you want me to come over?"

"Leave now, that'll put you getting here in about an hour. Don't bring Imani, though, 'cause that li'l bitch gets on my nerves. Let Queen Pen and her down-for-whatever clique stay on Flatbush until the cops run through again."

Monica took a deep breath. "Celeste, please. Not today. I'll be there in a little while: I have to drop Jamal off first." And she ended the call.

As Celeste hung up, she noticed Sharief walking into the kitchen. "The floor is wet." She gave him a quick once-over.

He looked down at the floor. "My fault."

"No problem," she said calmly, "it's almost dry anyway. So how are you this morning?"

Sharief appeared to be caught off guard and started to stutter. "I-I-I'm good, and you?"

"I'm well. Are you hungry? Would you like some breakfast?"

"You wanna cook . . . for me?"

"Of course. I'll cook it for you." Celeste slid off the bar stool and walked over to the refrigerator. She took out extra-sharp cheddar cheese, bacon, and eggs for an omelet. She placed the items on the island's countertop. Then she took a pot, filled it with water, threw in a dash of salt, and placed it on the burner before stirring the grits into it.

Celeste started to hum the gospel tune "Nearer My God to Thee" as she cracked the eggs open. Sharief stood in the doorway, not sure if he should come in and have a seat or back out.

"Have a seat, sweetie," Celeste said while pouring the eggs into the frying pan. "I missed you."

"Yeah?" Sharief said, moving slowly toward the bar. He unbuttoned the top three buttons of his sky-blue shirt, which revealed his wife beater and gave hints of the smooth hair on his chest. He sat down on the bar stool, on the opposite side of the center island from where Celeste stood cooking over the stovetop. Her hips swayed gracefully as she moved about, cooking the omelet and stirring the grits. Celeste wore a pair of CK jeans with a ribbed, sleeveless peach top, showing off the auburn freckles spread across her chest. Her hair had grown a little since she'd last cut it, and was now in an abundance of short natural curls.

"Celeste," Sharief said.

"Yes?" She turned the coffeepot on.

"You look nice."

"Thank you. Is your dick hard?"

"What?"

Celeste spoke slowly. "Is . . . your . . . dick . . . hard?"

"What the hell kinda question is that?" Sharief frowned.

"Look," she cut off the stove, reached for a plate, and slid the omelet on it, "you said I look nice so I wanted to know if I looked nice enough to make your dick hard. It must be soft." She leaned forward and squeezed his dick, looking him directly in the face. "It's real fucked up that your dick is soft, but not to worry, it'll be okay, sweetie, I understand." She fixed him a bowl of grits.

"Yo." Sharief chuckled in disbelief, shaking his head. "Chill with that shit. Celeste, I don't wanna argue with you."

"Me neither . . . me neither." She poured him a cup of coffee. "Milk or cream?"

"Cream."

"Can you grab it for me, sweetie?"

Sharief grabbed the cream out the refrigerator and placed it in front of her.

"Three sugar cubes?" Celeste asked.

"Yeah."

Celeste poured the cream and placed three sugar cubes in Sharief's coffee.

He took a sip.

"I'm sorry about the other night. I was a little out of line,"

Celeste said, cutting off the stove and bending over the island's counter.

"Yeah, I am too." Sharief kept his eyes on Celeste as he took a sip of his coffee.

"Is it sweet enough?" she asked.

"Yeah."

"As sweet as the cum that was sliding down your throat last night?"

Sharief swallowed hard. "Are you crazy? What the hell is wrong with you?"

"Oh, Sharief, darling," Celeste chuckled, sipping on her now cold latte, "nothing is wrong with me. I just figured that the bitch you're fuckin' must have some sweet cum because you're never here and when you are here, you play Daddy of the Year and that's it." She took another sip. "Honestly, I don't remember the last time you fucked me." She placed her cup on the counter. "Do you even remember what my pussy looks like?" She picked her cup back up and took a sip. "Uhmm, just so you know, I have a few gray hairs down there now. I'm thinking about dyeing it with some Just for Men, whatcha think?"

"I think yo' ass is crazy as hell," Sharief nervously chuckled. "Let me go take a shower, get my kids, and get out of here."

"There you go, planning to leave again!" Celeste slammed her fist against the counter, rattling the coffee cups. "What the hell is going on, Sharief? Just tell me who she is! That's all I want to know!" She opened her eyes wide. "Who is she? Is she somebody that I know? Would you do that, Sharief, are you fucking one of the neighbors? Is it Drew, is it Bree . . . Oh hell no, I got it, it's Veronica, that's why she moved from around here. I'ma kick her fuckin' ass!"

"I'm not fuckin' Monica! What the hell is wrong with you?"

"I didn't say Monica." She arched her eyebrows. "I said Veronica."

"Whoever the hell. All I know is that I'm not feeling this shit no more. I have tried, but I'm tired. Look at you, you act like you done lost your damn mind! Naw"—he shook his head—"this is some crazy shit."

Celeste picked up Sharief's cup of coffee and slapped the shit out of him with it, causing the cup to shatter and the hot liquid to splatter on the right side of his face. Some of it flew over his head and ran down his left cheek. Quickly Sharief took the palm of his hand and wiped the steamy coffee off his face.

After making sure the coffee hadn't burned him, Sharief reached across the island and grabbed Celeste around the neck. She flung her arms and knocked the hot grits off the stove as Sharief dragged her over the countertop. She tried to grab the edge of the island but couldn't grip it fast enough.

Everything seemed to be moving too fast. Not knowing what else to do, Celeste grabbed the butcher knife out of the multi-knife holder and swung it; immediately the top of Sharief's hand popped open and blood started running everywhere. "Awwwwwl shit!" he screamed, knocking her off the counter. "I'ma kick yo' fuckin' ass, bitch!"

Celeste regained her balance and jumped up with the butcher knife in her hand. "Let's roll, ma'fucker!" With the knife in one hand, Celeste picked up Sharief's plate of food with the other and threw it at him. Sharief ducked, the plate just missing his head.

"I hope that bitch is worth it!" Celeste picked up the coffeepot and threw it at him. The glass shattered and coffee splattered all over the wall, the steam still rising from it. If Sharief hadn't seen the pot coming it would've burned him in the face; instead it caught a small portion of his forearm. "What the fuck! You want me to kill you?"

"Kill me?" Celeste completely lost it. She threw what was left of the grits at him, breaking the kitchen window. "Kill me? I'm already dead, ma'fucker. I can't find shit that I like to do. I can't even remember what I wanted to be when I was a little girl. I've been reduced to staying home and being hidden in this goddamn house like I ain't shit while you pick yourself up and come and go as you please. You don't even fuck me anymore!"

"Fuck you?" Sharief screamed. "I wouldn't fuck you if your pussy was glued to my dick! This shit is a wrap! It's over!" Blood dripped from his hand as he grabbed a kitchen towel and wrapped it around the cut. Instantly blood soaked through the towel. As he tried to walk out of the room, Celeste ran in front of him and blocked his path. She still had the bloody butcher knife in her hand. She swung it and Sharief ducked.

"What the fuck!" Immediately Sharief drew his gun and pointed it at Celeste. "Now put that shit down!"

Celeste swung the knife at his head again. He ducked and cocked the gun. "I swear," he said, his finger on the trigger, "I will shoot you, bury you, and fuck a bitch this afternoon if you swing that fuckin' knife at me again!"

"You don't want me, Sharief? Just say it!"

"Why are you a glutton for punishment? I told you this wasn't working out before we left Brooklyn."

Celeste stood motionless with the knife still in the air. Flashbacks of him telling her how he wanted to just take care of his kids and leave the marriage ran through her mind. "How could you do this to me, Sharief?" Tears ran down her face.

"Put the knife down, Celeste." Sharief spoke as calmly as he could. The side of his face felt sore as he twitched his lips. He slowly moved his finger from the trigger.

"Celeste!" Monica called out, turning the knob on the unlocked front door. "Did you hear me ringing the bell over and over again? I've been out here"—she walked into the kitchen—"for ten minutes." She blinked and dropped her purse on the floor. It took a few seconds for her to register what she was seeing. She spoke slowly: "What . . . the hell . . . is going . . . on here?" As if she were under arrest, she slowly placed her hands in the air.

"Put the knife down, Celeste," Sharief said. Moving the barrel from her chest to her leg, he placed his finger back on the trigger, and the blood from his hand started to drip on the floor. "Please, Celeste," he begged, "I don't want to hurt you."

Seeing Sharief bleeding brought Monica out of shock. She put her arms down and slowly walked toward him. "What happened to your hand? Oh my God, look at all this blood, you need to go to the hospital!"

"Fuck that! Put the knife down, Celeste," Sharief ordered, cocking the trigger. "I will shoot you!"

"Celeste, sweetie," Monica said calmly, "please put the knife down. Please."

"I swear I should kill you," Celeste spat at Sharief. She took the knife and threw it on the floor. Sharief stepped on it as Celeste moved from in front of his face. Instantly his eyes locked with Monica's. Realizing that the gun was now pointed at her, Monica backed up. "Put that shit away!"

"I'm sorry." Sharief took the gun and placed it back in the holster on the side of his hip. "I swear to God," he went on, wiping the sweat from his forehead, "if you ever in your life pull a knife out on me again, I will arrest you!"

"You gon' arrest me?" Celeste snapped. She opened the cabinets above the sink and started throwing the dishes at him again. "Fuck you! Arrest me, ma'fucker! Do it! All this for some bitch in the street? Why did you marry me if you were going to cheat on me! I was fine all by myself!" Dishes were flying past Monica and Sharief like Frisbees.

"Celeste!" Monica screamed. "Stop it! *Stop it!*"

"Move, Monica, because I'ma kill him!" As Celeste said this one of the dishes shattered against the wall, and the flying pieces almost cut up Monica's face. Monica fell face-first trying to get out of the way. When she looked back up her nose was bleeding.

Sharief walked over to Celeste as she continued to throw dishes at him, blocking the hits with his arms. He grabbed her by the neck, lifting her slightly in the air, causing her to drop the dish in her hand. He squeezed the veins on the side of her neck so tight, she felt like her esophagus was being crushed. "What did I tell you? You think this is a fuckin' game?" He slapped her on the side of the head. "You think I'm playing?" He mushed her in the forehead.

"Sharief—Sharief." Monica got off the floor, holding her nose with the palm of her hand, some of the blood dripping between her fingers. She grabbed a dish towel off the counter. She was desperately trying to stop her nose from bleeding and her sister from being choked to death. "Come on," Monica pleaded, grabbing Sharief's arm, trying to loosen his grip. "Please let her go." Celeste was starting to cough as her tears rolled over Sharief's hands. "Sharief, just let her go! Let my sister go!" She ran and grabbed her purse off the floor, opened it, and shook all the contents on the counter. "Take my keys." She ran back over to him and stuffed her house keys in his side pocket; they were the same keys that he'd thrown at her earlier. "Just go." She wiped her nose, the blood starting to clog. She touched the bridge to ensure it wasn't broken.

"I came to get my children." He was still holding Celeste by the neck, blood dripping from his hand.

"Go get them. Are they upstairs?" Monica was desperate: Celeste's eyes were half closed.

"Yeah," he said, never taking his eyes off Celeste. "They're sleep."

"They're sleeping through all of this?" She looked around the kitchen. "Sharief, please, stay in New York tonight. Visit your mother and father, do something, because if you keep staying here like this, right now, somebody's going to die." He dropped Celeste to the floor. Celeste grabbed her neck and started coughing. Never taking his eyes off Celeste, Sharief started backing out of the kitchen. Monica ran over to him and grabbed his hand. She unwrapped the dish towel and looked at his cut. "You're going to need stitches."

"Look," Sharief huffed, "I know you mean well but I gotta get outta here!"

"Shut the hell up!" Monica screamed, tears running down her face. "Don't you need your hand to fuckin' work, *Detective,* or do you want an infection to seep in and lead to amputation?"

"Yo, I don't give a fuck right now. I gotta get outta here before I kill her. I'm straight!" Sharief snatched his hand away and briskly walked out of the room.

Celeste was crouched in the fetal position on the floor, and Monica stood there looking around. She had a bloodstained kitchen towel in her hand and a bloody butcher knife on the floor; every dish in the house was broken with the pieces scattered on the floor. There was coffee everywhere, eggs all over the place, and all of the cabinet doors were swinging back and forth. "Have you lost your fuckin' mind?" Monica looked down at Celeste. She wanted to kick her ass but thought better of it. "Do you hear me, Celeste?" she screamed. "Are you fuckin' crazy?"

"No! I just can't take it. He's cheating on me and I know he is!"

"So you try to kill him? You can't just leave or divorce his ass? You wanna go to jail?"

"I don't care!"

"You don't care? And who's going to take care of those three li'l grown asses you got? Get off that floor acting pitiful! If he didn't want your ass when you were sane, you think he wants you now when you're acting crazy as hell?"

"Monica—"

"Celeste, I don't even want to hear it. We are supposed to be having a bachelorette party for our mother and you don't have one fuckin' dish in the house, you look a hot-ass mess, and nothing is cooked. Get off the floor!"

Celeste got off the floor and started crying hysterically. "What does she have that I don't?"

Monica picked up the knife off the floor. "Who, Celeste?"

"The woman that he's with. Why is he choosing her over me?"

"You don't know if the man is cheating," Monica said as she put the knife in the sink. She grabbed the broom and began sweeping the floor, doing her best to avoid eye contact with Celeste. She bit the inside of her jaw. "Stop assuming." Shaking her head, she felt like shit.

"He told me he didn't want me," Celeste said. "Do you know the last time that he fucked me?"

"Look at how you're acting. Would you fuck you?"

Celeste didn't know what to say. She wiped her eyes, grabbed a sponge, and started wiping off the kitchen walls where the coffee, grits, and omelet had splattered. Half an hour later Sharief came down the stairs with the girls following behind him. The twins were both dressed in the same outfit: pink denim shorts, white baby-doll tees, and Dora the Explorer sandals. Kayla had on a white one-piece velour short jumpsuit with the matching visor. Sharief looked at Monica; his eyes told her that he loved her. Then he looked at Celeste. His eyes said nothing. "I'm out."

"Wow! Mommy!" Kai screamed in excitement. "You had a food fight!"

"Yuck!" Kayla frowned. "I heard yelling but, humph, this is nasty." She looked over and saw Monica. "Aunty!" She ran and hugged her around the waist, Kai and Kori following suit.

"Hey, Aunty's babies."

"Aunty," Kayla said, "when can we go shopping? Can I come spend the night with you?"

"Yes, next weekend, maybe. We'll see, okay?"

"That's a long time." Kayla pouted.

"No it's not. Now you get going with your daddy and Aunty will see you later."

"Bye, Mommy," the girls said, going out the door.

Monica turned to Celeste as Sharief and the girls left. "Let your children be the only ones that bring you to your breaking point. Understand? Men come a dime a dozen. Period. If Sharief doesn't want you then fuck him. But right now you need to get yo' shit together!"

"Monica—"

"Save it, Celeste, Ma'll be here any minute." Monica walked over to the refrigerator and opened it. "Where's the food for the party?" she asked.

"I didn't have a chance to get any."

"What? Why not?" Monica slammed the refrigerator door. "What did you do with the money I gave you?"

"I borrowed it. I needed to pay for my part of the flowers."

"And . . . how were you going to get the food?"

"I figured I could use my credit card and buy some ready-made platters from Costco."

Monica peered at Celeste. "I could slap the shit out of you! Does anything besides your unfaithful-ass husband run through your mind? Why would you use my money without asking? And on flowers? I paid my half for the flowers already. If you couldn't afford to help pay for this damn wedding then you *should not* have volunteered. Mommy could've taken her happy ass to the VFW! Shit!"

"I have children to take care of." Celeste looked Monica up and down. "Something you know nothing about. And I have a husband who is the only one who works."

"Then get yo' lazy ass a job!" Monica flopped down in the kitchen chair. "This is ridiculous. Where the hell is Costco? Let's go."

"It's an hour away," Celeste said nonchalantly, searching the ashtray for a decent cigarette butt.

"Why are you smoking cigarette butts? Just go get a damn cigarette!"

"I only have one pack left," Celeste said, lighting the butt, "and I'm saving it until tomorrow."

"Whatever," Monica said dismissively. "Wait a minute . . . Costco is how far away?" She looked at the clock: it was fifteen minutes before the first guest was due to arrive, and Starr was due shortly after. "I can't believe this! I really can't. The next time save your Desperate Housewife–Lorena Bobbitt attempt, because now everybody's affected by the shit! Now what are we supposed to do?"

"I don't know." Celeste blew out the smoke. "You figure it the fuck out. Shit! I can't do everything."

"Everything?" Monica screamed. "You don't do shit but complain!"

"Don't worry about me complaining. I've always had to do everything under the sun while you and Imani got to live your lives, so hell, I fuck up this one time and the world is coming to an end?"

"You are so selfish, Celeste. You were supposed to get this food days ago. I called and left messages for you."

"Messages? Oh please, what messages, the one you left on Sharief's voice mail? The one that said, *Sharief, tell Celeste to get the food . . . and I got some Audio Two concert tickets . . . blah . . . blah . . . blah?* Oh yeah, I meant to ask you, did Chauncey ask you to marry him that night or what?"

"You've been listening to Sharief's voice mail?"

"Of course, wouldn't you?"

"Why . . . would you do that?"

"Oh please, you are not that naïve. So did you tell Chauncey no? And if so, why? You need to go ahead and get married . . . do something with yourself besides layin' down and shackin' up with no-good niggahs. Humph, I was beginning to wonder if that threesome you had with your ex-boyfriend turned you out. I never looked at you the same after that. Sex with a man and another bitch, yuck! Does that shit make you a dyke?"

"Wait a goddamn minute here!" Monica slammed her fist on the kitchen counter. "I'm not a fuckin' dyke, you crazy bitch. And why should I get married? Who's setting the example, you? Oh honey, spare-fuckin'-me paleeze. And then you're listening to Sharief's voice mail? I should tell him. I can't believe this! You desperate fuckin' lunatic! You are certifiable."

"I'm certifiable? I'm not the one who needed Zoloft after she'd been left by a niggah."

"I didn't need Zoloft, bitch, that was your father when Mommy left his ass. Oh excuse me, he didn't need Zoloft. It was crack he turned to. Don't break bad with me, 'cause you will never win! You used to talk a buncha shit that made me cry, but not now I got somethin' fo' ya ass. Now try me."

"I don't have time to argue with you." Celeste mashed the cigarette butt in the ashtray. "Save the bullshit."

"Whatever, do you have anything in the refrigerator that can be thrown together quickly?"

"Yeah."

"What?" Monica got up and opened the refrigerator. "Celeste," she batted her eyes, "ain't shit in here but some damn breakfast food and Kid Cuisine."

"Well, there's some Care Bears fruit snacks and Oodles of Noodles in the cabinet."

"Oh . . . my . . . God . . ."

[Starr]

"HONEY-CHILE, I ain't had no reefer in about twenty years. For real—for real." Starr took a pull, the wet tip of the long and skinny joint glued between her lips. Relaxing her shoulders, she lay back in the recliner and crossed her ankles. "Buttah, this is the best wedding gift anyone could've given me." Starr was in her glory sitting in her living room, shooting the shit with her senile and soon-to-be mother-in-law, Mama Byrd, and Starr's oldest and dearest friend Buttah-Ann Askew.

"You know I had to get my home girl something," Buttah said, "and what better than a dime bag of smoke." Buttah placed the joint between her lips and pulled. "I just can't believe you getting married."

"I know." Starr blushed. "I've been engaged three times."

"Damn," Mama Byrd spat, "what the hell you tryna prove? We already know you a old ho."

Starr was offended. "How you figure?"

"Hell, all ya kids got different last names."

"Hush," Buttah snarled at Mama Byrd. "Lawd knows yo' senile ass is always talkin'."

Mama Byrd pounded her chest and stood up. "Make me shut up then, you so bad."

"Oh, don't get it fucked up." Buttah stood up. "I fights old ladies."

"Bring it then." Mama Byrd swayed from side to side.

"Wait a minute now," Starr said, getting between them. "Calm down." She turned to Buttah. "Now, Buttah, why you lettin' Mama Byrd get to you? You know she senile."

"You right," Buttah said, calming down. "I'm sorry, Mama Byrd."

"What you sorry for, baby?" Mama Byrd looked around. "And why is we standin'? We getting ready for the bachelorette party?" Mama Byrd smiled. "I hope they got a dancer who knows how get his grind on. 'Cause this seventy-five-year-old coochie need a fire-cracker!"

"Mama Byrd, be quiet." Buttah rolled her eyes, sitting back down.

"Bachelorette?" Starr's eyes lit up. "Is that what you said?"

"Sho'nough. And Buttah the one 'spose to be bringin' you." Mama Byrd sat back down and reached for the joint. She took a pull off the tip and spoke through the smoke. "Them niggahs say somebody gettin' married." She snapped her fingers as the burning weed hung from between her lips. "Who that is, who that is?"

"Who what is, Mama Byrd?" Starr asked, confused.

"Who gettin' married?"

"I am." Starr sighed. "I am marrying your son, *Red, tomorrow.*"

"Who the fuck is Red? Let me find out that ma'fuckers is still tryna say they know me."

"Mama Byrd," Buttah said, snatching the joint from between her lips, "if you gon' be acting senile, you ain't gon' be able to get ya blaze on with me no more."

"This is my shit, bitch. I'm the one with the prescription for it, not you. And who is you anyway?" Mama Byrd squinted her eyes.

"Awl hell naw!" Starr couldn't believe it. "Buttah, you mean to tell me this is Mama Byrd's shit?"

"Look, Starr, you know I'm on probation. The last time I was on the block tryna buy some reefer I got arrested for solicitation. So I had to take what I could get."

"Lord have mercy." Starr shook her head.

"So where is my bachelorette party? At the Foxx Trap?"

"Nawl, not there." Buttah took a pull.

"The Tremount?"

"Nawl, not there." Buttah let out the smoke.

"Madison Lounge?"

"Madison Lounge?" Mama Byrd interrupted. "Is you that bitch who stole my man from me?"

"Hush, ole lady," Starr said. "Now, where the hell is the bachelorette party?"

"At Celeste's house!" Mama Byrd spat out and then fell out laughing. "I know that's yo' daughter, but that ho is boooooorring! I bet all we gon' do is drink tea, hold our pinkies out, eat biscuits, and tell lies about how happy we is to be married. Well I'll tell you, men ain't shit, 'cause I ain't seen my husband in about ten years."

"Could that have something to do with him being dead for twelve years?" Buttah rolled her eyes.

"Well, how you know and I don't?" Mama Byrd pointed her finger toward Buttah's face. "I knew you was the bitch his stiff ass was cheatin' wit'."

"Mama Byrd, please," Starr said, agitated. "I don't understand how you can't remember from one minute to the next but you can remember a cuss word."

"Oh hold up, you don't want it wit' me, home girl! Better ask about me! Tell her somethin', Peaches."

"My name is Buttah." Buttah took one last pull off the joint.

"Oh, that's right." Mama Byrd frowned. "You that huzzie who

pussy-whipped my knee-baby boy, Jimmy. I believe you worked roots on him."

"I didn't work no roots!" Buttah screamed. "Jimmy loved me!"

"That's what they all say. But I know one thang, I was so thankful the day he left yo' ass. I ain't never believe them was his kids anyway."

"I'm tired of this coming up every few years, Mama Byrd. Like I told you before, De-niece and De-nephew are Jimmy's kids!"

"De-niece and De-who?" Mama Byrd frowned. "What kinda ghetto shit you got goin' on? And who the fuck is De-niece and De-nephew?"

"Enough!" Starr yelled, standing up from the chair. "You know De-niece and De-nephew are Jimmy's kids. Now we got other things to worry about, like what am I gon' wear to my party. I got to go get fly!" Starr stood and turned to go upstairs.

"Hell," Buttah yelled after her, "why you think I got this catsuit on?"

"Sho'ly ain't 'cause you got the body for it." Mama Byrd grinned. Buttah ignored her and mashed the remains of the joint in the ashtray; she felt like slappin' Mama Byrd upside the head. Just then Buttah's cell phone rang. As she flipped her phone open, Mama Byrd slipped the roach in her duster pocket.

"Hello," Buttah spoke into the phone.

"Buttah," Monica said, trying not to be nasty, "where are you and Mommy? You're an hour late! Everybody's here and we're all waiting."

"Oh baby, we're down the street. We'll be there in five minutes."

"She lyin'!" Mama Byrd yelled in the background.

"What did Mama Byrd say?" Monica asked.

"Nuthin'. Nuthin'. We're on our way."

Buttah hung up and shot Mama Byrd the evil eye.

"I wish you would!" Mama Byrd took her pocketbook and held

it in the air. "Look at me like that again and I'll tear yo' mouth out!"

"Hush." Buttah smirked. "Pull up them knee-highs, fix the snaps on your duster, take that purse down, and let's go!"

Mama Byrd fixed her clothes, grabbing her snuff and her empty spit cup. She placed them in her bag then went in the bathroom and rolled out her portable toilet with the metal railings. "Will this fit in yo' mini van?" She looked at Buttah.

"What the hell you wanna travel with a toilet for? Celeste got a bathroom."

Mama Byrd placed a hand on her hip. "Why is you all in my bid'ness, I ain't asked why yo' shoes lean to the side, so don't fuck with me about my porta-potty."

"Whatever you want, Mama Byrd, whatever you want."

A few minutes later Starr came downstairs dressed and ready to leave.

By the time they arrived at Starr's "surprise" bachelorette party, most of the guests were pissed. Not only had they been served Oodles of Noodles with a side of fried eggs, the guest of honor was three hours late.

As Starr walked in, everyone yelled a dry "Surprise."

Starr stood in the middle of the floor and fixed her catsuit as best she could. It was psychedelic blue and made out of paper-thin material, with one arm completely exposed and a shredded sleeve covering the other. Around her waist she wore a blue suede belt with a round silver buckle that was slanted to the side. Her three-inch white platforms were killing her feet but she was determined to strut her stuff. She was praying that her Visine kicked in as she placed her hand over her mouth. "All of this for me? Oh my God, what is this for?"

"Awl trick." Mama Byrd twisted her lips. "You know what this is for."

"My bachelorette party!" Starr smiled, ignoring Mama Byrd. She wiped the tears from her eyes as she looked around. Starr strutted her stuff across the room and kissed her family and friends on the cheeks. She mingled with them for a little while before Monica walked over to get her attention.

Monica shot a fake smile at the person her mother was talking to. "Excuse me," she said, grabbing Starr by the arm.

"Yes?" Starr said as they stepped to the side.

"Where have you all been and why is Mama Byrd telling people that the three of you were at home gettin' lifted?"

"Monica, you know the woman is senile."

"She might be senile, but she was just standing in the corner trying to light a joint. And now she keeps telling people about the batteries being low in her dildo. Get her ass right now!"

"Wooo, take that down, sweetie." Starr arched her eyebrows. "I'm still your mama. Now, where the hell is this old lady?" Starr looked around the room. She spotted Mama Byrd sitting at the bar with her legs gapped open and looking at a magazine picture of Steve Harvey. "I'm sayin', though," she snarled at the picture, "wassup with us, firecracker? Let me tell you I got a mean head game, and just so you know"—she winked—"a bitch's nickname is Lipton in case you ever need a tea bag."

"Oh my Jesus!" Starr snatched the magazine out of Mama Byrd's hand. "Let go and stop it!"

Mama Byrd jumped up. "You don't want it wit' me, Sun. For real you don't, better ask about me."

"My name is not Sun, it's Starr."

"Starr? Oh hey, Starr, how you doing today?"

Starr took a deep breath. "Just be good, Mama Byrd, just be good."

"Let's eat, everyone!" Celeste announced to the guests and led them into the dining room, where they each had their choice of popcorn chicken, macaroni and cheese Kid Cuisine, or fried eggs dipped in grits.

"What kinda shit is this?" Mama Byrd asked, looking around. "Eggs? I don't want no damn eggs! They make me fart! You ever smell a fried-egg fart, that shit is lethal. Y'all think I be around here shittin' now, humph. Y'all just some sorry asses! Goddamn eggs!" She picked up her Kid Cuisine. "Now somebody done microwaved the sprinkles under my chicken." She turned to Starr. "What the fuck is goin' on?"

Starr was so embarrassed she didn't know what to say. She looked at Celeste.

"Don't look at me," Celeste said, "I have enough problems."

Starr turned to Monica. "I'll be right back," Monica said, "I need to find Imani, she's got the party favors." Monica excused herself from the dining room. She called Imani's house and cell phone, but didn't receive an answer. As she went to dial Walik's mother's number, the doorbell rang.

Hoping and praying that it was Imani, Monica snatched the door open.

" 'Sup, niggah?" Imani's friend Sabrena snapped her neck. "Tasha parking the car and there go Quiana coming up the block."

"Hi, Sabrena," Monica said drily. "Have you seen Imani?"

"No, I thought she would've been here."

"Well, she's not. She was supposed to drop Jamal off with Walik's mother and then catch the train here."

" 'Sup, Monica?" Quiana and Tasha said, now standing beside Sabrena.

"Nothing, come on in, girls."

As soon as the girls walked into the living room Mama Byrd spotted them. "My niggahs! West Side."

"Mama Byrd," they whined in unison and ran to give her a hug.

When I find Imani I'ma cuss her ass the fuck out! Monica thought as she walked back into the kitchen and dialed Imani's cell phone again. No answer. She called Walik's mother.

The phone was picked up on the first ring. "Who dis?"

Monica knew right away it was Jamal. "Who *dis*?" Monica frowned.

"Yeah, that's what I said, who dis? Dis the 'Free Walik' party."

"I'ma beat yo' ass, li'l boy! Who you talkin' to?"

"Oh, Aunty, I didn't know that was you."

"I bet you didn't know it was me. Where is your mother? And what is all that noise in the background?"

"Imani right here talking to Walik. My grandma over here having a get-free party for my daddy."

"A what?"

"A party. He free."

"What do you mean he's free?"

"The niggah outta jail, Aunty."

"Watch your mouth. Now let me speak to your mother."

"Imani, phone!" Jamal yelled.

Monica was seething. Imani picked up the phone. "Who dis?"

"I swear to God I should just walk over there and punch you in the goddamn face! Why the hell aren't you here?"

"I'm coming. Jamal's grandmother was having a little get-together and I got caught up."

"Bitch! Stop lying! What kind of get-together?"

"A family gathering."

"For what?"

" 'Cause she wanted to have one."

"Is Walik out of jail?"

"Noooo, he's not. He'll be out next week, though."

"Stop lying! Jamal just told me that his grandmother was having a get-free party for Walik."

"That makes no sense, Monica. Why would she be having a get-free party if he's already home?"

"You tell me!"

"Monica—"

"Don't *Monica* me. What the hell is really wrong with you?

Where were they when he was beatin' yo' ass or better yet, when you were locked the fuck up for six months without a bail?"

"Oh God, here we go. These are my in-laws!" Imani snapped.

"In-laws! Bitch, you ain't married! You just a baby mama. Period. Get your shit untwisted. Trust me, they gon' be in-laws to you and whatever other bitch that lowlife got in the street. Just remember those'll be the same triflin' assess that'll turn on you when the shit go down again. I can't believe you would pull something like this!"

"Did I say I wasn't coming?"

"Are you here?" Monica yelled.

"No, but I'll be there. Plus, the wedding is tomorrow."

"Oh." Monica smirked. "I'm glad you remembered. Will you be here or is this get-free party lasting for two days?"

"Whatever, yo." Imani sucked her teeth. "You just hatin' 'cause you don't have a man."

"Don't you worry about it and furthermore, keep me lonely if I gotta have somebody like Walik's triflin' can't-stay-outta-jail sorry ass!"

"Monica, I don't have to listen to this!"

Monica was too disgusted to keep speaking to Imani so she hung up on her and walked back into the dining room. There she saw that most of the guests were even more disgusted than when she'd left. "These bitches is servin' Care Bear fruit snacks for dessert," Mama Byrd said, shaking her head. "And they call me crazy."

Before anyone could comment, spotlights shot back and forth across the room with one shining toward the door. In walked a six-foot-three-inch man with large muscles, cornrows braided straight to the back, and a well-fitted tailor-made gray Versace suit. As the man started to dance, Ready for the World's "Let Me Love You Down" began to play.

"Awwl shit!" Starr started bouncing her shoulders.

"Take it off!" Mama Byrd yelled, "take it *all* off!"

Slowly the dancer started peeling his clothes off. He stared at Starr seductively and pointed his finger, motioning her to come to him. Starr placed her hand over her heart. "Oh Lord, what are you going to do to me?"

"Stand here and watch me," the dancer demanded as the music played.

"Do that shit, baby!" Mama Byrd yelled.

"Hell yeah!" all the women in the room yelled, each of them starting to sweat. Once the dancer was down to his G-string he turned Starr around; with her ass glued to his shaft he bent her over and started pounding. She could feel his hard dick as her ass bounced in the air.

"Oh shit!" Mama Byrd yelled as Starr started panting. Slowly the dancer laid Starr on the floor. He moved his body like a snake, opened her legs, and made motions with his head as if he were eating her pussy.

Monica and Celeste couldn't believe their eyes. They didn't know whether to be embarrassed or in shock. Starr lay on the floor with her legs gaped open and shaking as if she suffered from epilepsy.

Once the dancer worked Starr over, he walked over to Buttah and pushed her against the wall. He bit each of her nipples. She felt chills running through her body.

The other women couldn't control themselves and started putting dollar bills in his G-string.

"Let me see that dick, ma'fucker!" Mama Byrd yelled.

"Oh, you want some?" the dancer asked Mama Byrd.

"Bring it on, baby boy, bring it on."

"Can you handle this?"

He walked over to Mama Byrd, and immediately she turned around, lifted her duster over her ass, and bent down. "Hit it, nig-gah, hit it!"

The dancer started banging her in the ass. She turned around, dropped to the floor, and spread her legs. "I want you to make me have a seizure."

"Mama Byrd!" Imani's friend Sabrena yelled. "What is that between your legs?"

"Gray carpet!" Mama Byrd yelled. "Now, come on, firecracker," she invited the dancer, " 'cause this ole clit need a flame lit!"

{ Monica }

"YOU KNOW WHAT I wonder?" Celeste spoke into a stream of smoke after the guests had left. She watched Monica hang up her electric-blue bridesmaid's gown and then pull out a black silk nightgown from her overnight bag. "I wonder if she ever thinks about what she's doing to my family."

Monica cocked her neck to the side. "Who is 'she'?"

"The other woman." Celeste took a drag.

"Why are you thinking about some shit like that?" Monica took the rest of her things from her bag. "Cool it with the bullshit, please. The guests just left and despite the grits used for dip, somehow we pulled this evening off. Now Ma and the rest of her old-ass-ghetto-wedding crew are downstairs trying to sleep. Why can't you just chill, damn!"

"Fuck chill. Chill ain't done shit for me but make me fat and have another bitch sleeping with my man."

"Oh God," Monica sighed. "Why don't you stop acting so in-nocent? Like everything is always so perfect until someone else comes along and messes it up. Take some responsibility."

"Responsibility?" Celeste mashed her cigarette in the ashtray and immediately lit up another one. "I can't believe you, but I forgot you don't know shit about how I feel because no man of yours ever stayed around long enough to count."

"I'm not the one being cheated on, sweetie. Let me inform you," Monica looked at Celeste and smirked, "I steal, I don't get stole on."

"And you're still alone." Celeste blew out the smoke. "So spare me. Need I remind you of what Mommy went through with yo' daddy?"

"Don't talk about my daddy!"

"Why shouldn't I? He's the one that fucked up our family!"

"Bitch, please!" Monica looked Celeste up and down. "Yo' daddy was a basehead and you look just like him with that cigarette stuck in yo' mouth! Mommy didn't want him, get the fuck over it."

"My father wasn't a basehead, tramp!"

"Tell it to the morgue, I don't give a damn."

"Bitch!"

"Correction, Ms. Bitch!"

"Yeah, Ms. Bitch with the rotten-ass womb. Let's see if your one fallopian tube makes you another baby!"

"What?" Tears rushed to Monica's eyes.

"Yeah, I said it and what?"

"I'ma get the fuck away from you because right about now I feel like punching you dead in the mouth!" Monica grabbed her car keys. "Dumb bitch!" She ran down the stairs and slammed the door behind her.

As Monica hopped in her car, Sharief parked his Excursion directly behind her. He threw the SUV in park, hopped out, and opened the back door to wake his sleeping children.

Monica rolled her window down. "Could you move, please!"

"Woooo, homes, slow it down." He looked at his watch. "Where are you going?"

"I'm getting the fuck outta here before I end up beating your wife's freckle-faced ass! I'm going to a motel—"

"Motel?" Sharief said. "Let me find out you got some niggahs up there tryna run a train on you," he chuckled, "tryna get a li'l short stay and shit."

"Do I have ha-ha-ha on my forehead? Do I look like I wanna fuckin' laugh? Get away from my car and back up that raggedy piece of shit you got."

"Don't talk about Abdul." Sharief shook his head. "Ab ain't never done shit to you."

"I have heard it all—a damn truck named Abdul!" Monica huffed, but she was even more pissed that she felt like laughing at Sharief. "Such a stupid ass!" she seethed.

Sharief walked over to Monica's car and opened the passenger's-side door. He slid in. "You still mad with me?"

"Being mad with you is not on my mind right now."

"Well then," he whispered, "tell me you love me."

"Are you crazy?"

"About you. Now tell me you love me."

"I will not," she said, tight-lipped.

"You don't love me?"

"Of course I do, but this is not the time. I can't stand this and I don't even know why I'm here. Celeste and I argue every time we see each other."

"Cut it out." Sharief frowned. "And stop acting ridiculous. You and Celeste need to stop arguing and focus on your mother. Now cut the engine off and get your ass back in the house."

"Psst, niggah, please." Monica waved her hand.

Sharief placed his hand on her knee. "What did I say?"

Monica glanced at Sharief's hand and saw that it was bandaged properly. "Did you go to the hospital?"

"Yeah, I went by my mother's and she had a fit . . . I told her I hurt it at work and she insisted that I go to the hospital."

"Stitches?"

"Yeah, twenty inside and out."

Monica couldn't hold it in anymore and started sobbing.

"Baby, don't cry; I've had stitches before." Sharief held his head down. "See this scar on the side of my head, my brother pushed me when—"

"I'm not crying because you got stitches!" she screamed, cutting him off.

"Well, damn, you gotta say it like that?"

"Be quiet." She chuckled in the midst of crying.

"Ahh, there it is, my smile." Sharief wiped Monica's tears. "Tell me what happened, ma."

"I just can't take it."

"Take what? Me?"

"No . . . yes . . . I don't know . . . ," Monica sobbed. "It's just that some of the shit Celeste said really hurt me."

"Oh baby, don't cry over that. It's me she hates, she's just taking it out on you."

"No, Sharief, you don't understand. She's obsessed with this other-woman bullshit. And it's driving me crazy."

"You can't fuck and feel guilty too." Sharief turned Monica's face so that she was looking him in the eyes.

"What?" Monica said, taken aback. "What is that supposed to mean?"

"Sometimes I wonder if you can handle this."

"Handle what? You are so selfish; why does everything have to be about you? Plus, correct me if I'm wrong, but didn't you tell me that I was only your sister-in-law? So what is there to handle?"

"Oh, so you want me to step?"

"You're the one who stepped. I didn't tell you to go."

"Yeah, ai'ight. I don't think you can handle this."

"You know what *I can't* handle?" Monica pointed her finger. "I can't handle our relationship going nowhere and knowing that I can never wake up one day and call you mine."

"Is that what you want?" he asked.

"In the midst of all this crazy shit—" She hesitated. "That's what I wish."

"Be careful what you wish for."

"Yeah." She smirked. "I just might get it." Tears flooded her eyes again and raced down her cheeks.

"Shhh." Sharief ran his index finger across her lips. "Come upstairs please. It's late . . . you can sleep in the guest room. Just chill."

"Don't tell me to chill."

"Look, it's late as hell, I'm not letting you leave. Your mother is getting married tomorrow. Just calm down; you don't need to be driving like this."

Monica looked at Sharief, and his eyes pleaded with her to stay. "Come on, baby," he assured her. "It'll be all right. I want you to come upstairs . . . please . . ."

She gave in. "Okay. I left my things upstairs anyway . . . Let me help you with the girls."

After Monica helped Sharief lay the girls down, she went in the guest room and changed into her nightgown. She sprawled across the bed with the echo of Celeste's cruel words troubling her mind. Somewhere along the way she'd settled with not being able to have children, but now that Celeste had tossed the reality of it in her face she didn't know what to do. Almost instinctively, she pressed on her abdomen and felt the hardness. She made a mental note to have an ultrasound done, then quickly changed her mind: denial seemed to be easier to deal with.

"Monica." Sharief peeked in the guest room after knocking repeatedly. "Are you sleep?"

"Damn, you scared me." She clutched her chest. "I was thinking about something."

"Like what?" He walked into the room, closed the door, and lay horizontally across the foot of the bed. "Tell me."

"Sharief, get off the bed. Don't you think that's just a bit much?"

"Girl, please," he laughed. "I'm not on no bullshit. I care about you. I really, really do. And you were so upset earlier that I wanted to check on you. I won't be in here too long."

"You checked, I'm fine, now go back to your wife."

"Cut that shit out. What things were you thinking about?"

She sucked her teeth. "You really wanna know?"

"Yeah," he turned his head toward her, "I do."

"I was thinking about the baby I had at fifteen."

"Baby?"

"Yes, a baby."

"And the baby is where . . . ?"

"Dead . . . And now I can't have any more children."

Sharief didn't know what to say.

"Speechless?" Monica asked.

"A little."

"I'll be all right. I just didn't expect Celeste to throw it in my face."

"How did the baby die?" Sharief asked.

"The cord wrapped around her neck in the womb, and she was stillborn."

"But why can't you have more children?"

"When I was seventeen, I had two fibroid cysts and my left fallopian tube had to be removed."

"Wow, baby, you've been through a lot."

"I know . . . Oh, and let me just tell you this: Celeste cussed me about my father. I could've slapped the shit out of her."

"Why would she do that?"

"Because we have different fathers and she acts like I'm responsible for her father's death because our mother loved my father and not hers."

"Don't take that on." Sharief curled his lips. "That's Celeste's issue, let her deal with it."

"Yeah, but damn. Hell, look at Imani, none of us knows who her father is. All we know is that her last name is Reid."

"Reid? All these years I thought Imani was a Lewis."

"No, Lewis is my father's name."

"Wait a minute, now, Jamal's name is Lewis."

"Yeah, 'cause that's his sorry-ass daddy's name. Walik Lewis. Imani is a Reid and Celeste was a Parker, trust me."

"Yo, that's deep."

"Well, it's not my fault, and I don't appreciate Celeste throwing it in my face!"

Sharief took two pillows and tucked them under his head, placed Monica's feet on his chest, and started massaging them. "Don't let that stuff bother you anymore."

"Why not?"

"Because you got me, and I love you."

"Oh, Sharief, please." Monica frowned. "You don't love me, you just wanna fuck me."

He chuckled. "I've been fuckin' you for months and truth be told, it wasn't that hard."

Monica took the pillows and snatched them from under his head. "Niggah—"

"Niggah what? Fucking you and loving you are different. I've been loving you for a minute. I can't put my finger on exactly when but it's been awhile."

"Shhhh . . . ," Monica said, "talking like that could only make this situation even more fucked up." She closed her eyes. "I'm going to sleep. Close the door when you leave."

[**Starr**]

S TARR STOOD ON the patio and took in the fresh summer air. It was eight o'clock in the morning, and today was her wedding day. She wanted to spend a few moments reflecting on her life and how far she'd come since her days of being a struggling single mother, looking for somebody to love her. "Thank God for better days." She chuckled, fanning her face with her hand. She sat down in the reclining patio chair and crossed her ankles. As she closed her eyes and started to think of her handsome groom she heard a slight grunting: *"Grrrrr."*

"What the hell is that?" Starr looked around but when she didn't hear it again she dismissed it as her imagination and instead started singing her favorite gospel tune, *"Oh happy day . . . oh happy day . . . when Jesus walked, He washed my tears away—"*

"Grrrrrrrrr . . ."

"Now, I know damn well I ain't losing my mind." Starr leaned forward but didn't see anything. *What the hell is that? Sound like somebody dyin'.* She got out of the chair and started looking around.

"Starrla—Starrla—I need you, Milkway—I need you."

"Mama Byrd, is that you?"

"Yeah."

"Where are you?"

"In the kitchen."

Starr's heart started racing. All she could envision was the old lady from the commercial who fell down but couldn't get up. Starr said a quick prayer hoping that nothing was wrong with Mama Byrd. Over the past five years since she'd been dating Red, she and his mother had gotten along perfectly. Mama Byrd was the closest person Starr had to a mother, especially since her own mother died when she was a little girl. Mama Byrd had been senile for years, but there was something about her that no one could resist.

Starr's heart raced as she ran in the kitchen. She didn't see Mama Byrd anywhere. "Mama Byrd," she looked around, "where are you?"

"Over here, in the corner by the 'frigerator."

"Awwwl! Oh, hell no!" Starr screamed, spotting Mama Byrd. Buttah and Celeste, who'd just woken up, both jumped when they heard Starr scream.

"Ma!" Celeste panicked, running into the kitchen

"Starr!" Buttah yelled, running behind her. When they found Starr standing in the kitchen doorway, they peeked over her shoulder. They were both speechless. Mama Byrd was sitting on her porta-potty taking a shit.

"I need somebody to dump this. And I need some tissue too. These paper towels is too hard for my ass." Then she started grunting again and passing gas. The cheeks on her face were sunk in and her eyes were bulging out. "Oh this is a big one." She held on to the metal rails on the side of the toilet. "Oh goddamn . . . oh goddamn . . ."

"I'ma throw up!" Celeste gagged, running into the bathroom.

"Oh hell the fuck nawl, Mama Byrd," Starr said. "Come on, Mama Byrd." She scrunched up her nose. "Get up and let's go clean yourself."

"All right, baby," Mama Byrd said. "I guess that enema worked." She got up from the portable toilet and pulled her pink floral duster down. Clearing her throat, she looked at Buttah. "Peaches, be a good daughter-in-law and dump that for me. And then tell Celeste to clean out the dried snuff from my spit cup."

"Oh my God," Buttah mumbled as they walked away.

After Starr helped Mama Byrd clean herself, she thought about Imani. *I'ma kick Imani's ass!* Starr thought. *Where the hell was she last night? If her li'l ass got locked up again I'ma turn that damn jail out!*

"Monica!" Starr yelled, helping Mama Byrd out of the bathroom. "Call that damn baby sister of yours! Monica!"

Starr started climbing the stairs with Mama Byrd behind her.

"Ma," Celeste said, walking up the stairs behind Mama Byrd, "Monica got mad last night—"

Before Celeste could finish Starr pushed open the door to the guest room.

"Monica! What in the world?" Starr said, shocked. Monica and Sharief lay on opposite ends of the bed, with Monica's feet on Sharief's chest and both of Sharief's hands wrapped around them.

"And y'all thought that I had some shit with me," Mama Byrd said, shaking her head.

"Monica!" Starr yelled, with her hands on her hips.

Monica was startled awake. She rubbed her eyes and looked around the room, seeing Celeste, Mama Byrd, Buttah, and Starr all staring at her like she was crazy. "What the hell is wrong with y'all looking at me like that?" As she tried to move her feet, she looked toward the foot of the bed and saw Sharief snoring, her feet on his chest, his hands wrapped around them. She nudged him with the heel of her foot. "Wake up." Praying that he didn't wake up and start sucking her toes, something he liked to do before planting kisses between her thighs, she said, "Sharief, Celeste been looking for you."

Sharief wiped the corner of his mouth and turned over to see the army of women watching him from the doorway. *What the fuck?* he thought. Immediately he sat up and glanced toward his lap, praying that he had his boxers on and his dick wasn't hanging out.

Celeste walked toward Sharief and stood in front of him. She looked at his lap and saw that his dick was hard. "You motherfucker!" She raised her hand.

"Don't put your hands on me." Sharief looked at Celeste. "I swear God it'll be on up in here."

"Well, we'll be rollin', Sharief," Starr assured him.

"Hump," Buttah seconded. "Bring it on, baby pa. Bring it on."

"It's not even that serious." Monica sucked her teeth.

"What the fuck is going on then? When did you come back here, Monica?" Celeste screamed.

"What do mean come back here?" Starr asked, confused. "When did you leave?"

"Last night—and nothing is going on!" Monica snapped.

"Monica was crying last night and I came to comfort her and see what was wrong," Sharief said.

"I'm your fuckin' wife and you go to my sister and see what's wrong with her? We're the ones with the damn problems."

"Watch your mouth, Celeste!" Starr snapped. "I told you 'bout your man sleepin' out too many nights anyhow."

"I second that motion," Buttah agreed.

"Uhmm-hmm," Mama Byrd interjected. "Tell 'em. And Buttah and you ought to know, 'cause that's how your man got stolen. And if you ask me, this look like a ménage del'rios."

"It's a ménage à trois." Monica rolled her eyes.

"Oh y'all just nasty, huh? Let me find out that y'all a family of freaks and ain't nobody hooked a old bitch up. I'll have y'all to know that I still got a clit."

"It's not that kind of party, Mama Byrd," Monica said.

"Yeah," Mama Byrd said, "it might not be, but one thing's for sure and two things for certain: pussy don't have a face, and in the midnight hour a stiff dick ain't related to nobody."

"Look," Sharief said sternly, "Monica was outside about to leave, it was late as hell, and she didn't need to be driving all upset and alone. I talked her into coming back into the house, then we started talking and I fell asleep."

Celeste looked at Sharief, her eyes filled with rage. "You have boxing shorts on and she has on a short-ass nightgown—"

"Your imagination is ridiculous! You need to write a book! I fell asleep, that's it. Period. Now I'm tired of explaining it." Sharief got off the bed.

"Hey big dog," Mama Byrd hissed, cocking her neck to the side and winking.

"Mama Byrd," Starr said, "ain't no dog in here, now hush."

"I wasn't talkin' to no dog, thank you."

"Who were you talkin' to then?" Starr asked.

"Sharief. The slit to his boxers is open." Mama Byrd grinned.

"Ai'ight, that's enough, Celeste." Sharief looked at her. "We fell asleep talking. That's it, nothing else!"

"That better be it!" Celeste screamed. "I ain't one for no bull-shit! I'm his wife, not you." She pointed at Monica. "Understand?"

"Oh how privileged you must be." Monica got off the bed. "Excuse me," she added as she approached the doorway, "I need to use the bathroom." She walked briskly into the bathroom and slammed the door. "Fuck y'all!" she seethed. She leaned against the back of the bathroom door and took a deep breath, the pit of her stomach in knots. Looking straight ahead and rubbing her temples, she stared at a picture of a smiling baby sitting on the toilet, tissue strewn all over the floor. *What the hell are you doing, Monica?* she said to herself. *This has to stop. Fucking a woman's husband that you don't know is one thing, but doing your sister's husband is triflin'.* Tears flooded her eyes. *I'm sick of crying! I'm sick of it!*

"Monica." Starr knocked on the bathroom door. "It's me, open the door for a minute."

Monica slowly opened the door and peeked through the crack. "Yes." She wiped her eyes.

"Let me come in."

"I'm using the bathroom."

"I'm ya mama, let me in."

Monica opened the door. Starr stepped in and closed it. "I don't want you to say a word, I just want you to listen."

"Ma—"

"Be quiet. Now, I'm not stupid, and whatever sparks are flying between *you and your sister's husband* better stop right now!"

"Oh God, what did I say? There is nothing going on!"

"This is the second time that I've seen you and Sharief in a situation that didn't look too copacetic. I don't expect to see it anymore. Understand?"

Monica sucked her teeth.

"Do you understand?"

"Yeah, I hear you."

{ Imani }

"OF ALL THE goddamn things to say, the bitch said she was married to you, Walik."

"On the real," Walik sighed, "I just let go of a serious nut and now I'm trying to get my sleep on. Aren't you tired? Don't me grabbing your hair and knocking the lining out your pussy make you tired?"

"No." Imani sucked her teeth.

"Well, I'm tired. Along with bustin' a nut comes sleep for me. So kill it with the bullshit. Matter of fact, ain't your mother getting married today? Go get dressed or something. Just leave me the hell alone . . . shit."

"Come on, Walik," Imani whined, "she had a ring and shit."

"I don't give a damn what she had. I been locked up for two years, where the hell I get a damn ring from, mess hall?" Walik turned over and buried his face in the pillow.

"A ring, Walik? A ring, come on now." Imani snatched Walik's pillow away. She knew she was pushing it, but holding this in burned her chest. She sat on the edge of the bed with her legs crossed and her blue silk gown resting on her cool chocolate skin. "This is not the time to sleep."

Walik sat up in bed. With his bare back against the wall, he stared at Imani. "What the fuck is your problem?"

"What the fuck is *my* problem? You niggah." She took her index finger and mushed him in the middle of his forehead. "I wanna know how come this *one bitch* don't never seem to go away. What, you in love with her or somethin'? You her goddamn man and forgot to tell me?"

"There you go with that bullshit." He sighed. "Don't mush me in my head again."

"Bullshit? The bullshit is that rotten-ass nut you let off in that bitch. Did you wanna sleep then, ma'fucker? I swear I don't want that bastard-ass baby in my house. I don't even wanna see that piece of shit."

"Yo, fall back," Walik said sternly.

"Fall back? Fuck you."

"If you would stop flappin' them lips and suck my dick maybe you would get a chance to. Look, Imani," Walik raised his voice, pointing his right hand toward her face, "all last night we talked about this. I fucked the shit outta you to show you that it was all about you. I came here last night and chilled with you and my son. And despite the fact that I saw a buncha crackheads peddlin' my shit, I didn't even stress you about my clothes or my guns being missing."

"I told you some niggahs broke in here."

Walik twisted his lips. "Ain't no niggahs broke in here, 'cause my boy Gill, my 5-0 niggah, was the one you donated my guns to, that's why he ain't ask your dumb ass no questions." Walik sucked his teeth. "You always fuckin' playin' yourself, ma. My guns is at my mom's, boo. *So chill.*"

"Chill? Who the hell is you talkin' to? I don't give a fuck about you or that crooked-ass drug-dealin' cop. Fuck both of y'all!"

"Ai'ight. Enough. I'm out." He threw the covers off.

Imani grabbed his wrist. "Where you goin'?"

"Gettin' the fuck outta here!"

"Bye, niggah. I knew you wanted to run off and be with that bitch anyway. Let me catch her and I promise you it's gon' be on all the time."

"Whatever, yo." Walik snatched his wrist from Imani's grip and slid out of bed. He picked up his boxing shorts from the floor. "See my dick." Walik held his dick in his hand. "This is what a naggin' bitch does to a dick."

"You and ya soft-ass dick can step! Get the fuck out!" Imani screamed. "Who the hell you supposed to be, John Gotti? You just a fuckin' hood rat, a mishap that stumbled across a li'l hustle. On the real your dumb ass couldn't even get a homemade porno fuckin' right, let alone knocking the lining outta pussy."

"Oh yeah?" Walik couldn't believe what he was hearing.

"And another thing," Imani continued, "you'd be better off sellin' bootleg CDs than makin' runs, you silly bastard!"

Walik reached for his jeans. "I ain't gotta listen to this shit." He slipped on his boxers and jeans, then reached for his cell phone. He flipped it open, pressed a button, said Shante's name into the receiver, and immediately the phone dialed Shante's number.

"Wassup?" Shante said groggily, answering the phone.

"Yo," Walik said, "check it, ma, wake up and fix me something to eat."

"You comin' over?"

"Yeah, I'm coming now."

Without warning a surge of wind made a *whoosh* sound as Imani fly-kicked Walik in the center of his chest, causing his back to hunch and his mouth to fly open. "That's right, niggah, you forgot what part of Flatbush I was from. Karate camp was fuckin' free. Niggah-what!" Before Walik realized what was happening Imani karate-chopped him twice across the forehead. He dropped his cell phone, and Imani could hear Shante on the line shouting his name.

"Oh, you just gon' call that bitch in my face!" As Walik rushed toward Imani she quickly stepped to the side and he ran into the wall. "Punk bitch!" she screamed.

"I'ma kick yo' fuckin' ass!" he said, checking to see if his nose was broken.

"Suck my dick!" Imani screamed. "Lick my ass! Ma'fucker, you gon' call that bitch in my house? You just gon' disrespect me?" She pounded two chops into the back of Walik's head, and as he went to turn around she poked him in the eye. Then she stomped on his cell phone and started crushing it to pieces. "Let's see yo' ass call the bitch now!"

As Imani continued stomping on Walik's phone, he was able to catch her off guard and grab her around the neck. "Oh, you think you fuckin' Bruce Lee? You gon' try that karate shit on me and think I won't beat yo' ass?" He squeezed the veins on the side of her neck and backed her up against the wall. "Stupid bitch!" Thick and blinding beads of sweat drizzled down Walik's face. He took one of his hands and wiped his eyes. "What the fuck is wrong with you!" He took his free hand and pushed her on the side of her head, causing her neck to jerk.

"Imani!" Jamal screamed, pushing the bedroom door open and running into the room. "What you doin' to my mommy, punk?" Jamal jumped on Walik and started hitting and kicking him on the leg. Before Walik could get a hold on Jamal, Jamal bit him on the knee. "Shit!" Walik screamed. He took his free hand and pushed Jamal to the floor.

"Oh hell naw!" Imani screamed. She tried to release herself from Walik's grip, so she kicked him in the dick as hard as she could. Immediately he let her go and grabbed his crotch.

"Don't you ever in your life put your hands on my baby!" Imani screamed.

Still in pain, Walik stood up straight and slapped Imani so hard that spit flew from her mouth and immediately she started coughing.

Jamal jumped up and down. "Niggah, you don't know me! King Kong ain't got nothin' on me!" He pounded his chest. "Now, don't make me regulate up in here!" He charged toward Walik. Stopping him midway, Walik grabbed Jamal by his pajama-top collar and twisted it with his fist. He lifted Jamal in the air and looked at Imani. "If you come over here I'ma forget who you are and I'ma beat the shit outta you!"

Walik turned to stare Jamal in the face. "I'm your fuckin' father and I will kill you before I ever let you beat my ass! Any li'l niggah that puts his hands on his father is a punk."

"I'm not no punk, I'm the man of this house!" Jamal screamed. "This is my hood, niggah, death before dishonor, remember that?"

"Hell yeah I remember that, I'm the one who told you that! But I'm home now, I'm the man of the house, and I'm your father. So don't you ever put your hands on me again, 'cause if you do I'ma beat you like a niggah in the street! Understand?"

Jamal didn't answer.

"Understand?" Walik repeated.

Jamal didn't know whether to answer or not, so he looked toward Imani. "I'm talkin' to you, not your mother!" Walik snatched his face around. "Now, do you understand?"

Not knowing what else to do, Jamal started to cry.

"Don't cry, niggah; you was all tough a minute ago. Now you wanna cry? You don't ever bring it to a man unless you can take him or you willing to take what the fuck he gon' give you. And see me, I'll break your chest open if you ever in your life jump on, at, or even look at me too hard. Understand?"

Jamal was silent, his tears splashing onto Walik's hands.

"Answer me," Walik said sternly, shaking Jamal.

"Yeah!" Jamal cried.

"Ai'ight then." He placed Jamal back on the floor. "Now go in your room. This is between me and your mother."

Jamal ran over to Imani and hugged her around the waist.

"I'm okay, Jamal," she assured him. "Go back to your room, we have to get ready for your grandmother's wedding."

Jamal was reluctant to leave. He walked backward out of the room, staring Walik down every step of the way. Walik slammed the door in Jamal's face and locked it.

"Imani! Y'all gettin' high up in this, ma'fucker? Trying to jump me? Do you know that niggahs die for less than this? Y'all some bold ma'fuckers, for real." Walik couldn't believe it. "I swear if y'all was niggahs in the street you would be resting in peace."

"Now you wanna kill us." Imani wiped tears from her eyes. "I don't even know who you are anymore." She broke down and started sobbing.

"Oh please." Walik started pacing the room. "Cut that crying shit out! You don't know who the hell I am?"

"No I don't." Snot ran from her nose.

"I'm your fuckin' man." Walik stopped in his tracks. "But I will leave yo' ass. I'm not gon' be going through this shit. Now, either you with me or you not. Shante is pregnant, period. I can't change that . . . and I'm sorry . . . but at least I'm a man and can admit it. And I'm trying, Imani, I am. But I'm not the type of niggah to have to keep beating yo' ass, 'cause I'll kill you. Remember that I will bury yo' fuckin' ass."

"Walik—"

"Don't fuckin' *Walik* me! Karate-choppin' me and shit." Walik ran his hand across his forehead. It was sore to the touch. "This li'l niggah," he pointed toward the door, "talkin' about King Kong ain't got nothin' on him."

"So what," Imani snapped. "I betchu he got heart."

"I betchu he get his neck broke and if he ever raise his hand at me, I will make sure that I break my fist in his chest. I can't believe that I wanted to marry your fuckin' ass!" Walik shook his head.

"Oh, we ain't gettin' married now?" Imani felt like kicking Walik's ass all over again.

"Yo, you stress a niggah too much and every time I turn around I gotta be puttin' my hands on you. I'm not trying to go to jail for some dumb shit."

"Now our relationship is dumb? I been with you for ten years and this is what the fuck you do. And to top it all off, this whole shit is dumb to you?"

"Spare me."

"Why you doing this, Walik?" More tears filled Imani's eyes. "I can't take it, we've been together for ten years, we have a son, and I wanna get married."

"Okay, you know what? You gettin' on my nerves! This is why I wanted to stop fuckin' with you. This is why I started fuckin' with Shante to begin with, 'cause she ain't fuckin' nag me. She know how to suck my dick and shut the hell up. But you—it's always an issue—always. You doin' karate on a niggah and shit. I just came home from a bid, I come scoop you and my li'l man, and *we* hang out over my mom's. Me, you, and Jamal, not some other bitch . . . not Shante . . . you. Who my family recognize as my girl?"

Imani held her head down. "Me."

"Ai'ight then. And Jamal look just like me, so that ain't even no question. But for real—for real—if you don't fall the fuck back and stop pressuring me I'ma straight leave yo' ass. I ain't come home for this."

"All right, Walik." Imani wiped her eyes. "I'm sorry." She walked over to him and started stroking his dick. She felt it hardening.

"Yeah whatever. I'm leaving." He was trying his best not to show how good Imani was making him feel.

"I don't want you to leave." She slid to her knees.

"Why not?" He felt her unzipping his pants.

" 'Cause I got something for you." She pulled his pants and his boxers down to his ankles. Then she proceeded to lick around his balls and the inner parts of his thighs. "You like that, daddy?"

"I don't know yet." Walik was fighting to keep his eyes from rolling to the back of his head. "What else you got?"

"Uhmm, let's see . . ." Imani started licking his dick and making popping sounds as she reached the tip.

"Oh shit!" Walik moaned. "Goddamn. You got a mean head game."

"Oh, I got a mean head game," she said in between licks and sucks. "You like it?"

"I love that shit, baby."

"What's my name?" Imani demanded. "Say it while I suck ya dick."

"Wifey baby . . . Ma'fuckin' wifey . . ."

"EVERYBODY GRAB YOUR man, the thief in the night is here!" Mama Byrd yelled as Monica walked into Celeste's bedroom. "Hey baby." She smiled at Monica while slipping on her cream-and-blue lace-trimmed duster for the wedding. "Peaches was just talkin' about you."

"Mama Byrd." Buttah cut her eyes while puckering her lips. "Don't lie on me."

"I thought you said your name wasn't Peaches." Mama Byrd smirked.

"It ain't."

"Well, then why you in this? Mind ya bid'ness."

"Would y'all please," Monica said, agitated. "Celeste, let me talk to you for a minute." She motioned Celeste to step to the side. "Look, I really need to apologize for last night and this morning. It really was nothing—really—I know *we* fell out—but Sharief was the one who talked me into coming back in because, as he said, this is about Mommy and not us. And for that reason alone"—she arched her eyebrows—"I came back in here. Yes, I'm still pissed—don't get it twisted. But I wouldn't do no crazy-ass shit in your house and disrespect you—to that extent—because I know what you've been going through. So I need you to understand that last night Sharief and I were just talking and we both fell asleep."

"Girl," Celeste caressed Monica's cheek, "no matter what we go through, you're my sister. I trust you and I know you wouldn't do anything like that."

Monica was expressionless as she replied, "*Like I said, Celeste,* last night was nothing."

"Celeste," Starr interrupted, "gimme my cell phone so I can call Imani." Tears filled Starr's eyes. "This is my wedding day and I gotta be looking for my child to see if she's coming, let alone be a bridesmaid. What did I do so wrong?"

"Look, Ma," Celeste said, turning away from Monica, "I really can't deal with a pity party today and quite frankly I don't wanna hear about Imani's li'l selfish ass. You're the only one with hope for the chick 'cause the way I see it, if you ain't some li'l bum niggah with a big dick who's selling drugs on the street then you don't mean a thing."

"Not today, Celeste," Monica said while helping Mama Byrd fix her duster. "Not today."

"I heard what you said," Imani announced as she entered the room, throwing her bridesmaid's gown on the bed and placing a hand on her hip. "Don't be worried about the size of my man's dick; you need to be concentrating on yo' niggah's dick, trick— excuse me, Jamal." Jamal covered his mouth and snickered. "You know what," Imani went on, rolling her eyes, "this a buncha bullshit, I'ma let this go for now. But don't think I'ma let y'all talk shit to me all day."

"Imani!" Starr stood with her fishnet stockings in her hand. "Do I look like a piece of the goddamn furniture? Watch your li'l nasty mouth before you get knocked in it! I swear if I wasn't getting married I would beat yo' ass down! Where have you been?"

"Mommy," Imani whined, "I'm sorry about cussin' but *some-*

body always got something to say. Anyway, wouldn't nobody come and get me yesterday. I called here but didn't get an answer."

"Imani." Jamal tugged on her arm. "Didn't you turn your phone off?"

"No, I didn't."

"Oh." Jamal stood quietly.

"Anyway, Ma," Imani continued, "I didn't have a way here."

"Stop lying," Monica chimed in.

"I'm not lying."

Jamal looked at Imani. "That sound like a lie to me, Imani. That don't sound like the truth." He shook his head.

"I'ma slap you!" Imani squinted.

"Oh hold up." Mama Byrd stood with her hands on her hips. "Ain't nobody gon' do no slappin' up in this ma'fucker."

"Imani," Monica snapped, "don't come up here lying. Just don't open your mouth. Just get dressed."

"Oh, you frontin' on me in front of everybody? Oh, you playing me?" Imani was shocked. "I thought we were better than that, Monica."

"You want to translate that into educated English?" Celeste smirked. "Otherwise, shut the fuck up!"

"You shut the fuck up!"

"Both of y'all shut the fuck up!" Starr yelled. "Now, Imani, how did you get here today?"

"Walik," Jamal said, with a frown on his face. "Walik got his boy car and dropped us off. Mama-Starr, you know I can't stand Walik. He had me by the neck and slammed me into the wall." Jamal balled up his fist. "Mama-Starr, he was like, *You li'l punk, I'll mess you up!* I was crying and everything—you shoulda saw me. And you know what? He and Imani were fighting too. I had to break free and save her."

"What?" everybody screeched.

"It wasn't even like that," Imani said defensively. "He ain't have him slammed up against the wall. Walik was just playing with us."

"That wasn't no game to me, Imani, I don't play like that. Plus, we were both crying," Jamal insisted.

"Shut up, Jamal!" Imani snarled.

"Remember, Imani?" Jamal continued with his story, oblivious to his mother's warning. "You were like, *Why you doin' this to me, Walik. I love you. I wanna be your wife . . . Ahhhh Ahhhh . . . God help me . . . Jesus Lord save me . . .* For a minute I thought you had the Holy Ghost. 'Cause you were like this." He fell on the floor with his arms stretched out. "*Help me! . . . Help me!* And then I came to save you, because if I didn't he was gon' beat us both down. You remember, Imani?"

"I remember that I told you about lyin'!" Imani snapped. "*And I told you* about tellin' my business. *And I told you* what goes on in my house stays in my damn house! Now don't get slapped. Matter of fact get your li'l ass off the floor, lookin' crazy. Take your tux and get yo' short ass downstairs with your uncle Sharief so he can help you get dressed." Imani yanked Jamal off the floor, gave him his tux, and pushed him toward the door. "Get yo' ass outta here!"

"But Imani—" Jamal said.

"What did I say?" Imani squinted. Jamal turned around and ran down the stairs.

Imani closed the door behind him, and Starr started yelling, "What the hell is going on with you! You were fighting *again* and carrying on in front of my baby?"

"What's new, Ma?" Celeste chimed in.

"Ma," Imani said, rolling her eyes at Celeste, "Jamal doesn't know what he's talking about. Jamal is always lyin'."

"He never lies, Imani," Monica interrupted. "He may exaggerate, but my nephew doesn't lie."

"Well, he's getting confused with the fight I had with Shante."

"That baby ain't confused," Starr said. "And what is he talking about with Walik bringing you down here?"

"Because he did." Imani twisted her neck.

"Girl," Starr growled, "you got the right one, 'cause it'll be live in this ma'fucker here! Now take it down. I thought that sorry sack of shit was in prison."

"He is not a sorry sack of shit, thank you!" Imani snapped.

"Ma, there was a get-free party for him last night," Monica said sarcastically, placing baby's breath in her hair and looking at Imani as she checked herself in the mirror.

"Oh, you trying to be funny?" Imani said as she started getting dressed.

"Does this sound funny to you?" Monica sucked her teeth. "I don't know about anybody else, but me personally, I'm sick and tired of you being so fuckin' irresponsible and my nephew being put through—"

"A buncha bullshit," Celeste blurted out.

"Exactly," Monica agreed.

Imani shot Monica the evil eye and said, "Don't speak to me!"

"Whatever." Monica sighed. "Whatever."

"See why I stay home? See?" Imani complained, zipping the side of her dress.

"Okay now," Buttah said, "every one of y'all need to hush."

"You're right, Buttah," Monica said as they all proceeded to put their finishing touches on for the wedding. Celeste dressed her girls in their flower-girl dresses and sent them downstairs to sit still and not get dirty.

Jamal came back upstairs so that Imani could see his tux. "It looks pretty in the backyard," he whispered to Imani.

"Good," she said, fixing his tie. "You look really handsome, but I'm still mad at you, so go back downstairs." Jamal turned around and went downstairs.

After a few minutes of silence Starr smiled and said, "I can't believe that I'm marrying the love of my life." She blushed as she fixed her furry blue garter around her thigh.

"Ma." Monica frowned. "You don't have any ultrasheer stockings?"

"Don't you worry about it. Anyway, I feel like all my life I've been waiting for a man like Red. Just think, I'll be Mrs. Redtonio Breaker Brown, lead singer of the Jam On Its."

"Ma," Imani sighed, "he's not famous anymore. He's a security guard and all he does now are What Happened to Them Old-Ass Niggahs concerts." She started laughing.

"You are so inappropriate," Celeste snapped.

"Oh hell no!" Mama Byrd said with her eyes bulged out. "Ain't nobody gon' be talkin' about my son." She looked toward Buttah. "The niggah is my son, ain't he?"

"Don't y'all worry about what he is." Starr rolled her eyes at Imani and placed her hands on her hips. "At least he ain't a sorry sack of shit. My Red is sweet, and he still does his thing." She snapped her fingers and shook her body. "On stage *and in the bedroom.* And to think *I'm* marrying him."

"Okay, enough," Celeste said, shaking her head and putting lipstick on. "I can do without hearing about Red in the bedroom."

"Don't mind her, Ma." Monica rolled her eyes. "You can talk about your man all you want. Can't nobody tell you who to love."

"That's right." Starr smiled. "And Red is kind and faithful—"

"Faithful?" Celeste looked at her mother, surprised. "I wouldn't quite describe someone who was still married to his wife when he asked you to marry him as faithful."

"For your information, they were separated," Starr said defensively. "And he's divorced now."

"He's been divorced for a month, Ma." Celeste waved her finger. "One month."

"What is it to you? As Red would say, you better hold ya roll, home girl. Sit back and listen. 'Cause one thing I know is men and from what I can see you need some old-school advice."

"Old-school advice? Ma, please, what can you tell me about a man? We each have different fathers."

"Why are you being so nasty?" Starr asked.

"Because she's not the bastard child of Redtonio Breaker

Brown." Imani frowned as she straightened her gown. "Her daddy was a crackhead."

"At least my father wasn't a fag."

"Oh please, you don't even know my father."

"Y'all don't have nothing else to do but talk about each other's fathers?" Starr asked.

"Whatever," Celeste said. "Ma—no disrespect—but I'm just getting tired of constantly having to hear about Red as if he's the only man that's ever been in your life. Or better yet our lives, because we all know that isn't true. Plus, ever since you been with him you act like he's all that matters. Like y'all are always one . . . *'Ma, can the kids come over . . . let me see what Red wants to do.'* Red-this and Red-fuckin'-that. You weren't born with Red, Red hasn't been around all my life, and he damn sure ain't perfect!"

"What is your problem, Celeste?" Monica asked.

"I don't have a problem—but if the truth be told I feel like a kid holding her breath trying to figure out what man is coming through the door next. 'Cause like we all know"—she pointed at both of her sisters—"none of us has ever known a man to stay around this long—not even our daddies."

"Mommy and Red have been together for five years. That's a long-ass time," Imani said. "So slow ya roll, home girl."

"I can't believe you're saying these things to me," Starr said, her heart feeling crushed.

"Ma, I'm only speaking the truth. Right, Monica?"

"Oh no, sweetie, you're in this one alone. I have no problems with Red. He already thinks I was making fun of his act, so I have nothing to say."

"I can't believe this, Celeste," Starr said. "Why would you insist on us getting married here at your home then? We could've stayed in Brooklyn and got married at the VFW."

"I wanted you to get married here because I thought that would make you happy, but I didn't realize it would make me miserable."

"Your ass is always miserable," Imani mumbled.

"Give it a rest," Monica said to Celeste. "This is not the time."

"I'm not talking to you," Celeste said. "And what are you worried about: she loved your daddy. I'm the result of a one-night stand. I would've been aborted if Mommy wasn't Catholic at the time."

"I ain't never been Catholic!" Starr screamed. "My daddy was a Baptist deacon! Is it a crime to simply not believe in abortion? And you were not the result of a one-night stand!"

"Then what was I?" Celeste screamed back.

"A pain in the ass, from what I can see," Imani said. "Shit, she raised you, didn't she? Paid for those expensive-ass bras you had to wear with them big-ass titties you got, shit."

"Imani," Starr said, "be quiet. Celeste, you were made out of love. I loved your daddy. I just didn't want to be with him anymore. I'm entitled to that!"

"But you were a mother—my mother. What makes people think that they can have children and just walk away from that child's parent? What about me? How could you expect him to stop loving you because you didn't want him anymore? He had a child with you. It's not that easy!"

"That wasn't my problem."

"And it's not your problem now, Ma!" Monica squinted at Celeste.

"You loved Monica's and Imani's fathers," Celeste said to Starr.

"It was my damn life, and I loved their fathers because I fuckin' loved them. I don't owe you any explanations. Get over it!"

"Well." Celeste sucked her teeth. "If I need to get over it then you need to know that the last thing I wanna hear is you confessing your undying love for Redtonio Breaker damn Brown."

"And that still won't make me love or wish I had been with your father," Starr snapped.

"Make you love my father? You should've already loved a man that you had a child by. It's called planning."

"And me slapping you in the mouth will be called painful if

you keep talking shit! I wish I had known before now that this is how you felt. But come rain, sleet, hail, or snow, I'm marrying that man downstairs because I love him and he's good to me. Understand? And just because I'm your mother doesn't mean that I should live my life revolving around you and what you want. And for your information, Ms. Married Lady, when you have a husband, you two are one. It doesn't take away my love for my children or my grandchildren, but I have to always consider my husband when I make decisions. As of this afternoon my last name will be Brown and that means we will all be family—whether you like it or not. Accept it and try applying this little bit of advice to your own life: if somebody doesn't want you—husband, wife, or baby daddy—then walk the hell away. Now shut up because I have heard enough! The next li'l nasty-ass comment that comes outta your mouth will be greeted by my fist slamming into your teeth."

"Ma," Imani said, "you a better woman than me because I wouldn't even talk that much. I would straight twist this broad's jaw." She turned to face Celeste. "Why don't you stop hating on Mommy and let her live her life? She ain't want your father; hell is she with mine? Just get the hell over it. Period."

"You know what," Starr yelled, trying to keep her eyes clear of tears, "just be quiet 'cause no matter what y'all think Red is a good man."

"He can be whatever you wanna believe he is, Mama. Whatever." Celeste frowned.

"Just put her out your wedding, Ma," Imani said, slipping her shoes on. "We don't need her, she's been a pain in the ass long enough."

Before Starr could respond, there was a knock on the bedroom door. "I'll get it," Monica said. She opened the door slowly. There stood Sharief dressed in a black three-piece walking suit with a starched white shirt and satin-trimmed three-quarter-length jacket. The cuff of his dress pants fell slightly over the back of his black alligator shoes. His bald head was smooth and reminded Monica of melted honey. His eyebrows were thick and his mustache well trimmed. His five-o'clock-shadow beard was perfect, and his white teeth set it all off. Monica took a deep breath. "Yes?"

Sharief tried not to smile as he admired Monica's royal-blue halter dress. The color didn't quite flatter her mocha skin, but she still looked as if the dress were tailor-made for her. It graced her wide hips and snuggled against every curve. Her waist was small but her ass was voluptuous and shaped like a full moon. There was a split on each side of the dress that showed off her thick legs and part of her thighs. Without thinking Sharief slid his hand in his pocket and slyly grabbed his dick. Monica peeped what he was doing, and her mouth started to water. She bit her bottom lip and nervously moved the Shirley Temple curls draping in her eyes from her face. "Yes?" she said again.

Sharief placed his bandaged hand on the door. "I wanted to speak with Celeste for a moment."

"Celeste—" Monica turned around and Celeste was standing right behind her. "Oh," Monica said, startled. "Sharief wants you."

Monica stepped away and Celeste stepped up. "What is it?" she said to Sharief. "What are you here to serve me?"

"Serve you?"

"Divorce and custody papers."

"Oh here you go. Damn, can I just speak to you civilly for a moment?"

Celeste sucked her teeth.

"You wanna step outside the door, please?" he asked.

"Are you asking me?"

Sharief took a deep breath. "If you don't mind, would you step out here for a moment?"

Celeste stepped into the hallway and closed the door behind her. "You have something you want to say?"

"Look, I'm sorry about last night. We had a big fight, the shit got way out of control, and I apologize for my part in that. I didn't intend to add anything more to the situation or make it even more fucked up. Monica and I fell asleep. I just wanted someone to kick it to, not to mention how upset she was."

"I'm your wife, me being upset is what matters—Monica will get over her shit."

"Celeste, I just wanted to apologize."

"Okay, whatever."

"You just insist on being nasty." Sharief shook his head. "Do you even know how to take a sincere apology? Do you have to always be nasty?"

"Me? *Nasty?* You're fuckin' nasty. You're nasty when you're fuckin' some bitch in the street and then you wanna come and bring your dirty-ass dick and place it next to me. You're nasty when you don't understand how much of my life I put into *you* and this is what you do? Your cheating ass has become a constant migraine in my asshole and they don't make Advil for the rectum—"

"Wait a minute, Celeste—"

"No, you wait a minute . . . It's like I woke up one day and suddenly I have become synonymous with you and now I don't know what the fuck to do because the you that I have glued myself to doesn't want me anymore. So fuck you and that sorry-ass apology." Celeste turned around toward the bedroom door.

"Why don't you just tell me to kiss yo' ass," Sharief snapped.

"Yeah," Celeste threw over her shoulder, "that too."

"Celeste, how can you say that you love me and want our marriage to work when you're always acting like this?"

Celeste spun around. "I'm hurt. Don't you see that?" Without warning tears fell from her eyes.

"I understand that, baby." He wiped her eyes. "I really do."

"Well then, why? Why did you let this get so far?"

"Time broke us apart."

"No, your wandering dick did it."

"I'm not even going to respond to that."

"Why do you hate me, Sharief?" Celeste wiped her eyes. Her stomach felt like it was caving in.

"I could never hate you."

"Then kiss me."

"What?" Sharief was surprised. "You just cursed me out and now you want me to kiss you?"

"Do you love me, Sharief?"

"Yes, you're my kids' mother."

"Then kiss me."

"Celeste, baby, it won't change anything."

"Yes it will." Celeste walked close to Sharief. She was surprised that he didn't take a step back.

"No matter what." Sharief closed his eyes as Celeste pressed her lips into his. "Always know that I loved you."

"Well thank God!" Starr yelled as she opened the door, with everyone standing behind her, looking at Celeste and Sharief. "Maybe you'll be happy now! Come on, it's time for the wedding to start. The preacher has arrived and *Mr. Brown is waiting for his bride downstairs.*"

[Monica]

MONICA'S HEART DANCED its way under Sharief's feet as she saw his lips pressed against Celeste's. *I gotta find a way,* she thought, *to get the fuck outta this.*

"Excuse me—I have to go to the bathroom." Monica flew into the bathroom, never making eye contact with Sharief.

As she closed and locked the door behind her, the lump in her throat started to ache. She didn't know how to stop the pain; all she knew was that she needed to soothe it. She walked to the sink, turned on the cold water, and splashed it on her face. The water slid down her cheeks and mixed in with her foundation, creating streaks of muddy tears.

Monica! her conscience screamed at her as she looked in the mirror and swallowed the lump's residue, *he is her husband.* She took a deep breath and snapped back, *But he's my man. But he's her husband.* She argued with herself, wrestling back and forth with her conscience, desperately needing a way to make this okay. *But he's my man. No, Chauncey has claimed himself to be your man. Celeste is married to Sharief; he's her man. But I love him. It doesn't matter he's her husband. But I love him—play your position—but I love him—it doesn't matter—What the fuck am I supposed to do with my love for him? What the fuck should she do with hers? Who cares, I love him. She's his wife. But I love him—but she's his wife: thank him for the dick, smile, take your skeleton and walk away.*

Monica took a cloth out of the linen closet and wiped her face clean. She opened the medicine cabinet and saw that Celeste had some clear MAC Lipglass and black eyeliner. She quickly lined her eyes, put the Lipglass on, and popped her lips together. "Fuck Sharief." Monica walked out of the bathroom and saw that everyone had left. She hurried down the stairs; they were all lined up by the French doors, waiting for her to come down.

She sucked in her stomach and walked briskly to take her position next to Sharief, who was her escort.

Sharief could immediately tell that Monica was upset. He could tell by the way she was chewing the inside of her jaw that either she wanted to break down and cry or slap the shit out of him. "Monica," he said as they locked arms. She ignored him and instead admired the beauty of the backyard, which had been transformed into sheer wedding bliss. Wildflowers, tulips, and roses were everywhere. All of the guests were seated in folding chairs with white satin covers and big draping bows in the back. There were ice sculptures of swans and hearts everywhere. There was also a multicolored rose-covered arch where the preacher and Red were standing. Red's backup singers from the Jam on Its were singing their rendition of the Isley Brothers' "For the Love of You."

"Monica," Sharief mumbled again, tugging slightly on her arm.

She ignored him and positioned her single calla lily in the fold of her arm while waiting on the musician's cue to walk down the aisle. Two seconds later the musician gave the cue and Monica and Sharief began to walk arm in arm. "Monica," Sharief mumbled.

Monica ignored him.

"It wasn't what you thought."

"Fuck you," she said under her breath.

"Oh." He laughed slightly as they continued down the aisle. "That means we're in good standing."

"I'm not fucking with you anymore." She smiled as the photographer took their picture. "Remember I'm just your sister-in-law. Let's hold true to the nasty-ass speech you gave me a few days ago."

"Be quiet."

"I can say what I wanna say!" She raised her voice a little but only loud enough for Sharief to hear.

"Then smile." He nodded toward the videographer. "You're on *Candid Camera*."

Monica almost shitted on herself praying that none of her conversation was caught on tape. *Damn, that's the last thing I need.* Instead of continuing to talk, Monica smiled as she walked the rest of the way down the aisle. Once she and Sharief arrived at the altar they went their separate ways.

Although Monica smiled at her mother's soon-to-be husband, Red, she couldn't help but shake her head. *What in the hell does he have on? Why does he have on that tight-ass metallic gold tuxedo with a white fishnet shirt? Is that why Mommy has on fishnet stockings? They can't be serious. Are they trying to match? I know they realize that this niggah is only famous in Vegas.* Monica chuckled a little, but did her best to maintain her composure. She held her head down so she could get her face together; when she looked back up, Sharief was looking at her. He motioned his eyes toward Red and as bad as Monica didn't want to smile at Sharief she couldn't help it.

Imani walked slowly down the aisle with an attitude. "These is some country-ass niggahs," she huffed under her breath, looking at the guests. *It's more sequins out this ma'fuckah than a li'l bit. God-*

damn. And this niggah here. She looked at her escort, Red's brother Jimmy, who was also Buttah's ex-boyfriend. *He about to pull my damn arm off.* Imani had a hard time keeping up with Jimmy's pimp-daddy strut. She looked at him and rolled her eyes a couple of times. *His ass know he look like Rick James reincarnated for Christmas. And I hope this long-ass jheri curl he got don't splash no juice on me and shit. Hold up . . . I know this ma'fucker don't stink . . .*

By the time Imani reached Monica all they could do was smile at each other.

Celeste and Buttah were the matron and maid of honor, so each walked down the aisle alone. Celeste was trying her best not to cry but she couldn't help it; tears ran down her face as she thought about her situation. She hoped that everyone would think she was emotional because of the wedding.

When Starr appeared behind the French doors, it was if Strongé had arrived on the helicopter with white horses and a chariot. Jamal rolled out the runner and opened the French doors. Kayla, Kai, and Kori came out and dropped white rose petals on the runner. Once the runner was completely covered, Starr made her grand entrance. Convinced that she was too old to be "given away," she chose to escort herself down the aisle. Starr stepped onto the runner, one three-inch stiletto at a time. The summer wind blew the asymmetrical hem of her dress up a little, revealing her fishnet stockings. "Whoo-wee! Look at you girl!" Red yelled down the aisle. "Oh yeah, baby, there it is. That's what I'm talking about! Bring it on over here."

The preacher tapped Red on the shoulder. "Excuse me—but you need to save that for the reception."

"Hold ya roll, Bruh Pastah—hold ya roll. I got this."

Starr's wedding dress was an all-white sequined halter-top gown. She had a small white veil hanging from her hat that she'd styled with a white feather on the side. As far as Starr was concerned, she was absolutely beautiful. She felt as if she were walking on diamonds. Staring at Red every step of the way, she switched her hips as she came closer to him.

"Now, that don't make no damn sense!" Mama Byrd smirked. "That ho knows she needs all black on."

"Hush," Red's cousin Lula-Baby said. "Be nice."

By the time Starr reached the altar Red was in tears. "You look good, baby." He sniffed.

"And so do you, boo." She smiled, wiping his tears.

As the preacher began the ceremony Starr and Red held hands. Red's backup singer Slick sang Freddie Jackson's "Jam Tonight" as his solo, and Starr's niece Sharay did a Christian rap. Afterward Starr and Red gazed into each other's eyes and recited their vows. "You know you my boo," Starr said to Red, "and you know that I'm feeling you like that. You are my light when it's a blackout and you are my ray of sun even when it's a thunderstorm. And I love you Red, I really do."

"All I can say"—Red sniffed—"is if loving you is wrong then I don't wanna be right."

"Man," Jimmy said, "you gon' make a pimp cry."

"Awwl, big daddy," Starr growled. "Plead guilty, baby." All of the guests fell out laughing. Monica, Celeste, and Imani just stood there watching, embarrassed and anxious for the ceremony to be over. Shortly after Starr and Red exchanged rings, the preacher pronounced them husband and wife, and it was time for Red to kiss his bride.

"Don't start nothin', daddy." Starr laughed. "You know how easy I am with you." She threw one leg in the air, meeting Red's waist. Red took one arm and supported Starr's leg; then he took his other arm and wrapped it around her waist. He pressed his lips against hers and they kissed long and hard.

"Oh hell no," Monica mumbled, mortified.

"Do yo' thang!" Imani's friend Sabrena yelled. "This shit is cracked—for real, for real. Starr got class."

"Would you be quiet?" Quiana poked her in the arm.

"My fault."

Monica made eye contact with Chauncey, who was sitting near the front. He winked and she smiled back.

Once Starr and Red finished kissing they turned toward their guests and everybody clapped. "Let's get it on!" Starr yelled. "It's time to party!"

{ I m a n i }

IMANI SAT WITH her back resting against the makeshift bar, her cell phone in one hand and an apple martini in the other. For over an hour she'd been blowing up Walik's extra cell phone; she hated that she smashed the main line to pieces. She'd called at least a hundred times and each time no answer. She was sick of listening to his dry-ass voice-mail message: "You know who this is and you know what to do." Every time she heard it, she felt as if the pit of her stomach were oozing through the bottom of her feet. *"Goddammit!"* she yelled, exasperated, aggravated, and fed up with the bullshit of loving this son-of-a-bitch. *"Something has got to give."* She'd tried calling him with her number blocked and with it unblocked, and she'd even text-messaged him; still nothing. She thought about calling from a number Walik didn't know but then she remembered that he didn't answer calls from unfamiliar numbers. So she sat not knowing whether to cry, scream, or shout. The only person she could really be pissed with was herself. She knew better than to leave Walik home alone, but hell, what else was she supposed to do? He didn't want to come to the wedding and he wasn't the type to be asked the same questions over and over again. So she took the chance of letting him drop her off, hoping, praying, wishing, and begging a Higher Being to please let this niggah behave and do exactly what he promised her he would do, which was take a shit and go to sleep.

Imani hit redial again and received his voice mail once more. She wanted to go off but she knew if she flipped on Walik's phone, she wouldn't hear from him for a week, and she didn't want to take the chance. So she swallowed her attitude and did her best to leave a message that would entice him to call her back: "Walik, where you at? I'm worried about you. Just want to make sure you're okay. You know I love you, boo. Call me, please." Imani hung up and as she went to press redial, a soft copper-toned hand slid her cell phone from her palm.

"Let me save my number in this piece before you lose your mind trying to call me."

Imani looked up and instantly she smiled. "Ahhh, Kree?"

"Ahhh, Imani?" He handed her back the phone with his number programmed.

She snapped her fingers. "Where do I know you from . . . ? Oh, I know," she said, answering her own question, "you was the niggah with the hard dick pressed into my ass the other night at the club. What? Are you stalking me?"

"Stalking you?" Kree laughed. "Ma, don't even do it to yourself. You know you liked my hard Puerto Rican dick rubbing against that fat ass, otherwise ya li'l nasty dance would've been a no-haps. Furthermore, on the real, you straight played ole boy's ass. If you was my wife I would've yoked yo' ass up. But on some real shit, don't use me as a pawn no more. I just got out the game."

"Or what?" Imani asked. "You gon' shoot my man?" She frowned.

"If need be."

"You don't even know me to be telling me that you'll shoot my man." Imani was pissed. "You got a lot of nerve."

"It was your suggestion, ma." He smirked.

"Whatever." Imani took a sip of her apple martini. "What the hell you doin' here anyway?"

"Damn, it's okay for you to calm down. I already know you like me." Kree smiled.

"Oh here you go."

"Anyway since you must know, I'm the DJ."

"The DJ?"

"Yeah, and had you stayed off the phone then you would've noticed me."

"You got a smart-ass mouth. Anyway, you're the one responsible for the soul-train line instead of the receiving line?"

"Now, you know I'm Puerto Rican, I would've had a freak fest to the macarena," Kree laughed. "But it's all good, the soul-train line was at the bride and groom's request." Kree smiled and Imani couldn't help but laugh. "So," Kree said, looking around, "where ya crazy-ass man at?"

"Don't call him crazy," Imani said defensively. "I shouldn't have been dancing with you like that in the club anyway."

"Oh you killing me," Kree said. "You still on that club shit, when was that? Like last year? Come on, ma, you see me tryna kick it to you." He folded his arms across his chest. "Don't you feel my Mac Daddy vibe comin' through?"

"Mac Daddy vibe?"

"Yeah." He cocked his neck to the side. "Tell me, girl, what your interests are, who you be with."

"Oh my God, are you serious?"

"It's a classic."

"What?"

"The line."

"It's not a classic." Imani sucked her teeth. "It's tired."

"I'll have you to know that what I just shot you was a line from Biggie's 'One More Chance,' ai'ight, Ms. Tired?" Kree stood directly in front of Imani and pressed his forehead against hers.

"Check it, let me know when you wanna get your grown and sexy on. I'll admit that my dick was hard the other night and it was so hard that it stayed on *your* mind. Don't fuck around and start wanting some of it, 'cause then I'ma have to give it to you. But for now I'll take your phone number or better yet I'll wait for you to call me."

"Excuse me, Papi." Jamal tapped Kree on the side of his leg. "We got a problem here, son?"

Kree turned his head, stood up, and looked down, "Oh, this you pot'nah?" He pointed to Imani.

"All day."

"What's your name?"

"Jamal."

"Ai'ight, man, I'm Kree." He held his fist out for a pound.

Jamal slid Kree a pound. "Ain't you the DJ?"

"That's what they say."

"Oh." Jamal's eyes lit up. "I like you. Look, me and my cousins Kayla and Kai wanna hear the cha-cha slide so we can get our dance on, and after that Kori said she can break down a new dance called the water sprinkler. So can you tell MC Old G," he pointed to Red's singer Slick, "to get off the mike."

"Ai'ight, no problem."

"That's wassup." Jamal looked at Imani. "Bye, Imani." He ran off to his cousins screaming, "Hey y'all, I met the DJ."

"That's your little brother?" Kree asked.

"No, my son."

Kree looked surprised. "How old are you?"

"Twenty-three."

"Word? So you been fresh for a long time, huh?"

"Wouldn't you like to know."

"Maybe—" he said. "Maybe not."

"Well, how old are you?"

"Twenty-six."

"Interesting," Imani said.

"Tell me, is ole boy your son's daddy?"

"Yeah, why?" Imani raised her eyebrows.

" 'Cause you got some shit on your hands."

"Why you all in mines? You act like I'ma really call you."

Kree laughed. "It's good, ma. If you feel to give me a call then hollah at me. If you don't—you're still sexy—so either way it's no problem." Kree kissed Imani on the forehead and walked back to his DJ table.

"Is that papi from the club?" Sabrena asked as she, Tasha, and Quiana walked over.

"Yeah," Imani said, staring at Kree.

"You gon' get with him?" Quiana asked.

"No, I have a man," Imani snapped.

"Good." Sabrena cocked her neck to the side. "Well, let's run a train on him and turn that niggah out! You know they say Puerto Ricans are freaks."

"A train?" Quiana laughed. "Sabrena, you stupid!"

Imani ignored the girls as they continued to go on about how sexy they thought Kree was. Instead she called Walik again, and still no answer. "Where is Walik at?" she huffed.

"Who?" Quiana asked. "Walik?"

"Yeah."

"Yo, fuck that niggah. You know he up to no good. You know a stray dog don't have a home—so he gon' roam. So either you shoulda brought his ass with you, or you shoulda just psyched yourself up to accept the fact the lady and the tramp is a true story."

"Why would you say some shit like that to me?" Imani snapped. "Why?"

" 'Cause it's true," Quiana said.

"How do you know it's true?"

" 'Cause it's staring at you." Quiana cracked up.

"Fuck you!"

Imani stormed off and went to sit next to Monica and Chauncey. As she sat down, they were getting up. "Where are you going?" Imani asked Monica. "I wanted to talk to you."

Monica raised her eyebrows. "You know I shouldn't be speaking to your li'l lyin' self, but Chauncey wanted to dance, is that okay with you?" she asked sarcastically.

"But I needed to talk to you."

"It'll have to wait. Period."

"I don't believe you!" Imani stormed away from Monica. As she went to find Starr, she spotted Red first. He seemed to be upset—he was stuttering and blinking. He was standing face-to-face with a woman who had finger waves in her hair and a spiked drawstring ponytail. She had red lipstick with black liner and red and blue eye shadow that covered both her eyelids and sprang from the sides like wings. She rocked back and forth. Her sequined babydoll mini dress was hiked up on one side and low on the other. She kicked her shoes off and looked at Red. "I'll bust yo' shit, fat boy!"

Imani had to do a double take because from the looks of it, this woman was serious and Starr was nowhere around. Once Imani was standing next to Red she noticed that this woman had arms that stopped just below her elbow and hands the size of a midget. *What the fuck.* And to make matters worse it didn't seem that she could control her arms very well because every time she moved they flapped around. Not to mention that one of the woman's legs was shorter than the other.

"Now, hold up," Red said to the woman, looking at how she was bouncing around. "What, you having a seizure? Why don't you go sit down? I'ma have to find Nadine to restrain you."

"Nadine!" the woman screamed.

"Yes, Nadine." Red stuck his chest out. "My sister, your counselor, Nadine, the one who brings y'all to every damn family function we have." Red pointed to the group of mentally and physically challenged people Nadine was responsible for. All Nadine's life she swore that her calling was to take care of the disabled, so she dedicated herself to opening up her own group home, caring for five and sometimes six mentally retarded and physically handicapped adults.

For the most part the people Nadine cared for were nice and quiet and talked among themselves, but this bunch was straight ghetto. Ever since they came they'd been loud, cussing, drinking, and eating everything in sight. One time they were even on the dance floor and making shoutouts on the DJ's microphone, which neither Red nor Starr particularly appreciated.

"Nadine!" Red yelled. "Come here, right now! Nadine!"

"Nadine—Nadine can't do shit to me. I'll beat her ass!" the woman yelled, rocking back and forth.

"Humph." Red smirked. "All you can do is beat yo' own ass with the way them arms and hands flappin' around."

"I ain't got to kick yo' fat ass with my hands, I can handle you with my feet."

"Oh, you wanna fight? Arms and hands lookin' like chicken wings and you tryna fight somebody!" Red said, taken aback.

"Chicken wings? Well, watch me cluck all over yo' tired ass! We can do this." The woman started skipping in place, like a boxer. She threw a couple of punches in the air, but to Red she looked to be throwing her body around.

"Oh yo' ass is crazy," he said. "Why can't you go sit down with the rest of the slow group." He pointed to a group of people on the other side of the backyard.

"Red," Imani said, still amazed. "What's going on here? Where's Mommy?"

"Ya mama had a li'l gas. She got a li'l lactose problem. But don't you worry about me, 'cause I'ma get Nadine to come and give this one here a tranquilizer."

"A tranquilizer? Why?"

"She asked for a beer."

Imani looked at the woman, who was still skipping in place. "You—can"—Imani spoke slowly—"not—have—any—al-co-hol—it—will—mess—with—your—me-di-ca-tion."

"Medication! Oh hell naw!" the woman screamed, kicking at Red. "Jimmy!" she screamed, "Jimmy! Let me tell you somethin', you played-out fat ma'fucker!"

"Oh hold up." Red was getting upset. "You better hold ya roll, home girl."

"He ain't played," Imani said, taking up for Red. "This niggah is retro."

"Jimmy!"

A few minutes later Jimmy walked over, his chest poked out. "What's wrong, Roxanne?"

"You better get fat ass," she cried, "and tell him something."

"Tell him what?" Jimmy looked Red up and down.

"I went to get a beer, and he gon' practically cuss me out talkin' about I'm one of Nadine's people and that me and my kids is the wild and retarded bunch."

"I ain't say nothin' about yo' kids," Red insisted.

"Yes you did." She pointed to the rowdy group that Red thought had come with Nadine. "Those is my kids and we ain't no slow group."

"Oh, Jimmy," Red said apologetically, "I didn't know. I just thought she had escaped from someplace . . . I thought . . . you know . . . that maybe she was a part of Nadine's group."

"Nadine didn't bring no people with her this year, Red." Jimmy looked him up and down. "So what exactly are you trying to say?"

"I'ma kick his ass," Roxanne said.

"Naw, baby, calm down." Jimmy said to Roxanne. "Ya man got this."

"Oh hell no," Imani said. "You on ya own with this one, Red. I'm going to check on my mother."

Before Red could respond he heard his name being yelled across the yard. "Redtonio! Redtonio! Come mere, Redtonio!"

Red looked around and saw that his aunt Sistah was calling him. "Redtonio! Redtonio! Come mere, right now."

"I'll be back," he said to Jimmy and Roxanne. "What's going on, Aunt Sistah?"

"This fool," she pointed to the white-gloved butler who'd been serving the guests cheese puffs and shrimp kebabs, "said I can't serve my fatback with pickle dip or fried chitlins on a stick."

"And do you know he stopped her," Red's cousin Lula-Baby said, "from setting up her food because he said her collard greens were dripping green water. I have you to know," Lula-Baby said to the butler, rolling her eyes, "that that's collard green juice. You get you some fried corn bread and you got a meal."

"It won't just the collard greens either, Red," Aunt Sistah said. "He also said that I couldn't serve my lima beans and neck bones. Will you tell this fool that I put my foot in my neck bones."

"What's the problem?" Red said to the butler. "Why can't they serve the food?"

"Sir, we were hired to serve the guests. I offered them the option of allowing us to take the food into the kitchen so it can be served properly with the other entrées."

"Y'all wanna do that?" Red asked his aunt and cousin. "My man here will hook it up with a li'l class. People'll be talkin' about how the butler was servin' chitlins on a stick."

"Now, what the hell wrong with you?" Aunt Sistah frowned at Red. "You know we don't let nobody go in our pots, now you know better than that."

"Anybody seen my porta-potty?" Mama Byrd yelled. "I'm warnin' y'all I need it."

"Oh Lawd," Aunt Sistah said, "let me go help my sister. Straighten this out, Redtonio. I expects that my food will be served."

Lula-Baby stood and watched Red and the butler. "Lima beans make you fart when they get cold, Redtonio."

Red looked at the butler. "Let them serve the food."

ONICA LAY HER head on Chauncey's shoulder as they swayed to Chaka Khan's "Through the Fire." For a moment her eyes connected with Sharief and she saw the hurt and anguish in his face, which only caused her to grip Chauncey tighter. Although she loved Sharief, Chauncey would do as a safe substitute.

Sharief sat at the makeshift bar, shaking the ice in his 7UP, wanting desperately to order a beer, or a rum and Coke, or anything that would calm his nerves and stop him from snapping on Chauncey as he rubbed his hands across Monica's ass.

"I've missed you, Monica," Chauncey whispered, stroking her back.

"Yeah right."

"I have. I've missed you a lot . . . and I've been wanting to talk to you for a while."

"Why didn't you call and tell me? I would've made time, or you should've come over."

"I didn't want to come over, because whenever I did your brother-in-law shot me nasty looks or did things like walk around with the butt of his gun showing. And I wasn't quite comfortable with that, so I stayed home."

"Is that why you haven't been calling me?"

"I've called you. You just never called back."

Monica placed her hands around Chauncey's neck. "I'm sorry."

"Don't be."

"Come again?" Monica stopped dancing.

"Don't stop dancing. Dancing will make this easier for me."

"Okay," Monica said as they started to slow-dance again, this time to Babyface's "Whip Appeal."

"Monica, I've been thinking about our relationship and how long we've been seeing each other. And it seems like the relationship isn't going anywhere."

"I thought we were past this." She took a deep breath. "We've already talked about that. I don't want a relationship right now."

"But I do. That's the problem," Chauncey said.

"But I don't. And I won't compromise my life to settle. I'm twenty-nine years old, and I'm happy. Don't try and take that from me."

"I don't want to take anything from you. And I didn't ask you to live with me or for your hand in marriage so take it down."

"Oh . . ."

"Listen." Chauncey stopped dancing and looked at Monica. "I'm seeing somebody else and I want to see her exclusively. You're not sure of what you want, you're always distracted and un-focused. I can't deal with that and neither do I want that. You seem to think that you'll be twenty-nine forever. Well I know better. So now I've said it. I hope we can be mature enough to be friends."

"Friends?"

"Yes, I like you as a person. I just can't be in a relationship with you."

"Oh." Monica swallowed hard. She absolutely couldn't believe this shit. "Well if that's how you feel, Chauncey, then I wish you the best." She kissed him on the cheek. "You can go home now."

"So now you're putting me out." He frowned.

"No, I just figured that you would wanna step, being that you just dumped me."

"I didn't dump you." He grabbed Monica by the waist. "I was just following your lead and you didn't want to be with me."

"I care about you, Chauncey."

"And I care about you." As Monica went to hug Chauncey his cell phone vibrated. He grabbed it and looked at the caller ID. His eyes lit up. "Excuse me, Monica, I need to take this." And he left her standing there.

"This bastard." Monica chuckled. "Just dumped me, ain't that some shit?" She walked over and sat at the bar by Sharief.

"You know I'm not speaking to you, right?" she said, bumping Sharief on the shoulder. "I'll have a glass of water," she told the bartender.

"Listen." Sharief stared at Monica with a serious look on his face. "I love you, I'm in love with you, and as fucked up as it may be, I would leave my wife to be with you. But don't ever in your fuckin' life play me by throwing a niggah in my face."

"You were fuckin' kissing your wife."

"She kissed me. It was nothing. Absolutely nothing."

"If you say so."

Sharief and Monica sat silent for a minute. The bartender handed Monica her drink. "Let me tell you." She pointed to Chauncey, who was still on the phone. "The square dumped me."

"What?" Sharief raised his eyebrows. "He did what?"

"The niggah left me."

"Oh, you were a couple?"

"No."

"Well, how did he leave you?"

"He said that he wanted to see someone else, because I didn't want to commit to him and shit like that. And . . ."

Sharief cracked up laughing. "And what . . ."

"The bitch called him while we were dancing and he stopped dancing with me to talk to her."

"Poor baby." He grinned. "You just got played?"

"Oh, you think the shit is funny?" She mushed him in the head. "Now that your competition has removed himself."

"I had competition?" Sharief asked seriously.

"No, baby, none at all."

"What competition?" Celeste asked, sitting down on the other side of Sharief. "What are you talking about? And why are y'all always holding li'l side bar conversations?"

"Don't start, Celeste," Sharief said sternly, "I'm not in the mood."

"Excuse me." The videographer stood in front of them. "Would you all like to say something to the bride and groom?"

"Sure, why not?" Sharief said.

"Thank you, sir. Let me get you and your wife first," he pointed to Monica, "and then this young lady." He pointed to Celeste.

"Excuse you?" Celeste frowned. "I'm his wife."

"Oh I'm sorry," the videographer said. "I didn't know . . . I tell you what, I'll come back." He turned and walked away.

"Everybody's your fuckin' wife but me, Sharief." She pointed to the bandage on his hand. "That's the root of our problems."

"You know what, Celeste," Monica snapped, "something's not quite right here. How did you go from confiding in me to accusing me?"

"I never accused you! It's not every day you wake up and your sister's in bed with your husband."

"It's not every day that your sister asks if her husband can live with you," Monica snapped.

"I never asked for him to live with you."

"Well hell, I can't tell; he's at my house every day!"

"Wooo, wait a minute—" Sharief held up his hand for Monica and Celeste to come to a halt.

"You know what? This is soooo for the birds, fuck both of y'all," Monica snapped.

Without thinking twice, Sharief snatched Monica by the arm. "Sit yo' ass down and stop running all over the place. Now, if y'all can't get along then fine, but this is about your mother and Red, not the two of you."

"This is about a buncha bullshit! I'm outta here!" Monica screamed.

Sharief squinted. "Sit yo' ass down and have a drink. What you want, a beer or what's that new drink you like? A Perfect Ten? Celeste, what you want? White wine?" Sharief took his fist and tapped on the bar to get the bartender's attention. "The ladies will have a Perfect Ten, a glass of Chardonnay, and I'll have a rum and Coke."

Celeste looked at Sharief. "You'll have a what?"

"A rum and Coke. I just need to breathe for once. That's it."

"I don't think that's a good decision."

"Damn, Celeste," Monica complained, "he's not your son, shit. Loosen up."

"You need to mind your business."

"This *is* my business."

{ Imani }

"COME ON, MA, talk to me."

Imani leaned back in the butter-soft gray leather front seat in Kree's Excursion. The *Proud to Be Puerto Rican* decorative CD that hung from the rearview mirror spiraled as Kree drove, reflecting streaks of light as he passed cars by. Imani stared at the side of Kree's face. He licked his lips and took a sip of his leftover Heineken. "You sleepy?" He put his beer back down and peeked quickly to the side.

"No, not really." She flipped the visor's mirror down and saw that Jamal had fallen asleep in the backseat. She pushed the visor back up and sighed. "I was just thinking."

"About what?" Kree asked, pushing his truck to almost ninety-five miles per hour up the dark turnpike. He had at least another hour left to drive from Celeste's house back to Brooklyn. Imani had been surprised when he'd asked if he could take her home. She'd agreed because it was right up her alley considering she wasn't speaking to Monica, couldn't stand to hear her girls' opinions about Walik, and everybody else was spending the night. And as far as Imani was concerned, spending the night was out of the question. Especially since she didn't know where Walik was and who he was with. Spending the night would've only made her restless, miserable, and sick to her stomach. All Imani really wanted was one phone call from Walik. Whether it was filled with lies or not, she needed it to at least sound legit. All she wanted to hear was, *I was sleep, ma, I didn't hear my phone ring, and I been at your crib this whole time.* Was that too much to ask? Her stomach was doing flips because she knew she'd been gone too long and didn't know what mood Walik would be in when she called him early in the morning. Or how he would feel about hanging out with her all day, since he had more than enough time to make up an excuse why he couldn't fuck with her too tough. For once Imani wanted to feel safe: as if all was well with the world and that Walik going to prison and coming home had somewhat changed him. After all, she'd stayed by his side the entire time, playing in her pussy and the whole nine, never fucking another niggah. In fact she'd only been with one other man, besides Walik, and that was when she was twelve and lost her virginity, but now that she was twenty-three she no longer wanted that to count. Besides, she'd lied to Walik and told him that he'd been her first and only one.

"So that's really ya man, huh?" Kree asked Imani. "What's up with that?"

"Why are you asking me all of these questions? I got one for you."

"What?"

"I ain't never met a Puerto Rican named Kree. What the hell happened to Rico Suave?"

"Oh no, you didn't say some stupid shit like that to me." Kree frowned.

"How is that stupid?"

"Why can't I be Puerto Rican and be named Kree? Now, if I flipped that shit and said something dumb to you like why is your name Imani and not Shanay-nay or Bey-Bey you would have an attitude. For your information my name is Kree Fernando Rodriquez. And I'm a full-blooded bronze-colored Puerto Rican. Don't be confused."

Imani felt stupid. "I didn't mean any harm. I'm sorry, I didn't expect you to get offended."

"It's good, ma, I checked you. Now we can move forward." He smiled. "But if you say something crazy again, then I'ma be convinced that that's a description of who you are."

"Are you calling me crazy?"

"I'm calling you tomorrow if you can act like you have some sense."

Imani couldn't help but laugh. "Ai'ight, Kree, you got that. So what's with you? You gotta girl?"

"I got some jump-offs that hang around, but I'm single."

For some reason Imani looked at his left hand.

"So how long have you been with ole boy?" he asked her.

"Since I was thirteen."

"Damn, that's a long time. So what's up with him? Why you play him the other night at the club?"

"It's a long story but we made up. Anyway do you hang out at NV a lot?"

"I DJ there on Saturdays."

"Oh, I didn't know that," she said, smiling.

"That's wassup."

"Wait a minute . . . Kree? Kree from Hot 97, rap, reggae, club and soca mix, that's you? I love to listen to that! Oh, you da bomb, boo. Aww shit, let me find out you Fat Joe on the low."

Kree laughed. "There go that mouth again."

"I'm just playing, big head."

"I know, baby." He blushed. "I guess I'm just not on my DJing shit like that. I do it because I love it."

"Damn, sweetie. I'm proud of you."

"You don't even know me to be proud of me."

"But you feel like my brother."

"Oh hell no." Kree smirked. "Don't even start that *brother* shit, 'cause I will commit incest. So stop it. Stop it right now. I'm too fine to be your brother."

Imani mushed him playfully in the head. "Punk."

"Don't you see me driving, girl?" Kree took a sip of his beer.

"I also see you sipping a beer, so hush."

"Ai'ight, ai'ight," Kree said, putting his beer down. "Yo, do you watch *Being Bobby Brown*?"

"Do I? That shit is off the hook. It's cracked-out love at its finest."

"Look, boo." Kree snickered. "Remember this?" He started singing, making fun of a line from the show: *"These work for me? These work for you? These work for me? These work for you?"*

"Hell yeah." Imani hunched her shoulders like she was doing the Cabbage Patch and started singing along, but instead she said, *"Crack work for me, crack work for you, crack work for me, crack work for you . . ."*

Kree looked at her. "Whitney gon' bust yo' ass, sayin' some shit like that."

"Well hell, it's my prerogative."

"You funny as hell, girl." Kree laughed.

By the time they finished singing, talking, and laughing they were pulling in front of Imani's apartment building. Kree double-parked his Excursion. "You know, you're a decent broad."

Imani playfully balled up her fist. "Oh no, you didn't call me a decent broad."

"What do want me to say, that you're not decent?"

"Just hush." Imani smiled. "I had a lot of fun with you. Thanks for making me feel better." She opened the truck's door.

"Well damn, it's a wrap? No kiss, no *I'll see you tomorrow*, no nothing?"

"I wanna kiss you. I do." She slid her hands down his cheeks, her palms meeting at his goatee. "But I have a man."

"Ai'ight, ma. You got that."

"Let me see your phone," Imani said to him, closing the door.

Kree handed her his phone. "Now"—she smiled—"my number is programmed. Call me."

"Later, baby. Let me help you with Jamal." Kree jumped out of his truck and opened Imani's door, then walked to the back door and woke up Jamal. "Come on, li'l man."

Jamal was groggy. "Where's my Imani?" He stretched.

"Right here," Imani said, helping him out of the backseat.

"We home?" Jamal asked.

"Yeah."

"Okay, I wanna get in the bed."

"Ai'ight li'l man and li'l mama." Kree hopped back in his truck. "I'll catch y'all another time."

"Bye, Kree." They waved.

Imani practically dragged Jamal upstairs. He was holding her leg as tight as he could. They rode the elevator to their twelfth-floor apartment. "Come on, boy," Imani said.

As she approached the apartment door, she heard the television playing. She breathed a sigh of relief. *Walik's here. Now I'ma go off because where the fuck has he been.* Before putting her key in the door Imani became pissed: she knew Walik was smoking a blunt because she could smell the weed floating underneath the door. *I'ma cuss his ass out! He knows I don't like that shit around Jamal.*

As soon as Imani opened the door, she spotted Walik sitting on the couch, sucking on the tip of a blunt. Jamal was so sleepy that he didn't even notice Walik. He walked directly to his room and fell out across the bed. Imani walked in behind him and pulled his pants off.

"What the fuck?" Imani screamed at Walik as she came out of Jamal's room. "What the hell I tell you about smoking if Jamal is home!" She knocked his feet off her coffee table and picked up the two empty bottles of beer he had sprawled on the floor. As she walked in the kitchen to place the bottles in the trash, she looked around and saw that the place was a mess: dishes in the sink and dirty plates on the table. "Damn, Walik, you couldn't clean up?"

"My fault," he bellowed out in between beer burps.

"Your fault, humph," she said sarcastically, walking back into the living room. She threw her keys across her glass coffee table and looked at the clock, which read four AM. "So where have you been all day?" she asked Walik.

"Goddamn, you walk in the door fuckin' naggin'."

"Walik, I asked you a question."

"And I asked you to stop stressing me." He mashed his blunt in the ashtray. "Damn."

"Damn what?" She frowned. "You know how many times I called you. I know you got my messages. You couldn't call me back?"

"I didn't hear my phone ring." He put his feet back on the coffee table.

"It's awfully funny how you never miss a call when I'm around."

"I been in prison for two years, you ain't been around like that."

"And from what I can see," Imani said, "you still the same grimy-ass niggah you were when you went in there."

"I was waitin' on it and there it is."

"What?" She placed her hands on her hips.

"That bullshit." He sat up and pointed his finger at her. "You just a fuckin' naggin' ass."

"So what, suck ya dick and stop flappin' my lips?" she said sarcastically.

"Basically."

"Fuck you!"

"Naw, I'll pass. Anyway, how you get home?"

Imani quickly blinked. "My mother—my sister, brought me home."

"Which one?"

"Celeste—Monica."

"Why you lyin'?" He cocked his head to the side. "I can't stand to be lied to."

"What?" She sucked her teeth. "What the hell I gotta lie to you for . . . and don't try and turn the shit around on me. Where the fuck you been? I been calling you all fuckin' day! You saw my number, you knew I was calling you, and you couldn't even call and say you're okay?"

"Yo." Walik got off the couch. "I should slap the shit outta you for standing in my fuckin' face lyin'! I saw your niggah drop you off a minute ago."

"What?"

"You heard me!" he yelled. "I saw that punk bitch drop you off and you had my son in the car!" He walked over to Imani and grabbed her around the neck. "I should knock your fuckin' head into the wall! This is exactly why I don't fuck with you for too long, fuckin' whore! You lie too much. I just got home from a bid and already I gotta put my hands on you." He took his hands from around her neck.

"Walik, it wasn't even like that!"

"Shut the fuck up! You stressing me. Y'all jumping me and shit all because I called some bitch, but then yo' niggah drops you off and you lie to me? I should break yo' face, yo'. I knew you was fuckin' his ass!"

"I wasn't fuckin' him. I don't even know him like that!"

"Imani, you was practically riding his dick in the club. When I asked you then how you knew him you should've been like, *This is my friend. You was gon' for two years,* yadda-yadda, and maybe, just maybe I would've understood."

"Are you serious? I've been more than faithful to you."

"Beat it, 'cause I'm not beat for it."

"It was a coincidence," she insisted. "He just happened to be the DJ at my mother's wedding. As a matter of fact, he DJs at NV and he's a DJ for Hot 97, the Friday-night nine o'clock rap, reggae, and soca mix."

"Why is you spittin' this niggah's résumé at me? You tryin' to throw that shit in my face? What, I ain't good enough for you no more, Imani? Now you got to have the local DJ."

"Oh . . . my . . . God!" Imani couldn't believe it. "What are you talking about? You probably made more money on the street than Kree has seen in a lifetime."

"So that's his name? Kree? What kinda bitch-ass name is Kree? What the fuck is that? Bitch ass!" Walik kicked the glass coffee table over, causing the glass to shatter all over the floor.

"Stop it!" Imani yelled. "You know Jamal is sleeping."

"You know what?" Walik picked up his wallet off the floor and stuffed it in his back pocket. "I'm sick of yo' fat ass!"

"I ain't fat. Shante's ass is fat. Yo' ass is fat, motherfucker!"

"She might be fat but at least she knows what to do."

"What to do? Do about what? All y'all fat asses can do is make sandwiches."

"Lyin' bitch!"

"You the liar, Walik."

"Kiss my ass, bitch!"

"What? You kiss my ass, open it up and lick the pink inside of it!"

"Imani!" Jamal ran into the room, wearing his white tuxedo shirt and Spider-Man underwear. His thighs were chubby and rubbed slightly together. "What is going on in here? I'ma call nine-one-one this time!"

"Let me get out of here, before I hurt somebody. I swear, don't come near me!" Walik yelled.

"Go back in your room, Jamal!" Imani screamed. Jamal didn't move. Imani ran in front of Walik as he walked toward the door and blocked his path. "Where you going, Walik?"

"What? If you don't get the fuck out my way—"

"Don't leave. We both got upset, and we can talk about it. Jamal, go in your room!"

"Naw, he ain't gotta leave. Seems to me that he's more of your man than I am. So you, ya kid, and the Rican can live happily ever after. I don't give a fuck."

"Yeah right. What, you wanna run to Shante?"

"At least she ain't got another niggah droppin' her off."

"Are you still messing with her, Walik?"

"What the fuck you think?" He pushed Imani out of the way. "Don't call me no more."

Imani quickly turned around and tried to grab Walik from the back, but she couldn't quite catch him as he slammed the door in her face. "Walik!" She opened the door and yelled down the hallway. "Walik! Come back! It wasn't even like that! It wasn't!" He pressed the button for the elevator. Imani ran down the hall trying to catch him, but as she got there he stepped onto the elevator. Within seconds the door closed and she was left standing alone in the hallway.

Imani felt like her whole head was spinning. She walked back to her apartment, sent Jamal back to bed, and crouched on the floor between the couch and the shattered glass of the coffee table. She held her head down and started crying. By the time she looked up, the sun was reflecting light from behind her and shining rays all over the living room.

"**B**ITCH! WHERE DE bumbaclot you been? And why've you been hiding from me the past couple of weeks?" Monica's best friend, Listra, snapped at her as she walked into Patsy's Café, a small West Indian restaurant on Flatbush that Listra and her mother owned. The restaurant was nothing fancy. In fact the word *café* in its name was fancier than the place. The restaurant was mostly a tight box, with a small air conditioner, four round kitchen tables with plastic floral tablecloths and matching chairs, a counter that doubled as a bar, a jukebox, and a soda machine that sold Trinidadian Chubbies. But no matter what, if you wanted the best West Indian food in Brooklyn, then Patsy's was the place to be.

Listra stood behind the counter with a cigarette hanging from the corner of her mouth as she pulled her shoulder-length hair into a ponytail. Monica sat down at the counter and slyly unbuttoned her denim capris. *Damn,* she thought, *when did these get too tight?* She did her best to pull her white DKNY V-neck tee over the waist of her pants as she reached over the counter to greet her friend.

They kissed each other on the cheek. "Look at you." Listra smiled, mashing her cigarette in the ashtray. "Humph, the dick must be delicious because your bumpsey is telling how well your coochie is eating it up."

"You are so fresh," Monica said, laughing. "But girl, my ass is gettin' big," she went on, resting her elbows on the counter, "I had to unbutton my pants just to sit down and believe it or not, for about three weeks, or at least since the wedding, I've been on a diet and I can't seem to lose weight for nothing."

"Girl, just give it up, don't nothing want a bag a bones but a dog and even he buries 'em. So to hell with being skinny. Fuck them skinny bitches." Listra leaned forward on the counter. She folded her arms underneath her large breasts and blinked. "You know what I'm sayin'?"

"Listra, you are a mess. I'm sooooo happy to see you. I've been needing somebody to talk to. Girl, I have a million and one things going on."

"What's going on?" Listra stood up and wiped her hands on her apron. "But first tell me what you want to eat."

"Akee and salt fish, rice with oxtail gravy, some corn soup . . . oh and some callaloo . . . and some dumplings . . . a currant roll too."

"I thought you were on a diet."

"I am. But I've been wanting some of your mother's akee and salt fish all week."

"You ordered a little more than akee and salt fish."

"Just get the food, girl." Monica playfully rolled her eyes.

"Patsy gurl," Listra called to her mother.

"Oh, ya callin' me Patsy, hauh?" She walked from the kitchen to the front, her eyes lighting up when she saw Monica. "Listra, ya mouth more hot dan it's sweet."

Monica laughed. "You must watch ya mouth, gurl," she said in a fake Trini accent. "Hi, Ms. Patsy."

Patsy walked over and kissed Monica on the cheek. "Hey dere, baby. Good to see ya, chile. How ya mummy and she new husband?"

"They're fine, thank you."

"Mummy." Listra smiled. "Monica wants some akee and salt fish, corn soup, rice with oxtail gravy, callaloo, dumplings, and a currant roll."

"What?" Patsy screeched. "Ya belly big, gurl?"

"No," Monica said, trying her best to hide her hurt feelings. "I can't have children." She lowered her eyes.

"Who told you dat? The good Lord tell you dat?" Ms. Patsy asked, placing her hands on her hips.

"No."

"Well until the good Lord tell you dat," she said as she lifted Monica's head up, "you remember that you a 'oman and if you got a man to screw you can have a chile."

Monica laughed. She knew Patsy was trying to make her feel better. "Okay, Ms. Patsy."

"I'm going to fix ya food now, chile."

"Mummy," Listra said as Patsy turned to walk back into the kitchen, "I'll take some crab and callaloo."

Patsy sucked her teeth, long and hard. "You own dis place here too, ya know." She shook her head and smiled. "Dis here chile of mine." She walked back into the kitchen.

"So tell me," Listra said, "what are the million and one things going on?"

"First of all, you remember Chauncey?"

"Yeah."

"Well, he dumped me."

"He did what?" Listra said, trying not to snicker.

"Girl, it's okay," Monica said, "you can laugh."

And with that said Listra stretched out in laughter. "He did what? Oh Gawd."

"But I figured it was for the best. I didn't really want him for my man. I just wanted him to hang around."

"I hear you, girl. So tell me, what else is up?"

"Let me tell you, the day my mother got married, Celeste flipped on her."

"I thought you said you all liked your mother's fiancé, well, husband now."

"He's okay. A little tired. He and my mother still think that he's famous. He's harmless, though. But Celeste still has some resentment about my mother and the many men she's had in her life."

"And you?" Listra poured Monica a glass of ginger shandy.

"Just some water, Listra, I can't take the smell of that."

"Of what?" Listra said, taken aback. "The shandy? You love shandy."

"I know, but not today. Just some water."

"Okay. Now go on, I'm listening." Listra sat the shandy to the side and poured Monica a glass of spring water.

"Well," Monica continued, "not until I really thought about how and why Celeste was going off did I really start to think about how many of my mother's ex-factors we've known. But shit, my mother and her boyfriends were just a part of life. Starrla Britt didn't let no grass grow under her feet, okay?"

"So . . . what's the problem with that? She took care of you, right?"

"Oh, hell yeah," Monica assured Listra, "in between her working and being on welfare at the same time, we wanted for nothing. My mother loved us, almost too much, but trust and believe she loved men too."

"And the problem would be?"

"I guess the problem is that we knew too much of her business, and all we ever saw was one man after the other, after the other. I remember one time, I was about . . ." Monica looked at the ceiling, then back at Listra, "eleven and my mother had a boyfriend, who had a daughter my age, I forgot her name, Rhonda I think . . . anyway, she and I played together all the time and her father was so nice to us, not to mention his daughter and I were best friends.

Well, one day I was hanging out the window, watching up and down the street, waiting for him to come and get me so his daughter and I could play. Well, after an hour of waiting my mother announced to me that not only was he not coming to get me, but I wouldn't be seeing him or his daughter anymore."

Patsy walked out of the kitchen and sat the plates of food on the counter. Listra sat down in the chair behind the counter, and she and Monica sat face-to-face, eating.

"So your mother and her boyfriend broke up?"

"Yeah," Monica said with her mouth full.

"Did she tell you why?" Listra took a sip of the shandy that she'd previously poured for Monica.

"Hell no and I didn't ask, unless I wanted to be slapped in the mouth for being too grown."

"What about you and how you felt? Didn't your mother understand that? You said how nice he was to you."

"Oh chile please, the way my mother saw it, they were all nice. Once thing about Starr is, if you didn't like us, or treat us nice, then she didn't fuck with you. And to this day, even with her new husband, that's still the deal. But when we were kids, what my mother didn't understand is that we had feelings and when these men were nice to us and introduced us to their families, took us places, and made us feel good, we became attached to them. And sometimes we couldn't deal with them breaking up." Monica took a sip of water. She broke a piece of salt fish and stuffed it in her mouth. "Oh this is sooo good . . . ," she moaned.

"Would you finish talking?" Listra laughed.

"Okay, listen, what you need to understand is that yes, my mother loved us; and yes, she took care of us. And no, she didn't let nobody fuck with us, but what she didn't realize is that we couldn't take the breakups with her men. We were little girls, what were we supposed to do with heartbreak? It was bad enough that we all had different fathers and kids used to ask, 'How come you and your sisters have different last names?' Then on top of that, not one of us had a responsible father and every time my mother brought a new man home, especially someone we liked, we were all hoping that Mr. Well-Liked would stay around long enough to become our daddy. But it never happened, so I guess when your mother is doing her thing, those are the breaks."

"So your fathers just never came around."

"Nope."

"Do you at least know what your father looks like?"

"No more than what I see in the mirror every day. From the pictures I've seen, I look exactly like him, the dark mahogany skin, almond eyes, thick curly hair."

"Not to change the subject." Listra swallowed her food. "I saw Walik around the corner on Church with a newborn baby girl."

"Get the hell outta here!" Monica couldn't believe it.

"At first I thought Imani had another baby."

"Hell no, I would've kicked her ass!" Monica stuffed a piece of fish in her mouth. "When *Imani* has a baby, *we* have a baby. And I don't want any more kids, okay?"

"I hear you. Sounds like my sister. But anyway as I went to speak to him, some chick walked up and started talking to him, so I left it alone and kept on going."

"That niggah is sorry as hell. I'll be so glad when Imani gets rid of him," Monica said.

"She's been with him forever."

"I know." Monica rolled her eyes. "And forever is too damn long. She's been calling me every day. That's how I know she's miserable. Because when all is well in paradise, I don't hear from the wench, other than when she's dropping Jamal off."

"Well, how's Celeste?"

"A fuckin' lunatic."

"She still thinks her husband is cheating?"

Monica stared at Listra for a moment and took a sip of water. "Yes. She thinks he's cheating."

"Is he? You would know, he's still staying with you during the week, right?"

"Yeah, he does."

"Well hell, does he act like he's cheating?"

"Uhmm, sometimes."

"Oh hell no, bitch, cough it up. Since high school you have told me everything."

"I know but . . . I want to tell you something . . . but I don't know how or what you'll think of me, and what you think is important."

"Don't tell me, you're fuckin' him." Listra laughed. "I'm just playing girl, tell me. He's cheating, ain't he? Pussyclot! I knew any man that looked like Common was way too fine to be faithful."

"Yes, he is." Monica swallowed hard.

"What? Too fine to be faithful?"

"No . . . he's cheating."

"Oh my God, and you didn't tell Celeste?"

"I can't."

"Why not? That's your sister. I know y'all don't always get along but still, she is your sister."

"I know . . . but . . ."

"But what, just tell me," Listra urged.

"I fucked him," Monica spat out. She looked Listra directly in the eyes in an attempt to read her mind and see her reaction.

"Yeah right." Listra curled her lips. "I know we said his ass was cute and joked about him probably having a big crooked dick but you didn't . . . fuck him, right?"

"I did."

Listra leaned back in her chair as if she were lost for words. "Where my bumbaclot cigarettes?" she said. She grabbed her purse from the shelf under the counter, lit her Newport, and took a strong pull. Listra's Trinidadian accent was in full effect. "Now what de fuck really wrong wit' you, gurl?"

"I fucked him. I did. I did. I sucked his dick. He ate my pussy, I let this niggah fuck me in the ass. I did it. I was the biggest ho in the fuckin' world. A stupid no-good slut. I know. I fucked my sister's husband. I know I was wrong. I know."

"Wait a damn minute. Don't try and put yourself down in hopes that I won't follow up, because I'ma tell you that that is some bacchanal shit you got goin' on! In my country my sister might've killed you for dat, gurl."

"It wasn't planned. I always had a slight thing for him, but he was Celeste's husband and I just tried to brush it off . . . well, we tried to brush it off."

"We?"

"Well, I always felt like he had a thing for me too, because he always stared at me too long. Or he laughed at too many of my corny-ass jokes and he noticed intimate things about me like a new hairstyle, makeup, shoes, and shit."

"Hell, I would've assumed he was a batty man—gay or someting. Not dat he wanted to horn his wife with me."

"No. I knew he wasn't gay. Look." Monica paused. "When Celeste and Sharief first moved to Jersey, Sharief ran off the highway."

"And fucking you comes in where?" Listra raised her eyebrows.

"Would you listen," Monica snapped. "You know that Sharief is a detective and his shift didn't end until two and sometimes three o'clock in the morning. And then he had to drive an hour and a half home. So one night, when he was driving home he fell asleep, and totaled his car by slamming into the barrier."

"Oh Gawd, was he all right?" Listra asked concerned.

"Yeah, he walked away with some bruises from the airbag. Shortly after that Celeste asked me if I would mind Sharief staying with me for a few days during the week, or when he had to work."

"And you said yes?"

"Of course I said yes."

"Why didn't she ask your mother?"

"Girl, don't nobody wanna stay with Red's nonsingin' ass, practicing dance steps and shit all night."

Listra laughed.

"Anyway," Monica continued, "at first I did well, he and I both did well. We had opposite shifts. When he went to work I was at home, when he was home I was at the hospital working. No problems. Barely saw each other. He had his own key and we kept it moving."

"Get to the point." Listra mashed her cigarette in the ashtray.

"I'm getting there," Monica huffed.

"Don't get vexed wit' me, 'cause I'm waitin' for you to get to the part where Celeste kicked yo' ass."

"Look, my shift changed and I started working nine to five with every other weekend off, and I noticed how Sharief never seemed to eat any home-cooked food, always fast food. So I started cooking for him. And I would always make sure that he had dinner in the microwave when he came home at night. And if I didn't feel like cooking, then I would order Chinese and have it delivered to him at the station. And we started to get close after that."

"Uhmm-hmm." Listra sucked her teeth. "So you were laying down the bait?"

"It wasn't like that."

"I can't tell."

"You wanna hear the story or not?" Monica asked.

"Go ahead."

"So one night we were talking and I found out that he liked old-school hip-hop. Well, his birthday was coming up, so I surprised him with tickets to an old-school concert: Naughty By Nature, MC Shan, Lyte, Lateefah, Moni, the Jungle Brothers . . ."

"How long ago was this?"

"Three—almost four months."

"And you fucked him before or after the show?"

"After—the same night—but it just happened. We came home, ate dinner, watched some ole Bruce Lee karate movies, and fell asleep. When we woke up we were lying on the couch and my head was on his chest. He kissed me on the forehead to wake me up. 'Get up baby,' he said.

"I stared at him long and hard and I wanted to kiss him so bad. I did. I really did, but I just sat up and said, 'Wow, I didn't realize we fell asleep.'

" 'Me either,' he said. And Listra, he stared at me and he kept looking at my breasts and my face, and back at my breasts, and then he tucked his lips inside his mouth. I can't even lie, my pussy was dripping. As I went to stand up he said, 'Come here.' I turned around and he kissed me . . . and I kissed him back, I couldn't help it. Then he slid his hands down over my breasts and started feeling my nipples. He started kissing me on my neck down to my cleavage and then he started sucking my titties through my shirt.

" 'Sharief,' I whispered to him, 'we gotta stop, baby. I want to, I really want to, but we can't.'

" 'I know.' He stopped sucking my nipple and started unbuttoning my blouse. 'We need to stop, but I can't . . . unless you absolutely want me to stop.'

"But by then, girl, I was undressed. My mouth couldn't speak so my body had to do the talking."

Listra took a deep breath. "Look, don't do it again. Just take the skeleton and tuck it in the closet. It happened once, that's more than enough, just forget about it. But let me warn you: if you try anything with my husband, I'ma beat yo' ass."

Monica laughed. "Shut up, girl."

"Listen, you were wrong and I have to tell you that I'm disappointed, but just don't let it happen anymore. It was *only once,* right?"

"No." Monica hesitated. "I've been fucking him like he's mine."

"But what de hell! Gurl, I thought it was just some forbidden dick. Not a damn love affair! Monica, are you in a relationship with this man?"

Monica looked down and then she looked back up again. "Yes. Look, Listra." She took a deep breath. "I didn't mean to fall in love with him. I didn't mean for this to ever happen . . . or to get this far . . . I love my sister. I do . . . I do . . . but I'm in love with Sharief and I don't know how to give that up."

"Do you want to?"

"No . . . and I know it's fucked up and the more I lie the worse it is. Every time I see Celeste, I feel horrible. And lately I don't see her as being my sister as much as I see her as being his wife. I can't lie, Listra, I love him. He's perfect. He's beautiful, his smile, his laugh, his teeth." She giggled. "The dick, all of it. He has a wonderful career, he's a good father, a good provider, if I ask him for something—anything—and he has it, I have it. He's all that I've ever wanted in my life. And quite frankly I don't know what the hell is wrong with Celeste."

"Celeste?"

"Yes, Celeste. She gained weight, I swear all she does is smoke, eat, and complain."

"That's not a reason to fuck your sister's husband. Anyway, does Celeste know?"

"No."

"Well, den you in a mess. She's his wife. She is the Mrs. to your Mr." Listra looked disgusted. "Come on, Monica, you and your sister are fucking the same man?"

"No—he's not fucking her—he wants a divorce."

"And so does every other cheatin'-ass man."

"No, this is different. I know both sides because Celeste tells me all her business, no matter how nasty she is to me."

"Get the hell outta here! Oh, this shit has got to stop."

"What has to stop?" Celeste asked, walking into the café wearing a pair of jeans and a tank top. "Tell me."

"How did you get here?" Monica said, surprised.

"I drove here. Hi, Listra." Celeste looked around. "Damn, Listra, when are you all going to decorate in here? Goodness."

"When you pay for it." Listra smirked.

"Anyway." Celeste snickered. "I just stopped in to get something to eat. I know Sharief likes West Indian food, so I figured I would stop in and get him something."

"How is Sharief?" Listra asked Celeste.

"He's fantastic! I can't wait to get home. I have the candles lit, the whipped cream and strawberries in the refrigerator, and the Boney James on repeat. Oh let me tell you, when I get home me and my husband gon' make a baby!"

Monica almost choked on the water she was sipping.

"Are you okay?" Celeste asked.

"Yes," Monica coughed out. "Where are the girls?"

"With Mommy."

"I'm surprised that you're here," Listra said. "When's the last time you were in Brooklyn?"

"A few months ago, and just looking around I see why I don't come back. But I called and asked my mother to keep my children tonight so that Sharief and I could spend some time alone. Let me tell you, I even brought a new negligee. It's white, see-through, and trimmed in fox fur. I'ma screw his brains out, you hear me?" Celeste smiled. "Listra, can I have two orders of curry chicken to go."

"No problem." Listra went into the kitchen and fixed the food.

"Look, Monica," Celeste said, "let's try and get along, after all we are sisters."

"You should remember that when you're being nasty to me. Don't try and be nice now because you have plans to get some dick. Just make sure you pay me my money back from Mommy's bachelorette party and then we'll call it a truce."

Listra quickly returned. "All right, Celeste, two curry chickens." Celeste pulled out her wallet.

"It's on the house," Listra said, waving her hand. "No worries. Have fun tonight."

"Thanks, Listra, I appreciate it. Okay, see ya later." Celeste waved good-bye and left.

"If you don't stop"—Listra looked at Monica—"it's only a matter of time before all hell breaks loose."

"It already has." Before Monica could go on, the walkie-talkie on her Nextel went off. "Monica—Monica over and out."

"Who the hell is that?" Listra mumbled.

"My mother," Monica mumbled back. "Ma," she clicked the walkie-talkie button on her phone, "just call me on the phone. I can hear you better." A few seconds later Monica's phone rang. "Wassup, Ma?"

"Monica, I need you to come and get these kids for me. Red got an important gig."

Instantly Monica caught an attitude. "What?"

"Don't say *what* to me. Anyway, the Chi-Lites, Blue Magic, some of the living members from Earth Wind and Fire, and Pips gon' be at Symphony Hall in Newark, New Jersey, and they invited the Jam On Its to be their opening act. Red, Jimmy, and Slick on the come-up, baby! Mama Byrd is going with Nadine, but I need you to keep Celeste's kids."

"Call Celeste and tell her to keep her own kids. I have something to do."

"Celeste has a special night planned for her and Sharief. She's trying to save her marriage."

"Oh please. She should've thought of that before she tried to chop his hand off."

"That ain't none of your business. When you get your husband, you worry about that. Now, look, I gotta do Red's hair and let out the waist in his glow-in-the-dark catsuit. And then I gotta go help Jimmy and Roxanne out. The poor woman, she tried to let out the waist in Jimmy's catsuit but given the situation with her hands, she ended up sewing the ass to the elbow. So what time are you going to be here?"

"Ma—"

"Ma, what? You mean to tell me that you can't help me out? You can't rearrange your plans for one night? I'm your mother and if I had a mother still alive I would jump through hoops to do whatever she ask me to."

"Okay, Ma. Just tell them to get ready because I'm around the corner at Patsy's."

"Okay, tell Patsy and Listra I said hello. Love ya, baby."

"Love ya too, Ma."

"Look, Listra," Monica said, hanging up, "let me go. I need to get my nieces so Sharief and my sister can get their fuck on. All of a sudden Red has an important gig. The Chi-Lites and the fuckin' Pips. Gimme a break."

"All right, girl. Remember," Listra said, "no matter what you are my best friend in the whole world, but stop messing with Sharief. Believe it's you to catch in the end."

"Bye girl," Monica said, ignoring her friend's warning. They kissed each other on the cheek, and Monica left.

＊　●　＊

WHEN MONICA PULLED up in front of her mother's house, Starr, Red, and the girls were waiting outside for her. Monica couldn't believe her eyes. Starr was dressed in a long red skintight dress, showing off every single voluptuous curve that God had blessed her with. Starr wasn't the type to care about her love handles; as far as she was concerned that was a part of her beauty. Red's glow-in-the-dark yellow catsuit was supertight. And the cape that hung from it was trimmed in red feathers. His Afro looked as if it had been doctored up with jheri-curl juice and was now wet and stringy, hanging almost to his shoulders. He had a red-and-yellow feather tucked behind his ear and at first glance looked like a mix between

Nick Ashford and the black man from the Village People. *Oh my Lord,* Monica thought.

Looking at the girls, Monica could tell that Kayla had an attitude. Kayla walked to Monica's car, opened the door, and sat in the front seat. "Aunty, they look absolutely ridiculous."

Kai and Kori kept laughing and pulling off the feathers that trimmed Red's cape. "Y'all stop it now!" Red growled. "Leave my cape alone."

"Come on, Kai and Kori," Kayla snapped, "get in the car!"

The twins ran over to the car with hands full of feathers. "Aunty Monica!" Kori said, "Pa-pa Red is a bird." Kai fell out laughing. After a few minutes Monica started laughing. "We shouldn't be laughing, girls. What you're seeing there is a classic."

Kayla rolled her eyes in her head. "Let's just leave, please."

"Bye Ma and Red," Monica said as they pulled off.

"Aunty," Kayla said, "did my daddy call you?"

"No. Why?"

"Because I called him earlier to come and get us so we could go over my other grandma's house. He said he was coming. And when I called him back to tell him that we were going to your house, he didn't answer his phone."

"He'll call back. Don't worry."

"Aunty, can we order pizza?" Kori asked.

"I want Chinese!" Kai demanded.

"Shut up," Kayla said, "we're getting Taco Bell. You'll eat a burrito and be quiet about it!"

Monica quickly looked at Kayla and then quickly back at the street. For a moment she thought Celeste was talking. "Don't talk to them like that!" she said to Kayla. "That's not nice. Now, what I suggest is that you apologize right now!"

"I'm sorry," Kayla mumbled.

"You didn't mumble when you told them to shut up, miss, so don't mumble now."

"I'm sorry," Kayla said with tears in her eyes.

"Don't cry. You can have Taco Bell, just be a little nicer about it."

"Okay," she sniffed.

"Now, look," Monica said to the girls, "we'll all get what we want and then we'll go back to my house and pig out!"

"Yeah! We did it! We did it!" Kai and Kori started to sing.

"I am so sick of them," Kayla mumbled.

*　•　*

MONICA TOOK THE girls to get what they wanted to eat; on the way home she stopped by Junior's and grabbed a strawberry cheesecake that she'd been craving since she'd left Patsy's. Back at home she and the girls took their clothes off and slipped pajamas on. "What DVD do you guys wanna watch?"

"I wanna see *Disappearing Acts*," Kayla insisted. "My mommy says that my daddy acts like Franklin."

"Your mother shouldn't tell you that," Monica said. "We'll watch the Cheetah Girls. That's a little more appropriate."

She sat down on the floor with the girls and started eating a slice of pizza. As she took the first bite she felt her stomach starting to rumble and her mouth beginning to water. *I'ma throw up,* she thought. *It was all that shit I ate earlier at Patsy's. Damn!* Monica got off the floor and walked to the bathroom as quickly as she could. She leaned over the toilet and started throwing up what felt like every particle of food she'd ever eaten in her life. Afterward she ran water in the sink, washed her mouth out, and splashed it in her face. When she looked in the mirror she saw Sharief standing behind her.

"You scared the shit out of me!" she cried, jumping.

He kissed her on the back of the head and caressed her behind. "What's wrong?"

"I just feel sick. I think it was something I ate. What are you doing here?"

"Kayla called me earlier when I was at work to come and get them. She wanted to see my mother. But I ended up working later than I thought—and to think, today was supposed to be my day off. So I stopped by your mother's and when nobody was there I came here."

"Okay." Monica splashed more water on her face. "Damn, I feel flushed."

"Daddy! Daddy!" Kai called. "Come mere."

"Go see what she wants," Monica said, "I'll be there in a minute."

"Aunty," Kayla called, "telephone. It's Aunty Imani."

Monica rolled her eyes at the ceiling. "Tell her I'm coming." She walked into the kitchen, sat down at the table, and picked up the cordless phone. "Y'all want popcorn?" she asked the girls before saying anything to Imani.

"Yes!" they screamed.

"Hello?" Monica said, putting the popcorn in the microwave.

"What, my son can't come over your house?" Imani was pissed. "The Desperate Housewife does us all a favor and blesses Brooklyn with Raven Symone and the Olsen twins and all of a sudden Jamal can't come around? What, my son too gully for you?"

"What are you talking about?" Monica opened the window; the smell of the popcorn was killing her. "Red had a gig, that's how the girls ended up over here, thank you."

"Yeah, I bet."

"I don't have time for this. What is it?"

"I just called to talk. Now I have to have a reason to call?"

"No, but don't call here questioning me about why I don't have my nephew, who by the way I keep all the time. I have a headache, my stomach hurts, and I'm not in the mood to deal with the kids in my house. So no, Jamal can't come over here. Call his daddy— Mr. Wonderful."

"We broke up," Imani paused, "the same night of the wedding."

"Again? Well good, time to take the trash out. But what does that have to do with Jamal? Jamal is still his son. Now call him."

"He won't answer when I call him."

"Wait a minute, Imani, say that again."

"He won't answer when I call him."

"That sorry son-of-a-bitch. I can't stand his fat cheatin' ass! And what is this about Walik and some baby girl?"

Imani hesitated. "How did you hear that?"

"Don't worry about it. But the person told me that he was holding a newborn baby girl."

"Oh." Imani felt like she wanted to break down and cry. "Shante must've had the baby."

"What? She and Walik had a baby together? This sorry-triflin'-good-for-nothin' niggah had a baby on you? Wait a minute . . . didn't he just get out of prison after two years?"

"So?"

"So? How the hell is he making babies in prison?" Monica couldn't believe what she was hearing.

"He was fucking her in prison. Believe me, whatever you do out here, you can do in prison."

"Well, I have heard it all. Either you gon' have to leave him alone or you need your ass beat. With his fat-ass self—oh I can't stand him!"

"He's not fat," Imani said defensively.

"He's not fat? Well I know what he is, he's a no-good, inconsiderate, cheatin'-ass deadbeat bastard. Let his ass go! Jamal don't need him either. I'm sick of this!"

"How do you think I feel?" Imani started crying. "You would think that his mother would be on my side. As much as I have done for her, loaning her money, going with her to the doctor, anything she asked me to do I did. And when I called her to talk about what Walik was doing, she told me that she had nothing to do with our nonsense. That a man will be a man and that I should just either understand him or leave him alone. And then come to find out, Walik's mother has been babysitting and she and Shante are now hanging out."

"Imani," Monica said, "what did you think Walik's mother was? Your girlfriend? I told you about men and their families. His mother will like you and any other chick he brings to her house. Stop falling for the okeydoke! And get it together!"

"This is why I don't like telling you nothing," Imani sobbed. "Because you're always judging me."

"Oh shut the hell up! And be quiet. You're my sister and I love you but I don't like the shit you're doing. I don't care about Walik. I care about you and Jamal. Now, school is starting in a few weeks, do you have money for Jamal's clothes?"

"No."

"When do you get paid?"

"My check"—Imani sucked up snot in the bridge of her nose—"doesn't come until the first of next month. It's the fifteenth of August and we don't have no food either."

"Oh come on, Imani, what are you doing with your money? Damn, you work and get welfare."

"I don't work anymore. I quit my job."

"You did what?" Monica chuckled in disbelief. "I know yo' ass is lyin'."

"No I'm not," Imani snapped. "Humph, my supervisor got on my damn nerves, she was always telling me what to do."

"She . . . was . . . your . . . su-per-visor. What the hell do you mean, she was telling you what to do?"

"Well, I ain't like her attitude when she was telling me to do it. So I told her she could kiss my ass because I had had it with her and her fuckin' job."

"Oh no you didn't."

"Yes I did," Imani said. "And then I got my shit and told her to pick up her lip and go suck a big black dick!"

"And now since you've told your supervisor off, you've proved what?"

"Well, I was going to ask you to help me out and loan me some money until next month."

"How much money?"

"A thousand dollars."

"Oh hell no. I'll never see it again."

"Yes you will. I wouldn't do you like that."

"Whatever. After this I'm not loaning you any more money—"

"Monica." Sharief walked into the kitchen. "The girls said you made them some popcorn?"

"Excuse me, Imani. It's in the microwave, Sharief."

"Sharief!" Imani screeched. "What the hell is he doing there? Ain't his wife home tryin' to get her coochie knocked out?"

"How do you know that?"

"When I spoke to Celeste this morning she told me."

"*You* called *Celeste*?" Monica couldn't believe it.

"Yeah and? That's my sister."

"Oh, you must really need somebody to talk to."

"Whatever, and like I said, why is Sharief at your house instead of at home hittin' his wife off? He don't have nothing else to do but to be in your house talkin' about popcorn and shit? Is that niggah gay? I'ma tell Celeste she better watch him."

"Oh Imani please, he is not gay. But I can't make him go someplace he doesn't want to be."

"What, that sounds wack as hell."

"What you mean that sounds wack? I didn't tell him to come here!" she said defensively.

"Maybe not, but you need to encourage him to go home. Believe me, Celeste is waiting for him."

"I bet she is. Look, Imani, I have to go." Monica hung up and rubbed her aching stomach.

{ Celeste }

CELESTE SAT AT the dining room table and watched the trees blow outside the picture window. She was dressed in a black trench coat with a white fur-trimmed see-through negligee underneath. The negligee stopped midway on her thighs; underneath she wore a pair of white crotchless panties. She sucked on the tip of her cigarette and blew the smoke toward the ceiling.

She was beginning to sweat with the coat on. The ensemble was actually a surprise for Sharief. Something he'd been begging her to do for years. He'd told her that one of his fantasies (besides simultaneously fucking two women, which he'd fulfilled in high school) was to see her come to the door with a black trench coat on pulled tight around her waist with a see-through negligee underneath. He swore to her that she would feel beautiful, but she knew that was another one of his lies. Because instead of feeling beautiful at this moment, she felt stupid sitting in the house in ninety-degree weather wearing an oversized trench coat and a too-small negligee that squeezed her E-cup titties and made her thighs look as if cottage cheese had taken control.

She tooted up her lips as the saxophonist, whom she'd hired for a serenade, looked at her like she was ridiculous.

"Don't worry." She lit a cigarette. "I won't burn this ma'fucker up, at least not with you in it."

The saxophonist blinked. "Miss. I'm just wondering if he's coming."

"What the fuck do you think?" Celeste snapped, blowing smoke toward the ceiling. "Why are you asking anyway, you want some pussy? Here, take your money." She placed her cigarette in the ashtray and reached for her checkbook. She wrote him out a check for two hundred dollars and handed it to him. "Now get the fuck out!"

After the saxophonist left, Celeste paced from one end of her living room to the next, nervously shaking and peeking out the window like a paranoid crack addict. *I could kill him. I asked him this morning to please come home. "Sharief," I said, "I have something special for you—for us—please come home as soon as possible. The kids will be at my mother's."*

"Okay, Celeste," he nodded and said. "I have to get my stitches taken out, after that I need to run to the station and then I'll be back."

Celeste stopped pacing and walked back in her dining room. She looked at her table. The bowl of whipped cream now looked like sour milk, all of the frost had slid off the chilled bottle of wine and made a puddle underneath it, and the candles that once lit up the table were down to the last of their wicks.

"I'ma end this bullshit tonight! Tonight! I'ma find his ass. Fuck staying in the house crying, heart aching, pussy dry, titties need to be sucked. Fuck it! This time I'ma confront him in the bitch's face!"

Celeste slipped on her pink Old Navy flip-flops, wrapped her hair in a scarf, grabbed the keys to her Cherokee, and stormed out the door. She was determined not to cry; besides, she had no tears left. She didn't exactly know where she was going; all she knew was that whatever it was, whoever it was, that kept Sharief away from her was in Brooklyn. And if she had to search from one end of the borough to the next she was determined to find his ass and make him pay for all of her lonely days, horny nights, and never-ending heartache.

I'm here sucking my own goddamn titties, she thought, *and I'm married to a man with a big and functioning dick. Oh hell no. I've been in love with this man since I laid eyes on him. I was the one who cultivated him into being the marrying type. Now somebody else will reap the benefits? I cooked his food, washed his shitty-ass drawls. Stood by him when he fucked up and needed help. It was me and not this ragamuffin that he wants to run all over town with. I had his babies. I smelled his farts and heard him strain when he had to shit. Me. Celeste. I've seen slob slide out of his mouth when he was sleep and turn into crust before he wakes up. I've seen his pants up his ass, holes in his T-shirts, and I've seen him scratch his balls and then want some head. Me. Celeste. Not this two-bit tramp that he's galloping around Brooklyn with. Not her, but me!*

An hour's drive suddenly felt like five minutes as Celeste flew up the turnpike. She lit a cigarette and let down all the windows in her Cherokee. The back of the paisley Jackie O scarf that she wore wrapped around her head and tied under her chin floated in the air. Once she hit the Brooklyn Bridge, her phone rang. She peeped the caller ID. It was Kayla.

"Kayla," Celeste snapped, "what did I tell you about using that cell phone when you're in the house?"

"I know, but Daddy was on the Internet and Aunty Monica has dial-up."

Celeste slammed on the brakes, causing the cars behind her to scurry, screech, and suddenly halt. As the passing cars started blowing their horns and flipping Celeste the bird, she picked up speed. "What did you say, Kayla?"

"I said"—Kayla was probably rolling her eyes at the ceiling— "that Daddy's on the Internet and Aunty Monica only has dial-up. Did you hear me?"

Celeste couldn't believe it. "Monica?"

"Oh boy . . . ," Kayla whined. "Now you don't know who Monica is? She's your sis-ter." Kayla spoke slowly. "And your sis-ter is with your hus-band . . . and your chil-dren, Kayla, Kai, and Kori. Do you hear everybody laughing in the background?" Kayla held the phone in the air then put it back to her ear. "That's us. Do you know who we are now?"

As Celeste tried to respond, visions of Monica and Sharief started to flood her mind. "I'm on my way!"

• • •

CELESTE STEPPED ONTO Monica's porch feeling numb. All her thoughts about Monica and Sharief fucking around raced into her mind like jolts of lightning. As much as she tried to shake it, she couldn't stop envisioning Monica and Sharief having sex. Celeste pressed on the bell as hard as she could and tapped her foot. She needed something to calm her nerves, so she pulled out a ciga-rette, lit it, and took a drag, still tapping her foot steadily as she pressed the bell once more.

"Celeste!" Imani called from the front seat of Tasha's car. "Ce-leste."

Celeste looked back and saw Jamal walking onto Monica's porch. "Tell Monica that I'll pick Jamal up in the morning."

" 'Sup, Aunty?" Jamal grinned. Celeste didn't answer. Instead she resumed tapping her foot and ringing the bell again.

"Who is it?" Monica asked as she turned the locks. Once she opened the door, she and Celeste locked eyes and then they looked each other up and down. Instead of a sisterly look it was one that said, *This is what he wants?*

"What are you doing here?" Monica asked, wondering what the hell Celeste had on. Monica was so busy staring, she didn't re-alize Jamal was standing there. The wind blew Celeste's trench coach open and revealed her white negligee.

Celeste peered at Monica, who was dressed in a short baby-blue nightgown and leaned against the door with one leg stretched forward to reveal a tattoo of a butterfly. It was the same tattoo that Sharief had begged Celeste to get and located in the exact spot where he wanted it.

Instantly everything went black for Celeste. When she came back to her senses, she'd slapped Monica through the front door of her house. "What the fuck! You fucking my husband? You fucking my husband!"

Sharief ran from the back of the house, and the kids who were in the kitchen eating ice cream ran into the living room. Jamal stood in the doorway, shocked.

Sharief pushed Celeste off Monica. "What the hell are you doing?" Monica said, standing up. Once she was able to regain her balance, she quickly moved to Sharief's side and jabbed Celeste in the face. "What the fuck is wrong with you?"

Celeste lunged for Monica, but Sharief caught it instead. He didn't flinch; instead he took the punch. He turned toward Celeste and grabbed her by the arms. "What are you doing?"

"You're fucking my sister! I know you are!"

"Excuse me, y'all"—Jamal looked around—"but what kinda *Jerry Springer* shit is this?"

"Go upstairs!" Monica yelled at the children. "Go!"

"Don't tell my kids what to do!"

"I think you need to calm down," Monica said to Celeste as she rubbed the side of her face.

"For what? My sister is fucking my husband! How could you?" Celeste started to fall to her knees.

"I'm not fucking your husband!" Monica screamed. "You are crazy! Fuckin' crazy!"

"Celeste." Sharief shook his head and pulled her off the floor. "Why would you come out the house and charge over here like this? I told you I had to work."

"You told me that today was your day off."

"I also told you that I still needed to go in to the station and take care of something."

"I needed you to come home," Celeste sobbed. "I waited for you. I had everything planned: dinner, saxophonist, everything. I had everything! I wanted to fuck you! Don't you see this hot-ass trench coat? This was your fantasy, not mine. You're my husband!" she screamed at the top of her lungs. "You belong with me! I didn't marry you for this. And my sister? You would stoop so low as to fuck my sister?"

"Celeste, don't be crazy. I'm not fucking your sister, or anybody else for that matter. I just needed some time. I couldn't take the constant nagging and the accusations. I just couldn't, so I stayed away."

"I'm not nagging. I'm just trying to understand what's going on with my life."

"Understand that we've talked about this," Sharief snapped. "And understand that you're pushing me away."

"*I should understand*—and what about you? You are such a liar; if you had to work, what are you doing here?"

"Kayla called me."

"No she didn't! Monica called you here. She knew what I had planned and she wanted me to be by myself, because she wanted to be with you. Don't say my child called you because she didn't!"

"Yes, Mommy, I did," Kayla insisted, standing at the top of the stairs. "I really did. Aunty had nothing to do with it."

"I thought I told you to go upstairs!" Monica yelled.

"I am upstairs."

"But you don't need to be in this!"

"But I have to tell her the truth. Mommy, I called Daddy to come and get us because I don't always like staying with Nana-Starr and Pa-pa Red. I wish somebody would understand that he can't sing and he needs to give it up! I called my daddy and I asked him to pick us up. But Nana-Starr called Aunty Monica, because Pa-pa Red had a concert. How could you hit Aunty? She brought us food and movies, and popped us popcorn! My daddy was on the Internet!" Kayla started crying. "What you did wasn't nice, Mommy! We were having lots of fun!"

"Mommy's mean," Kai said to Kori.

"I told you," Kori said.

"Don't talk to your mother like that!" Sharief and Monica said simultaneously. Monica looked at Sharief as he continued to speak. "And your mother's not mean, so stop it! Get your things!" He looked at Celeste. "Go home."

"Not without you!"

"You've been without me for a long time."

"Sharief, please . . ."

"Celeste, what do you want me to do? We've already talked about this."

Celeste looked at Monica and tears rolled down her face. *I know that he's fucking her,* she thought. She wanted to run over to Monica and knock the shit out of her but for some reason her feet wouldn't move.

Monica felt like shit. She was embarrassed, ashamed, and confused. She didn't want to see her sister like this, but she didn't want Sharief to leave either. *Sister or no sister,* Monica thought, *I can't give him up.* "I don't know what to say to you, Celeste," she said. "Maybe I should just pray for you."

Celeste grabbed Sharief by the hand. "Don't let it end like this."

Sharief looked around and saw everyone looking at him. He felt like nothing. He felt as if he were missing and had been replaced by a coldhearted bastard. He wanted a drink—he needed a drink—he needed something to coat this feeling of being a user, a cheat, a no fuckin' good. Here he had a wife who loved him, and he couldn't stand to look at her. Something was wrong with this picture, and he needed a way to make it right. He turned around and looked at Monica. "I'm sorry you had to go through this but I need to go home and be with my family."

Instantly Monica's heart filled her mouth. "If that's what you want," she mumbled.

"Let's go," Sharief said to Celeste.

"Bye, Aunty," the kids said one at a time to Monica, kissing her on the cheek on their way out.

"Aunty," Kori said, standing at the door, "can I take the rest of the pizza home?"

"Nawl, Chief." Jamal snorted. "I'm 'bout to eat that."

"Yes, baby," Monica said, pushing her heart to the side. "Go and get it."

Kori ran back into the kitchen, grabbed the pizza box, and ran back out.

"Monica—" Sharief said, standing on the stoop as he turned around to face her. She stared him in the eyes and slammed the door in his face.

{ Imani }

"LOOK Y'ALL!" IMANI danced in her seat, pointing to the DJ booth. "See Kree?"

"Goddamn, do I?" Quiana said, checking Kree out from head to foot. "That's a pretty motherfucker."

"Hold up, bitch, don't get it twisted, that's me right there," Imani snapped.

"Oh ai'ight, Imani, you got that." Quiana smiled.

Imani blushed as she looked Kree up and down. He was dressed in all white in honor of the all-white Dons and Divas party they were at. Kree wore slightly baggy Versace dress pants with a cuff that fell over the top of his matching square-toed gators. His rayon pointed-collar shirt lay on the side of the DJ table, while his wife beater clung to his well-defined chest. The tattoos that ran down both of his muscular arms forced Imani to lick her lips. His long braids swayed back and forth over his shoulders as he held the earphones to one ear, listening for the precise beat to blend the next song into. He bounced his shoulders. "Awwl shit ladies," he said into the mike, "it's coming . . . it's coming . . . get ready . . . get set . . . 'cause here it is . . . the end-of-the-summer anthem . . .

and to all the men, don't be mad, just do better the next time!" Instantly Keyshia Cole's "(I Just Want It) To Be Over" bombarded the speakers and everybody in the club started dancing.

"This is my shit!" Sabrena screamed, dancing and sipping on her Cisco martini.

"Fa sho'," Tasha agreed. "This that same shit I was singing to Fuquan's ass last night." She did a spin, her dollar white Chinese slippers helping her to slide. "I told him, *Beat it, niggah . . . it's over!*"

"Y'all already know who I need to sing this shit to," Imani said, dancing and tossing her layered flip to the back and over her shoulders.

"Home girl," Sabrena said, "I cut the shit out this flip." Sabrena was proud of herself. She knew for a fact that she was the fliest bootleg in-house beautician around.

"You sure did, Brena," Imani said. Hell, and tonight, if no other night since Walik left, Imani knew she was fly. She wore a white linen halter dress with a deep V-cut in the back and the front. The cut in the front dipped all the way to her navel and the one in the back stopped at the top of her ass.

Kree watched as Imani did the damn thing, making his dick pulsate with each movement. All he could envision was bending her over and fucking her from the back.

Once the song finished playing and another song blended in, Imani took a deep breath and sat down. "Yo, this shit is fiyyah!"

"Oh hell no." Sabrena giggled as she, Tasha, and Quiana took their seats.

"What happened?" The girls looked around.

"See them niggahs right there?" Sabrena pointed. "I have fucked all four of 'em."

Imani, Quiana, and Tasha looked at her as if she was crazy.

"This is why I don't like to get high wit' yo' ass." Tasha rolled her eyes. " 'Cause you start fucking up my shit."

"Bitch, my buzz is steady, it's yo' shit that's questionable. I know exactly what I'm saying. See them two, they're brothers."

"What?" they all screeched.

"Hell, I ain't know they were brothers. They got different daddies or something." She paused. "Although their dicks do look alike. And see that older guy over there? That's their uncle. He got the biggest dick of 'em all. I ain't know he was related to them until I went to their family reunion and spotted the niggah. He was cool, though, he was there with his wife anyway. And see the one standing beside him, that's their baby cousin, I was his first."

"Ai'ight," Imani said, "that's enough. Look, y'all." She crossed her legs and sipped on her apple martini. "My sister told me that somebody told her that Shante had her baby."

"Oh, is that right?" Quiana said, pissed off. "I can't stand that bitch. My cousin did tell me she saw her over on Rogers and she didn't look pregnant anymore."

"You should call that ma'fuckin' Walik," Tasha said, rolling her eyes, "and cuss his ass out! Who the fuck does he think he is? Have you heard from him?"

"No." Imani looked down.

"Has he come to get Jamal?"

"No."

"Has he given you any money?"

"No."

"But he's having babies by this trick?"

"Yup." Tears started to form in Imani's eyes.

"Well, that niggah is owed a cussin'-out! Here," Quiana handed Imani her cell phone, "call that niggah."

"He doesn't answer numbers that he doesn't know and if I call from my phone he won't answer at all."

"Oh hell naw, I don't give a damn. You better take this phone and call that niggah!"

The music was so loud that the first time Imani dialed the

number and the phone rang she could barely hear it. "I'ma have to go outside and call him. I can't hear." She looked toward the DJ booth and mouthed to Kree, *I'll be right back.*

The girls walked outside, and Imani pressed redial. Walik's phone rang three times before his voice mail came on.

"Make sure you cuss his ass out!" Tasha yelled.

"Uhmm-hmm," Sabrena agreed.

"Walik," Imani began, "this is Imani." She turned her back toward her friends. "I'm real sorry about what happened between us. I miss you. Jamal cries every night and we need you in our lives. Whatever it is we can work through it." After that she hung up.

"I should punch you in the face!" Quiana snapped.

"Hell yeah," Sabrena and Tasha said simultaneously. "I can't believe that you just played yourself for that pussy-ass-soft-ass niggah . . ." Sabrena rolled her eyes. "Why you always gotta be the stupid one?"

Before Imani could respond, Quiana's phone rang. Imani looked at the caller ID and saw that it was Walik calling back. "This is him now. Hello?" Imani anxiously answered the phone.

"Yo." After hearing the voice Imani realized that it was Shante who'd called her back. "Look darlin', Walik is eating my pussy, so that makes him busy. And he don't give a damn how sorry you is. And as far as that li'l fat-ass kid you got, Walik will be getting a paternity test. The only kids he can be sure of are the two he got by me. So like I told you before, play your fuckin' position!" She hung up.

"I gotta—I gotta—go kick ha ass!" Imani shuddered.

"Who was that?" Sabrena put on the screw face.

"Shante."

"What the fuck she say?"

"She said that Walik was eating her pussy . . . and she called my baby a fat-ass li'l boy!"

"He is a li'l chubby, Imani," Sabrena said, "so don't worry about that. But what else the bitch say?"

Imani rolled her eyes. "Bitch don't talk about my baby! Anyway she must've stolen Walik's phone because he don't play with nobody checking his messages and he especially don't play with nobody talking about his son. Wait till I tell him, I know he gon' gank that bitch!" A sly smile ran across Imani's face. "Y'all, I don't have time to argue no more. I gotta fuck her up."

"Oh I understand," Tasha snapped, "I understand quite well, 'cause I'ma be the one to put that ugly bitch in a choke hold. Best believe dat."

"Plus," Imani chuckled, "that bitch looks mad stupid because I know for a fact that Walik don't even eat pussy."

"Yo." Sabrena frowned. "Let me inform you, home girl. I have heard many chicks swear up and down that their man don't eat pussy but when I fuck his ass, he can't keep his tongue off my clit. Don't ever fall for no shit like that."

"Whatever." Imani brushed Sabrena off. "Let me finish, the bitch had the nerve to say that Walik would be getting a paternity test for Jamal—"

"Oh no, the bitch didn't!" Tasha snapped.

"And she told me to play my position because he had two kids with her."

"I knew that other li'l kid was his. I knew it, that ma'fucker looks too much like an alien not be a mix of Walik and Shante!" Sabrena screamed. "Oh we going over there. That bitch is doin' too much talkin' and we need to put up the hands now!"

"Oh, now y'all feel me?" Imani said.

"Damn real," Quiana agreed. "Let's be out."

The girls—all dressed in different variations of white linen dresses—removed their earrings. All of them but Tasha, who wore her Chinese slippers, agreed to take off their stilettos if need be.

"You better slap her ass as soon as she opens the door," Sabrena snapped. "My cousin lives in the building so he'll buzz us in and then we'll proceed right to her apartment."

Imani was quiet on their ride to Shante's. She was determined to bust Shante's ass immediately. Enough of the mouth. It was time for Shante's ass to be dragged . . . again.

The girls parked in front of the building and each got out the car. Sabrena pressed her cousin's buzzer. "G-G," she said, "it's Brena." A few seconds later he buzzed them in. They caught the elevator to Shante's apartment, and once they were in front of the door, they made Imani stand behind them in case Shante looked out the peephole. Then when Imani snuck up from behind, Shante wouldn't know which direction the whup-ass was coming from.

"Yo," Sabrena said as she pounded on the door, "this that 5-0 knock, make a niggah jump out their sleep."

"Imani," Quiana said, "you better pull that bitch's eye socket out!"

"And if you don't," Sabrena chimed in, "I got a knotted shoe-string in my purse. I'll put it around that chicken's neck and cut that ho's air supply off. Have her ass lookin' like SpongeBob!"

"Shhh, y'all, here she comes," Tasha whispered. The girls stood still as they heard the heavy footsteps approaching the door.

The door flew open and to their surprise, there was Walik, with no shirt on and his boxers twisted to the side. "What the fuck y'all fat asses want?" He looked them up and down. "What, y'all came to do somethin'?"

"Oh hold up, niggah," Sabrena spat, " 'cause I'll beat yo' ma'-fucker ass, ain't nut'in'!"

"Wait a minute, Sabrena," Imani said as she stepped to the front. The first thing she noticed was how Walik's boxers were twisted. *This niggah been fuckin'.* Immediately a chill came over her.

"Didn't my girl tell you that I was eating her pussy?" Walik said nonchalantly, looking at Imani. "Now, what the fuck is you at my door for?"

Caught off guard, all Imani could say was, "You talkin' to me?"

"Oh we 'bout to throw!" The girls grunted and groaned; Sabrena took off her shoes.

"Wait—wait," Imani said. "Just let me talk to him. Walik," she repeated, "are you talking to me? Did Shante tell you to say these things to me?"

"Shante?" Walik frowned. "Do you understand the words that are coming out of *my* mouth?"

"So you really are talking to me?"

"Who the fuck else am I talkin' to, ma? Yo, check this, you must be stupid! With your dumb-ass friends, all in my grill. What you bring 'em around here for? So they could hear the truth? Listen, I told you that I don't want yo' ass, so stop sweating me. Take ya lazy ass and go get a job! I hope you can work better than you can suck a dick, you dry-mouth bitch! I swear to God yo' tired ass is just a used-up jump-off! On the real you like a stray dog around here, any niggah that feed you can keep you."

"Walik—"

"Don't *Walik* me, ma. See a niggah can't be nice to you. Naw, I gotta get gully. Now I'ma tell you this only once, don't come back around here, ya bum bitch! 'Cause I ain't got nothin' for ya Work First ass. Go get a job or go get a pimp. But then again a pimp can't do nothin' for you, ya head game is ridiculous. Rotten-ass-fishy-ass-infected-ass-pus-leaking pussy. And to think you use to beg a niggah to eat that shit. Fuck off, tramp! Ya bum bitch! All I can do for you is come around from the first to fifth, take ya money, and give it to my wife. Other than that . . . what's the use?"

"I'ma beat yo' ass!" Sabrena took a swing at Walik.

"Sabrena!" Imani yelled. "Stop it! Fuck him. Fuck you, Walik!"

"Fuck me?" Walik chuckled in disbelief. "What's left to do with you other than run a train on you? The only thing yo' stank ass can do for me is play like Imodium AD and drink the shit from my asshole. You knew your place was on your knees, now you tryin' to stand up? Stop playin' ya'self!"

"You got two kids with her, Walik?" Imani cried.

"Yeah, bitch, he sho' do," Shante snapped, stomping to the door. Once she was standing next to Walik she placed her hand on her hip, twisted her lips, and placed her neck in full motion. "And what? And he married me when he was locked up—"

"You married her?" Imani was in disbelief. "I can't believe this!"

"Believe it," Shante said. "Ya played ya'self. Dumb ass! I told you I ain't goin' nowhere!" Shante's eyes looked as if they could pop out of her head. Imani peered at her. She looked shorter and stockier than Imani remembered, but still and all she wouldn't hesitate to beat Shante's high-yellow ass. Imani took a swing at her and Walik blocked her fist out of Shante's way. "What I tell you about disrespecting my babies' mother?"

"Babies' mother?" Imani couldn't believe it. "She wasn't your babies' mother when you followed my ass in the club. She wasn't your babies' mother when you were lying in my bed fucking me! Babies' mother?"

"Bitch, beat it," Shante yarned, "can't you see he's tired of you?"

"What the fuck you think yo' light-bright ass is, special?" Imani frowned at Shante. "All his ass gon' do is come runnin' back to me when the clearance sale on irregular pussy is over."

"Irregular pussy?"

"Irregular pussy, damaged goods. That's what the hell I said and I ain't stutter! Now come wit' it."

"I'm the wife, trick."

"The wife? Bitch, please, you was just an address for the parole board. 'Cause if you were all that, he would've stayed with you when he first got outta prison and you would've been at his mother's for his get-free party."

"Whatever," Shante blew Imani off. "Wasn't no party, so stop lyin'. Dumb ass!"

"No, sweetie, you're the dumb one. At least I don't have fifty-five kids by his ass."

"Whatever. I ain't on welfare."

"I guess not, since I reported yo' ass for fraud."

"You reported me?"

"Anyway." Imani turned her attention back toward Walik. "I can't believe that you really have two kids by this trick and you married her? I've been with you since I was thirteen and you married her?"

"Maybe I did, maybe I didn't, don't even worry about that. And as far as my kids, yes, I got two with Shante. Now skip yo' ass outta here and go find yo' punk-ass li'l DJ."

"Oh, so that's what this is about? You mad over a niggah I ain't even fuckin' wit'? And here you having babies by this bitch! You really got two kids with her ass?"

"Did I stutter? Yes . . . two kids. Shante's last two kids is mine. So go away. I have a family, ya fuckin' retard!" Before she could open her mouth, he slammed the door in her face.

"Why the hell did you stop me from busting his ass!" Sabrena turned on Imani and pushed her on the shoulder. "Now I wanna bust yo' ass! Why the fuck you let him talk all that shit to you and you ain't say or do nothing? I could've kept my earrings on for this bullshit! I should beat yo' ass!"

Imani did her best to hold the tears back. She felt like the epitome of stupid. She felt as if all the air in her body had been stolen and all she had left was a hollow shell filled with the echo of Walik's harsh words: *Get ya lazy ass a job, ya bum bitch!*

Truthfully it never mattered to Imani before about being on welfare and only having a job when she needed some extra money for clothes and shoes. Hell, who really wants to work anyway? Especially if you can stay at home, get money, put ya feet up, and get fucked, then what's the use of wasting your time having a job?

But now it felt different. To hear ya man call you lazy and to tell you to *get a job!* and your position was *on ya knees anyway,* and to say it not only in front of your friends but in front of the girl he'd left you for, felt as if you'd welcomed death and kissed its feet.

"I promise you if you take that niggah back that I won't say shit else to you!" Sabrena spat as they got into the car.

Imani didn't respond. Besides, taking him back wasn't the issue. She would take him back in a heartbeat . . . but it was his words that couldn't be taken back. And the embarrassment; that was the issue. He'd taken her heart, opened it up, and pissed inside.

She never felt the car move as Tasha drove to her and Sabrena's building and dropped them off. Imani and Sabrena caught the elevator and quietly went their separate ways.

Imani walked into her apartment and flopped on the couch. She took her hands and covered her mouth as she screamed . . . and screamed . . . and screamed.

Half an hour into screaming she wiped her face. As she went to go to the bathroom her phone rang.

"Hello," she sniffed, trying her best not to sound upset.

"Wassup, ma, I thought you were coming back? That's fucked. You just jetted on me."

"I'm sorry, Kree. I really am. I wasn't thinking. It's just that things got crazy and we left in a hurry. It's a long story."

"Yo, where ya li'l man at?"

"My sister's." *Damn, that bitch gon' cuss me the fuck out,* Imani thought, remembering the drive-by drop-off she did with Jamal.

"Ai'ight," Kree said. "Well, look, Papi got you some chocolate cheesecake and some Cristal. Let me come check you."

"Ai'ight." Imani sighed.

Ten minutes later Kree was knocking on her door. As Imani opened the door, she could smell the sweet aroma of Kree's Eternity for Men cologne. Although he smelled good, she never expected him to look so sweet—his long braids hanging on his shoulders. At first glance you would think he was a black man, but something about the look in his eyes or the mixture in his skin let everyone know that he was Latin. He stepped into her living room, still dressed from the night's festivities, but his shirt was now thrown over his right shoulder, supported by the tip of his index finger. "Goddamn, you look good as hell." Kree kissed Imani on the forehead as he glided into the apartment, one hand holding his shirt and the other hand holding the bag with the cheesecake, Cristal, two plastic forks, and two plastic champagne glasses. "You look sweet as hell, too, ma."

Imani looked down. "Thank you."

"Don't be looking down when I give you a compliment. I want you to look me in the eyes and be like, *That's right, ma'fucker, and don't get it confused.*"

"I'm spose to be that bitch, huh?" Imani chuckled slightly.

"Damn real." He handed Imani the bag, and she placed it on the floor. "You got a cute li'l spot," Kree said, looking around.

"It's ai'ight," Imani said, unsure.

Kree looked at Imani. "Wassup, ma, why you sounding all down?"

"I'm not down." She sat down on the couch and took the cheesecake and forks out of the bag.

"Yes you are." Kree sat down beside her. "The other day you were Ms. Confidence, looking at me like, *Yeah, niggah, what?* But today you look like somebody stole ya bike and shit. Wassup?"

Imani sucked her teeth. "It's nothing."

"Talk to me." Kree turned her face toward him. "I'm a good listener."

"The night that you brought me home after my mother's wedding, Walik and I had a fight . . ." Imani told Kree everything, from Shante being pregnant on the prison bus to Walik cussing her out like a dog. She spared no details and Kree didn't make a sound; all he did was listen. "Sometimes I wonder if it's the dick," Imani said, eating her third slice of cheesecake.

"The dick? Whose dick?" Kree asked, taken aback. "His dick?"

"Yeah. It's like, he was my first, unless you count that other shit, but I was twelve and that was nothing. But I haven't been with anybody but him. I mean, you should've heard him. *Get a job, you lazy bitch!*"

"You don't work?" Kree asked, surprised.

"No, I don't work. The last job I had I quit. I don't do shit."

"Take that down, ma. Don't beat up on yourself. You don't have to front for me, I'm cool. I'm saying, though, you have a son, and you're young. You need to think about what you wanna do and do it. Don't ever let no niggah play you like that. And on top of that the chick was talking shit to you? Don't sweat it, ma, all he gon' do is cuss her ass out later."

"Yeah right."

"He will, but you wanna know what I'm trippin' off of?"

"What?"

"That you tellin' me about his dick being good. Fuck that Russian-roulette dick. All you can get from that niggah is infected. Trust me, he don't give a shit about you. You got a baby by him and that's how he treats you? Oh hell no. Ain't no way the sex was that great."

"It was good. He wasn't no freak or nothing."

"What you mean, he wasn't no freak?"

"All he wanted to do was fuck, no foreplay, he ain't wanna go down or nothing."

"He ain't wanna go down? They still make ma'fuckers like that? Come on now, I know you was six o'clockin' his ass."

Imani laughed. "I am sooo not answering that."

"Look, ma." Kree smiled. "I didn't exactly expect you to answer that. It was a statement. Not a question."

"Oh. Anyway, I don't wanna talk about that anymore."

"Well, what you wanna talk about?" Kree smiled.

"What's up with the DJing. You got any of your hot-ass CDs that are flying off the streets?"

"How you know about that?" he asked.

"I have my ways."

"I bet you do. Well, I got a demo that this CD company wants to buy."

"For real?"

"Yeah, one of those companies that sells the deluxe slow jams on TV. The commercials come on late at night. They offered me a contract to create CDs for them."

"Well, where's the CD? Let me hear it."

"Ai'ight, let me run downstairs and get it."

·   •   ·

KREE WENT DOWNSTAIRS and came back. He noticed that Imani had lit some candles. "Wassup with the candles?" he asked, cutting the CD player on.

"Ambience," she assured him, "nothing else."

"It's your show, baby. It's all yours." Kree popped the CD in and instantly Joe's "All the Things Your Man Won't Do" came on.

"This used to be my song." Imani smiled, singing along.

"Yo, I'm supposed to be singing this song, not you."

"Oh, is that so?"

"Uhmm-hmm." Kree sat next to Imani, held her chin in his hand, and started singing to her.

"You're embarrassing me."

"Why?" Kree said, moving his face closer to Imani.

"I don't know if I'm ready . . ."

"For what?"

"To be with somebody else right now."

"I didn't ask you for all of that." Kree kissed Imani on the eyelids. She could feel her clit jump. "Kree," she whined, "maybe we shouldn't . . ."

"Shhh, let me show you something." He stood up and sat on the floor. Gently he pulled Imani's hand. "Come here." Imani sat on the floor next to him, and he started to kiss her soft and slow. He took his tongue and licked the outline of her lips. Then he sucked her lip in and out of his mouth. As he slipped his hand underneath her dress, he soon discovered what he thought were silk panties was actually the wetness of her pussy.

Kree laid Imani down and kissed her from the top of her head to the tip of her clit.

"Kree . . . ," she moaned.

"Be quiet," he insisted.

He opened Imani's legs and began to suck on her inner thighs, going from one to the other. Her eyes rolled to the top of her head; she didn't know whether to be nervous or act like an expert. He slid his tongue into her slit and graced her clit with its warm wetness, sucking it slowly and slurping the flowing juices as if it were melting ice cream. Her juices glazed his lips as he ran his tongue from one end of her pussy to the next. Imani placed her hands on top of his head.

"This is what ya man is supposed to do," he said, softly biting her pussy lips.

Imani had never imagined that having someone go down on you felt like this. She knew that her friends had always bragged about it. And Sabrena had even told a story about getting the bomb head and passing out, but never in a million years did Imani imagine that it felt like this. This was ecstasy. This is what made you dream . . . dream about being a down chick for life. This is what carried your mind to a place you never knew existed.

Kree licked and sucked until he felt Imani's body start to tense. He knew she was cumin'. And he wanted her to. He needed her to . . . to cum . . . so that he could show her sometimes making love was about getting pleased and not always having to be the one to do it.

The music continued to play as Imani came long and hard, screaming Kree's name. She started to get fidgety after she came, wanting him to stop kissing her pussy and instead take his dick out and put it in, but he continued to eat her out and even more aggressively than before. Forcing her, two seconds later, to cum again.

"Kree," she moaned.

"Yes, baby."

"I want some dick."

"You can't handle this."

"Yeah, please. I want it."

As Kree undressed Imani he used the soft glow from the candles as his light. Once they were both undressed, he sucked her breasts and then slipped his ten-inch dick inside. He took both of her legs and threw them over his right shoulder. Imani felt as if she'd been blindsided. She never expected his dick to feel like this. For once she felt as if she were being made love to and not fucked.

Kree moved with expertise, as if he were a pianist, stroking each key with precision. As Imani's pelvic muscles started to contract, Kree flipped her over. "Imani," he said, breathing heavy.

"Yes."

"Don't ever—"

"Don't ever what?"

"Talk about another niggah's dick to me." He turned her to the side, spreading her legs like scissors. "Understand?"

"Kree," she whined.

He flipped back over; now she lay on her back. "Understand?"

"Yes." She moaned, "Kree . . ."

"Yes, baby."

"I'm cumin'."

"That's what you spose to do. Now cum on."

[Starr]

"STARR!" ROXANNE CRIED, "Starr!"

"Come on big girl and do that rodeo show for daddy," Red said, as he entered their bedroom, interrupting Starr's conversation.

"Hush," Starr said, giving him the evil eye, "Roxanne on the phone crying. Now Roxanne," she turned her attention back to the phone, "What's wrong?"

"Jimmy—"

"What about Jimmy?! Where are you?"

"At the hospital."

"She at the hospital," Starr mumbled to Red. "Why are you at the hospital? What happened?"

"I was—I was—oh I'm embarrassed to say—"

"Just say it," Starr said as calmly as possible.

"Well you know my arms is little . . . and I feel like I gotta be a freak to make up for my elbows being next to my ears . . ." Roxanne let out a long sigh. Starr could hear her shuddering tears.

"Roxy, please tell me what's wrong?"

"Well . . ." Roxanne sniffed, "Jimmy was giving me a golden shower and he tumbled on top of me—"

"A golden who?" Starr asked in disbelief.

"A golden shower."

"Jimmy was giving Roxanne a golden shower," Starr whispered to Red.

"Oh my lawd Jesus!" Red sucked his teeth, "I knew anybody with they hands that close to their mouth was a freak! Get off the phone with that backwards heifer. Tell her don't be callin' over here startin' no shit. Next thing I know you'll be tryna get me to eat grits out ya ass! Hang up on her right now, Starrla!"

Turning her attention back to Roxanne, Starr could hear her moaning in the background. "Roxanne," Starr said shaking her finger at Red, "How's Jimmy doing now?"

"Oh, Starr . . . he's dead!" Roxanne screamed, "He's dead! He had a heart attack and died."

Starr was in shock as she held the phone in her hand. Not knowing what was wrong, Red became concerned. "Look, Starr,"— Red cleared his throat—"what Jimmy and Roxanne do is one thing, but I just can't bring myself to piss on you. Why don't we try swingin' instead?"

"Hush, Red," Starr said wiping the tears streaming from her eyes and hearing Roxanne continue to scream on the phone. "It's Jimmy."

"What about Jimmy?"

"Sit down, Red."

"I don't wanna sit down, just tell me."

Starr swallowed hard. "Jimmy passed, Red. Roxanne said he had a heart attack and died."

Red started to cry as he flopped down on the bed next to Starr, who was trying her best to calm Roxanne down. "Roxanne," she said, "hang up the phone, baby. We're on our way to the hospital . . . Let's go, Red." Starr wiped her tears. "I need you to be strong, we still have to tell Mama Byrd."

• • •

"MAMA BYRD," STARR said, as she and Red walked into the living room. Starr was practically holding Red up straight. "I have something to tell you."

"Can a old ho shit in peace, please," Mama Bryd said, holding the metal rails on her porta-potty.

"Mama Byrd," Starr continued, "I don't know if you'll understand this, but I need to tell you something."

"What is it, baby?" Mama Byrd said seriously, "You can tell me anything."

"All right, this is hard for me to believe and even harder to say. But Jimmy—Jimmy—he died."

"Jimmy? My knee-baby-boy Jimmy?"

"Yes."

"Oh hell to the nawl!" Mama Byrd crouched to her knees.

"It's all right, Mama Bryd," Starr assured her.

"It ain't all right, 'cause now I got to worry 'bout the pastor's wife tellin' Jimmy that Deacon Jones was really his daddy."

* • *

AT JIMMY'S FUNERAL Starr tried to comfort Red as best she could. Roxanne couldn't speak. At most, all she could do was rock back and forth, whispering Jimmy's name, over and over again.

"Excuse me." Mama Byrd tapped Roxanne on the shoulder. "Yo' sleeves too long."

"Hush up!" Starr said to Mama Byrd. "Hush!"

Starr wiped the tears from her eyes as she walked around for one last look at Jimmy's casket. She stooped and kissed him on the forehead. *I'ma miss you, Jimmy,* she thought, rubbing his cold hands, *I'ma miss you.* As Starr walked to the back of the church she couldn't stop thinking about the way her girls had spoken to her on her wedding day. Hell, she couldn't help it if things didn't work out with their fathers. After all, Starr was never one for letting children dictate whom she should and shouldn't be with. Her philosophy was, *One day their asses will be grown, and then I'll be stuck with some niggah I don't like.*

As soon as Starr got home, she started cooking for the repast and then called her daughters on the phone. "You ain't got to like Red, but you will respect him. Now his baby brother Jimmy died and I expect you to be here. I don't wanna hear nothin' about no get-free parties, about how far you live, or any other nonsense, and since y'all selfish asses didn't show for the funeral, I expect you to be here."

"All I wanna know," Mama Byrd said, spitting snuff into her spit cup, "is who was that niggah in the casket? It wasn't Red, was it? Now, Jimmy, if he got to go, he got to go. But Red, that niggah owe me some money."

"Mama Byrd," Buttah said, fanning her hand, "my man died, my kids' daddy. Jimmy . . ." Buttah started crying. "Jimmy! Jimmy! Oh, Jimmy!"

"Shut the fuck up!" Mama Byrd frowned. "Goddamn, them wasn't his kids no way."

"That ain't true!" Buttah screamed. "De-niece and De-nephew are his kids! Jimmy loved me!"

"Who the fuck is De-niece and De-nephew?"

"Mama Byrd, be quiet." Starr rolled her eyes. She hated that Mama Byrd didn't know any better because then she couldn't tell her off like she wanted to. "I don't know what I'ma do about my Red," Starr said, sliding the corn bread into the oven. "Red is torn up. I thought he was gon' fall in the casket. He and Roxanne both. Jimmy was their backbone, not to mention the Jam on Its will never be the same."

"I guess they'll just be Jam now." Mama Byrd frowned. "Can a bitch get a beer around here?"

"Mama Byrd, Jimmy was your son!" Starr said, upset.

"I knew he looked familiar. Was that my knee-baby Jimmy?"

"Yes."

Tears filled Mama Byrd's eyes. "You mean my knee-baby-boy Jimmy Jack Daniels Brown?"

"Yes."

"Oh Lord!" Mama Byrd shot up from her seat. "Jack Daniels!

Jack Daniels! Oh why they had to go and take Jack Daniels, that was my knee-baby!"

Roxanne walked slowly into the kitchen as if she were numb. She was wearing a long black dress, with a long veil hanging from a large garden hat that tied in a bow under her chin. She looked like a mourning southern belle. Cutting her eyes at Buttah, she fell to her knees. "My man . . . My man is gone! Oh Jimmy! Oh Jimmy. Oh Lawd! I can't lose you and Luther at the same time. I can't do it!"

"Luther?" Mama Byrd said, wiping her eyes, "Luther died too? Oh no!" she screamed. "Oh hell no! This house will never be a home! Oh this is too much! Luther!" Mama Byrd screamed. "Luther!"

"Jimmy!" Roxanne screamed simultaneously. "Oh, Jimmy!"

"Oh Jesus!" Starr screamed. "Please, my nerves are bad!" First she helped Mama Byrd off the floor, and then she helped Roxanne up. She handed Roxanne a cold compress. "Take that hat off and go lie down, baby . . . It's all right." She turned to Mama Byrd, who was still sniffling and calling Luther's name. "Mama Byrd, Luther and Jimmy both in a better place."

"I need," Mama Byrd sniffed, "my porta-potty."

"I'll get it!" Buttah said. "I can't clean up no mo' shit. Please."

"Why you got to call me out?" Mama Byrd sucked her teeth. "It ain't a secret that my bowels is loose."

"Ma, do you have any Extra Strength Tylenol?" Monica said, walking into the kitchen. "My back is killing me." She sat down at the kitchen table, and the smell of the squash, corn, and tomato pudding that sat on the table started to make her feel even worse. *This is not going to work.*

"I'm glad you're here. Are you feeling okay?" Starr asked Monica. She handed her a glass of water and two Tylenols. Afterward she pressed the back of her hand against Monica's forehead. "You feel a little warm, baby."

"Hey, Ma," Celeste and Imani said, walking into the kitchen. They walked over to Starr and gave her a kiss on the cheek.

Afterward Imani kissed Monica on the cheek. "You know you're my favorite sister in the whole world."

"Get outta here, heifer!" Monica chuckled. "You make me sick. I'ma kill you about the drive-by you did with my nephew the other day."

"I thought you told me he could come over."

"Stop lying."

"My sister loves me so much," Imani teased, pinching Monica's cheeks.

"Where's Jamal?" Monica said playfully, slapping Imani's hands down.

"In the living room with the twins."

"Celeste," Starr said, "has my wedding tape come to your house yet?"

"No, Ma," Celeste said, "not yet." As Celeste turned around she frowned at Monica. "Hi," she said drily.

Monica didn't respond. As far as she was concerned Celeste had already won, and she didn't need the shit thrown in her face anymore. "Can I have some more water, Ma?" Monica asked.

Starr poured Monica a glass of water and handed it to her. "Have you gone to the doctor?"

"I'll be okay. I'm a nurse, remember, all I feel is miserable." For a brief moment Monica thought of her fibroids.

"Humph." Celeste snickered. "Funny how the tables turn."

"Don't start." Monica got up from her chair and walked over to the kitchen sink. As she turned around to sit back down, everyone's eyes darted directly to her protruding stomach.

"Monica, are you pregnant?" Imani blurted out.

Monica sucked her teeth. "You know I can't have children."

"The doctor never said that," Starr said, taking a fork and tasting some of her collards out of the pot. "I was there. All he said was with one fallopian tube it would decrease your chances of having children. He never said you couldn't get pregnant."

"Ma, please I don't have time for that," Monica said.

"Celeste," Starr said, "where's Sharief?"

"Why?" Celeste snapped. "What, are going to ask *him* if she's pregnant?"

"Oh here we the fuck go!" Monica snarled. "Give it a rest."

"Wait a damn minute!" Starr screamed. "What is going on here? All I want is for Sharief to carry some of this food into the dining room!"

"You should feel good and stupid." Imani rolled her eyes at Celeste. "I'll get him, Ma."

"I'm getting a little sick of you two," Starr said. "First my wedding day and now today! I'm not gon' have it."

"Ma," Celeste said, lighting a cigarette, "this has nothing to do with your wedding day."

"Well, what the hell is going on? Are you two still upset about me not being with your daddies?"

Imani walked back into the kitchen. "Sharief's coming, Ma. He was using his cell phone."

"Who was he talking to?" Celeste asked Imani.

"How the hell am I supposed to know," Imani said. "I don't keep tabs on your man."

"Remember that," Celeste snapped, "when you're looking for Walik's sorry ass!"

"This is not about Walik."

"I can't tell. Walik was sorry from the jump," Celeste said.

"And so was yo' daddy."

"All right now," Starr warned.

"What's all the screaming about?" Sharief asked as he walked into the kitchen. "How come it's always a war zone when y'all get together?"

"Don't worry about it." Starr pointed to the food. "Just get that food over there."

As Sharief reached for the first pot, he made eye contact with Monica. He could tell she was upset. He wanted to comfort her and ask her what was wrong, but decided that he would just leave it alone.

Monica couldn't stand looking at Sharief. She felt as if she wanted to cry; the man she loved was untouchable. "I can't breathe in here." Monica walked toward the kitchen's doorway. "I need to get some air."

Sharief watched Monica leave and immediately noticed her stomach. Almost instantly he tried to remember the last time she had her period.

Celeste watched Sharief intensely as Monica walked past him. Sharief knew Celeste was watching him. "How's Red, Starr?" he said, frowning at Celeste.

"As well as to be expected," Starr said.

"Ma, you think Monica is really pregnant?" Celeste said, giving Sharief the evil eye.

"I don't know, chile." Starr took the end of her apron and pulled her sweet-potato pies out of the oven. "I had a dream about fish, so somebody is pregnant." She peeked at Imani.

"It ain't me," Imani said. "Humph, 'cause if it was, nobody would know about it but me and the doctor."

Starr rolled her eyes. "You just say any damn thing! Imani, grab that corn bread, Celeste, get them greens, and Sharief, take that pot and then come back and get the rest of this food, please."

As Celeste sat the greens on the dining room table, she looked around for Sharief. "Where's your father?" she asked Kai, who was playing with Kori and Jamal.

"I don't know. I think he's outside." Celeste walked into the living room and pulled the curtain back. She saw Sharief on the porch talking to Monica. She snatched the door open.

"Celeste!" Starr called. "Come here, come here."

Celeste looked at Monica and Sharief. "Celeste!" Starr called again. "Everybody come here and see my babies! They said they

got a little play for Nana-Starr and Pa-pa Red . . . Come on, Red."
Starr squeezed him around his shoulders. "This'll make you feel
better."

Monica and Sharief came into the house and stood on opposite
sides of the room.

"Come on, babies," Starr said to Kai, Kori, and Jamal, "make
Pa-pa Red feel better."

"Do that shit, Jamal!" Mama Byrd yelled. "West Side, show
'em how we do!"

Jamal winked at Mama Byrd then gave everybody else thumbs-
up. "Okay, Mama Byrd." He smiled. "We got something for you."

"Y'all gon' do that Eddie Murphy fartin'-my-ass-off impres-
sion?" Mama Byrd asked. "If you need to you can borrow my
porta-potty."

"It's okay, Mama Byrd." Jamal smiled. "We got one even better."

Jamal, Kai, and Kori all huddled together and whispered out
their act to one another.

"Y'all got it?" Jamal asked, breaking up the huddle.

"We got it!" The twins cheered.

"All right then," he said. "All for one and one for all."

Jamal walked to the back of the living room, where everyone
stood wondering what they were going to do. Kai stuck a crayon
between her lips and let it hang from the corner of her mouth. She
tapped her foot and pretended to be ringing the doorbell. "Ding
dong," she said. Nobody answered. "I said *ding-to the-dong*!"

Kori hiked her skirt up to show off her thighs. "Who is it?" she
said as she pretended to open the door. Immediately Kai pretended to punch her in the face, and she fell down.

Getting back up, Kori said dramatically, "Oh my Lord! What
the fuck is you doin'!"

"My husband," Kai sobbed. "You fuckin' my husband!" She
placed her hands over her eyes like a sun visor. "Oh Lord! Oh
Lord. Jesus. Help me!"

Jamal walked over toward the girls as if he were a cowboy. "Now, what's going on here?"

"My husband!" Kai clutched her chest. "I can't believe y'all doing this to me!"

"Listen, tricks." Jamal cleared his throat. "Ain't no need to argue, it's enough of big daddy to go around. Who wanna ride big daddy's train?"

What kinda shit is this? Starr thought. *This is not what I had in mind.*

"You fat ho!" Kori yelled at Kai. "He don't want you. You look like a greasy-ass monkey-dog with your mean and nasty self! I'ma punch you in the face the next time you say I have to go to bed at eight o'clock, to clean up my room, or to eat all my vegetables."

"Kai, Kori, and Jamal!" Starr yelled. "What the hell is going on?" She turned toward their parents. "What the hell kinda shit y'all teaching my grandbabies?"

"Jamal," Imani said, "I told you about cussin'."

"They off the hook," Kayla said. "That's not right y'all making fun of the fight Mommy and Aunty Monica had over Daddy!"

"Fight?" Starr screeched. "What fight?"

"Y'all is some disorganized niggahs," Mama Byrd said.

"It's *dysfunctional,*" Kayla snapped at Mama Byrd.

"Oh hold it, home slice, you gettin' fly? Better ask about me."

"Y'all had a fight?" Starr asked, still stunned. "Answer me!"

"I'm not answering shit!" Monica yelled. "I'm tired of this." She grabbed her purse and stormed out.

Celeste looked at Sharief. "I'm ready to go."

"Get the kids," he said, " 'cause I've been ready to leave since I got here."

"Well, I don't care what they say," Mama Byrd said. "That li'l skit was the shit. Call 'em tricks again, Jamal."

"GO 'HEAD, CELESTE. Celeste, please go ahead," Sharief begged while sifting through the mail and walking from the living room into the kitchen. "Here, here's the tape of your mother's wedding. It came in the mail today." He threw it at her. "Go sit the fuck down and watch it!"

"What the hell you want me to watch the tape for? So I can replay how you walked down the aisle with my sister while I walked by myself?"

"Goddamn!" Sharief said as he turned, Celeste right on his heels. Celeste took the palm of her hand and mushed Sharief in the face. He grabbed her by the wrist and squeezed the bones on the side. "You want me to break your fuckin' hand off? Please just go sit down." He walked out of the kitchen and into the bathroom. He knew that if Celeste continued to follow him around and try to hit him, he would knock the shit out of her.

Celeste was angry, and she became even more enraged every time he walked away and refused to answer her. It had been more than an hour that she'd been following him from room to room, mushing him in the head, punching him in his back, and tortur-

ing him with words. "I already know you fucked her!" Sharief ignored her and walked into the bathroom. "You no-good piece of
shit!" Celeste continued. "Young ass! I should've known you
wouldn't be a man. Fuckin' drunk! Does she know you're an alcoholic? Did you tell her your drunk ass is on desk duty? Or is she
in love with your sober representative? Why don't you just admit
it, she's pregnant!" Celeste punched Sharief in his back. "Say it!
Say it!"

Sharief tripped out of the bathroom. "I'm begging you, Celeste, please go ahead."

The kids were in their respective bedrooms, and they each had
grown used to the constant arguing and fighting. They buried
their heads under their comforters and eventually fell asleep.

Celeste mushed Sharief again.

"I'ma knock you in the fuckin' mouth," Sharief warned her
while walking down the stairs to the basement. All he wanted was
to get away from Celeste. He couldn't stand the arguing; all it did
was make him hate her more, and he desperately wanted to keep
a small portion of love for her on reserve. "Get the fuck out my
face!" He pointed his index finger into Celeste's forehead. "I'ma
smack the shit out of you!"

"Fuck you! Smack me, then! Is she pregnant? And what were
you talking about on the porch? What was it? Was it me? Were
you laughing at me? Were you cursing me? Did you say you
wish you hadn't married me? You no-good niggah. I hate you! I
hate you!"

"Then let me leave, Celeste."

Celeste balled her fists up and ran toward Sharief. Before she
could attack him, he caught her by her throat. Pressing her head
into the wall, he asked her, "Are you trying to see if I can actually
kill you or not? Do you know if I punch you hard enough in your
throat, it's over for you?"

Celeste looked in Sharief's eyes and saw tears, which turned
her on.

"It's not a crime to not be in love with you anymore, Celeste." He let her neck go. "The crime is staying here and hating you. Doing all kinds of shit to you, because I can't stand to look at you."

"What can I do . . . to make this work?" she begged.

"Nothing."

"Don't say that." Celeste started kissing Sharief on the side of his neck. Her pussy started to tingle as she caressed the outline of his shoulders, feeling as much as she could of his well-toned body, from the thumping vein on the side of his neck to the veins running down his arms and into his hands.

"What are you doing?" He hated that her kisses made his dick tingle. She continued to kiss him. Then her tongue made a trail up to his earlobe. Her nipples hardened and he could feel her breasts against his chest and for a moment he thought about how he used to love to suck them. "Is this what you want," Sharief asked, "some dick?"

"I wanna fuck you."

"This is sick."

"Let me see your dick. Please, I need to feel you inside me. Fuck me. I'm begging you to fuck me."

"Celeste, we can't keep doing this." He started popping the buttons off her shirt. Lifting her bra, he remembered sliding his dick in between and cumming all over her dark brown nipples. Instantly his dick was hard. Celeste started unbuckling his pants and sliding his boxers down. Once his pants were down Sharief picked Celeste up, and she wrapped her legs around his waist as he slid his dick in.

Celeste started to moan and Sharief fought hard to not envision Monica. He closed his eyes but all he continued to see was Monica's face, the sound of her voice and the way she whispered in his ear about how big and hard his dick was. *Grab my hair,* Monica would say, *and make me work this dick.* Sharief started grinding Celeste as hard as he could. He placed one of his hands at the back of Celeste's head and as he went to pull her hair, his hand slipped through her short curls.

Celeste started to moan as she felt Sharief's fingers playing in her hair. "I like that, baby."

Instantly Sharief's dick deflated. He was hoping that Celeste didn't feel it, but as she moved her hips it slipped out. Never making eye contact with her he put it back in. Celeste gyrated her hips and started to moan and call his name. Again his dick went soft. He put it back in and a few minutes later, the same thing happened. This went on at least three more times.

Eventually her pussy dried up and Sharief felt like his dick was a brittle tree bark, breaking apart, and landing in the midst of a stick bush.

"I can't, Celeste. I just can't." Sharief pulled his pants up. "I'm leaving. Don't try to stop me. I'll be back in the morning for my things and to let you know when I'll want to see my children."

Celeste slid down the wall in silence. She knew it was over, the way Sharief walked out the room and never looked back. The way his voice rang with finality and the way it kept a steady rhythm as he said, *I'm leaving.*

She could still smell sex in the air, mixing in with the stinging echo of Sharief's announcement. She thought of running up the stairs behind him but she knew this time if she kicked him in his back, he would continue to walk away and never turn around. And she wasn't sure if she could stand up to the pain of him leaving and the pain of him staying gone.

[Monica]

"SO WHAT'S THE deal?" Listra said, pissed off that she was having this conversation. She crossed her legs while sitting on the couch and listening to Monica vomit into the toilet.

As the vomit hit the toilet water, splashes of it hit Monica in the face. She rested her hand on the side of the sink, took a deep breath, and spit out what remained in her mouth. *I'm too old for this shit,* she thought.

"This is one time," Listra said, hearing the toilet flush, "that I agree with abortion."

"What?" Monica said, taking a piece of tissue and wiping specks of vomit from her face and the corner of her mouth. "I'm not having an abortion. Fuck that."

"You can't have a baby by your sister's husband."

"Listen. If I hear one more time about whose husband he is I'ma scream. He was her husband when he fucked me. He was her husband when he told me that he loved me. And he's her husband now that I'm pregnant. Do I look like I give a fuck anymore whose husband he is? My guilt is long gone. She's the one who chopped up his hand and shit. Fuck her. She's had her babies, now let me have mine." Monica walked out the bathroom and lay on the couch, resting her head on the arm. Her curly hair fell over the edge as she threw her right arm across her forehead.

"Have an abortion," Listra stressed.

"Listra, I've lost one baby and now you think I should kill the other?"

"Yes." Listra mashed her cigarette into the ashtray. "I think this is one nut you should flush."

"Listra, I thought I couldn't have kids." Monica sat up and looked at her.

"And that was your own homemade thought. You have more than one egg. Hell, wait three, four months, ovulate, and fuck somebody else. Trust me. This is not what you need right now."

"How'd I get myself into this?"

"Because you opened your legs and fucked him. That's how it happened. That's why you need to have an abortion."

"I'm not having an abortion. I don't give a damn."

"Well, that's obvious."

"Look, Listra," she pointed out, "either you be my friend and support me or maybe we don't need to speak anymore."

"Bitch, are you crazy?" Listra sucked her teeth. "Being your friend is not always agreeing with you. What you did was fucked up and what you're contemplating is even worse."

"You think I'm doing this to keep him?" Monica was pissed.

"No," Listra shook her head, "I think you're doing this so that Celeste can't."

"Fuck Celeste! This is about me! I already said that I won't tell Sharief."

"Yeah," Listra huffed, "and that damn baby'll come here looking just like him."

"Don't say that. Besides, he asked me earlier was I pregnant, and I told him no. Then I told him to leave me the fuck alone. He looked at me and said, *Never.*"

"I know that's a lie." Listra laughed. "What is he supposed to do with his wife?"

"His cell phone number is 718-555-1212. Call and ask him, I don't give a fuck."

"You're a real live bitch."

"I'm not a bitch!"

"Yes you are. You're the mistress from hell. I'm telling you, if I were Celeste I would beat yo' ass. For real—no lie."

"Well, you're not Celeste. I'm done with her husband. Therefore she can have him. *And* I'm having my baby. Anyway I don't even know how far along I am. I only took the test this morning. My doctor's appointment isn't until next week, my period is irregular, which all translates to mean I really don't know how far along I am. I could easily be three, four months. I'm fat-ass hell, and if nobody wants to support me, then by all means fuck 'em!"

"You're talking an awful lotta shit for somebody who needs friends."

"Whatever."

Before Listra could go on she and Monica heard keys jiggling at the front door. When they both turned to look at the door, the lock and the doorknob were turning. "Monica," Sharief called.

Damn, I forgot this niggah had a key, Monica thought. Sharief stumbled inside but tried to play off his clumsiness by holding on to the door. "Yo," he said, looking at Listra with bloodshot red eyes and a dripping wet lip. "Time na roll, home girl. Y'all li'l fuck-that-niggah session is over."

"Don't talk to me," Listra snapped.

"Listra," Monica said.

"What? Fuck him. Can't you tell he's drunk?"

"Whooo," Sharief slurred, "am I fucking you and you forget to tell me? Whether I'm drunk or not is none of your business. Better fall the fuck back, broad! Don't worry about me, I'm good."

"Have you been drinking, Sharief?" Monica asked.

"Yo." Sharief chuckled. "Don't do that, ma. Don't play me in front of ya girl. Don't."

"Have . . . you . . . been . . . drinking?" Monica repeated.

"Yeah, I had something to drink, and what?"

"I can't stand this pussyclot!" Listra rolled her eyes.

"Pussyclot my ass, speak fuckin' English!" Sharief snapped.

"Don't say that, Sharief," Monica said, annoyed. "And Listra, please."

Sharief looked at Monica and ran his hand across his head. "I need . . . I need . . . to talk to you." She couldn't help but stare at his body. She hated the fact that he always turned her on. Sharief was dressed in baggy jeans, a white V-neck T-shirt, and Tims.

"What the hell is wrong with you coming to my door drunk? Are you fuckin' crazy?"

"You want me to embarrass you? Now, I said I wanna talk to you."

Monica sucked her teeth. "Listra, let's just—"

"Don't say no more. It'll be my pleasure." Listra picked up her purse and kissed Monica on the cheek. "Call me." She rolled her eyes at Sharief as if to say, *Fuck you.*

He looked at her and frowned, catching her drift. "Yeah, you too."

Watching Monica lock the door behind her friend, Sharief said, "What's her problem?"

"It's you," Monica said.

"Why?"

"I'm fucking you and you're my sister's husband." Monica frowned, sitting back down on the couch.

"You telling that chick our business?"

"What difference does it make now? Your drunk ass wasn't speaking in Morse code when you stumbled in here."

"Whatever," he said dismissively. "What I wanna know is when you start lyin' to me?"

"What are you talking about?"

"Don't play dumb. You know what I'm talking about!" He flicked his hand across her stomach, pointing out her unzipped jeans, her T-shirt tucked under her breasts, and her semi-hard and protruding pouch. "Look at you." Sharief took the back of his hand and wiped the beads of sweat popping on his forehead. "Of all the goddamn things to do, how did you fuck around and get pregnant?"

"What?"

"You heard me. You told me that you couldn't have kids? *I can't have kids. I suffered from fibroids-blah-blah-blah* . . . That ain't no damn fibroid you carrying—or is that the new lie that bitches are telling now?"

"Bitches?" She felt like slapping the shit out of him. "You the bitch!"

"Oh, now I'ma bitch. After you've lied to me? Well I don't want no more kids. So what you gon' do?"

"Fuck you! I'm having my baby!"

"I can't believe this! Look at you." He pointed. "Look at you—fulla games. I asked you five times," he held his hand up, "on that porch were you pregnant and all you could say was *What you talkin' about, Sharief? What you talkin' about?* You knew what the hell I was talking about! I can't believe you would do this."

Monica raised her eyebrows. "You can't believe that I would do this? Every time I turned around, you wanted to fuck. *Let me stick it in ya ass, Monica.* Remember that?"

"You didn't get pregnant from me shootin' off in yo' ass. Don't lie."

"Sharief, get the fuck out! Get . . . the . . . fuck . . . outta here!" She stood up and pointed to the door. "Leave!"

Sharief walked over to the door and leaned against it. "My life is fucked up. It's like I'm on crack and shit. Just when I make up my mind to leave you alone, I start thinking about you being with other niggahs and shit. And then I think about how you look at me when I'm fucking you. How you make me laugh. How I look forward to seeing you. Then I start going crazy . . . it's like I can't get over you."

"You're not trying hard enough."

"Listen, baby. I walked out on my wife to be with you."

"What are you talking about?"

"I left Celeste."

Monica looked perplexed. "You left Celeste? When?"

"Tonight. And listen, I tried to fuck her."

"I don't wanna hear that, Sharief." Monica sat down on the couch, starting to feel light-headed.

"I need you to hear this. I never touched Celeste the whole time I was trying to make things work with her. I couldn't stand to look at her." He walked over to Monica and kneeled before her, placing his hands in her lap. "I couldn't fuck her. But tonight, tonight was different, and for a moment I thought maybe, just maybe it could happen. So I tried to fuck her . . . and all I could think of was you. And every time she went to call my name, I remembered that it wasn't you and my dick went soft." He started to laugh. "I'm twenty-eight years old and I was trying to fuck with a soft dick."

"Oh please."

"You got to know that I love you."

"You're drunk. You'll feel differently in the morning."

"Monica," Sharief said, "let me love you. We don't have to have any kids. We can keep this between us and keep it moving. Have the abortion, baby."

"You selfish motherfucker! I should slap the shit outta you!" She pushed his hands off her lap. "You think this is about wanting you and wanting to keep you? Celeste can have your cheating drunk ass. I'm good. You can't tell me not to have my baby and instead be with you in secret. No, niggah, you ain't that fly! You and my child are not an even exchange. And if you can't accept that, then oh well—not my problem. Now, my advice to you is to get the fuck out because I'm through with you!" Monica stormed up the stairs.

"Monica!" Sharief shouted, "Monica!"

"Fuck you!" She slammed her bedroom door as hard as she could.

Sharief flopped down on the couch and held his face in his hands.

Twenty minutes later he got up and climbed the stairs. He quietly opened Monica's bedroom door. She stood with her back to the doorway and a towel wrapped around her. He could tell that she'd just gotten out of the shower because her skin was still wet.

Monica closed her eyes as she heard Sharief come up behind her. He started to kiss her on the neck while pulling her towel down. He kissed straight down her back, over her ass, and down to her ankles. Tears streaked her face. "Why can't I just leave you alone?" she said. "I'm tired. I'm tired of the lies, of the games, of pretending that it's okay when my sister goes home with you. I'm tired of being tired. Just let me go—You let go and I'll go too—"

"Shhh . . . I can't."

He kissed her feet and came back up the front of her body, showering her with the same kisses that he'd laid down her back. Once he got to her pussy's lips, he immediately went to licking, kissing, and biting her clit until all she could do was scream.

After he made her cum, he picked her up and carried her to the bed. He laid her down and then undressed. Climbing on top of her, he nursed her swollen nipples slowly, circling his tongue over and over again. Her clit started to jump as his hard dick brushed across her thigh and parted her pussy lips. "I can't keep doing this," she whispered.

"Hush," Sharief kissed her on the lips, "I told you that I was gon' be fucking you forever." He slid his dick in as far as he could and instantly felt at home.

"Sharief—"

"We gon' work this out, baby. Somehow, we have to." He grabbed her hair and she looked him in the face. "I love you . . ."

"I know you do," she said, melting in his arms, "I know you do."

* • *

"SHARIEF," MONICA SAID, excited, waking him up the next morning, "I changed my doctor's appointment to this afternoon so we can go together."

"Go where together?"

"The doctor."

"What doctor?" he asked, wiping the corners of his mouth.

"The ob-gyn, silly." She laughed, playfully pushing him on the shoulder.

"You didn't hear what I told you last night or what?" He sat up. "You think this is a game? I'm not fuckin' playing with you. I don't want no baby."

"But last night, you came upstairs and we made love." Monica was confused.

"Yeah, we made love and? I told you I didn't want any more kids. Let me shine some reality on this bullshit. I have three kids with your sister. Kayla may not biologically be mine, but she's mine, feel me? I don't have money like that to be having babies all over the place. Now, it's one thing for us to be on some downlow bullshit and fuck around, me and you exclusively, but it's another thing to have a baby. That's just fucked up and I don't wanna hurt Celeste like that."

"Celeste? I can't believe you're saying this to me."

"And I can't believe you wanna have this baby. What the hell is wrong with you? Are you thinking straight?"

"I . . . really . . . can't believe this . . ." Monica got out of bed.

"Don't you feel bad? Goddamn! How are we supposed to do something like this?" Sharief was disgusted, disappointed, and pissed. "What the fuck, Monica? I can't have a baby on my wife!

Now you throwing salt in the game. You were not supposed to get pregnant! Shit!"

"Excuse me?"

"I tell you what," Sharief continued, "don't start thinking I gotta buncha fuckin' money and shit, 'cause I'm not letting you drain me fuckin' dry. So get that child-support shit outcha head."

"Child support! How fuckin' dare you talk to me like that? You know what?" Monica blinked. "Get the fuck out! Right now. All of a sudden your fucking me comes to light because I'm pregnant and now you're Mr. Self-Righteous? I can do bad by myself! Hell, that's my sister, not yours. I didn't fuck your brother. I can't explain to my mother how I'm pregnant by my sister's husband. She'll never accept this shit, but what am I supposed to do? I thought I couldn't have kids and now everybody thinks I should give my baby up because of Celeste. Fuck Celeste! What about me? What about Monica? Celeste has three kids and here I can't even have one? Kiss my ass, Sharief, you have to go. Get your shit and get the fuck out!"

"Whatever you want." Sharief got dressed, picked the rest of his things up, and left.

[Celeste]

CELESTE GOT OFF the floor at five in the morning. She crept into the kitchen, made herself a cup of coffee, lit her cigarette, and took a drag. She stared at the copy of Starr's wedding tape and decided to play the uncut version. All she wanted to see was Monica and Sharief. She felt obsessed, betrayed, and buried alive. No matter what Sharief's mouth said, his face told the truth every time. The other woman was Monica, and Celeste had to know why. She wanted to study Monica's face, her hips, her lips, the arch in her back, and figure out what it was that made Monica sufficient and her insufficient. Hell, was it a wife's duty to dress up all the time, to always be pretty, perfect, and ready to fuck? Was there any room to gain weight, any room to want a different hairstyle, any room to not like to suck dick, fuck in the ass, or be on top? Or was the rule, anything you won't do somebody else will?

Celeste popped the tape in and fast-forwarded it to Monica and Sharief walking down the aisle. Monica looked upset and Sharief started to whisper to her. *"It wasn't what you thought."* Their voices were low but thanks to the stereo surround sound, Celeste could hear clearly.

"Fuck you," Monica mumbled under her breath.

"*Oh*"—Sharief laughed slightly as they continued down the aisle—"*that means we're in good standing . . .*" After that their voices muffled and Celeste could no longer make out what they were saying. So she fast-forwarded again. What Sharief said to Monica still wasn't enough to make the pain stick. Celeste needed more, she had to have it, otherwise there was a chance she would convince herself that she'd misunderstood or heard wrong. And that's not what she wanted; she wanted something concrete. Something strong enough to make her feel as if a poisonous dagger had sliced the middle of her face open.

Everyone on the tape moved in fast-forward motion as Celeste placed the video on ultrahigh speed. Once she spotted Monica walking over to the makeshift bar and sitting next to Sharief, she slowed the tape down and let it play.

"*Listen.*" Sharief stared at Monica with a serious look on his face. "*I love you, I'm in love with you, and as fucked up as it may be I would leave my wife to be with you.*"

Celeste pressed rewind and played the tape again. "*Listen.*" Sharief stared at Monica with a serious look on his face. "*I love you, I'm in love with you, and as fucked up as it may be I would leave my wife to be with you.*"

And again. "*Listen.*" Sharief stared at Monica with a serious look on his face. "*I love you, I'm in love with you, and as fucked up as it may be I would leave my wife to be with you.*"

One more time. "*Listen.*" Sharief stared at Monica with a serious look on his face. "*I love you, I'm in love with you, and as fucked up as it may be I would leave my wife to be with you.*"

Celeste snorted as she stared at the tape. Her first thought was the bottle of Aleve tucked away in the cabinet. She thought about swallowing all the pills, but then she realized that they would build up a chalky residue in her throat and perhaps cause liver damage but nothing more. She knew the sweetness of death wouldn't be so kind as to snatch her breath away simply because she took one too many pills.

Then she thought of slitting her wrist but figured in the end she would feel the pain, have the scars, and everyone would always think she was insane, even though she wasn't.

Celeste called Greyhound and made arrangements for her children to take the eight AM bus ride to Port Authority, something she'd never done. She called Starr, who promised that she and Red would be there as soon as the kids stepped off the bus and, since it was a straight ride with no stops, there was nothing to worry about.

After putting the kids on the bus, Celeste came back home, went upstairs to her bedroom, and fell across the floor. "How did I get myself into this? Here I am thirty-two years old with no friends, nobody to talk to, no nothing. My sister's fucking my husband. What did I do, God? Was it because I didn't go to church like I was supposed to? But I still prayed, I still believed. And no, I can't recite all of the Ten Commandments and so what if all I know of the Twenty-third Psalm is, 'Yea though I walk through the valley of the shadow of death I shall fear no evil . . .' " Celeste started to scream in agony. "Oh my God, I can't believe this . . . this was not supposed to happen. He wasn't supposed to leave. He was supposed to beg for my forgiveness and promise to never cheat again. He was supposed to hold me close and say, *I'm soooo sorry, baby. I love you, and I don't want to lose you or my kids. I swear I'll never do it again, just forgive me.* He was supposed to want me not to leave, not the other way around."

Celeste wiped her tears, got off the floor, and walked over to her closet. "You see this shit." She pulled her white fur-trimmed negligee out of the closet and slipped it on. "This shit made me look like a damn fool and here I been dressin' like a fool, actin' like a fool, and being a fool fo' yo' ass way too long. I'm tired now." She grabbed her purse and went in search of her cigarettes. Once she found them, she realized she had only two left. "Damn."

Without thinking about the negligee she had on, she slipped on a pair of pink matted bedroom slippers and walked out the door. She got in her car and headed for 7-Eleven.

When Celeste walked in wearing her negligee, no bra, and a pair of pink bedroom slippers, no one in the store could believe their eyes. The cashier frowned as Celeste walked by. The last time she'd seen anyone who looked and dressed like this was two years ago, and they had robbed the place.

Celeste's big breasts flopped against her stomach as she walked into the store. She had to smile thinking of the money she was preparing to withdraw from the store's MAC. A few weeks ago in the midst of searching through Sharief's things, she'd found two bank books with matching debit cards: one for checking and the other for savings. The checking account had a balance of five thousand dollars and the savings account, twenty-five thousand. Celeste knew she couldn't withdraw more than five hundred dollars from the MAC machine, so she decided to take what she could get this morning and go for the rest later this afternoon. And since Sharief's code was always the same, 0411, transferring all his money into his checking account would be a cinch.

Once her banking transactions were complete, Celeste sauntered around the store in search of a Pepsi and two banana Moon-Pies. The bottoms of her bedroom slippers slapped against the floor as her ass bounced in the air. Her nipples hardened as she spotted a tall, fine chocolate brother. She winked. "Wassup, cat daddy?" He couldn't help but smile as he watched her nipples stick out.

Celeste took a pen out of her purse, wrote her cell phone number down on a piece of paper, and slid it to the man. She noticed the ring on his left hand. "Don't worry," she said seductively to the fine brother, who was watching her breasts the whole time she spoke, "I won't tell if you won't. Call me, so you can suck these." She winked again and walked away.

Usually at this time of the morning 7-Eleven would be filled with the hustle and bustle of passing motorists stopping in just long enough for a buttered roll and coffee. But not this morning; instead the crowds seemed to linger around so they could get a bird's-eye view of the big-tittie woman with the flat ass floating from one freezer to the next.

Once Celeste found the coldest Pepsi she could, she turned around and walked toward the front, never noticing the people standing around and staring.

Celeste smacked her lips as she spoke to the cashier. "Cigarettes, babe . . . a carton."

"These not free," the cashier said to her. "And you can't beg for no money in here either." She rolled her eyes, disgusted at the crust in Celeste's eyes and the dryness around her mouth. "You need to leave the drugs alone."

Celeste looked around. "Who you talking to?"

"You." The cashier pointed. "Out my store!"

"I asked you for a carton of cigarettes!"

"Nasty, filthy wench! Everytime you people come in here you steal!"

Celeste looked at the cashier and slapped the shit out of her. Immediately the cashier jumped on top of her, causing Celeste to fall back and hit her face on the corner of the metal shelf. "Not this time!" the cashier screamed, "I won't be robbed again! I promise you!"

The store was in an uproar. One of the men watching the fight snatched the women apart. By now Celeste's negligee was in shreds and her breasts were hanging out. Celeste stood in silence for a moment as she watched the lady kick and scream. Thinking that she needed to get out of the store, Celeste turned away from the crowd and simply walked out. In the midst of all the commotion no one even noticed that she was leaving. She hopped in her car and took off. As she was driving home she pulled to the side of the road to see where the blood dripping in her lap was coming from. When she looked in the rearview mirror she realized that there was a large bruise covering the side of her face and a cut over her eye. *I must've cut it when I hit the shelf, 'cause I know for sure that bitch didn't kick my ass!*

Celeste pulled up in her driveway and walked across her yard practically naked. As soon as she walked in her front door, she ran to the bathroom and looked in the mirror. She couldn't believe it: her face looked as if someone had beaten her with a bat. *If I didn't know better,* she thought, *I would think that I had my ass beat!*

"Celeste!" Sharief called, "Celeste! Why the hell is the front door wide open and the car still running?" he yelled, storming through the house. Once he found Celeste he looked her up and down. She stood in the bathroom doorway in the tattered negligee, her titties hanging out, with bruises and cuts on her face. "What the fuck happened to you?" He frowned. "Who the fuck beat yo' ass? You been assaulted or some shit?"

Instantly a lightbulb went on. Celeste took a puff off her cigarette. "You think I was assaulted? You really do? Well I got something for yo' ass then." Celeste walked past Sharief and into the living room. She grabbed her cell phone, flipped it open, and hit 9-1-1. She smiled at Sharief, while he looked at her like she was crazy.

Celeste pressed send on her phone and the operator picked up right away. "Nine-one-one, what's your emergency?"

"Oh God!" Celeste screamed, "somebody please, come get me, my husband! My husband he's beating me! He's beating me. Sharief, stop! Please stop! He's trying to rape me!" Celeste placed her cigarette in the ashtray and started banging her fist on the wall.

"Ma'am," the operator said, trying to remain calm, "your address, please."

"Hang up that fuckin' phone!" Sharief snapped, realizing what was going on.

The operator could hear him yelling in the background. "Ma'am."

Celeste could hear a little panic in the operator's voice, so she played on it and started breathing heavy. "I live at 555 Willow Clark Drive."

Sharief tried to snatch the phone. "What the fuck are you doing?" The operator could hear Sharief's voice escalate as she dispatched the police to their address. Celeste grabbed Sharief by the collar and tried to rip his white T-shirt off. When she saw she couldn't get it off easily, she jumped on top of him and started fighting him, causing the gash above her eye to reopen and drip blood all over Sharief's shirt.

Sharief pushed Celeste in the center of her chest; she fell off him and slid across the floor. As he got off the floor and stood up, in rushed five police officers—one with a German shepherd, the rest with their guns drawn—and three EMT workers.

Celeste was stretched out on the floor. The blood dripping from the cut above her eye slid down her face and dripped between her lips, giving her mouth the appearance that it was bleeding.

"Get on the fuckin' floor facedown!" one of the officers yelled at Sharief.

"I'm an officer!" Sharief screamed.

"Stop lying!" yelled one of the cops. "Now get down!"

Scared that the officer might shoot if he made any subtle movement, Sharief hit the floor, facedown. "Spread your legs apart! Stupid ass likes to hit on fuckin' women!" The cop placed his knee in Sharief's back while another officer pointed a gun at his head.

"You lowdown stupid son-of-a-bitch!" the officer with his knee in Sharief's back yelled. "You like to beat on women?" He pressed Sharief's head to the floor with the palm of his right hand while he took his left hand and slapped the handcuffs on him. Then he started searching Sharief while the other cops looked around the house.

"I didn't fuckin' hit her!" Sharief clinched his mouth tight.

"You gettin' tough, niggah?" the cop said as he found Sharief's gun on the side of his hip. "Look at what we got, boys!"

"That's mine," Sharief said as the cop pressed his palm harder into the side of his face. "I'm a detective. Look—look around my neck you'll see my badge. I swear to you I didn't put my hands on her. I didn't hit her! I don't know how she got beat like that but I didn't do it. That's how she looked when I got here!"

Celeste, whom the EMT workers thought was unable to speak, started screaming, "He attacked me! Whenever he has a bad day he does it! I try . . . I try so hard to be a good wife and nothing is ever good enough!"

"You know I could lose my job over this bullshit!" Sharief screamed, tears running down his face. "You know if I lose my job I won't have shit!"

"You're really a cop?" the officer took his knee off Sharief's back and the palm of his hand away from his face, but he left the handcuffs on. The officer with his gun pointed at Sharief's head withdrew it and helped Sharief stand up. They could see Sharief's sterling-silver badge clearly now.

"Yes. I'm a detective in Brooklyn, New York," Sharief said. "My captain's name is Kevin Lassiter."

"Oh God!" Celeste screamed. "I know you gon' let him go! I know he's going to kick my ass again! I knew as soon as you found out that he was a cop that you would let him go! That's why I never said anything before, but I can't take him beating me anymore. Please I can't take it! Please, help me!"

"Celeste," Sharief said, "are you having a nervous breakdown? Why are you doing this? You got these people thinking I'm fucking crazy and that I beat you when I didn't touch you!"

"With all due respect, Detective," the officer interjected, "we have you on a nine-one-one tape struggling with her, and we saw you throw her into the wall. You're under arrest."

"I can't fuckin' believe this shit!" Sharief said as one of the officers grabbed him by his arm and started walking him toward the door. "You fuckin' set me up," he screamed at Celeste.

The EMT workers placed Celeste on the stretcher and carried

her out the door after the cops marched Sharief outside. It seemed as if everyone in the neighborhood stood outside watching. Sharief held his head down and slid into the backseat of the police car. The police started the blaring sirens and took off.

Tears rolled down Celeste's face and she did what she could to fight back her smile. She lay in the back of the ambulance and listened to the sirens that were sounding like music to her ears. *Good fo' yo' ass,* she thought. *Now let's see how well you sleep tonight.*

[Monica]

"I SWEAR TO GOD, Sharief," Monica screamed into the voice mail on his cell phone as she sat in her car in the ob-gyn's parking lot, "I don't care if Celeste is checking your messages, I'm not fucking with yo' ass anymore! Don't call me, don't nothing!" Her head felt like it was going to explode. Her doctor's appointment was over; she was officially four and a half months pregnant, and if the surprise of that wasn't fucked up enough, Sharief wanting her to give the baby up was. *Why, Monica,* she thought, *why do you keep playing yourself?* She started recapping his conversation with her this morning and suddenly it felt like her body was shutting down. Remembering that her body was needed to support the baby, she started backing her car out of the parking lot. As she went to make a left into traffic, her phone rang.

"Hello?"

"Hey dere, gurl." It was Listra. Monica knew that Listra was either mad or listening to reggae music since her full Trinidadian accent was in effect.

"Hey, Listra," Monica said with a drag.

"What's wit' de attitude? First I call Mummy and she attitude nasty and now you. But what de hell?" Monica could hear Listra taking a pull off her cigarette.

"I'm just pissed off with Sharief."

"Why?"

"He doesn't want the baby. He wants me to have an abortion."

"Well, he wasn't that damn drunk after all. We finally agree on someting."

"I gotta go," Monica snapped. "The last thing I need to hear is a buncha smart-ass shit falling out of your mouth. Please!" She hung up.

In an effort to not think about the bullshit that had now become her life, Monica turned the radio all the way up and started singing.

By the time she got home her face was drenched with tears. She parked in front of her house, walked inside, lay down on the couch, and closed her eyes. Trying desperately to remember what she liked to do before she started fucking with Sharief, she opened her eyes and turned on the TV to see if her favorite show, *American Justice,* would still interest her since she hadn't watched it in months. She turned the channel only to see that cable had switched the networks around and A&E was no longer channel 23. Instead channel 23 was HBO, and they were premiering a new movie, *Flip Side of the Game. Humph,* Monica thought, sitting up, *now ain't this some shit?*

• • •

MONICA GOT OFF the couch and stretched. *What the fuck am I doing?* she thought. No matter how hard she tried, Sharief clouded her every thought. She sat back down and flicked through the TV channels again. Hell, if she was forced to think about him, then she needed to think about how to let him go . . . and how to breathe without him . . . and how to piss, shit, sleep, and just be without having to see him, feel him, or fuck him. It was two o'clock in the morning and she was miserable. "So Ms.," she said in an animated and deep voice, holding the remote control to her mouth like a microphone, "you are officially a part of the ex-factor, so tell me how does it feel? Is he still the bomb or what?"

As soon as she went to answer her own question the telephone rang. "Hello?"

"Monica?"

"Sharief," she said as calmly as possible, "let me inform you. Sorry will not work and your lick-and-stick game ain't that great. I'm what you would say . . . sick of yo' shit—"

"Monica—"

"I'm four and a half months pregnant and I cannot have an abortion."

"Monica—"

"Did you hear me?" she yelled.

"Monica . . . shut . . . the . . . fuck up! This is not about your selfish ass, for once, goddamn!" he said, exasperated.

Sensing the panic in Sharief's voice, Monica immediately switched gears. "What's wrong?"

"Celeste had me arrested."

"What? What happened? What do you mean arrested? Where are you?"

"At the police station. The cop let me use the phone at his desk. But she had me arrested for assault."

"Oh my God!" Monica couldn't believe it.

"Monica, baby, I swear," he started to get upset, "all I did was walk in the house and she was beat the fuck up and shit. But I never touched her. I asked her what happened and the next thing I knew she was callin' nine-one-one and the police ran in the house like a fuckin' SWAT team!"

"I don't understand." Monica was confused. Her heart started to race and her palms started to sweat.

"Listen, baby, all I know is that I didn't touch her. I'm being held at the police station. I want you to come and get me before they move me to the county jail. My bail is ten thousand cash. I keep my checkbook locked in the glove compartment of my truck. I need you to get down here this morning. Go by my house and my truck is parked out front. Get my checkbook, and write yourself a check for ten grand so you can pay my bail."

"And what if Celeste is there?"

"She won't be."

"Where is she?"

"In the hospital."

"What? My sister's in the hospital?"

"Oh, now you're concerned. She's in the hospital because she lost her fuckin' mind, not because of anything I did. Please, baby, I need you."

"I'll be at the bank as soon as they open."

.   •   .

"I'M SORRY, MISS," the teller said, "but we can't cash it. Insufficient funds."

Monica's heart stopped. "What?"

"Insufficient funds."

Before she could respond, her phone rang. It was a collect call from Sharief. She was thankful that her call forwarding worked. She pressed 2 and accepted his call. Instantly she began to cry. "Sharief, you don't have any money in the bank."

"Calm down, baby, now what did you say?"

"You don't have any money. I'll just spend my money and come get you."

"No . . . don't do that. Where the fuck is my money?" he mumbled. "Okay, baby, something is not right. Walk over to the MAC machine and check my account's balance. Inside the pocket in my checkbook is a duplicate MAC card, my code is zero-four-one-one."

Monica got out of line and walked over to the MAC machine. She checked Sharief's balance. "Your checking account is negative." She started to get upset again.

"Baby," he took a deep breath, "I gotta get the fuck outta here. Check my savings."

She checked his savings. "It's two dollars left."

Sharief pounded his fist. "What the fuck!"

"I'm coming to get you," Monica insisted.

"No, I'ma need your help with an attorney."

"Are you sure Celeste is still in the hospital? Did she come and get the money outta the bank?" Monica asked.

"Look," Sharief said, ignoring her, "come down here and wait for me. I'ma call my captain and see if he can call in a favor to the judge to get me the hell outta here."

•   •   •

MONICA LEFT THE bank and drove to the Somerset County police station. Once inside she walked over to the processing officer's desk. "Excuse me," she said, "I'm here for Sharief Winston."

"One moment, have a seat, ma'am. I'll check for you . . . Excuse me, are you the one pressing the charges against him?"

"No." A voice floated over Monica's shoulder. "That would be me."

As Monica turned around, Celeste, Starr, and Red were standing directly behind her.

"What are you doing here?" Starr asked Monica, her eyes moving from Monica's face to her stomach. "And don't lie."

"I-I-I . . ."

"You were what, Monica?" Celeste said, with a bandage over her eye and a large bruise covering half her face. "You were what? You fuckin' slut! How could you take and sleep with my husband! How could you! I trusted you!"

"You didn't trust me, you don't even like me!" Monica screamed.

"You're my sister!"

"And whose fuckin' problem is that? You know what, Celeste"— Monica pointed her finger—"you got fat and fuckin' miserable. You cut all your damn hair off, looking like a man. You! All he tried to be was a good man to you and all you did was go from project shit to trailer-park trash—"

Before Monica could go on, Celeste slowly lifted her hand in the air, bit her bottom lip, and hauled off and slapped the shit out of her; Monica stumbled, almost falling to the floor. "You tryin' to play me crazy! This fat bitch will kick yo' ass!" Celeste screamed, placing her hands on her hips.

Monica put her hand over her mouth. "I can't believe that you just did that." She made eye contact with the officers who were walking up on them. "What's the problem?" the officer asked.

"None of your damn business!" Celeste screamed.

"I'm sick of this!" Monica screamed. "I'm sick of this pretend shit! Pretend-it's-all-grand shit. Well it's not! And I'm glad you know because now I can move on with my life and my man!"

"Ya man!" Celeste lunged at Monica. "That's my husband!"

Red grabbed Celeste's arms and pulled her away from Monica. "Monica—you better hold ya roll," Red insisted. "You can't go around violatin' marriage vows. You ever heard of a jezebel? I need a Bible right now, somebody need to pray for you!"

"The Bible?" Monica said. "You just found the Bible. So be quiet!"

"Oh wait a minute now," Starr said. "I ain't Celeste. I'll beat yo' ass over my man!"

"And that's all you've ever been concerned about was your man. So you know what," Monica spat, "I don't have time for this. Sharief didn't do anything to Celeste. She's lying. I know she's lying. And I hope she burns in fuckin' hell. And if you're here to help her press charges then to hell with all of you."

"Monica—" Starr couldn't believe it.

"No, fuck that!" Monica stormed away and started walking toward a bench. As she sat down, she spotted an officer escorting Sharief.

"Have you been released?" Monica asked, running toward him.

Sharief nodded and walked closer to her. Once he stood next to her, he yoked her by the arm and pulled her back toward Starr, Red, and Celeste. "What the hell is going on here? I could hear you all the way in the back. This is ridiculous!"

"You got a lot of nerve," Starr growled at him. "You fuckin' both of my daughters? You wreck my family—"

"He didn't wreck anything, Ma. Monica is grown!" Celeste insisted. "She's the home wrecker."

"Pussy don't fuck alone, Celeste," Starr reminded her.

"Pussy don't fuck alone? This ain't about pussy, this is about her being my sister!" Celeste screamed at the top of her lungs. Tears flooded her face, and her vision was blurry. "Here I was asking you for advice. Asking you what you thought, if he was cheating, if it was me, was it this and was it that, and here you were suckin' his dick and fuckin' him." Celeste reached for Monica but Starr jumped in the way. "Move, Ma, 'cause I'ma kill her."

"We're in the police station!" Starr screamed.

"I don't give a fuck!" Celeste completely blacked out. "You stinkin' no-good-rotten-eggs, half-a-fallopian-tube slut. And if you're pregnant, I hope your fuckin' baby dry-rot just like the other one and then your infested-ass womb fall to pieces! This niggah know you had crabs? This niggah know you had a threesome, fucked a bitch just to keep yo' man, and the man still left your skeezin' ass—"

"Monica!" Starr screamed, cutting Celeste off. "On top of all this I know you ain't no dyke!"

"Oh we gon' need some anointing oil for this one, baby!" Red said.

"Did you tell him that he ain't the first married man that you've fucked," Celeste continued, "did you tell him that? You gon' tell me I got fat, I cut all my hair off, that it was me? That's why your fuckin' daddy didn't even want you. I hate you, Monica, and I swear to God and if Mommy and Red weren't standing here I would bury you!"

"Now, wait a fuckin' minute, Celeste," Sharief said. "You better fall the fuck back. Don't blame Monica, blame me. It's my throat you comin' for, not hers. I told you I didn't want you. I never meant to hurt you. I just wanted you to leave, but good-bye was never good enough, it always had to come with an explanation. Just go someplace and sit the fuck down. 'Cause guess what? I still don't love you. I still don't want you and after what you did to me I hate you! I hate you! And if you want to press charges on me for something you know I didn't do, then go ahead, because I will win. Now, get the fuck out my face!" He turned to Monica. "I'm ready to go."

Monica looked Celeste in the face, grabbed Sharief by the hand, and turned to leave.

"You son-of-a-bitch!" Celeste screamed. "You son-of-a-bitch!"

Starr grabbed Celeste as she went to run toward Sharief. "He ain't worth it, and right about now neither is she."

[Monica]

IT WAS SIX o'clock in the morning and Monica had been watching Sharief sleep for close to an hour. As far as she was concerned, everything about him was perfect. From the way his lips curled when he took deep breaths to the way a light coating of drool glazed his lips. As she brushed her hands across his soft cheeks, her phone rang. Without looking at the caller ID she answered, "Hello."

"I'ma try real hard," Starr said into the receiver, "to not call you a bitch, ho. But in a minute I'ma take it there!"

"Excuse you?" Monica said. "What did you just say to me?"

"Oh, you heard me, dammit! And I tell you what, you got an hour to get that high-yellow niggah out yo' bed and out yo' house before I wreck shop on yo' ass. What the fuck is really wrong with you? Have you lost all of your common sense? I don't give a damn about how good that dirty-dick niggah can fuck, eat pussy, or suck a tittie, that is your sister's husband and if I was Celeste I would've stuck my foot so far up yo' ass, you would be eatin' the crust off my calluses! Now, when I warned you about sister's husband the first two times you should've stayed away, but nooooo, not you. If he ain't gone in a few minutes, so help me all y'all niggahs will get fucked up! And just for the record, I know that you are my child, but Celeste is my child too and when she hurts, I hurt, and I don't like to feel pain. So wake that niggah up and tell him he needs to step!"

"Ma, please."

"Did you hear me? Don't make me come over!"

"Do what you gotta do," Monica said dismissively.

"Do what—what." Starr couldn't believe it. "Bitch, I will come over there and stomp a mud hole in yo' ass so deep that all the black will slide off you. Matter fact, put your sneakers on and come outside, ho. Mama Byrd," Starr said, "grab ya porta-potty, I got to go and kick Monica's ass . . . Monica, be sure you put some Vaseline on yo' face 'cause I'ma fuck you up. And you better not hit me back 'cause then I'ma bust yo' ass like the home-wreckin' bitch you are! And in case you think you can possibly take me, just know that I have always lived, breathed, and will die in the hood, so when you come, come correct 'cause it's the fuck on!"

"Ma, I'm not fighting you."

"Oh, you don't wanna fight? Hell you may as well 'cause this gon' be an easy one. It's gon' involve two kicks: me kicking you and you kicking his ass to the curb. You better recognize whose child you playin' with. Celeste is my child and the moment you decided to fuck her husband is the moment you declared war!"

"I can't believe you're saying this to me! You have always loved Celeste more than me anyway! So I'm not surprised that you would want to fight me because she's crying. But what about me, I'm your child too!"

"You sure are, and when that niggah dogs you, we'll deal with that. But since you're my child, no matter how grown you get, I always reserve the right to kick yo' ass!"

"I really can't believe this." Monica felt like crying.

"Monica." Sharief turned over and looked at her. "Who are you talking to? Are you crying?"

"My mother"—Monica's tears began to pour—"is calling me and cursing me out."

"I sure am!" Starr said. "And what?"

"Monica, you don't need this kind of stress," Sharief said, concerned.

The more Starr heard Sharief's voice, the more infuriated she became. "Monica!" she screamed. "Did you tell that niggah it's on?"

"Why are you talking to me like this? You're my mother."

"I know who I am. And you are my child but right now you are my wrong child. And this is unacceptable! Now, if I don't say something to you, especially how you showed yo' ass in the police station, then that means I'll stand for any damn thing. And the next thing I know you're comin' after my man. So before it gets that far, we gon' nip this in the bud right now!"

"Listen, Ma, I'm not going through this. I love him."

"Oh hell no!" Starr screamed. "So what are you saying? Fuck me? I just told you to do something and you're not going to do it? Are you choosin' this niggah over me too? Is the dick that damn hypnotic? You done lost yo' damn mind. You know what, maybe I better get on board with Red and this religious thing he trying to get started. I need to remember that my daddy was a deacon, 'cause I swear to God you gon' make me lose so much of my religion that I'ma have to be baptized again. So you know what, Mama Byrd go put your porta-potty back, I'm not going over there because if I do, I'ma going to jail for murder. But don't be confused, me not coming to kick yo' ass is no punk move. It's just that God is still working on me and I need to pray for you, 'cause if I don't you'll be buried tomorrow." And Starr hung up.

Monica took the phone away from her ear and looked at the receiver. She had expected her mother to go off, but never in a million years did she think Starr would lose it to that degree. Now she questioned how she could mend things with Starr and keep Sharief at the same time.

Monica placed the phone back on the base, turned over in bed, and lay her head in the center of Sharief's chest.

[Imani]

FOR THE PAST month Kree and Imani had been inseparable. It was something about Kree that Imani couldn't let go of. The more he was around, the less she thought about Walik. The less she held her breath wondering if he would be coming to see her or wondering if he wanted to see her. Kree was different. He made no bones about how he felt and caused no confusion with her heart. For once Imani could close her eyes and not think about her man fucking somebody else.

And Kree didn't just love Imani, he loved Jamal. He would take him shopping, play video games with him, and just kick it with him like only a male child and a man could. And somehow the more time Kree spent with Jamal, the more Imani loved him and had the feeling as if she finally had her own family . . . so she tried her best to avoid anything that reminded her or forced her to face how she still loved Walik.

"Now, Imani." Kree turned over in bed, watching Imani's Beyoncé ass bounce as she locked her bedroom door. He stroked his hard dick a little then watched her hard and dark violet nipples as she turned around, walked toward him, and slid into bed. He turned to face her. "Tell me that shit again."

"What?" Imani asked, surprised.

"Walik was what now?"

"Broke," she said matter-of-factly.

"What was he pushing? Weed?"

"One leaf at a time."

Kree fell out laughing. His hair was wild and loose. Imani ran her fingers through it. "I thought you said he was doing his thing?"

"He was doing his thing, but somehow, his ass was always broke. Every time he tried switching and pushed diesel somebody got locked up. After a while I was like, *Fuck it, give it up and be a weed man.* Truth be told, I was the one paying all the bills. Sometimes I was even the one buying the supply, and believe me, my shit was limited . . . humph, still is, really. Anyway, Walik ain't never been no grand hustler in the street. I use to soup him up and tell him that. But shit, on the real he would've been better off pushing Benadryl."

"I should've known that niggah was broke." Kree laughed. "A broke drug dealer is worse than a crooked cop."

"Why?"

" 'Cause he'll snitch first." Kree stared at Imani. "You know, Mami," he said with an enhanced Puerto Rican accent, "I want you to speak Spanish."

"Yeah right."

"I do." He pulled her on top of him. "Say this." He caressed her nipples. "Uhmm . . ." Kree said seductively. *"El papá que quiero joder."*

"El papá? What you got me calling you, Daddy?"

"Just say it."

"All right. *El papá que qui-qui-quie-ro."* Imani chuckled as she stumbled over her words. *"Joder."*

"Uhmm, Mami, I wanna screw you too."

"You're soooo nasty."

"Hearing you speak Spanish"—Kree stroked the side of her face—"turns me on. I'ma tell you what to say and then I'ma show you what it means by doing it to you."

"Ai'ight."

"Bésame." He licked his lips.

"Bésame."

Kree pulled Imani close to him and started kissing her long and hard, running his hands up and down the small of her back. He turned her over and lay on top of her. *"Uhmm, Papi,"* he said, *"quiero tú tomar mis seno y chupar mis pezones agradable, y lento."*

"What's with all this *papi* and *papá*? What, you got a fetish?" Imani laughed.

"Imani," Kree said, fighting back his own laughter. "Say it, boo."

"Kree, I can't say all of that."

"Tell me what you like for me to do to your breasts and then you'll know what I said."

"I love the way you suck them."

Kree took her breasts and sucked them both simultaneously, softly biting them as if he were eating cotton candy. Then he took his finger and started playing in her pussy.

Imani started to moan, "Kree—"

"Sí."

"How do I say, I want you to eat me?"

"Uhmm . . ." Kree took his finger from her pussy and licked it. Opening her legs and kissing her pussy, he said, *"Kree, quiero tú comer mi coño."*

Imani struggled to say it as Kree started sucking her clit. *"Kree, que-que qui . . ."*

"Sí, Mami," he said, sticking his tongue in her cum. "No worries, I got you."

"Imani! EEEmaaannnniiiiii!" Jamal yelled, banging on the door. "You finish rappin' 'cause Aunty Monica on the phone."

"Shut up, Jamal! I told Sabrena to call me before she sent you downstairs," Imani yelled from behind her bedroom door while throwing her housecoat on. "And for your information, I wasn't rappin'!" She opened the door and Kree pulled the covers over his head until she closed it. He didn't want Jamal to see him lying in Imani's bed.

Jamal looked confused. "You wasn't rappin', Imani? But with all that screaming you were doin', you sound just like Ludacris. I was thinking," he placed his hand under his chin, "my Imani could do a remix with the Jam On Its."

"Go to bed, Jamal." Imani looked at the clock. Eight PM. *Kree needs to get up. He has to be in the studio in an hour.*

Jamal handed her the cordless phone. "Excuse me," he said, "but don't be too long."

"Why not?"

" 'Cause Kree is supposed to call and tell me when to get ready. I'm going to the radio station tonight. I'ma be makin' shouts."

"It's *shoutouts* and who told you that?" Imani looked confused. "Monica," she placed the phone to her ear, "let me call you back." And she hung up.

"Kree told me that," Jamal said.

"When?"

"When he took me school shopping and to the arcade. He said that he would take me to the studio before I went back to school."

"Oh, for real?"

"Uhmm-hmm. That's wassup."

Imani shot Jamal a high five. "Yup, that wassup."

Imani pushed her bedroom door open slowly. Jamal spotted Kree slipping on his boxing shorts and pushed the door completely open, almost catching Kree with his dick swinging. Kree looked at Jamal with eyes filled with shock and embarrassment. "Imani, Kree," Jamal called, "was y'all gettin' a li'l freak on?"

"I'll slap you in the mouth!" Imani said.

Jamal ignored her. He placed his hands behind his head and

started moving his body like a hula dancer while rapping "The Whisper Song" by the Ying Yang Twins: *"Girl wait to see my/ohh-hhhh . . ."*

Kree walked over to Jamal. "Yo!" he said sternly, "stop it! Now, I'ma tell you this while your mother's standing right here." He shook his head. "Look, man, I wish you hadn't seen me in here like this, but let me make this clear to you. Don't you ever in your life disrespect your mother—or me for that matter—again. You are a little boy and you stay in a little boy's place. All that you did and said about getting a freak on, I didn't like it. And that song you were singing, do you know how disrespectful it is to women?"

"No. I just heard it on the radio and saw the video. So don't blame me, blame BET." Jamal held his head down. "Now I wanna rap 'Watch Me Roll.' "

Kree scooted down next to Jamal. "This is the agreement. When your mommy's door is closed, you knock. Can we agree on that?"

"Yeah." Jamal smiled.

"Now give me a high five." Jamal started to give Kree a high five and Kree moved his hand. "Too slow!" he laughed, pointing at Jamal.

"Dag." Jamal snapped his fingers. "Imani, I always fall for that."

"Stop calling your mother Imani too, man," Kree said. "Now go and get ready for the studio."

"Oh I can't wait!" Jamal said, excited. "I'ma wear my Spider-Man T-shirt, my Hawaiian shorts, and my light-up SpongeBob flip-flops."

"Oh hell no." Kree looked at Imani and mouthed, *He ain't wearin' no shit like that.* "Jamal," Kree yelled as Jamal turned to close the door, "check it. I want us to dress alike. Why don't you grab your Negro League throwback I bought you, those long Ro-cawear shorts we got the other day, and ya Tims."

"Oh, we thuggin' it?" Jamal asked.

"All day long, man. All day long."

As Jamal closed the door and Imani locked it, Kree smiled.

"You know that was my jam he was rappin', but still and all baby, I had to make a point."

"It was a good point." Imani smiled back, taking her housecoat off and walking over to Kree, who was now sitting on the bed. "Shut up and lie down," she demanded.

"Awwll shit . . . now you wanna get freaky—knowing I gotta leave."

"I know, just let me do something I haven't done for you." She pulled Kree's boxers all the way down and showed him her mean head game. When she was done she smiled. "Now you get up."

"Oh you tryna trap my ass," Kree said, laughing. "Keep giving me head like that and I'ma marry you."

"Get outta here!" she laughed.

Kree went in the bathroom for a quick shower and Imani went into Jamal's room to check on him. Jamal was completely dressed. He looked so cute with his throwback jersey—although it clung to his chubby stomach—and his long and slightly baggy denim shorts, and his beige Tims. His hair was freshly braided, which was a new thing that he and Kree had started doing together. "Look at my man," Imani said, kissing him on the cheek.

"Well, what can I say?" Jamal said, flicking his nose.

"Jamal!" Kree called from the living room. "Let's be out."

"Imani," Jamal said, excited, "make sure you call everybody and have them listen to me on the radio. I'ma make shouts."

"It's *shoutouts,* Jamal."

"Yeah that too."

"Okay, boo-boo," Imani laughed. "I love you."

"Ai'ight, baby," Kree said to Imani, giving her a peck on the lips and a sly pat on the ass. "Later."

· ■ ·

IMANI RAN INTO the bathroom and took a quick shower. Afterward she slipped on a pair of jeans and one of Kree's wife beaters. *Damn, my mother was right,* she thought, *the replacement for one man is always another.* Imani had done well with pushing Walik out of her mind. Besides, thinking of Walik was too much to handle, too much history to consider, too many broken promises, dead dreams, and unfulfilled fantasies.

For a moment she thought about calling him and asking him if he remembered that Jamal was his son. But as quickly as she thought about it, she changed her mind. The last thing she needed was Shante on her phone again, giving Imani her ass to kiss. *Fuck both of 'em. They deserve each other.*

As Imani went to pick up the phone to call Sabrena downstairs and invite Tasha and Quiana over, her phone rang. "Hello?"

"You know what, bitch!" Shante spat, "you think you slick but I saw you and Walik riding down the street in your new green Honda. But best believe I'ma blow that ma'fucker up! I ain't goin' nowhere, bitch, so why do you continue to hang around?"

Imani couldn't help but laugh. "You dumb bitch! I haven't seen that fat ma'fucker and apparently you either! Good for yo' ass!" She hung up.

Imani clicked over and called her girls on the three-way.

"Ain't she stupid, y'all?" Imani laughed.

"Dumb bitch!" Sabrena said. "I betchu she feels good and stupid!"

"She needs to," Quiana agreed.

"Oh," Imani said, "before I forget, y'all turn on the radio. Kree took Jamal to the studio with him and my baby gon' be making shoutouts."

They each cut their radios on. "Wassup Tri-State?" Kree said on the radio. "I got my li'l man right here . . . say wassup, Jamal."

"Wassup y'all. West Side! I'm in the place to be with my main man Kree." Jamal laughed. "How I do?" he said before moving away from the mike.

"You did ai'ight, man," Kree laughed. "Ai'ight, now let's make it happen New York, New Jersey, and Connecticut . . . to all my

Latina, Black, and Blanco *boniquas* I wanna get-get-get it pop-pin' . . ."—which led directly into Fat Joe's new song.

"That's my baby!" Imani said, excited, to Sabrena, Quiana, and Tasha. "Both of 'em! Did you hear them!"

"We heard 'em," they all said.

"Oh I know y'all ain't hatin'?"

By the time Kree's show was getting ready to end, the girls were still on the phone laughing at Shante.

"Ai'ight, Tri-State," Kree said on the radio.

"Be quiet y'all," Imani said, "here comes my baby."

"My li'l man got some shoutouts that he wanna make." Kree pointed to the mike. "It's all you, baby," he said to Jamal. Kree looked at the engineer. "Just give him thirty seconds and then play the outro music. I gotta pee bad as hell." Kree ran out the room and Jamal stepped to the mike.

"Allow me to reintroduce myself. My name is Jamal Lewis and I wanna make some shoutouts to some people that my Imani is always talkin' about. To fat-ass Bookman aka 'Bubble Butt' in maintenance for not telling the old lady next door that we set off roach bombs every other week, which is why the roaches keep moving into her apartment. Another shout goes out to Mae Smith at Section Eight, for puttin' us at the top of the list and helpin' me and my Imani make moves. And I wanna make a shoutout to our welfare caseworker, Ms. Phyllis Whitaker, for not reportin' us or cuttin' off our food stamps when Imani said she wasn't beat and refused to go to the Work First program."

When Kree walked back in the studio, everybody's mouths were dropped open. Kree looked at Jamal. "What you say, man? What you say?"

[Imani]

"WHO THE HELL is that banging on the door this time of the morning?" Kree wiped the side of his mouth and nudged Imani.

"I don't know—go back to sleep," Imani said.

Kree and Imani both closed their eyes, but the banging continued. Imani threw the covers off. "Let me go see who this is."

"You do that," Kree said smiling, " 'cause I'm going back to sleep."

Imani playfully mushed Kree in the head. "Punk. It could be somebody tryna kill me."

"Yeah right." He twisted his lips. "It ain't nobody but one of your friends wantin' to bust a niggah's ass, talk trash, or make sure she can hang out all day. Which just reminded me, that I've been wanting to talk to you about that."

"About what? My friends? We've been friends since high school."

"I don't care about you having friends, you just need to do something besides hang out with them all day—every day."

Imani was starting to get pissed. "Let me go answer the door."

"Yeah, you do that."

Imani grabbed her robe and closed the bedroom door behind her. "Who is it?" she asked, looking through the peephole. Once she got a clear view she snatched the door open. "What the fuck you want, Walik?" She tried her best not to make eye contact with him, because seeing how good he looked always made her pussy tingle. *Damn,* she thought. *I hate I'm still feeling this niggah.* "What is it?"

"I came to get my son."

"Niggah, please, it's seven o'clock in the morning. And he hasn't seen your ass all summer, so step."

"I'm taking him to breakfast first and then I'ma come back and see you."

"You can't come see me."

"Why?"

"Go see Shante. And let that bitch know if she calls my house again, I'ma stab her in the mouth."

"Shante? We ain't together no more."

"Oh, boo-hoo-hoo. I'm so upset."

"Yo." Walik smiled. "Why you always giving me a hard time, knowing I'm trying to apologize."

"You? Apologize? Niggah, please."

He grabbed her by the waist. "I miss you."

"Fuck you."

"I want to," he looked her up and down, still holding on to her waist, "I swear I do."

"Look, I'm not feeling you. You cussed me out like I wasn't shit, treated me any kind of way, had two babies on me. And word is, you really married to that bitch. So naw, I can't get over that."

"Imani, you gotta forgive me. Listen, baby, if I didn't cheat on you would you take me back?"

"Maybe." She brushed his hands off her waist. "But you'll never know." And she slammed the door in his face. As she turned around, Kree was staring at her.

"That was your broke weed pusher, huh?" he asked sarcastically.

"Kree, please, don't start and why are you on me today?" Imani rolled her eyes.

"On you? I'm lying in the next fuckin' room and you tellin' this niggah maybe if he didn't cheat on you, you would be with him."

"What did you expect me to say? I don't know what the future holds."

"Oh get the fuck outta here, you need to tell that niggah, *I got a man. And you could hit the hustler's lotto, niggah, and I still wouldn't want you.*"

"Oh, so that's what this is about?" Imani walked past Kree and into the kitchen. "This is about me not mentioning you. Look, that's Jamal's father, and I'm not going to disrespect him."

Kree followed behind Imani. "Disrespect him? He cussed yo' ass out like a dog and you're worried about you disrespecting him?"

"Look." She turned to face him. "You knew what the fuck you were getting into. Jamal is only six and I have to deal with Walik for twelve more years so get used to it. I was with him for ten years. My son deserves a father."

"A father? Where was his father when I was taking him to get his hair braided?"

"What?" Imani snapped. "You want your twenty dollars back?"

Kree stood speechless for a moment. He looked at Imani and said, "You know what, ma, I'm too much of a man for you. You still a weed-smokin', trash-talkin', corner-store li'l broad—destined to be an around-da-way jump-off, and I am so not beat. Take your broke-ass hustler and live happily fuckin' after, 'cause me and you—we're over!" Kree went into Imani's bedroom, slipped on the rest of his clothes, put on his boots, and grabbed his car keys. "I'm out."

"Where are you going?" She tried to block his path.

He picked her up by the waist and moved her out of his way. "Stay the fuck out my face!"

{ Celeste }

"WHAT I DON'T understand," Celeste expressed to the TV while watching Sanaa Lathan play Zora in the movie *Disappearing Acts,* "is what the fuck will break this niggah? I had him arrested, thinking that maybe just maybe he would look at her with disgust and despise her because of what he had to go through . . . then I thought that if I could punish him enough, he would regret the day he cheated on me. Well, I'll tell you, Zora," Celeste tapped on the TV, "the shit didn't work. He walked out the police station arm in arm with that bitch, and they looked at me as if to say, *Now do something!* And you know what? I stood there like a damn fool telling all of her business, and guess what, the niggah still didn't do shit . . . not a fuckin' thing."

Celeste flicked her cigarette. "But ooooohhh noooooo, this niggah thought that I was crazy and stupid. I got his ass, though. Wrote myself a fuckin' check and cashed it courtesy of his bank account."

Celeste picked up the phone and called Starr. "Ma, I'm dropping the kids off with Monica."

"What?" Starr looked at the clock and saw that it was eight AM. "The kids should be sleep and you too."

"Sleep? Sleep? My husband just left me for my sister and you tell me to go to sleep? Fuck sleep."

"Watch your mouth."

"No, I'm tired of watching my mouth. It's always about somebody else and what they think, and never about Celeste. Well, I'm tired of that."

"You're tired of that? You created that, Ms. Thing. When you married that no-good high-yellow niggah I asked were you sure and you swore by him. When I used to tell you to go out with your friends and have a good time, enjoy their company, get you a spare tire."

"A spare tire?"

"Yes, a spare tire," Starr snapped, "I told you that the secret to a good marriage is a side niggah."

"I can't believe that you said that to me!" Celeste screamed. "Other people in my marriage is what has me in this situation—"

"No, honey, you were a part of it too. Now, I feel bad, because the other woman is your sister, also my child. But there are times, Celeste, that when a man cheats on a woman that the woman has to wear some of the responsibility. No man wants you underneath his arm all the time. When I told you to get a job, you told me that you wanted to stay home. When I asked you how did Sharief feel about that, you told me it didn't matter. When the man told you that he felt like you were gaining too much weight, all you did was eat more. If the man wasn't happy in bed then you shoulda talked to him and found out what he likes and perfected it. You married him and he married you. Now look at you two. You got three kids and a damn circus act! And I'm sick of it! So if you wanna drop your kids off with Monica then goddammit, do what you got to do!" Starr began to cry. " 'Cause quite frankly I don't give a damn. Ever since Jimmy died Red feels as if it's his calling to turn the Jam On Its into a gospel group and that's what

I need to focus on, not this devilish mess! Now, I love you, Celeste, and I love Monica too, but I will not get in between y'all! And I will not hear of you leaving or watch you wallow in pity one more minute."

"Well look, don't worry about me. I just need to get myself together." Celeste took a drag. "I love you."

"Celeste, you need to stay here and deal with this."

"No, I know what I have to do. I love you and I'll call you."

　　　　　·　•　·

THE KIDS WERE half asleep when Celeste made them get in the car. By the time they arrived in Brooklyn, they were exhausted. As they walked onto Monica's stoop, Celeste lit a cigarette and rang the doorbell. She was dressed in a loose-fitting yellow sundress with spaghetti straps, a scarf wrapped around her head, and marble Jackie O sunglasses. She had a big straw bag on her shoulder and a cigarette hanging from the corner of her mouth. Celeste rang the bell again.

Who is this, Monica thought. She cracked the door halfway open, thinking it was Imani doing a Jamal drive-by.

"What?" Monica snapped. Once she realized it was Celeste she instantly became defensive, determined that pregnant or not she would kick Celeste's crazy ass if need be.

"Look." Celeste slid her glasses down the bridge of her nose. "Since you wanted this niggah so bad, I decided that you needed to know that there's more to him than a big dick and a fierce tongue. He's a package deal and I'm not talking about his scrotum. He also has three kids." She tapped each of them on the head. "One . . . two . . . three . . . and they need to get to know their new stepmother. Don't thank me now, thank me later. You wanted my life, so here you go." Celeste took a drag off her cigarette and blew the smoke in the air. She pointed to the three suitcases on the porch. "There are some school clothes, school transcripts, and a bag of sanitary napkins because Kayla just started her period. You will need to buy school supplies, the Wal-Mart by my house is not open twenty-four hours."

"Are you fuckin' for real?" Monica asked.

"I'm as real as it gets. And now Monica *Lewinsky,* you've got Bill and a couple of Chelseas too." She tapped Monica on the stomach. "Be sure to avoid stress. I'm so praying you have a boy."

Monica couldn't believe it.

"Now, kids, give Mommy a kiss." The girls kissed Celeste on each cheek. "You'll be staying with Aunty Monica and Daddy for a while."

"Yippeeeee!" Kai yelled. "Pizza every night!"

"And we can play with Jamal more!" Kori said.

"Whatever," Kayla said. "I just need to use the phone."

"I'ma miss you," Celeste said, stepping off the stoop.

"We gon' miss you too, Mommy!" the girls yelled, walking into Monica's house. "Have fun!"

(Imani)

"CELESTE DID WHAT, Monica?" Imani was trying to understand what Monica was saying through her tears. At the beginning of the conversation Imani really didn't give a damn. She was more concerned with missing Kree than the bullshit Monica was crying about.

Monica went on, "And the baby is Sharief's. And I cussed everybody out . . ."

"Wait a minute, what you say? Start from the beginning." Imani's eyes darted toward Jamal, who'd been sitting at the window and watching outside for over an hour.

"Are you listening to me?" Monica demanded.

"Yeah, but what is all that damn noise in your house?" Imani asked.

"It's these kids!" Monica screamed.

"Oh, you tryin' to be funny again and not invite my son over?"

"You don't understand, Celeste brought these kids over here to live."

"To live? What the hell is wrong with her? You keepin' kids now? You a foster parent or something?"

"No, I'm no damn foster parent!"

"Well then, how long have they been there?"

"Two weeks!"

"What? What the hell? Where's Sharief?"

"Here!" Monica snapped.

"Don't get nasty with me. I'm trying to understand. And why is Sharief living with you?"

"Look," Monica stressed. "Sharief and I had an affair, we fell in love, I'm pregnant, and we're together."

"What kinda nasty-ass shit is that?" Imani couldn't believe it. "You fucked Sharief? Your brother-in-law? Your sister's husband? Have you lost your damn mind? You know Celeste should bust yo' ass."

"Oh my God, have you heard a word that I've said? It wasn't meant to happen."

"Damn, Monica." Imani was disappointed, "I know we've never really liked Celeste that much, but that is our sister. How am I supposed to defend you and you wrong as two left shoes? You couldn't just fuck the niggah and bury the shit in the closet? Did you have to make him your man? Mommy is gon' flip."

"She already has."

"What?" Imani leaned back on the couch and propped her feet up. Jamal was still looking out the window.

"We had a big falling-out at the police station. And she called and cussed me out over the phone," Monica said. "Celeste pressed charges against Sharief for assault. They had a court date today, but she didn't show up. Nobody knows where she is."

"Assault? Did he?"

"No—the bitch is buggin'."

"Well, she has a right to be. I know damn well I couldn't leave you around Walik now."

"Walik?" Monica was insulted. "I don't want that fat-ass deadbeat ma'fucker, please."

"Speaking of deadbeat, he's supposed to be coming over here

today. He promised Jamal that he was going to take him to the movies."

"Oh, here we go with his promises again."

"Excuse me, Ms. Aunty's having a baby by Daddy."

"Damn, you sound like Listra."

"Well, what do you expect? Being pregnant by your brother-in-law is not exactly something to brag about. Shit, if you wanted a bitch's man, you shoulda picked another bitch, not your sister. I love you, Monica, but niggahs get killed for less than that."

"Look, I'm not asking for you to understand. I just want you to be my sister."

"I'm your sister regardless, but wrong is wrong."

"Look, this is my life."

"Yeah, you sure right, so don't be mad when you get what your hand calls for."

"I gotta go, Imani," Monica snapped.

"Yeah, I'm sure you do."

Imani hung up and looked at Jamal. "Jamal, what are you doing and why have you been sitting at that window all day?"

"Is Walik coming? He said he was coming this morning."

"Well, Jamal, it's going on eight o'clock. I don't think so."

"Can I call Kree?"

"Kree?" Imani couldn't believe it. She hadn't mentioned Kree since they'd broken up two weeks ago.

"Yeah, Kree. I wanna talk to him. I miss him," Jamal said.

"No, you can't call him. And you may as well get him off your mind because he's not coming over here no more! I broke up with him."

Instantly Jamal started to cry. "Why you do that? Why did you break him?"

"I didn't break him. I just don't date him anymore. He's not my boyfriend, so you won't be seeing him again. So stop crying over his ass. You have a father." Imani picked up the phone and called Walik's cell but didn't get an answer.

"Imani," Jamal whined, "can you call Kree please?" He started biting his bottom lip and rocking back and forth.

"What did I just tell you!" The more Jamal asked her to call Kree, the more aggravated Imani became.

"Please!"

"No!"

"Why, did he say he didn't like me anymore because of the shouts I made on the radio?"

"He never said he didn't like you, Jamal."

"Did he say he didn't like me because I couldn't speak Spanish? I can speak it now, listen." He spoke slowly. "Geraldo . . . Rivera."

"Boy, shut up and go play a video game." Imani was trying desperately to fight off her memory of speaking Spanish.

"Can you call him please," Jamal continued to beg. "I've been saving my candy, I got it from the Puerto Rican store, see, Chico Sticks."

"Boy!" Imani yelled, "if you don't leave me alone—"

"Why would you do that, Imani?"

"Do what?"

"Break Kree."

"I didn't break Kree and why you in my business?"

"I love Kree."

"You have a father."

"I don't like Walik! You're the one who likes Walik, not me!" Jamal yelled. "Call Kree, Imani, please. I just wanna say good-bye."

Imani got off the couch and walked into her bedroom. She was sick of Jamal. He followed behind her. "Please . . ."

"I'ma smack the shit outta you!"

"I can't believe this!" Jamal started to cry and stomp. "I loved Kree, he was my daddy. He said I was his boy and that we could do some things! How could he just leave me!"

"Jamal, you have your Pa-pa Red."

"Red makes me sick!" Jamal kicked over the chair in Imani's room. "I've been waiting by this stupid window"—he pounded his fist—"saving this stupid candy"—he emptied his pockets and crushed his candy with his feet—"and all this time he wasn't coming back! I'm mad, Imani!" His tears started flying everywhere. "I'm so mad! Kree was my dad and he just left me."

Imani couldn't believe it. What the hell was she supposed to say? "Jamal . . . I-I didn't think you cared whether he said goodbye or not. I thought you would just get over it. I mean, you got me, and all I had was my mother."

"Is that what your daddy did, Imani, he just left you?" Jamal asked.

"Yeah, Jamal." Imani wiped her eyes. "I guess he did."

[Monica]

"**I**'M GETTING READY to leave for work, baby," Sharief said to Monica, kissing her on the forehead. "What time are you leaving?"

"In a minute. I'ma get up now." She stretched. "Have the kids left for school?"

"Yeah, I saw them off a little while ago. All right, I have to work a little late today. So I'll call you." He kissed her again and left. As Monica heard the front door close, she turned over in bed and called out sick. She'd plan to call out since last night, she just didn't want Sharief to know she'd be home. Lately money had been extremely tight, and she didn't want to hear him complaining.

First I'm going food shopping, Monica thought, *and then I'ma come home and sit my fat ass on the couch and watch the soaps all day.* She dressed and headed for downtown Brooklyn. She went to Key Food first and brought three bags of snacks. She couldn't wait to get home. All she could think of was a day alone. For a moment she thought about Sharief, so she called the station to see if he wanted something to eat for later.

"Detective Winston, please."

"Detective Winston is not here."

"Will he be back . . . this is his-his-his fiancée." Monica figured that *fiancée* had a better ring to it than *girlfriend*.

"Ma'am, you need to speak with the detective about that. I have no idea when he'll be back."

Monica could tell the officer was getting agitated. "Just one more thing. Can you please tell me the last time he was at work?"

"Almost a month ago, ma'am. Now I really need to go."

Monica stood still for a moment. Trying to think of what was going on in her life a month ago. She couldn't put her finger on it . . . for some reason she felt like she'd been fat, broke, and pregnant forever.

Monica jumped in the car and drove home. She tried her best not to think much because she knew it would only make her head pound. She opened her front door with grocery bags in her arms and there was Sharief, lying on the couch. His feet were stretched over the arm with a beer in his hand and two empty bottles on the floor. He gave Monica a crooked smile as she stood in front of him. She placed her hand on the side of her protruding stomach. "What the hell are you doing here? I thought you were at work."

"Naw," he said.

Monica could tell he was half drunk. She ran her hands over her eight-month belly. "Why not?"

"I decided to take the day off so I came back home."

"And how many days have you been leaving and coming back home?"

"What is that supposed to mean?" He took a sip of his beer.

"I called the station and they told me you hadn't been to work in a month, so why are you lying?"

" 'Cause I knew this is how you would act."

"Don't put the shit off on me!" she screamed.

"See." He sat up. "Look at you. Do you know how hard it is for a black man—"

"Save that bullshit! Why aren't you at work and where have you been?"

"I been coming home every day. You know Celeste pressed charges on me."

"That was months ago. You told me that she hasn't been in court. And you said that the same lawyer I spent all my money on promised the case would be thrown out."

"Well, when you're black man in the police force—"

"I don't wanna hear no shit about you being black, save that. What the hell is going on that you aren't working? We need money, Sharief. I'm a nurse and I only make so much money— not enough to support five people. Now, you better talk and talk quick because I can't take it and I need to know something!"

"My captain suspended me."

"Suspended you?" Monica was stunned. "What happened to desk duty?"

"My captain didn't find me fit, so he suspended me."

"But you said that since he called in a favor for you, he wouldn't suspend you."

"Well he did."

"Why?"

"Because he did!" Sharief snapped. "Shit!"

"But you said desk duty," Monica pressed.

"Look, I was already on desk duty."

"Why?"

"A few months ago I was making an arrest and accidentally shot the guy."

"So what, you're a cop, y'all are always accidentally shooting somebody."

"They accused me of being drunk when I did it. But I wasn't. Come on, baby, I don't even drink like that. So when I went to re-port to work a month ago, my captain announced that I had to leave, that administration made a decision to suspend me without pay, pending Celeste's charges."

Monica looked around her house, her eyes darting from one

piece of furniture to the next. "I'm having a baby, Sharief. I can't take care of you, my baby, and three other children."

"Oh, a niggah down on his luck and now he and his kids gotta step?"

"I never said that. I just said that I can't do it all."

"Look." Sharief walked up to Monica and placed his hand on her stomach. "It's gon' be all right, baby. Just trust me."

"I'm trying to." Monica's eyes welled up with tears. "I really am trying to."

{ Imani }

"I'MA BEAT YOUR ass, Jamal!" was the routine statement that Imani had been screaming at her son all week. "What the fuck is wrong with you?" All week long Jamal had been in everything. From fighting the kids down the street to breaking things around the house. And Walik making promises every day and never keeping them was making the situation even worse.

As Imani looked out the window she heard a knock on the door. She walked over and looked out the peephole. It was Walik. "What?" she said, snatching the door open.

"Wassup?" Walik stepped inside. "I came by to see my son."

Imani looked at her watch. "It's ten o'clock in the morning on a Thursday. He's in school."

"Oh," Walik said, sitting down on the couch. "I'll wait for him."

"That wasn't an invitation for you to come in," she said sarcastically.

"Whatever, yo." Walik looked around the room. "So wassup? You can't never call a niggah?"

"You keep waitin' for that phone call." Imani rolled her eyes. "Anyway, when Jamal comes home from school maybe you can talk to him about the way he's been acting."

"Yo, he don't listen to me. His ass is spoiled."

"Why don't you take him out so y'all can get your hair braided together. He gets out of school at three. You can walk down and pick him up."

"What? Yo, I don't do that. When I get my hair braided that's my time."

"What about his time?"

"I spend time with my son."

"When?"

"When I spend time, shit. I'm here now."

"But why are you here? He's in school. You ain't come here to see him, you came here to beg for some pussy, which you ain't gettin'. You know what, just step."

"What, bitch?"

Imani rubbed the temples of her forehead. "I tell you what." She looked at Walik. "Be gone."

"You putting me out?" Walik couldn't believe it. "Ai'ight, it's good, I can check Shante anyway."

"Okay," Imani said, holding the front door open. "You do that."

As soon as she slammed the door behind him her phone rang. "Hello?"

"Ms. Imani Reid, please."

"Yes."

"Ms. Reid, this is Ms. Wilkerson. Jamal's teacher."

"Is everything okay?" Imani started to panic.

"Well, no. I really need to see you. Jamal's being suspended from school for fighting. And for the past two weeks, he's been disrupting the entire class."

      ·   ●   ·

I'MA BUST THIS *li'l niggah's ass!* were Imani's thoughts on her way to pick up Jamal. *When the hell did he become a terror at school? A class clown, yeah. But a terror? Hell no.*

"Ms. Reid," Jamal's teacher said. "Lately Jamal's been out of control."

Imani did her best to control her anger and embarrassment.

"While Jamal is a good child," the teacher continued, "he seems to be having trouble with listening, which seems to affect his behavior. Is there anything going on at home?"

I wanna fight this bitch, Imani thought, *I really do.* "Excuse me?"

The teacher went on, "He's not doing well with following directions and the fighting must stop. We will not tolerate that here. Please talk to him. He can come back in two days."

· • ·

"GO TO YOUR room, Jamal!" Imani screamed at him as soon as they got home. "Go to your damn room!" Imani picked up the phone and called Monica on her cell phone. "Monica."

"Yes, Imani. I just got off work," Monica said, sounding annoyed.

Imani started crying. "I don't know what to do with Jamal. Every day it's something different with him. Today he got suspended from school."

"What? Why?"

"For fighting."

"My nephew Jamal?" Monica couldn't believe it. "Are you sure?"

"Oh, Monica, please, I just went and picked him up."

"What about your new boyfriend, Kree? You said that Jamal loves him. Maybe you should have him talk to Jamal and see what's going on."

"I wish I could," Imani snapped. "I don't go with him anymore."

"I thought Jamal really liked him."

"So what? Jamal'll like the next man."

"Well, just how many men do you plan on introducing him to? What the hell is wrong with you? You don't just up and introduce your son to man after man and think that he should just deal with it when you break up. Stop it and stop it right now. You know what we went through. I will not have my nephew going through that shit. It's hard enough not having his real father; don't take every man that he loves and trusts away. Get your shit together, Imani. I have enough problems of my own, believe me."

"Humph, speaking of your problems, how's Raven Symone and the Olsen twins?"

"Getting on my fuckin' nerves. I can't stand it. My house is never clean. All they do is argue and fight. All I hear all night is, *Leave me alone, don't copy me. I'm telling, and get outta my room.*"

"Whose room?"

"Nobody's room, how about that's my fuckin' office and your room is in New Jersey. I'm sick of 'em!"

"Well, what I wanna know is why do you sound like a single parent? Hell, you got ole boy there, shit. You snuck Celeste for his ass, make good use of 'im."

"I don't even want to discuss that."

"Me either, because every time I think about it, I get pissed off."

"I have to go."

"I'm sure you do. Bye." Imani held the phone in her hand. She looked toward Jamal's room and shook her head. *Fuck it,* she thought, *what's the worst that can happen?* Imani dialed Kree's number and a soft female voice with a Puerto Rican accent answered on the first ring.

Oh hell no, Imani thought as her throat filled with an iron fist. Instantly her stomach started doing back flips and she felt sick. Imani thought about hanging up but she couldn't bring herself to do it, so instead she bit her bottom lip, took a deep breath, and said, "Why the fuck is you answering Kree's phone?!"

"Who is this?!" the soft Puerto Rican voice suddenly became harsh.

"Why bitch? This ain't yo' phone! Now put Kree on the line!"

"Quién es ése?" Imani could hear Kree speaking Spanish in the background.

"Kree," the girl shouted in Spanish, *"no sé quien es, pero ella quemará si yo cojo esta perra . . ."*

"Oh hold it," Imani snarled, "you talkin' a whole lotta ying-yang trick." Imani was pissed that she didn't understand what the girl had said about her. "If you so bad, why don't you speak English, fuckin' lifeboat refugee! Go win a green card lottery or some shit. Translate *that*, bitch! Dumb-ass plaintain banana speakin' ho!"

"Oh you done lost every bit of your little-ass mind?!" Kree laughed in disbelief. "You loco, *Mami*?"

"Oh you just screwin' anything movin', huh?"

"Why? You jealous 'cause she don't need no help speaking Spanish?" Kree said sarcastically, as he moved his mouth from the receiver and began speaking Spanish and laughing with the girl in the background.

"Kree!" Imani screamed. "I know you not talking about me!"

"What, *no hablo Español?*"

"You know what, fuck you, Kree!"

"Ai'ight peace." Kree hung up.

Immediately Imani started to cry. After a few moments of feeling sorry for herself, the phone rang. "Yeah," she sniffed.

"Yeah, look, whatever man," Kree said defensively. "Wassup, what is it, and get to the point. I got shit to do. I brought some new sneakers and I need to lace 'em, so don't keep me on the line with you breathing in my ear and shit too long, 'cause in a few minutes I'ma hang up on you."

"Kree—"

"And skip all the hood-rat dramatics too, ma, get to the point."

"What the fuck is wrong with you?" Imani asked, taken aback, "Your dick grew or some shit?"

"You got five seconds and you've already used up two."

"You know what?" Imani took a deep breath. "Look, this is not about me, this is about my son."

"Wassup with my li'l man?" Kree asked seriously. "He ai'ight?"

"No. He's been crying for you. He's acting up in school and all kinds of shit and he got suspended today."

"Where's his father—the one that's going to be around for twelve more years?"

"Look, he keeps making him promises that he never keeps. Jamal loves you—he don't give a fuck about Walik—but you . . . he needs you."

"You know I'll do anything for Jamal. He has nothing to do with this bullshit."

"Well . . . can you come see him? Please, he needs you." Imani took a deep breath. "I know you're not his father. I know that. And if you don't want to be bothered, I understand. But I'm asking you, please, to come and see my son." Her throat welled up with tears and she started to cry uncontrollably. "I feel helpless, like I'm a horrible mother who can't control her son."

"I wouldn't say all that."

"Kree, all Jamal's life I've been running the streets, smoking weed, hanging out, and treating my son like he's a grown-ass man and not a little boy. But he is, he's only six years old and he doesn't understand that I've made bad choices, which seem to be fucking up his life. I'm begging you and I've never begged a niggah before. Please come see my baby. I know you may not want to see me. I can go in the other room when you come, but please. And I know I have a lot of shit I need to get together . . . and I will be . . . but for now it's about Jamal. Please."

"I'll see what I can do."

* • *

KREE STOOD IN front of Imani's apartment door, hoping his dick wouldn't rise when he saw her, but as soon as she opened the door, he knew that his dick staying soft would be a difficult task. She wore a pair of tight jeans, and a blue T-shirt with a picture of Angela Davis with her Afro outlined in rhinestones.

When Imani looked at Kree, her nipples instantly became hard. He looked thuggishly exquisite in his gray sweat pants, matching hoody, black goose-down vest, and Tims. His hair was braided straight to the back and the scent of his Dolce & Gabbana cologne filled Imani's nose. Kree walked in and frowned when he looked at Imani. He started walking close to her until he backed her into a corner. "Let me hit you with this real quick," his warm breath blew like a summer breeze across her face. "Don't you ever in your short-ass life call my sister a fuckin' lifeboat refugee, 'cause I promised her that the next time, I would let her left-hook the shit outta you! Now"—he took a step back—"where's my man at?"

Although Kree had just went off on her, all Imani could concentrate on was that he said the girl was his sister—she couldn't care less about anything else he'd said. Imani did all she could to keep from smiling. "Damn, hello to you too."

"Don't be smiling at me and shit." Kree smirked. "Where is Jamal?"

"In his room."

Kree knocked on Jamal's room door and slightly pushed it open. When Jamal turned around and saw Kree's face, his eyes lit up. "Kree! Imani didn't break you! I'm glad you came back! Kree! Yeah, Imani! Kree is here!"

"I'm sorry I stayed away from you so long, man. I'ma have to do better with that. But check it, what's this I hear about you acting up in school?" Kree said sternly.

Jamal held his head down. "I got suspended for punching Jahaad King. He makes me sick."

"Yo, you know it's a punk move to be fighting and messing up in school, right?"

"Yeah, I know."

"And I expect you to apologize, understand?"

"Yes."

"School is for you to learn, not fight."

"Yes. I'm sorry."

Kree hugged Jamal, he ran his hand over his braids and noticed that they needed to be done. "Grab your jacket, man." Jamal ran and grabbed his Power Rangers jacket.

"Man if you don't put that back . . ." Kree laughed. "Where's your goose-down vest I brought you?"

"In the closet."

"Well put it on and let's go. We need to get our hair braided."

"Is it ai'ight"—Kree turned to Imani—"or his father gon' mind?"

"Don't be smart."

Imani stood back and watched Jamal's face light up as Kree grabbed him by the hand and they walked out. *I'ma dumb bitch*, she thought to herself, *how the hell did I fuck that up?*

*   *   *

"YO, IMANI," SABRENA yelled while banging on the door.

"Wassup?" Imani opened the door.

"Come upstairs." Sabrena popped her lips. "I got some smoke."

Before Imani could answer, Walik walked up behind Sabrena. "Excuse me, big gurl."

"Oh hell no." Sabrena turned to Walik. "I'ma bit sick of yo' evicted ass!"

"Shut the fuck up!" Walik snapped, pointing his hand in Sabrena's face.

"You shut the fuck up! My cousin told me that yo' crazy-lookin' ass along with yo' crazy-lookin'-ass gurl and her fifty-five kids got put the fuck out, which must be the reason you been over here beggin'."

"Walik." Imani couldn't believe it. "That's why you came over here? You stupid no-good ma'fucker, don't even think you movin' back in this piece."

"Who the fuck you talkin' to?" Walik pointed in Imani's face.

"I'm yo' fuckin' man. I been with you for ten goddamn years and you let your girl try and play me? You better get her the fuck out my face before I fuckin' smack the shit out of her."

"Do it, boo," Sabrena dared Walik, "ain't nothin' between us but air and opportunity." She cocked her neck to the side. "Bring it."

Imani stepped between them. "Brena, calm down. Let me talk to him for a minute, please."

"You can talk all you want, but you need to check this niggah, 'cause I ain't in love with his ass, I will stab him."

"Sabrena," Imani said sternly, "I'll be upstairs in a few. Please take it down."

"Yeah, ai'ight." Sabrena sucked her teeth and walked toward the elevator while Imani and Walik walked inside the apartment.

"What you want? I need to do something." Imani sucked her teeth.

Walik squinted. "Why is you actin' like this? Yo, I know I've done some fucked-up shit."

"Oh, you know this?"

"Yeah. And I'm willing to change."

"You're willing to change? So if I ask you something you'll tell me the truth and won't lie."

"Yeah, baby," he assured her, "anything you wanna know."

"Did you marry Shante?"

Walik didn't answer.

"You can't hear?"

"Listen, a minute ago Shante and I caught a case together."

"What the fuck you mean a minute ago?"

"The last charge I caught, she was with me. I took the rap."

Instantly Imani's heart felt like it was oozing out of her chest cavity. "I was pregnant with your child and you wouldn't even claim your own shit, but you take the rap for her?"

"Only so the feds wouldn't make her testify against me."

"You caught state charges. I was the one who got caught with your federal shit."

"You don't have a record, shit, you were considered a minor."

"Ten thousand dollars and a crooked lawyer later, ma'fucker. Walik, just go home. Go somewhere and just leave me alone. Please."

Walik grabbed Imani by the waist. "I love you."

"Well," she pushed his hands off her, "don't love me no more."

"All I have to do is be faithful." He pulled her back into his embrace.

"Faithful." Imani twisted her lips giving him the screw face. "It's so beyond you being faithful. I just wanna be at peace. I don't want to be with you. Damn." She pushed him in the center of his chest. "Just go home!"

"Go home? You don't wanna try anymore?" Walik was taken aback. "Wassup with that?" He placed his hand under his chin. "Oh I get it, you fuckin' that Rican niggah, right? You fuckin' him?"

"Go 'head, Walik!"

"You got my son around his ass?" Walik took his index finger and pointed into Imani's forehead, causing her neck to jerk back.

She slapped his hand. "Keep your fuckin' hands off me!"

"What you gon' do? Karate-chop me?"

"Go home!"

"Don't you wanna love me again?"

"I don't wanna love you. I just wanna leave you."

"What you sayin'?"

"I want it to be over. You make me fuckin' crazy. Get . . . the . . . fuck . . . out!"

"Get the fuck out? Is that how you talk to that niggah? Is that what you say when you suckin' his dick?"

"Walik, just go home." Imani turned to open the door. Walik walked up close behind her and yanked the back of her hair, pulling her to the floor.

"I'ma beat yo' ass!" He snatched his belt from around his waist and slapped her across the face with it.

Somehow Imani was able to grab the end of the belt long

enough to get off the floor. "What the fuck is wrong with you? I don't want you!" she screamed, her face feeling as if the belt had snatched off a strip of her skin.

The apartment was dark and Imani's eyes darted around the room. Trying desperately to find a way out, she thought about running down the fire escape, but remembered that she had it blocked by the air conditioner. "Walik, please," she begged. "Please."

"Please what? All these fuckin' years I was with you, bitch! And you think just because you get a new niggah, I should fuckin' go away. I ain't goin' nowhere, bitch!"

"Go home, Walik! Goddamn, can't you just leave me alone?"

"Hell no, I ain't good enough no more? You got this li'l DJ niggah and you got this niggah around my son."

"You didn't spend no time with your son. He needs a father, Walik, and you ain't it!" Imani reached for her cell phone. "I swear to God if you don't leave I'ma call the police."

"Oh, now you gon' call the police on me?" Walik rushed toward Imani and slapped the cell phone out of her hand. He grabbed her by the hair and dragged her across the floor. Her follicles felt as if they were being snatched out. She could feel the roots ripping away from the scalp as clumps of her hair tangled between his thick fingers. "You stupid bitch! You think you just gon' fuck around and leave me. It ain't over until I say it's over!" He grabbed the belt off the floor and again slapped her with it, the buckle splashing in her face like water.

"Awwwwlllllll!" she screamed, her eyelids feeling as if they were being forced shut. Struggling to fight back, Imani started swinging her arms wildly, but instead of seeming to gain control she appeared to be drowning while doing backstrokes. "I'm begging you to get off me. Please," she cried. "Okay, okay we can work it out. Anything you want. Anything."

"Too late!" Walik kicked Imani in the neck. "I should fuckin' kill you!" She closed her eyes as the pain of his steel-toed-boot felt like a boulder crushing her vertebrae.

"I got something fo' yo' ass, bitch!" Without warning Walik took Imani and swung her across the room.

She took her arms and covered her face as she slammed into the wall.

"Watch this shit, bitch!"

Imani struggled to get off the floor as Walik kicked in her bedroom door. He snatched all her clothes out the closet. "I bought this shit, bitch! I did! Me! Not that new niggah!"

"Walik, please," Imani begged, her vision coming and going. She knew she was bleeding but she didn't know from where. "Walik, what are you doing?"

His arms were filled with her coats, pants, shirts, and dresses. He took his foot and kicked the air conditioner out of the window; it made a loud thud as it fell back on the fire escape. Imani put her hands to her head and started to scream, "What are you doing?" She grabbed the tail end of one of her coats but Walik yanked the coat so hard that she cracked the glass in the window as her shoulder slammed into it. Walik threw her clothes on the fire escape, some of them flying over the ledge and floating in the air like parachutes. He turned around and kicked Imani out of his way. He opened her dresser drawers and took out her bras, her panties, and all her other clothes, throwing them onto the fire escape. Once he was done he reached for the lighter fluid that Imani kept on the windowsill for when she and her girls grilled food.

"Walik," Imani said, exasperated, "what are you doing?" She grabbed him by the arm. "Please stop." He pushed her back and she fell onto the bed. He took the lighter fluid and shot it onto her clothes. He placed one foot on the window ledge so he could completely empty the bottle. Once he was done, he struck a match and set all her clothes on fire.

As he turned around, Imani took the folded metal chair that

she kept in her bedroom and slammed him across the head with it. Walik stumbled as he lost his vision. She hit him again, causing him to fall to the floor. She could see her clothes going up in a single stream of smoke before turning black and exploding into flames.

"Imani?" Sabrena and Tasha knocked on the door. "What the hell is going on in there?"

Imani slammed the chair against Walik's head again. Blood was everywhere. As she began to take another swing, he charged toward her, knocked her on the bed, and punched her in the face with a closed fist.

The room smelled of fire as the flames snuck in through the cracked windowpane. Quickly the curtains caught on fire, causing the bedspread to ignite. Walik yanked Imani off the bed, pulled her into the living room, and left her lying on the floor.

Walik knocked Tasha over as he ran out the door. Immediately Tasha and Sabrena ran in and spotted Imani on the floor, drifting in and out of consciousness.

"Imani," Sabrena cried.

"We gotta," Imani struggled to say, "get outta here . . ."

"Sabrena!" Tasha screamed, pointing to Imani's bedroom where flames were soaring out. "Let's go!"

Tasha and Sabrena each picked Imani up by an arm and ran out the door with her.

Before they could think to call for help they could hear the sirens blaring outside. People were everywhere as they exited the building. Imani started coughing. She could barely see as Sabrena and Tasha carried her toward the EMT workers. Once the workers spotted Imani they lifted her out of the girls' arms and placed her on the stretcher.

"I'ma kill that niggah," Sabrena said to Tasha.

• • •

"MAN," KREE SAID as he and Jamal walked around the corner to Imani's building, "your mother is gon' be so mad that I kept you out this late . . ." Kree's speech started to slow down as he looked to see the building on fire. He looked around for Imani but didn't see her. Once he spotted Sabrena, he grabbed Jamal's hands and rushed toward her. "Where's Imani?"

"Walik." Sabrena started crying. "I left them downstairs and some shit jumped off."

"Where is she?" Kree panicked.

"In the ambulance. We gotta go with her, they're getting ready to leave."

"What's wrong with my Imani?" Jamal said, crying.

"It's gon' be all right," Kree assured him. He looked at Sabrena. "Can you drive?"

"Tasha can." She pointed.

Kree tossed his keys to Tasha. "My truck's around the corner, meet me at the hospital and take Jamal with you." He jumped in the ambulance with Imani. The sirens started blaring as they took off.

BETTY WHITE'S *Tonight Is the Night* flowed softly from the Bose speakers in Starr and Red's bedroom ceiling, as the disco ball, which doubled as a light fixture, sent metallic streaks across the room.

The black leather chaps that Red wore hugged his thick thighs, while the spiked leather suspenders enhanced the tiny balls of salt and pepper hairs on his chest. He snorted and licked his lips, "Is ya ready for Pa-pa Red, girl."

"What you say, Daddy?" Starr growled, wearing a crotchless red leather leotard, while cracking her whip and stretching her legs out as if she was doing a warm-up exercise. "Ask me again," Starr said, as she did a ballerina spin into Red's arms.

"Girl." Red looked into Starr's eyes. "I want you to spank Pa-pa Red good."

"Well she ain't gon' have to spank you," Mama Byrd yelled through the door, " 'cause in a minute I'ma kick ya ass. I been listening to you growl, snort, and crack them whips all night long and I'm tired. Now instead of fuckin', you need to be answering this damn phone that won't stop goddamn ringin'. Old lady can't even shit in peace . . . dumb-ass, dry-ass pussy li'l dick bitch!"

"All right, Mama," Red said.

"I got yo all right, motherfucker. And the next time I feed Chocolate Thunder some recharged Duracell, don't y'all knock on the bathroom door! Jack ass! Now answer that damn phone 'cause it's ringing again . . . show off!"

Starr rolled her eyes at Red. "I'ma ignore her, so just let me answer the phone. Hello?" she said into the receiver.

"Ms. Starr!" Tasha screamed in panic.

"Who is this?" Starr asked. She looked at her clock and saw that it was midnight. She turned to Red, "You ain't give this number to no groupies, did you?"

Before Red could answer, Tasha said, "This Tasha, Ms. Starr," she started to cry, "Imani's in the hospital."

"What?"

"Yes, Kings County."

"What happened to my baby?"

"Walik. Walik beat her and set her apartment on fire."

Starr threw the phone across the bed. "I got to go!" She looked at Red. "My baby, Imani, my baby's in the hospital! Walik beat her and set her apartment on fire!"

"Oh no!" Red jumped up and started to panic. He fumbled around the dresser for his car keys. Afterward, he and Starr, still dressed in their leather bondage outfits, flew down the stairs.

Mama Bryd was on her porta-potty in the living room as Starr and Red stormed past her, "Well damn, Red, I ain't never seen so many bubbles in one ass!" Mama Byrd screamed behind them.

• • •

STARR STARTED TO hyperventilate once she got to the hospital and Tasha and Sabrena recapped for her what happened. Jamal was crying so bad that his eyes were swollen. People passing by were staring at Red and Starr, but nobody in their immediate circle had noticed because they were so upset.

"I got to see my baby," Starr cried.

Kree, who'd been in the emergency exam room with Imani, walked into the lobby. Instantly he spotted Starr and Red and couldn't believe his eyes. *What kinda nasty shit?!* Kree walked over to them. Before he could whisper to them about their clothing the doctor walked over. "Just want you to know, she has a broken arm and collarbone. She has serious brusing around her neck and across her face, all of which will heal. I will need to keep her for a few days, though. She's sleeping right now, and that's what I want her to do. You can see her for a few minutes, but just so you know, her hair is pulled out in a couple of places."

"Is my Imani gon' die?" Jamal cried.

"No, young man." The doctor squatted down to face him. "Not at all." He stood up again. "The police are over there," he pointed, "and they would like to get a statement from everyone."

"To hell with the police," Starr said, "I need to see my baby."

"Right this way." The doctor pointed.

"Well, I'm tellin' it all," Sabrena said, wiping her eyes, "every bit of it. I didn't see him beat her but I know he did it and I know for a fact he set that damn apartment on fire."

Kree didn't say much. He stood with his arms folded. "Yo," he said, "watch my li'l man real quick. I need to go take care of some business. Call me if Imani needs anything before I come back." And he took off.

"KAYLA!" MONICA SCREAMED. "How many damn times have I told you that when you're on your period you have to turn around and look at the toilet seat for blood? Stop being so fuckin' nasty!" Monica wanted to slap Kayla upside her head. She understood that Kayla was young and had to learn to care for herself when her period was on, but damn, how many times did she have to keep telling her the same thing?

Monica rubbed the sides of her stomach. She'd been feeling pain all day, but tried to dismiss it as normal uterine cramps. She didn't have enough energy to sit down and figure out why it hurt so bad; she just prayed she wasn't in labor. Monica barely had any money to buy the few supplies she had. And she wanted desperately to hold on a little longer until her disability kicked in. Then maybe keeping money wouldn't be so difficult.

Ever since the girls moved in, her house had been turned upside down . . . and now that the honeymoon of visiting Aunty Monica versus living with Aunty Monica was over, the girls became more consumed with where their mother was and when she was coming back. Not to mention, Monica was starting to feel resentful. She was having her own baby and *Is it too selfish,* she wondered, *to want to keep it that way? Is it too much to ask that my child be afforded the privilege of being the only one, instead of one among many?* Besides, these were her nieces and not her daughters. They were Celeste's and Sharief's responsibility, and it seemed that neither one of them wanted to do shit.

"Monica," Sharief said, walking into the kitchen and feeling Monica on the ass, "I'ma get some tonight?" He rubbed his nose into the side of her neck, something that used to drive her wild.

She looked at him and rolled her eyes. "If you don't get the fuck out my face!"

"Goddamn." Sharief smirked. "What's wrong?"

"I'm tired and I'm ready for your children to go home to their mother."

"As far as I can see, you're their mama now and this is their home."

"No!" She pointed her finger. "Their home is in New Jersey. And when are you going back to work?"

"Once Celeste's charges are dropped, I can go back."

"And until then, what?"

"Look, baby." Sharief grabbed Monica by the waist. "I know this is hard. And it seems like everything is on you. But I love you and we fought for this. Everything will work out."

"Sharief, we need some money." She looked at him and sniffed. Thinking she smelled alcohol, her nose started to twitch. "Why can't you sell that damn house you and Celeste were living in? At least sell it before they foreclose on it, I know the mortgage hasn't been paid."

"I have unemployment insurance on my house. It defers the mortgage for six months."

"So what's stopping you from selling the place?"

"I can't sell it without Celeste."

"Why not?"

"I just can't." He turned to walk away.

"Where the hell are you going?" She pulled him by his shoulder. "I'm talking to you!"

"The fuckin' house isn't in my name! Okay? I can't sell the house because it's not in my name! And in case you forgot, I have no money because somehow Celeste cleared my bank accounts."

"Well, if you changed your goddamn codes and used more than zero-four-one-one she wouldn't have guessed it! Shit!" Monica slammed her fist.

"That was my wife. I didn't care if she had my codes."

"Your wife? But you were married to my pussy, niggah, so get the hell out my face with that! I'm you're fuckin' wife for all intents and purposes and I ain't staying around for better or worse. So either you get a job or you leave."

"Get a job? Leave? And do what?"

"I don't give a damn. Get a side hustle, deliver newspapers, QuickChek, McDonald's, be a Moonie and sell flowers on the side of the street, I don't give a damn, but I can't keep living like this."

"Well, guess what? I ain't doing any of that and all I got right now is me and my children. And if we're not good enough for you, Ms. Monica, then I don't know what the fuck to tell you."

Monica stared at Sharief's face. She wanted to slap him in the mouth. As she thought about how she could backhand him, she noticed slob sliding out the side of his lips; his eyes appeared to be hellfire red and more slanted than usual. She walked up close to him. "You're drunk?"

"I'm not drunk! Just leave me the fuck alone. Call Listra or one of your li'l friends so you can talk about me. A man's down on his luck and all of sudden you can't shut the fuck up. If I knew it was gon' be all of this I'da stayed with my wife." And he walked out of the kitchen, leaving her there alone.

"Aunty! Aunty!" Kori came running in. "Are you a tramp-ass ho?"

"And ask her if she's a slut too!" Kai said, running behind her sister.

Monica spun around to face them, stunned. "What? What did you say to me?"

"Are you a tramp-ass ho?" Kori repeated innocently.

"And a slut?" Kai chimed in. "Don't forget that."

"Where did you get that from?"

"Kayla," Kai said. "Aunty, she on the phone with her friend Ronneasha talkin' about Mommy, and you, and Daddy. She said that Daddy is pimpin' both of y'all bitches!"

"My sister said," Kori joined in, with a hand on her hip, "that the reason my mommy ran away is because you and Daddy were fucking each other. And she said that that baby in your stomach is a basket." Kori folded her arms across her chest. "How could a baby be a basket, Aunty?"

"Where's Kayla?" Monica was fuming, and tears started to fill her eyes. Living with Kayla felt like living with Celeste all over again.

"Kayla's on the phone," Kai said.

Monica marched out of the kitchen with the twins following close behind. They walked up the stairs to what used to be Monica's home office but now doubled as the girls' bedroom. Monica could hear Kayla's conversation as she approached the room. "Although I miss my mother, I'm real pissed off with her," Kayla was huffing to her girlfriend on the phone. "She just up and left us here with this low-life prostitute. And my daddy—that niggah—you know he ain't even my real father. They think I don't know, but I can read and I saw my birth certificate, so you know I ain't doin' shit this niggah say—"

"Get your ass off that phone!" Monica yelled, barging into the room.

"Excuse me." Kayla rolled her eyes. "I'm on the phone, don't come in here tryna flex." She sucked her teeth and returned to her phone conversation. "See what I mean?"

Monica snatched the phone out of her hand and threw it across the room. "I said hang up the damn phone and I mean it!" she yelled.

"I hate this place!" Kayla screamed at her. "Oh, you get on my nerves!"

Kai and Kori placed their hands over their mouths and started giggling.

"You get on *my* damn nerves and you better shut the hell up!"

"I don't have to shut the hell up. You know it's the truth. You just a low-life home wrecker and like my mother told me you just a skeezer. A tramp-ass—" Before Kayla could finish what she was saying, Monica had slapped her in the mouth.

"Let me tell you something. I will not tolerate you being disrespectful to me, you hear me? The next time you call me a tramp-ass ho—"

"And a slut," Kai interrupted.

"And a slut," Monica continued, "I'll break your little freckle-faced ass open, you understand? I'm tired of your li'l grown and nasty ass! If you don't like it here, then call your grandmother and go live with her, because quite frankly I'm sick of you!"

"And I'm sick of you too!" Kayla spat.

"Well then, get your shit and get to steppin'! Get outta my face!"

"Hold up!" Sharief slurred. He stormed into where Monica and the girls were. "What the hell is gong on?" He rested his beer on the dresser. "Damn, Monica, you have to talk to them like that?"

Kayla ran over to Sharief and started crying. "Daddy! Daddy! She slapped me!"

"What?" Sharief looked at Kayla's face and saw the redness. He was pissed. He looked at Monica. "Have you lost your damn mind?"

"Do you know what she said to me?" Monica couldn't believe he had taken Kayla's side without hearing her out.

"Just don't put your hands on her no more!"

"You know what, this is getting real, real tired." Monica felt the pain in her stomach intensify. She started to double over. "Something has to change," she tried to say.

"Monica, what's wrong?" Sharief asked, seeing her bending over.

"I need to go to the hospital, Sharief. Get the car keys."

"What's wrong?" Sharief started to panic.

"I think it's time, so please get the keys, we have to go."

Sharief stood there.

"Did you hear me?" Monica screamed.

Sharief stumbled as he pulled the keys out of his pocket. He wiped the drool that was sliding out the corner of his mouth. "Ready?"

Monica looked at him and started screaming, "You're drunk! I can't believe that you're fuckin' drunk!"

"I'm all right, baby." He grabbed her by the arm.

"Get the fuck off me!" She snatched her arm away. "Just go."

Monica grabbed the phone and called 9-1-1. She explained her situation to the operator, then called Listra. "Listra, please come and go with me to the hospital."

Listra didn't ask any questions. "I'll be there in a minute."

By the time Listra got to Monica's house, the ambulance was already there. "Where's Sharief?" she asked.

"He's drunk." Monica cried, "He's drunk."

"COME ON, SHARIEF!" Celeste blew on the dice as she rolled them across the craps table. "Mama needs some fuckin' Manolos!"

"It's a hit!" the dealer yelled, raking the dice back.

"Hot damn!" Celeste cheered. She took a pull off the silver tip of the long brown cigarette tucked between her fingers, blew out the smoke, and collected her chips. "Do it again, baby. Five hunnid this time." Celeste had been in Atlantic City, New Jersey, all weekend, contributing to Donald Trump's fortune by gambling half of Sharief's money away. Hell, what else was there to do? She was exhausted from staying at home, crying, cussing, having visions of stalking Monica and Sharief. Tired of Starr calling her cell phone and begging her to please come home.

So fuck it, Celeste thought. *Monica and Sharief have moved on and I need to do the same thing. Besides, how many tears can I waste on unchangeable shit?*

Sharief had already admitted to cheating, that was half the battle; she knew who he was cheating with, that was the other half. And now that he was gone, Celeste knew her battle was lost. Her James Bond instincts were downhill from there. There was no more looking through his shit; no more listening to his voice mails; and no more waiting up with wild eyes, wondering just how long she could stand for them to burn, before she lay down and accepted she was alone.

But no matter what, the hardest thing for Celeste was trying to figure out when the dick flipped and turned the extramarital affair into a relationship. What happened to her being the wife, number one, numero uno—was that just for show? Or was Celeste sleeping or fucking herself with a beaver dildo when the exchange took place? Was she in the kitchen cooking his food, washing his clothes, bathing his kids, or sucking his dick? And that's when it clicked: that his cheating didn't bother her as much as his leaving did. And it wasn't him having sex with another woman as much as it was him falling in love with her. And it wasn't so much that it was another woman, but it was her sister. The same sister she'd confided in about Sharief cheating, the same sister who'd advised her on whether she should kick in the bitch's door or not. The same sister whose words of advice were, *I think you should chill . . . he's not cheating . . .* The same sister who was now pregnant with her husband's child.

For a moment, as Celeste watched the dice pop up snake eyes across the craps table, she thought about her children. She missed them and realized being away from them wasn't the answer; it only made things worse. At least her children would have clouded her thoughts so she could pretend to be happy.

After having Lady Luck dump her, causing her to lose five hundred dollars, Celeste looked around, wondering if she should hit the blackjack table or the slot machines. As she turned around, she felt someone brush up against her right shoulder. "Mind if I stand next to you?" a deep and raspy male voice asked her.

"Not at all," Celeste said, never looking at who was talking to her. "I'm leaving anyway."

"Well, hello to you too." He peeked around at Celeste's face.

Celeste turned to greet him. *Oh my God!* she thought, *this is the niggah from 7-Eleven. The same ma'fucker that I told to suck my titties. Shit.*

"Aren't you wanted for assaulting the cashier in 7-Eleven?" The guy laughed, massaging his chin. "Listen." He looked her in the eyes. "You ai'ight tonight? Or do I need to warn the dealer?"

Celeste laughed. "Do I know you?"

"Oh," the guy chuckled, "you know damn well you remember me. 'Cause I never forget a beautiful face, even when it seems a little out of wack."

"So now you're calling me out of wack?"

"Well, something was going on," he insisted.

"Why are you all in my business?" Celeste snapped. "Don't you have a wife or something? Go find her."

"I'm divorced." He placed a hundred-dollar chip on the table with his left hand, which was no longer wearing a wedding band. "And you?"

"I was almost a widow, until the police got involved."

"What?"

"You asked." Celeste batted her eyes. "Ola!" She walked over to the slot machines, dropped a chip in, and pulled the handle. "Come on, seven, seven, seven, come on and make Mama proud." The machine dropped a cherry, banana, and an orange. "Shit, damn, motherfucker!" Celeste dropped another chip in. "You better be good to Mama!" She pulled the lever.

"Excuse me," a voice purred over her shoulder, "what you said to me a few minutes ago, were you for real?"

Celeste jumped and spun around on the stool. "What the hell is really wrong with you?" It was the 7-Eleven guy again.

"You." He smirked. "I'm tryna put my thang down on you and you playin' me."

She turned back toward the slot machine. "Let's see." She stared at the machine. "I've lost my money since sitting here, and lost time because you scared the shit outta me. You called me wack, crazy, and have asked me several times am I okay. Why would you want to keep puttin' your thang down on me? Are you the one crazy? Or you looking for some pussy?"

"Look, on the real I ain't never had no shit like that happen to me."

"What?"

"What happened in 7-Eleven. And I swear ever since then I can't stop thinking about you. I was scared to call you, so I was hoping to one day see you again, and when I saw you here I had to come up to you."

"Okay, now listen." Celeste dropped in another chip and pulled the lever. "My husband fucked my sister, fell in love with her, and got her pregnant. I have three kids, a house I can't afford, and without warning my life left me and nobody declared me dead in the process. So there I was, trying to get in where I could fit in, and at that moment it was with my titties shaking as I walked half naked through 7-Eleven. So, Mr. Stalker, can you leave me to play my game?"

"Damn, baby, you've been through a lot."

Finally Celeste spun around and prepared her mouth to tell him off, but then she noticed how fine he was: six foot two, perfect teeth, and broad shoulders. He had a shadow mustache, big round eyes, regal nose, and sexy African lips.

"Damn, you're cute," she said, looking him up and down.

"Oh, now I'm cute?" He laughed. "After I've been called a stalker."

"Look, let's call it a truce. What's your name?"

"Myles."

"Well, Myles, I'm Celeste."

"Listen, I can't hold this back any longer." Myles took a deep breath. "You're absolutely beautiful." He licked his lips admiring her copper skin, large breasts, and sharp haircut.

Celeste couldn't believe it; instead of feeling complimented, she felt self-conscious. She looked down at all the cleavage she had, but decided there was nothing she could do about it. She tried to pull the split that was in the front of her sleeveless red rayon dress together praying it didn't show the cellulite that dimpled portions of her thighs.

Myles noticed Celeste covering up. "I'm sorry. I hope I didn't embarrass you or make you uncomfortable."

"No—no." She took her hands off her dress and let her split fly open. She saw Myles look at her thighs and again lick his lips.

"So what's a beautiful young woman like you doing here alone?"

"Oh," she chuckled, "I could ask you the same thing."

"That's true, so is this a vacation?"

"More like a personal retreat."

"Okay—okay. Have you eaten?"

"As a matter of fact," Celeste said as she smiled, "I haven't."

"Wanna go out on the boardwalk and grab something?"

"I would like that. I've been dying for a funnel cake."

Myles and Celeste walked the boardwalk; they grabbed two funnel cakes, a glass of white wine for her, and beer for him. Once they were done eating they strolled along the beach. "So you really think I'm crazy, huh?"

"I'll admit, at first I was like, *This chick has flipped her lid.*" He smiled. "But now I know that you've been through a lot—"

"So do you think I'm crazy?" Celeste asked him again, as if she were looking for a definition of herself.

"I don't think you're crazy; I think you're beautiful."

"Stop it." Celeste held her head down.

"I'm serious." Myles lifted her head back up.

Suddenly they started to hear thunder, and when they looked at the sky rain started to pour. Celeste had never seen it rain on the beach. The drops were different from the ones she was used to seeing. These raindrops were clear and heavy, and when they splashed they seemed to dent the sand and scatter into wet dia-monds. "Come on!" Myles ran with Celeste, grabbing her by the hand. "Stand over here with me. When the rain comes, it's like a river coming down." He pulled her under an open wooden stand, where most people prepare picnics or simply lie back and relax when they hit Atlantic City's beach or need a break from the casi-nos. Since there were no chairs, they were forced to stand. Celeste leaned her back against Myles's chest. Although it seemed strange leaning against a stranger, Celeste felt at peace. She grabbed Myles's hands and pulled them around her waist.

Once the rain let up, Celeste turned and smiled at him. "I'm staying at the Taj Mahal."

"You're leaving?" He seemed disappointed.

"Yes. Come with me?" she asked.

"Yes."

They both laughed.

I hope he has a big dick, Celeste thought on their walk to the hotel, *because I wanna fuck him sooooo bad.* She looked at Myles and smiled.

* • *

ONCE THEY WERE in the suite, Celeste opened her balcony doors and let the breeze pass through. She sat on the edge of the bed. "Look," she said, "I hate to be so direct, but all I really wanna do is fuck. No strings attached, just some nasty-ass wet-ass ball-slappin' groovin'."

"Damn." Myles couldn't believe it. "You're bold as hell."

"Just direct. I don't know you well enough to want anything other than dick."

Myles walked over to Celeste and extended his hand. She ac-cepted and stood up. He wrapped his arms around her waist and started dancing with her, moving slowly from side to side.

Didn't I just tell this niggah I wanted some dick? Celeste thought.

Why is he trying to romance me? "Myles, I don't mean any harm, but I don't want to dance. I would like to get down to business."

"Look." He stopped dancing and stood still, facing her. "Calm down and stop being so aggressive. You act like you're scared to be made love to. Allow me to be a man and take care of you."

Celeste didn't know what to say.

"I'm not going to be a one-night stand," Myles continued, "so let me give you a sample of who I am." He started kissing Celeste softly on the lips and then gradually slipped his tongue in her mouth, kissing her the way she longed to be kissed. Instantly her nipples hardened. He could feel the fullness of her breasts pressed against his chest; he couldn't wait to take her nipples, have his tongue bow down and treat them like royalty. "Let me take care of you," he said as he lifted her dress above her head. He unsnapped her bra, and she stepped out of her panties. Myles couldn't believe her body. She was perfect. Her love handles, her stretch marks, her breasts that sagged just a little, her thighs, dimples and all, were like artwork, carefully put together, creating the masterpiece of a real woman. He laid her down slowly. Before he undressed he took one of her breasts and sucked it until her nipple felt like silk in his mouth.

Celeste felt like a tug-of-war was going on inside her, wondering when she was going to see his dick. Myles took his clothes off, revealing a dick that more than matched his height. *Thank you, Lord,* she thought, looking at the ceiling, *but I hope that big dick isn't just for show.* Celeste reached across the nightstand and handed him a condom. "I want you"—she looked him in the eyes—"to fuck the shit out of me."

"There you go with this getting fucked. Why not make love?"

"I don't wanna make love right now. Check with me tomorrow on that. Right now my pussy is aching. I ain't had no dick in I don't know how long and I can't help it but I need you to turn me the fuck out."

"Damn, Celeste, I'm not that kind of man."

"If you ain't that type of man, then hand me my beaver underneath the bed."

"Now, Celeste, I know you're not telling me that a portable dick is better than a real one."

"Then you"—Celeste pointed—"better take that big dick and work me overtime."

Myles started smiling. He started kissing Celeste on her stomach and was working his way down toward her pussy to give her some head. Celeste tapped him on the shoulder. "I don't want no head right now. I said fuck me."

In all of his forty years, Myles had never been with a woman so aggressive, but something about it turned him on. Without warning, Celeste flipped him over and got on top of him. "Let me show you how to bang up a pussy. You're taking too long." She threw her hands in the air, took her left leg and stretched it over his shoulder, causing her pussy to expand to its full capacity, then leaned back and got her seesaw on. "When I tell you to fuck me, I mean get on top and tear this pussy up."

"Goddamn, baby," Myles said, trying his best not to nut, but Celeste was driving him wild.

Celeste took her leg down and flipped around backward, throwing her ass in his face, practically having his lips kiss her cheeks. Before he could get hold of the way she was riding his dick, she bent down, slipped the condom off, and started giving him some head, pushing her pussy up toward his face and instantly creating a 69. Celeste surprised herself with how freaky she was, especially since she'd never liked to suck dick.

Myles started to shiver. Celeste could feel that he was about to nut, so while she continued to give him head she reached for another condom, slipped it on, and turned back around to face him.

"Stand up," he demanded. Celeste complied and he bent her over, her hands touching the floor. He slipped his dick in and immediately went to work, pounding into her wet pussy. He reached his hands forward and grabbed her bouncing titties.

"That's it, motherfucker, that's it!" Celeste screamed. She could think of nothing other than seeing stars when she came. Myles's dick filled up every inch of her pussy and even more. She loved the kaleidoscope of pleasure and pain that came each time he pounded into her, his balls slapping generously against her. "I'ma—I'ma—" she started to stutter, "I'ma cum."

"Cum on, and make sure you keep standing, 'cause I got some more shit for yo' ass. Let me show you how to toss a salad."

Is this niggah trying to be funny talking to me about food? Celeste thought. Suddenly she felt the soft hairs in her ass lifting: it was Myles running his wet tongue between her ass checks. Celeste could do nothing but close her eyes. *I feel like I owe him some money,* she thought. *This is the best freak session I could've ever imagined . . .* And this went on for hours.

When Celeste woke the next morning she pinched Myles's arm to make sure he was real. "Ouch, sweetie." He smiled. "What was that for?"

"I wanted to make sure you were real. You know," she laughed, "I know nothing about you."

"Yes you do, you know I shop in 7-Eleven and you know I can keep up with your freaky ass."

"Yeah, you were all right," she chuckled, moving her hand from side to side, "but for a minute there you had me worried."

"Worried? Well, let's go again this morning." He arched his eyebrows.

"Naw, I wanna talk to you. Like I said, I know nothing about you. I'm sorta embarrassed."

"Don't be. My last name is Cochran. I'm forty years old and divorced. I have two children, both grown. My daughter is eighteen and my son is twenty. I'm a computer software engineer and I split my time between Atlanta and South Jersey. You should come to Atlanta—you would like it."

"Who knows? Maybe one day I'll move there."

"I would like that. Now, Celeste your turn."

"Okay, my last name is Winston—well, Parker, like I said I'm getting divorced. I'm thirty-two. I have three girls—Kayla is eleven, and my twins, Kai and Kori, will be five. And I miss them like hell. Oh, I need to get a job, and somehow figure out if I can afford this house that I live in . . . did I mention I need a job?"

"Yes, you did." He smiled. "Now, what about needing love."

"Well honestly, love and I don't get along. So before I fuck somebody up, I'll pass on love right now. Besides, I need to get to know me, spend some time with my children, and become okay with Celeste. I buried everything in my husband and when he left me, I was a mess. I can't go through that anymore."

"So you're scared?"

"No, I just want to be careful."

"I can understand that. So will I get to see you again?" he asked.

"I hope so."

"So we can be friends?" he pressed.

"As long as we're friends with fuckin' benefits." Celeste laughed.

"Uhmm . . . ," Myles said, rolling on top of her, "that sounds good to me."

{ Imani }

IMANI WAS SORE as she tried her best to drag herself down the hall to the bathroom. She'd gotten out of the hospital yesterday, and since her apartment wasn't livable she and Jamal had to stay with Starr and Red until they were able to move out on their own. Imani twitched her cheek only to be met with excruciating pain. Once in the bathroom she stood in front of the mirror and stared at herself. Immediately tears fell from her eyes. Her hair looked like untamed grass: wild, loose, patchy, and matted. Her once flawless face was bruised and wore the imprints of a leather belt. Her right arm was in a cast, and her shoulder was numb.

She heard someone creep into her room, so she patted her hair down as best she could, only for it to spring back up. She took her left hand and wiped her eyes. As she stepped out of the bathroom, she saw Kree sitting on the edge of her bed and instantly she felt embarrassed.

"Hey, beautiful." He helped her to the bed and kissed her on the forehead. His long braids brushed past her face, tickling her nose.

"Beautiful, yeah right." She tried not to grin as Kree sat back down on the edge of the bed.

"I know you wanna smile. Go 'head," he kissed her again, "let me see you smile."

"Shut up!" she said playfully, unable to resist a grin. "I feel like Miss Celie after Mister kicked her ass." Tears started to form in her eyes. "You see how Walik yanked my hair out and beat me across the face with his damn belt. You know I be having dreams about that shit?"

"Damn, I thought I was the only one." Kree shook his head. "Every time I think about how that niggah beat you I wanna fuck him up again. I swear I shoulda shot his ass."

Imani looked confused. "What? Fuck him up again? You shoulda shot him, what are you talking about?"

Kree stared at Imani. He didn't want her to know that after he'd left the hospital the day she was admitted, he had some of his boys find Walik and bring him to an abandoned building. Kree was there to greet him with a ski mask on. With his boys watching, Kree stood over Walik, imagining what he'd done to Imani, and started beating him the same exact way. He took his belt off and slashed him across the face, but instead of hitting him with a leather belt he beat him with a spiked one. Instantly blood shot everywhere. Walik tried to fight back but was no match for Kree, who stomped him with his boots and dragged him around on the ground. Afterward he made Walik strip naked then burned his clothes, his pants catching on fire before they were completely off him.

Once Kree finished beating Walik's ass, he left him on the floor, his burning clothes next to him. Then he went to the nearest pay phone, disguised his voice, and turned Walik in to the police for the warrant he had for beating Imani and setting her apartment on fire.

Kree shook his head. "Don't worry," he told Imani, "I didn't mean anything by it. I'm just saying how I really wanna beat his ass."

"Did you do something to him, Kree?"

"Don't start, Imani."

"I'm not starting. I just don't want you in any trouble, please." She held her head down. "We need you too much."

"We?" He lifted her head up. "Don't start that holding-your-head-down shit."

"Yes, we. Me and Jamal."

"Naw," he laughed, "you cussed my ass out, remember?"

"I'm sorry . . . I hate myself for that. Look at me. Just look at me. All because I told him I didn't want him. He couldn't take it and this is what he does to me?"

"Look, ma, sometimes it takes certain shit to make us see what we were doing wrong and what we need to change."

"It still doesn't give him the right to try and kill me. I really thought I was going to die. I really, really did." She started crying. "I gotta get my shit together, Kree. I have to. I have a son, I don't want to hang out on the stoop no more, smoke weed, and carry on. I can't believe this, I don't have shit. He burned up all of my clothes, my bras, my panties, everything. I have nothing."

"Shhh baby." Kree scooted up close to Imani and placed her head on his chest. "Don't cry, baby, I got you. I do."

"Yo, yo, yo, wasuuuuuppp!" Sabrena yelled, coming into Imani's room. Tasha and Quiana were behind her, each with three shopping bags in her hands. Sabrena's bags were from the Gap, Quiana's bags from Banana Republic, and Tasha's bags from Neiman's.

"Oh, Imani." Sabrena stood still, watching her cry. "I didn't know . . ." She pointed to the door. "You want us to come back?"

"No," Imani sniffed.

"Okay, good," Tasha said. The girls walked over and gave Imani a group hug. Meantime Sabrena slipped Kree his credit card and the receipts for the clothes. He stuffed them into his pocket.

"Girl, let me show you what we found for yo' ass at the mall." Sabrena laid the clothes out on the bed. "Ain't this shit sharp?"

"Damn, Brena," Imani said, "you picked this out?" She held up hip-hugging jeans and a turtleneck.

"Look at this," Tasha said, showing her a mint-green Donna Karan peacoat.

"I can't believe this," Imani said, smiling.

Kree looked around Imani's room; all he could see were clothes everywhere. Without anyone noticing he pulled out the three receipts that Sabrena handed to him and looked at the total. He had to do a double take when he realized that they spent well over three thousand dollars.

"Imani," Kree said, getting up from the edge of the bed, "I'ma come back later. I need to get to the studio. I'll be calling to check on you. I promised your mother I would stop by since she and Red were at the T. D. Jakes Explosion."

"T. D. Jakes?"

"Yeah, The Jam on Its have converted to Jammin' for Jesus. And it looks like they gon' be taking off. Red might come back with a bangin' CD after all."

"Oh please." Imani frowned.

"Finally," Sabrena said, after Kree left, "I'm glad he's gone so we can give you the lowdown. First off," she continued, "that fat fuck, Walik, is in jail, tryna cop a plea for what he did. Shante, that skank, is living with Saraah, from Utica, her cousin Fatima's baby father. And it's about to be a war over that ma'fucker. You know Shante's fat ass is a user, worried over some baby Walik is spose to have."

"And yo," Tasha interrupted, "word is that Kree beat Walik's ass! Don't sleep on Kree, I know he a DJ and all, like to dance and shit, but he put his thug-thizzle down. My new boo told me when I bailed him out that he saw Walik coming up in there naked and beat the fuck up. And when he asked Walik what happened, he said some niggahs with ski masks robbed him and burned his clothes up."

"Say word?" Imani cracked up.

"Word."

"And look," Sabrena said, giving Imani the eye, "I don't know what you plan on doing with Mr. Kree, but you see all this shit here? That niggah bought it. And honey, it's more where this came from. He bought Jamal all new shit. I tried to get that niggah to take my shit off layaway but he looked at me like I was crazy. Yo, his ass is a keeper."

"You see how fucked up my face is," Imani stressed. "I can't imagine being able to keep a man like Kree."

"Girl, please," Sabrena said, "Kree loves yo' ass. And listen, your face is still pretty. But that hair is another story. As soon as I walked in here, I couldn't wait for Kree to leave so that I could cut this shit even and give you two goddess braids with a zigzag part down the middle. And next week I'ma get some pony hair and we gon' hook you up with some invisa-braids." Sabrena took her hair supplies out of her bag. She took the scissors out and cut Imani's hair as evenly as she could. After that she took two packs of hair and completed Imani's hairstyle. "That'll hold you for now."

"Look," Tasha said, looking at her watch, "I need to pick up my daughter, so we'll be by here tomorrow."

"All right," Imani said, sad to see them leave. They kissed her on the cheek and waved bye.

"Remember what we said about Kree," Quiana said. "Don't sleep."

[Monica]

SHARIEF HAD BOTH of his hands filled with packages of Pampers and baby bottles as he pushed his back against the door, holding it open for Monica and his newborn son, Jeremiah Winston.

The orderly pushed Monica and the baby outside next to Sharief's truck. Monica could feel the truck rocking as she stood up, preparing to place the baby in his car seat. Sharief opened the door. All the kids were jammed into the backseat: Kayla was pushed into the corner, with Kai, Kori, and Jamal practically sitting on top of one another. Kayla sat with her mouth poked out and rolling her eyes.

Jamal looked at her. "You too grown, Raven Symone!"

"Shut up! Fat boy!"

"Yo' mama fat!"

"Don't talk about my mama!" Kayla screamed.

"Jamal!" Monica said, giving him the evil eye. "Stop it."

Sharief opened the door Kayla was sitting next to. "Hold the baby's bags."

She folded her arms across her chest. "I ain't holding no bags!

You got me messed up! Get it offa me, he ain't my brother! And where my mother at? I'm tired of this!"

"Kayla!" Sharief said sternly, slamming the bag down on her lap. "He is your brother! And your mama off spendin' my damn money! Now be quiet and take these bags!"

"I hate this!" Kayla screamed.

"I hate this," Kai said mocking her sister.

"Stop it, Kai!" Kayla yelled.

"Stop it, Kai!"

"Uhmm." Kayla took her fingers and plucked Kai in the head, and Kai started screaming. The baby, whom Monica had just placed in his car seat, started crying. "Awl, hell to the nawl!" Kori said. "Aunty, can you tell him to be quiet?"

"No!" Kayla said. "Tell him to shut the hell up!"

"I'ma slap the shit out of both of y'all," Monica said, giving the baby his pacifier.

As she hopped in the front seat, she looked at Sharief. "You couldn't find no babysitter? And why do you have Jamal?"

"No, I couldn't find a babysitter, and Imani just got out the hospital."

"Why?"

"Your mother didn't tell me why," Sharief said. "You know Starr can't stand me, so she says the bare minimum."

"Jamal," Monica turned toward the backseat, "why was your mother in the hospital?"

" 'Cause Walik got mad, punched her in the face, and burned the whole block down, now all of Flatbush is homeless."

"Y'all homeless?" Kori asked, excited. "I wish I was homeless."

"You are homeless," Jamal insisted. "Don't get comfortable at Aunty Monica's. She told my Imani that y'all got to go."

"We got to go, Aunty?" Kai asked Monica. "Oh good, then it must be the bomb to be homeless."

"Yeah," Jamal said, filled with confidence. "BK to the fullest, you know how we do. But me and my Imani'll only be homeless until she finds another building that take Section Eight. But it might be hard finding someplace that take all of what Section Eight give, 'cause you know rent is high these days."

"You could move in with Aunty," Kai said. "Don't nobody sleep in the kitchen yet. Most of the time my daddy be in the living room, though."

Oh hell no, Monica thought. "I'll call my mother," she said to Sharief, "that is, if she's speaking to me. Being she didn't come see me in the hospital."

"Well, Monica, she did come see the baby," Sharief said. "And she dropped off a lot of things for him."

Monica didn't say a word; she simply looked out the window as Sharief started to drive.

"Hey," Jamal said, "I got a question and being that we all family and everything, I wanna know something. What y'all gon' call the baby: Li'l Bruh or Li'l Cuz?"

"Shut up, Jamal!" Monica said. "Just shut right up!"

"BUTTAH." STARR TOOK a deep breath while frying chicken. "I need me some damn weed."

"Well, you sure can't get none of mine," Mama Byrd snapped. "Anybody seen my porta-potty, my stomach is rumblin'."

"It's in the bathroom where it needs to be," Buttah snapped.

"Who the hell is you? Is you the ho that stole my husband?"

"Mama Byrd, please," Buttah said.

"Oh yeah, you the bitch that tried to say them ugly-ass kids you got was my knee-baby-boy Jimmy's. I believe you worked roots on him."

"I didn't work roots on Jimmy!" Buttah screamed. "Jimmy loved me! And De-niece and De-nephew are his kids!"

"Buttah," Starr said, "why do you always argue the same damn thing with Mama Byrd? Give it up, girl. Please, we know De-niece and De-cousin—"

"De-nephew," Mama Byrd corrected.

"Yeah," Starr said, "De-niece and De-nephew are Jimmy's kids."

"You're right, Starr. She just gets under my skin."

"Ain't nothin' got under yo' skin," Mama Byrd said, "but three hundred and fifteen pounds of Oreos, Crunchy Cheez Doodles, and chocolate cakes."

"Be quiet, Mama Byrd!" Buttah screamed. "Now, what's on your mind, Starr, why you need some weed?"

"Buttah," Starr sighed, "all my girls have gone crazy and I never thought I would say this, but Imani seems to be the one with the most sense."

"Well, have you talked to Monica and Celeste?"

"No I have not," she said matter-of-factly, "I just can't bring myself to do that. I can't get over Celeste using her children as pawns to ruin this bullshit Monica and Sharief got going on. And now she's God knows where doing God knows what. She pressed charges on the man. Cried to me about how he beat her, and now she never shows up in court. What that look like—"

"Some bullshit," Mama Byrd said, "straight-up-and-down bull-shit."

"Exactly," Starr agreed. "And Monica, oh my God, Lawd Jesus how do you lay up with your sister's husband? I can't even lie, I wanted to beat her ass! Had it been my man, I woulda tore this motherfucker up!"

"You and me both!" Mama Byrd yelled as she walked toward the bathroom to grab her porta-potty.

"And I got a new grandbaby, you know." Starr felt tears coming to her eyes. "He's almost a month old and I haven't seen him. I mean I saw him at the hospital but I couldn't hold him and give him that Nana-love-you talk. And Monica ain't never had no baby before. Buttah, what she know about a baby?"

"Nothin'," Mama Byrd yelled from the half-bath next to the kitchen. "I betchu she know who the daddy is, though."

"Well, Starr, you need to go and talk to her," Buttah said, ignoring Mama Byrd. "Hold your grandbaby and let Monica know how hurt and disappointed you are, but you need to say something to her. She still is your child."

[Monica]

OR THE PAST month Monica had walked around carrying her newborn in her arms. His days and nights were completely mixed up, and Monica felt like she hadn't been to sleep in weeks. Heavy bags rested under her eyes and her once curly Afro was now frayed and tangled.

"Hand him here," Sharief said, reaching for the baby. For once he was sober. "Let me hold him for a while. Go upstairs and get some sleep and maybe tomorrow, since it's Friday, you should hang out with Listra, leave Jeremiah here with me and the girls while you go getcha groove on."

Monica looked at Sharief and laughed. "Yeah right, and I'll come back and meet my damn house in an uproar."

"No you won't, baby. I'm trying to do better. I know it's hard with me not working yet and you being out on maternity leave but we'll make it. The last couple of times Celeste hasn't shown up for court. The judge said if she doesn't show up at the next hearing he'll dismiss the charges."

"Sharief, I want you to stop drinking. I'm concerned."

"About what?" he asked. "You're the one that goes overboard, all I do is have a beer or two."

"But Sharief, you drink until you get drunk. And there was a time when you didn't drink at all."

"Listen, don't stress me. I don't have a job right now, I have a woman and four kids but I can't contribute shit to the household. How do you think it makes me feel to see bills come up in here late and to hear you arguing with bill collectors trying to make arrangements? Hell, Monica, I have a brand-new baby, the son I always wanted, and I haven't been able to give him shit, nothing."

"Sharief—you still don't have to drink so much."

"Monica, I'm good. With the shit I got going on, I need me a drink right now. And I would like to spend some time with my son."

Monica handed him the baby and watched Sharief place Jeremiah on his shoulder. Immediately Jeremiah started crying. "Sharief, give him back," Monica said, holding her hands out.

"No," he said sternly, "I'm his father and he needs to get to know me. All you do is carry him around. Your tittie stays in his mouth enough. It's time for him to share the wealth." Sharief slapped Monica on the ass. "He'll be okay, Monica."

She did her best to swallow what Sharief said and walked upstairs. She washed her hair, took a bath, and ended up falling asleep in the tub, only to wake up to Jeremiah screaming at the top of his lungs. She jumped out the tub, wrapped a towel around her, and ran down the stairs. When she looked to see what was wrong with her baby, Kai had him laying faceup on her lap while she tried to feed him with her baby doll's plastic bottle. Monica rushed toward Kai and took the baby from her; instantly he stopped crying. She looked around the room for Sharief and spotted him lying on the floor asleep, with a beer next to him. Monica kicked him in the shin as hard as she could.

"What the hell is wrong with you, Monica?" Sharief screamed.

"Kai had my fuckin' baby! And yo' ass lyin' up in here sleep! She could've dropped him!"

"I wasn't even sleep." He got off the floor and wiped the sides of his mouth. He took a swig of beer. "I was watching Kayla the whole time."

"Stop fucking lying!" Monica snatched Jeremiah's bottle off the table. "Kayla didn't even have the baby, it was Kai!" She stormed up the stairs and yelled over her shoulder, "Stupid motherfucker!"

"I ain't gon' be too many more ma'fuckers. And I'm gettin' a little tired of you cussin' me out!" Sharief said, following Monica up the stairs.

"Then leave!" She got to her bedroom and spun around in the doorway. "Get the fuck out my face and leave me and my child the hell alone!"

"Leave?" Sharief was stunned. "Oh, that's what this is about. You got your baby now, so I can step?"

"And take your grown-ass kids with you!" Monica stepped into her bedroom so she could change the baby's Pamper and place him in his crib.

"Well guess what?" Sharief snarled. "I ain't goin' no fuckin' where. Didn't we fight for this? You gon' see me when you go to sleep and when you wake up. You wanted me, now here the fuck I am."

"I can't do this anymore," Monica said with tears in her eyes. "I'm broke, I can't be alone with my baby, my house is always nasty, Kayla is tooooo fuckin' grown, and you are an alcoholic."

"You don't give me no pussy, what you expect me to do!"

"Pussy? As much as you fuckin' drink your dick can't get hard. Plus, I just had a baby. I ain't fuckin' you."

"Monica, you used to give me head just because I sat next to you, now I can't even get you to look at my dick."

She squinted her eyes tight. "I wish I would suck your li'l nasty dick. Fuck you!"

"Oh God!" Kayla yelled as she slammed her door. "We didn't have to break up our family for this! We could've stayed home! Shut up!"

"You see?" Monica pointed to the door. "You see? Too fuckin' grown. You better go catch her before I slap the shit out of her again."

"Don't put your hands on my child!" Sharief said, walking out toward Kayla's room. "You better not touch her!"

＊ • ＊

"WHAT THE HELL has Mommy gotten us into?" Monica stared at Jeremiah's face. If it weren't for his cocoa skin he would be the spitting image of Sharief. "Everybody hates me, you know. Everybody. I took a big chance having you . . ."

"You sure did," Starr said, walking into Monica's bedroom. She placed her purse down on Monica's dresser and said, "Let me see my grandbaby." Starr held him in her arms, and he smiled at her. Instantly her heart melted. She couldn't help but love him. She placed Jeremiah on her shoulder and looked at Monica. "You know that you have started a whole heap a shit, right?"

Monica bit the inside of her cheek and stroked her hair to the back.

"And you know that you were wrong?" Starr continued.

"But I loved him," Monica said defensively.

"No, you wanted to fuck him and went too far. He stayed here too long without his wife and y'all figured if you fucked nobody would know. But Monica, you can look at your daddy and know that whatever is done in the midnight hour will come to light by noon."

"I don't want to talk about my daddy, he has nothing to do with this!"

"Yes he does, and me too. I think that by your daddy being a married man and you knowing it, somehow I gave you permission to fuck married men. I somehow told you it was okay to mess up families and always be a thorn in their side. Well, since this is my fault," Starr said, pointing to her chest, "then I'ma tell you now. It's not okay to do that. You leave women and their husbands alone. When you find out the man is married step the hell off, 'cause in the long run you always get smacked with the dick rather than fucked with it."

"Ma—"

"I ain't finished. Now, the next thing, your sister's husband? Your sister?" She squinted, rubbing the baby's back. "You don't fuck with your sister's husband. That is a complete no-no."

"But we fell in love. It was more to it than that."

"I don't give a flying fuck! That was your sister's damn husband! Ain't no lovin' his ass. When I told you that I didn't like what was going on between you two, you should've canned it, put it away, but instead you continued to mess with him, doing whatever and never thinking of your sister. Let me tell you something, Monica, when that big-dick niggah is long gone and layin' it on some other ho, having babies with her, Celeste will still be your sister."

"Well, Ma, my baby is already here. What do you want me to do?"

"I want you to make peace with yourself so when this baby starts asking why are his cousins also his sisters you can explain it to him."

"Ma." Monica started to cry. "Do you still love me?"

"Me loving you ain't the issue. I'm ya mama, nobody will love you like I do. But your sister is a different story." Starr looked around. "You need to clean up, this house is a mess."

"Ma, I just need a break." Monica shook her head.

"Well, it's nine o'clock. Call up Listra or one of your other girl-friends and go out for a little while. I wanna spend some time with my grandbabies, anyway. Don't worry, I'll stay here until they fall asleep."

"Thank you, Ma." Monica kissed her on the forehead. "I love you too."

She pulled her hair to the back and placed it in a curly Afro ponytail. She placed big silver hoop earrings in her ears, slipped on a tight denim dress with a fringed bottom hem, put on her red patent-leather stilettos, and stepped out the door. For the first time in a long time, even if she didn't feel it, she was fierce. Monica didn't know where she was going or who she was going with but knew she was going somewhere, even if she had to do it alone.

As she got in her car she pulled out her cell phone and called Listra. "Hey, gurl!" Monica said, excited, as Listra answered the phone.

"Hey, Monica! How are you?"

"I'm fine. You haven't been by to see your godson."

"I know, girl, but the truth is I can't stand Sharief and I can't be around him."

"But you don't have to talk to him."

"Monica, what de hell? Gurl, I'm not comin' no place that man payin' bills and be vexed with him, I can stay home for dat."

"Look, I don't want to get into it with you, I'm calling so we can hang out. I'm dressed and ready to go."

"You wanna bust a lime now?" Listra said, surprised.

"Yes, come on out."

"I can't gurl. I got de worst cramps in de world. I can't drink nuthin', I'm sorry, baby gurl."

"Damn. All right, I understand."

"Will you and Jeremiah come see me tomorrow?" Listra asked.

"Yeah."

"Good. Look, I'll call you at home later on or if I feel better I'll make an exception and ride by. Maybe we can hang out then."

• • •

MONICA SAT WITH tears in her eyes, determined not to go back in the house. She couldn't believe this is what her life had come to. She couldn't take it and she didn't want it anymore. *I can't deal with this right now,* she thought as she placed her car in gear and took off. By the time she stopped driving she was pulling into a parking lot and walking across the street to the Cherry Lounge.

As soon as she walked in, she noticed the men. *Goddamn, look at these men in here. One thing's for sure,* she thought as she sat down at the bar, *that ma'fuckin' Sharief knows he cleans up rather well.* As Monica went to order her drink, she noticed that the bartender was setting an empty shot glass in front of her.

"My friend over there," he said, pointing, "would like to say hello."

Monica looked up and the guy waved. He was average looking, nothing to write home about, but Monica appreciated the drink and the attention. He walked over and extended his hand. "Milton," he said. As she shook his hand, she noticed a thin gold band on his left hand. He caught her looking and smiled. "Don't worry about that, what's your name?"

"Well it damn sure ain't Desperate, Need to Be Fucked, or Chick on the Side."

"Excuse me?"

"I don't need to excuse you, your wife does. Now beat it, I have enough problems." Monica was pissed. She got up from the bar and headed toward the dance floor. As soon as the club song "One Night Love Affair" came on, she started gettin' her groove on.

Monica stayed in the club for a few hours then headed home. By the time she got there, she noticed that her mother's car was gone. She hoped that Jeremiah was still sleeping peacefully.

"Where the fuck you been?" Sharief yelled as soon as she walked in the door.

Although he scared her she still tried to ignore him. He spun her around. "I asked you a question. Where the fuck you been?"

"I was out with Listra."

"Stop lying," he pointed in her face, "because that nontalkin' bitch was over here looking for you, so how did you go out with her?"

"I hooked up with her after that."

"What time?"

"At ten thirty."

"Stop lying, she came by here at eleven." Sharief got into Monica's face and pinned her against the wall. She could smell the alcohol on his breath. "You were out with some niggah?"

"Get out my face."

"Answer me!"

"Get the fuck out my face!" she screamed.

He grabbed her roughly by the chin. "Answer me."

"And if I was?"

"I'll kick your fuckin' ass, you cheatin' on me?"

"Fuck you."

"Fuck me! Since when I get left at home alone with the goddamn kids in this nasty-ass house while you go fuck some niggah?"

"Why I gotta be fuckin' somebody?"

"You ain't fuckin' me!"

"I don't wanna fuck you! How about that?" She pushed him in the center of his chest. "I don't want you no more. Don't you see I fucked up my family to be with you. I fucked over my sister to be with you and what the fuck are you? Some drunk-ass, unemployed nothing with kids that get on my damn nerves! I need you to leave. I don't want to work at this. I don't want nothing for Jeremiah! I have to get away from you, because I feel like I'm in a battle."

"So you want me to step? Where the fuck am I supposed to go?"

"Find someplace, besides a liquor store, you drunk motherfucker! You have a mother, go stay with her. But you have to leave here. I want your shit packed and you gone. I can't do this anymore." She started to cry. "Please. Please leave. I'm begging you to go."

Sharief kicked over the wicker truck and threw a chair across the room. "I don't believe this!"

"Stop it!" Monica screamed. "Stop it." She slid down the wall, tears pouring from her eyes. The kids ran to the top of the stairs and watched as Sharief tore up the living room and Monica cried, begging him to leave.

"Daddy!" Kai yelled. "What you doin'? If Aunty wants you to leave, why don't you just go? Maybe then we can find my mommy."

As if Kai had said the magic words, Sharief stopped instantly and turned to Monica. "You know I love you." He chuckled slightly, tears racing down his cheeks. "I love you so much that I didn't give a fuck about nothing and nobody and now look at this. Look at this." He wiped his eyes and looked at Monica. "Me and my kids'll be gone in the morning. I won't say good-bye, because we've already said that."

Monica wiped the tears that covered her face. "And don't wake me when you leave." She walked up the stairs and went to bed.

(Imani)

"WHERE YOU WANT us to go, Tasha?" Imani said, watching Sabrena roll a blunt as she, Tasha, and Quiana sat around Sabrena's living room. The music was blasting and Tasha was trying to talk the girls into going to a club over in Jersey.

"Come on, y'all," Tasha said, "I heard the Arena is supposed to be fiyyah."

"I'll pass," Imani said, "but look, I wanna tell y'all something."

"What?"

"I've been thinking about enrolling in this X-ray technician program. It'll be like going to school and having a job at the same time. The program is out of the hospital and I'll be working at the hospital during the day and going to school at night."

"I could see the school part, 'cause you is smart," Quiana said. "Remember you used to write them poems and shit?"

"But a job?" Sabrena said as she finished packing the blunt. "You don't need no job, Christmas done passed already."

"God-Lee, y'all," Tasha said, "maybe it's somebody birthday."

"No, that ain't it." Imani sighed. "It's just time to get off the stoop smoking weed. And I want a career. My face is healed, thank

God, and my cast came off yesterday. Plus, I can't stay another day with my mother and this nonsingin'-ass Redtonio Brown and his Jammin' for Jesus clique. You know they tryin' to get a recording contract. I told my mother his Top Ten days are over."

"Get the fuck outta here." Sabrena went to pass Imani the blunt. "Jammin' for Jesus?"

"Naw, I'm good." Imani said refusing the smoke. "But y'all, you should hear 'em." She laughed. "They be in the basement doing the remix to Terror Squad's 'Lean Back.' "

The girls almost choked off the weed smoke, they were laughing so hard. "Tell me—tell," Quiana coughed out, "how that shit go."

"Damn, Quiana," Imani said, "you spittin' and shit. But look, the remix goes like this, *'Lean back—lean back—lean back for Jesus He comin' through . . .'* Then Roxanne jumps out—she took Jimmy's spot." Imani stood up, laughing so hard she was crying. "And Roxanne says, *'R to easy Jesus ain't greasy.'* Girl, me and Jamal be on the floor."

"That's is funny as hell." Tasha wiped her eyes. "Now tell us, wassup with Kree?"

"I can't even lie, I love that niggah, but I have to get my life together. And I swear to you I haven't even fucked him in months."

"What? No dick in months and you still breathing?" Sabrena took a pull of the blunt. "Busting a nut is like oxygen for me."

Imani laughed. "The next time I fuck him I wanna be able to offer more than a big butt and a smile. But all I want is a career and a spot for me and my baby right now. I was thinking about moving uptown; there's a new building on Hundred Forty-second and Covenant."

The girls all looked at one another. Tasha put the blunt out. "Imani, you done fucked up my high."

"Why you say that?"

"Don't pay Tasha no mind," Sabrena said. "You know she gon' rep for the BK till the end."

"And you know this," Tasha said.

"They take Section Eight?" Quiana asked.

"Yeah," Imani said, "I would just have to contribute two hundred dollars more to the rent every month."

They all cracked up laughing.

"Yo, you crazy, to be paying shit extra," Sabrena said.

"It's just two hundred dollars."

"Yeah," Tasha said, "but it's far as hell."

"No it's not, it's just a train ride away," Imani assured them.

"You ain't gon' be hangin' out with us no more?" Sabrena asked. "What, you gon' be reppin' with an Uptown crew?"

"Look, y'all my niggahs and we down like four flats. Ain't no replacing that. I just don't wanna sit on the porch and smoke weed every day."

"Yeah, I feel you," Tasha said.

Just then Imani's cell phone started ringing. She wasn't going to answer because the person was calling from a blocked number but she did anyway. "Hello?"

"Imani, this Shante."

"Oh God no! Shante, sweetie," Imani said condescendingly, "why are you calling me? What do you want? Is Walik outta jail, y'all having another kid? You want me to drop the charges, if so then no. I'm not. As a matter of fact the state picked them up."

"No, Walik ain't outta jail." Shante sucked her teeth. "His PD is tryna get him to cop a plea anyway. So I'm not calling for any of that." Shante sucked her teeth again. "And I'm not calling to argue. All I wanna know is this, did you know that Walik had another baby?"

"A what?" Imani couldn't believe it. "A who?"

"A baby, by this chick named Lizette. I just had a fight with her the other day because she came outside talkin' a buncha smack about Walik was her baby father and a buncha ra-ra and shit."

"How old is the baby?"

"About six months."

"Well hell, don't be mad, welcome her to the club, let her know the rules, get y'all visiting days straight, and keep it movin'. Shit, either go hard or go home. Tell that bitch to play her position."

"Oh, you tryna be funny?"

"Shante, leave me outta that bullshit. I don't give a damn and don't call me no more." Imani hung up.

"What happened?" Sabrena asked.

"Shante come calling me."

"Oh, do we need to put up the hands?" Tasha asked. "You wanna go bust her ass?"

"Naw, fuck her!" Imani waved her hand. "But listen." She stood up and stretched. Reaching for her DKNY peacoat, she went on, "I'll get up with y'all later, I need to go past the hospital to see when I'll be able to start classes."

"You really going, huh?" Sabrena asked.

"Yeah. It's time for a change." Imani hugged her girls and kissed them on the cheeks. "Ai'ight, mamas, catch y'all later."

＊　•　＊

"KREE," IMANI SAID sitting on the edge of the full-sized bed that she shared with Jamal at Starr's house, "have you ever been scared?"

Kree sat on the floor, as Red walked by every five minutes looking in and out of Imani's room to make sure that Imani was the only one seated on the bed and that the door stayed open. Kree shook his head and laughed as Red passed by for the third time. Imani mushed Kree playfully in the back of his neck. "Are you listening to me?"

"What, baby?" He turned to face her. "I'm sorry, what'd you say?"

"I asked have you ever been scared?"

"Hell yeah, of different things, why?"

"Ever been scared that you were going to start something and then somehow not complete it? Or that you were going to make big plans to be something and it not happen?"

"Sometimes. Why?"

"Because I feel scared as hell. Like everything is new to me. I'm used to sitting in the living room, being at Sabrena's or Tasha's or Quiana's, or sitting on the stoop smoking weed, going to the club, fighting with Walik, chasing behind Walik, beating Shante's ass 'cause of Walik, and talking shit. I ain't never just chilled. And ever since I came out the hospital, I've been feeling like, *Imani, that niggah could've killed you, yo what you really doing?*"

"So what are you going to do about that?"

"Well . . . I didn't want to tell you in case I got stupid."

"What?" Kree didn't know what to expect; he was just praying it had nothing to with her having feelings for Walik. Kree hadn't placed any pressure on Imani, but he wanted to be with her. It was something about her that he loved and was willing to accept, as long as she stepped up to the plate . . . and then there was Jamal, who had become like his son. He still took him shopping, he picked him up from school, and every Thursday afternoon they went and got their hair braided together. One thing Kree was sure about was if nobody else loved him, he had a little boy who loved him unconditionally. "Yo," he curled his lips, "don't tell me nothing crazy, Imani."

"Crazy?" She frowned. "No. I don't think it's crazy."

"Then what?"

"I enrolled in an X-ray technician program. One where I work at the hospital for four hours during the day and go to school for four hours in the afternoon."

"Say word." Kree smiled.

"Word." Imani blushed. "And I'll be finished in six months. Then I'll be employed at the hospital full time."

"Jamal must not know."

"Why?"

"Because that's my ma'fuckin' man and if he knew, he would've told me. Damn, I'm proud of you, baby, but what's to be scared about?"

"What if I get tired of working or I just don't want to do it anymore?"

"Imani." Kree grabbed her hands just as Red walked by and cleared his throat. "You have to believe in yourself and be determined. I told you before that you needed to find something that you liked and that you wanted to do. It's about growing up and maturing."

"It's something else."

"What?"

"I put in an application at this building in Harlem for an apartment."

"Harlem? What happened to Brooklyn in the house?"

"Yo." She smiled. "I'm not about reppin' for no boroughs anymore, I have to be about what's best for me and my son. And I want my independence back. I love my mother and Red but I cannot live with them. Mama Byrd shittin' on the porta-potty all over the house, all this music playing, and Red's ass practicing dance steps and shit in the middle of the night, it just ain't gon' cut it, baby. I got to go."

"Well damn," Red said as he passed Imani's door, "the homeless is awfully choosy."

Kree laughed. "I can understand you wanting your own place." He peeked out the door and Red said, "I'm still here." Imani rolled her eyes and Kree smiled. "Look," Kree went on, whispering, "maybe I can get some pussy now."

Imani placed her arms around Kree's neck. "Oh you want some? You want some pussy or you want some head?"

"Both. And I wanna taste you again." As Kree placed his lips against Imani's, Jamal ran in the room and jumped on his back. "This a jack, niggah, gimme your candy!"

Kree quickly kissed Imani and let Jamal place him in a pretend choke hold. "Awwwl, man," Kree screamed, "where'd you come from?"

"Me and Mama-Starr just came back from the store. Now be

quiet, this is a jack!" Jamal pulled Kree to the floor as Kree fell out laughing. "Oh you laughing, punk?" Jamal said. He playfully punched Kree in the head. "Imani—get him."

"Get him, Jamal?" Imani asked, ready to attack.

"Jack 'im!" Jamal shouted.

Imani got off the bed and started moving from side to side like a sumo wrestler, then without warning she playfully pounced on top of Kree as Jamal had him in a choke hold. "Uhmm, take that!" She tickled Kree in the stomach. "Take that, punk!"

"Oh, I'ma punk?" Kree said. He was laughing so hard that tears were coming from his eyes. "Oh, I'ma punk? Jamal, Jamal," he said, "remember you gon' want that new Madden game, remember who gon' play it with you."

Jamal loosened his grip on Kree's neck. "Ai'ight, ai'ight. You're right, you're right. You wanna get her?" Jamal asked.

"You talkin' about me?" Imani couldn't believe it.

"Who else?" Kree and Jamal turned the tables and jumped Imani. Kree started tickling her and Jamal took the palms of his hands and played in Imani's hair, causing her micro braids to fly all over.

Imani swept them out of her face. "Okay, okay I give up. I give up."

"You give up?" Kree asked.

"I give up," Imani said as Jamal continued to mess in her hair.

"You give up?" Kree asked again.

"Yes." She laughed.

"Well, who you give in to?"

"You. But what y'all beating me up for?" She laughed as Jamal took her braids and tossed them back into her face.

"Because we love you," Kree said seriously.

Imani brushed her braids out of her face and suddenly her grin was replaced by a serious look. "We love you too," she said. "We really do."

{ Celeste }

CELESTE LISTENED TO *The Miseducation of Lauryn Hill* CD as she nervously drove up the highway. She took one last puff off her cigarette and plucked it out the window, slowly releasing the smoke behind it. She felt cold and turned up the heat. The winter frost had taken over, and after all winter in New York was colder than most places.

As Celeste exited the Manhattan Bridge and entered Brooklyn, she knew there was no turning back. Besides, she was done with counterfeiting reality. Now was the time to welcome the difference in bullshit being real but not being defining.

She parked on the corner of Monica's block and walked up the street. She felt as if her tight, fitted Seven jeans held her together. She straightened the collar on her purple cowhide sweater and matching jacket. Her signature Coach purse was tucked snugly under her right arm and her red curls were wild and free. She took one last breath and rang Monica's bell.

Monica had just laid Jeremiah down and prayed that whoever was ringing the bell wasn't Sharief. She hadn't heard from him in almost a month and that was the way she needed it to be, to keep her feelings intact and not worry about sympathy and desperation getting together and disguising themselves as true love.

Monica looked around the living room and was pleased to see her house was clean. The bell rang again.

Once Monica saw it was Celeste, she opened the door. She and Celeste stared at each other for a moment. Monica's eyes admired her sister's beauty while Celeste tried her best to block Monica's out—that way her mind could resist comparing—but she couldn't help noticing that Monica was no longer pregnant. Trying to keep herself from wondering about the baby she said, "I just came to get *my* children."

Monica stood speechless. Without warning, tears came to her eyes and she started crying.

"What are you crying for?" Celeste asked. "Did something happen to my children?" She peeked around Monica and looked into the living room. "Where are they?"

Monica wiped her eyes. "They're not here. I'm sorry, Celeste." She bit hard on her bottom lip.

"Where are my children?" Celeste started to panic.

"With Sharief. They all live with his mother, including Sharief. Celeste, I really want to apologize," Monica said.

"For what? Did the sober representative leave and you found out that *yo' man* was a drunk, or was it the desk duty that killed it?"

"He was suspended without pay for the bogus charges you pressed against him."

"I see. Y'all didn't have any money." She chuckled. "Well, touché. Oh and another thing, don't tell me what the hell my charges were. 'Cause technically I should've pressed assault charges on you too."

"Me?"

"Weren't you his co-defendant? Didn't you help him to assault me?"

Monica held her head down. "I really want to apologize for what I did."

"You can look at me," Celeste said. "You looked me dead in the eyes when you told me that my husband was *yo' man.* And what are you apologizing for?" Celeste squinted. "You had a baby, didn't you?"

"Yes. A boy, Jeremiah."

"You named him Jeremiah? That's the name Sharief and I were supposed to name our son . . . Well hell"—she tapped her index finger against her full lips—"that makes the shit even worse, doesn't it? From what I can see, Sharief always wanted a son, you always wanted a baby, yet you're apologizing? Are you apologizing for having your baby?"

"No—I love my baby," Monica said defensively.

"Then what are you apologizing for?"

"Don't make me rehash it."

"Look"—Celeste cleared her throat—"you're not apologetic. Sorry, yes, triflin', yes, apologetic, no. I looked at you and Sharief and I studied your vibe around him and the way you looked at him. You loved him and you didn't give a fuck about me, my marriage, or my feelings. I am struggling right now not to tell you that I hate you. That I resent you. And I'm struggling even more not to love you and want to see my nephew. My heart tells me that you're my sister but my mind figures what fuck does that mean if there are no boundaries? Truth be told, I can't stand you, but I love you. But right now I don't want a happily-ever-after ending with you because that's bullshit. Therefore, your tears mean nothing to me. I have a life to live and taking on the burden of your apology only causes me grief." Celeste turned around and walked off the porch. She got in her car and headed for Queens to pick up her children.

Once Celeste arrived in Queens she spotted Sharief and the girls getting out of Sharief's truck. Kayla noticed her right away. She ran to her mother and hugged her tight. Kai and Kori followed suit.

"Mommy," Kayla cried, "I have missed you so much. I thought I would be mad when I saw you but I love you."

"Yeah, Mommy," Kai said, "I'm ready roll up outta here."

"Let me go get my things right now," Kori insisted. "I'll be right back."

Sharief stood back and watched the girls hug their mother and at that moment, he realized that he'd missed Celeste. He wasn't in love with her, but he'd thought about her and wondered how things could have turned out differently.

"Celeste," he said walking over to her, "you look wonderful."

"Thank you." She forced a smile, trying her best to look him in the eyes and not feel anything. "I'm not here for a long conversation and if you want to apologize, save it. I don't want to hear it."

Kori came back with a teddy bear and a small radio. "I'm ready," she said, tapping Celeste on the leg. "We ain't got much. Daddy and Aunty Monica stayed broke."

"Kori"—Sharief looked down at her—"where are you going?"

"With me," Celeste said, "I came to get my children."

"Yeah," he said sarcastically, "and take care of 'em with my money."

"Oh please," Celeste smirked, "you got off light. I officially dropped the charges so smile and shut up about it."

"I'm not trying to argue with you, Celeste."

"Then good, don't. Where are their things?"

"You don't have a place to stay."

"Excuse me, but is that a question or a statement?"

"Well, do you?" he asked.

"Let me make this clear to you. I am no longer depending on you for shit. I'll be staying with my mother tonight. And just so you know, I took the time I needed to collect myself and now I have a new place to live; the closing for our house was yesterday. And I'll be moving into my new house . . . in Atlanta . . . tomorrow."

"Whoa-whoa-whoa, wait a minute. What?"

"You heard me. I sold the house and my children and I are moving."

Sharief couldn't believe it. "That house belonged to both of us, so how did you sell it?"

"Sharief, you're not stupid. The house was in my name, what'd you expect me to do? Now look, like I said, I'm moving to Atlanta." Celeste felt tears starting to flood her eyes, but she was determined not to cry. "And I really would ask you not to give me any problems. I don't want to keep your children away from you, I just need to go someplace and live my life. New York and New Jersey have too many memories, too many things that I'm tired of. I don't have a job yet, but I'll find one, I have enough money from the sale of the house to take care of me and my children for a while."

"You don't know anybody in Atlanta."

"Hell, I didn't know you and we were married. Besides, I have a friend there."

"A *friend*?"

"I can't have friends?"

"A man?" Sharief frowned.

"You have a lot of damn nerve. Didn't you just get finished playing house with my sister? Get the hell out my face talking stupid!"

"Celeste," Sharief said, practically begging, "can I please say one thing to you?"

"No. Come on, girls," she said. "Let's go."

{ Imani }

"WHY DID YOU insist we come over here, Kree? What, you got tired of Red?" Imani chuckled while looking around Kree's studio apartment. "This is a mess." Kree had the epitome of a bachelor pad: an abundance of clothes strewn on his black futon, a couch, two candleholders on the wall, a fully equipped and computerized CD player, mountains of CDs, along with state-of-the-art engineering and DJ'ing equipment. In addition, next to his refrigerator was a poster of Bob Marley with a blunt in his mouth and smoke rising from his lips, and on the back of his front door was a Puerto Rican flag.

Kree lit the candles and cut the lights off. "Don't talk about my spot." He sat on the couch and motioned for Imani to come over. "This is the secret Bat Cave, so be quiet. Not everybody gets up in this piece. So don't look at the mess, look at me." He grabbed Imani by one of the belt loops in her tight and fitted jeans and pulled her toward him. "I spent this afternoon at your mom's already, now I wanna spend the night here . . . with you. We need some time alone."

"Why?"

"Why?" Kree lifted Imani's shirt and massaged her waist. "Because we're grown and the last time we fucked was too long ago. *And* something tells me that out of that 'I'm scared' conversation we had, you left out being scared of me." He took his tongue and licked in and out of her belly button. "True story?"

"True story." She sat down on his lap and straddled him.

"Why we keep playing around?" He kissed her on the neck. "You ain't ready for me?"

"I don't know."

Instantly Kree stopped kissing her. "You don't know?" He didn't want to show his disappointment over Imani's unexpected answer. "Wassup with that?"

"Kree, there's no greater feeling than being with you. But yo, for real I'm scared as hell. I loved Walik hard. I mean hard as hell and now I'm looking at you going, *I feel like I could love this niggah even more,* what the hell is wrong with this picture? So yes, I am . . . scared of that. The last thing I need is my heart killed . . . again."

"You think I'ma kill your heart?"

"I don't know but I keep worrying that if my heart dies, then how am I going to revive myself? I can't deal with no more Shantes." She rolled her eyes. "Not having to put up with that bullshit is like being able to breathe fresh air. Truth be told, I just don't want any more ex-factors, that shit is like a tug-of-war, he is pushing, I'm pulling. We both end up scared. I can't be in love and always in some shit. That mix doesn't turn me on. I am not drama chasing anymore. I just wanna chilled-out love. My heart is all I have and believe me, love is one niggah that I can't seem to trust."

"I love you, Imani, and I have no intentions of hurting you. But if you feel like you still wanna be with Walik then I'll step."

"How did you get me wanting to be with Walik out of that?" she asked with her eyebrows raised. "I love you, I wanna be with you, I'm just scared. Fuck Walik, if I never see him again it'll be too soon." She brushed Kree across the lips with a kiss.

"Imani," he said, responding to her kiss, "I just don't wanna play any games, and I don't wanna set myself up to be a part of no rebound shit. This is about me, you, and Jamal. And on my word, I can't see past you and I don't want to."

"Are you sure?" she pressed.

"Yes," he assured her. "Now stand up."

Kree picked up the remote control to his CD player and turned it on. Instantly LSG's "My Body" filled the room. "Take off your clothes," he said softly.

"Kree . . . ," Imani whined.

"Don't be shy."

Slowly Imani started unbuttoning her blouse, revealing her creamy cocoa skin. Once her pants and panties were off, Kree started kissing her on the stomach, leaving the trail of his wet lips from her belly down to her sweetness, where he softly pulled a few of her pubic hairs through his teeth. Imani felt herself getting weak.

"Keep standing," Kree demanded. He started massaging her clit. "I wanna watch your face while you cum all over my hands." Taking his left hand, he slipped two of his fingers into her wetness, easing them back and forth in her warm flesh. Then with his right hand he started massaging her clit in a circular motion. Imani pressed her top teeth into her bottom lip and closed her eyes.

"Open your eyes and look at me," Kree said as he continued to create an erupting volcano between her thighs. Imani opened her eyes, but squinted tightly. The orgasm she felt building up was like no other. His fingertips continued to seduce her pussy to drench his hands. Imani felt a hurricane rumbling in the pit of her belly as the nut started to release, easing its way from the top of her head to the bottom of her feet . . .

"You want me to be your man?" Kree asked Imani, after she came, dripping cum between his fingers. He licked her pussy-made candy from them and pulled her on top of him.

"Yes. I want you to be my man."

"I'ma love the hell outta you," he said.

"You promise?"

"I do."

"And I'ma love the hell outta you," she said, now on top of him, "right after this."

"Right after what?"

"Right after," she smiled, "I fuck the shit outta you."

TIRED OF WATCHING the cars pass by and listening to the wind whistle across the stoop, Sharief decided that not only had he stayed away long enough, but he'd been sitting in his car for way too long wondering when the right time would come for him to ring the bell. The embarrassment of being a drunk and a failure started to flood him as he exited his car, but this was something that he had to do. No matter the ending with Monica, he couldn't help his love for her. Yet he wasn't there to try to win her back. He was there to smooth the situation because he needed to see his son and he knew he couldn't go another day without him.

Sharief ran his right hand over his lips and rang the bell. Suddenly his gun holster felt like it was stabbing him in the hip. He knew it had to be his nerves that heightened the sensitivity in his skin. He cleared his throat and rang the bell once more.

"Uhmm," Listra said as she opened the door. She sucked her teeth and started filing her nails. "Wait, don't tell me," she blew residue from her cuticles, "you've been raised from the dead because they didn't have AA in hell?"

"Do I know you?" Sharief said sarcastically.

"Listra," Monica yelled, "who are you talking to?" Monica stood at the top of the stairs and saw Sharief standing at the door. Feelings that she swore had been washed in the sea of memories covered her body, causing her to become nervous. She looked down at her clothes and remembered that she looked exquisite in her sleeveless sky-blue cocktail gown and matching stilettos. Then she remembered that she no longer had to impress Sharief.

"Ask him what he wants," she yelled.

Listra started filing her nails again. "She said, what de ras clot you want?"

"I came to see my son," Sharief responded.

"Monica, gurl," Listra yelled, "he suddenly remembered he had a son!"

Instead of responding, Monica stormed down the stairs. Standing beside Listra, she noticed that Sharief wore beige pleated and cuffed dress pants with a lavender rayon shirt and matching square-toed gators. His Kangol snap cap was cocked to the side, his beard was laid, his skin was smooth, and his eyes were clear and no longer red from drinking every day. He was beautiful, but now that Monica knew his beauty had many complicated layers to it, she didn't feel her clit jump or her heart get out and take over her speech.

"Hey," Sharief said, "how are you?"

"Cold standing at the door," she responded.

"You want to step . . . inside?" he asked.

"I do. Good-bye." She turned to leave, and Listra prepared to close the door.

He grabbed her by the arm. "I love you and I'm sorry."

"What?"

"I love you and I'm sorry. I needed to tell you that."

"Don't do this, Sharief." She was begging her eyes not to release the tears.

Listra was pissed. "Look, I'm going into the kitchen," she said.

"Yeah, you do that," Sharief snapped.

330 • Tu-Shonda L. Whitaker

"Monica." Listra rolled her eyes. "Call me when you've taken the trash out."

"Monica." Sharief stepped inside as Monica held her hand out in an *after-you* fashion. "Just hear me out." He continued, "I am in love with you, but I know that we're no good together and besides our son, and the sex, I can't remember anything worth saving other than our friendship. I fucked up, in more ways than one, and I'm sorry. All I want now is to be a father to my baby. I need him and he needs me. I know that you and I are through and I'm strong enough to place my love for you in perspective, but don't deny me my child."

Monica looked at Sharief's face and studied his eyes—the same eyes that Jeremiah had. "That's really sweet," she blew him off, "but don't try and make me feel guilty because the abortion that you wanted me to have has come to life and is suddenly the son you've always wanted." Monica placed her hand on the knob. "Red is having a CD-release party at the Hilton. Listra is babysitting and I have to go."

"I know about the party," Sharief said, picking up Jeremiah from his swing and kissing him all over his face. "Kayla called me and told me. Of course she called asking for some money."

"Well, I know that answer was no," Monica snapped.

"Damn, you cuttin' a niggah deep." Sharief smirked. "Just so you know, I'm working now. I got my job back—"

"Thanks for telling me, now I can file for child support."

"I'll take care of my son, don't worry. And I want you to know that I'm off desk duty, and I attend AA every Wednesday night. I have a little studio apartment in the Bronx and now that I have my son back in my life I'm good."

Monica raised her eyebrows, one arching higher than the other, "Your son . . . back in your life. You think you gon' be coming over here because suddenly you're not drunk anymore? Negro, please. How about this: even when you were sober, you were confused, I was confused, and together we were fucked up! And I don't want you back."

"You don't mean that." Sharief placed Jeremiah back in his swing and walked up close to Monica.

"Yes I do. I tore up my family to be with you and all I got was sheer agony. I would love to see you change . . . but with somebody else. Now, you can see your son anytime you would like, but just remember that being in a relationship with me is not a part of that equation." Monica opened the door and motioned Sharief to leave. "If you will excuse me, I have to get going."

[Imani]

IMANI WAS RUNNING late from her X-ray technician program. She'd hopped on the train bound for Brooklyn before she remembered that she and Jamal had recently moved to their new apartment uptown, so she jumped off the train, ran across the street, and caught the A train going in the opposite direction.

By the time she walked in her front door, Kree was straightening out Jamal's tie. Jamal and Kree had on the same black Sean John walking suit with the long jacket and tailor-made dress pants. Their hair was braided the same way, and Imani knew instantly from the smirks on their faces that they were pissed with her.

"Before y'all start complaining I ran late because I hopped on the wrong train."

"Uhmm-hmm," Jamal said, "sure you did."

"Be quiet, Jamal." Imani laughed.

She walked over and gave both of her men a kiss on the lips. Then she dropped her bags from work on the couch and flew in the bathroom to take a quick shower.

Ten minutes later she was in her bedroom getting dressed. And a few minutes after that she was in the living room ready to go. She was dressed in a tight and fitted black tube-top gown. Kree looked Imani up and down and was happy that he was her man. "Damn, ma," he said, "you look so good you make a niggah wanna do a remix of fine."

Jamal slid across the hard wooden floor in front of Kree, picked up the remote control, and started rapping: *This is the remix, R to the easy Imani ain't greasy.*

"Lean back, lean back for my Imani she comin' through," Kree said, joining Jamal.

"Red gon' kick y'all asses!" Imani laughed. "You know that's his shit." Before Imani could go on, her phone rang.

"I'll get it," Kree said.

"You have a collect call from—" the recorded operator said.

"Her baby daddy motherfucker!" Walik spat.

"If you wish to accept," the operator continued, "press two. If you wish to decline please hang up."

"Imani," Kree said, tossing her the cordless phone, "ya baby daddy on the phone."

"How he get this number, Imani?" Jamal asked. "Tell 'im you ain't beat, Imani."

Kree and Jamal stared at Imani as she pressed 2. "Yes," she said.

"This Walik, boo. I miss you."

"Are you crazy?" Imani asked, turning her back to Kree and Jamal.

"What the hell you mean am I crazy?" Walik asked. "I'm doing three-to-five for arson and assault over you."

"So what the hell you callin' me for? What, you need some cookies, some cigarettes, some socks? Niggah, get you some Vaseline so you can be ready for one of them punks to dick you in the ass and get the fuck off my line."

"Who you talkin' to, Imani?" Walik couldn't believe it.

"Do you understand the words that are comin' outta my mouth?"

334 • Tu-Shonda L. Whitaker

"So after all we been through, after ten years and a son, you ain't down for a niggah no more? I'm not fuckin' with Shante no more. Imani, if I be faithful will you take me back?"

"No, niggah. I got a man." Imani turned and looked at Kree. "You could hit the hustler's lotto and I still wouldn't want you."

"You forgot to tell him you ain't beat," Jamal whispered.

"And by the way, I ain't beat! Now press that fuckin' bunk and don't call me no more!" She slammed the phone down.

"Now." Imani looked at Kree and Jamal. "Let's go."

{ Celeste }

CELESTE WAS DRESSED in a glued-tight sleeveless silver cocktail gown that fell to her ankles with slits around the bottom. Her chiffon scarf was thrown loosely around her neck as she strutted her stuff with a wrapped red box topped by a white bow. Although Myles was her escort, Celeste made it perfectly clear to him that he wasn't her man and that she wouldn't be ready to commit anytime soon.

Myles held on to her arm as he wore his double-breasted tuxedo and the girls walked in front of them in their off-white lace dresses. Each of them walked into the party as if they were running for political office.

The music from the *Jammin' for Jesus* CD was blasting. Balloons floated everywhere, streamers were all over the place, and several reporters were snapping pictures.

It may have only been a month since Celeste moved to Atlanta, but she felt refreshed. Yet there was one last thing that she needed to do.

"Celeste! Celeste!" Imani said, excited, running over and hugging her. "I'm sooo happy to see you." Imani looked at Myles, who stood next to Celeste and smiled. *Who is this?* she thought.

Kayla, Kai, and Kori kissed Imani on the cheek and ran across the room toward Starr and Red, who were arguing with Red's aunt Sistah and cousin Lula-Baby. "I could've tolerated you drinking Thunderbird," Red said, "and you playing spades, and yelling 'my book,' but the pickled pig's feet and apple vinegar has got to come off the table."

"Y'all gon' stain the folks' linen tablecloths," Starr insisted. Lula-Baby got up from the table and tapped the butler on the shoulder. "You got any foil paper? I need to wrap this." She pointed to her plate.

"Hold ya roll now, Lula-Baby." Red turned to his cousin. "Don't be asking people for aluminum foil, you can't take the people's china to go. Come on now, Lula. Damn."

* • *

ACROSS THE ROOM Celeste introduced Myles to Imani: "This is a friend of mine, Myles. Myles, this is my sister. The safe one."

"Imani." He extended his hand. "How are you?"

"I'm fine, thank you . . . Can I speak to you for a minute, Celeste?" Imani asked, smiling at Myles.

Celeste said, "Excuse us one minute, Myles."

"No problem. I'll wait here for you."

Imani and Celeste stepped a short distance away. "Celeste." Imani felt a little awkward with what she was about to say, but she believed she didn't have a choice. "I know that we haven't always gotten along and for the most part we didn't speak, but you are my sister and I love you. And what Monica and Sharief did to you wasn't right and I told Monica that. I really did."

"Get outta here." Celeste couldn't believe it. "I thought you saw Monica as the great black hope."

"Now, don't get it twisted, that's my sister and I love her dearly, and she has always been there for me, but wrong is wrong and you're my sister too."

"Well, thank you, Imani."

"Do you think you'll ever speak to her again?" Imani asked.

"I've spoken my peace."

"But Celeste, there's Jeremiah, and he's innocent in all of this."

"He's not my innocence, Imani. He's my husband's guilt. Listen, I know you mean well, but don't worry about it, I'm only here for a short time today and then I'm leaving. I don't have to deal with it."

Starr walked over and interrupted their conversation; she had a local journalist who was interviewing and photographing Red and his family in tow. "This is a reporter," Starr said to Celeste and Imani. "He's interviewing the wives of the rich and famous—well, in my case, the famous. Now smile for the camera." Imani and Celeste quickly posed.

"Thank you, Mrs. Brown," the reporter said, walking away.

Starr spotted Monica as soon as she walked in the door. As Monica walked toward them, Celeste walked away.

"Monica," Starr said once she was standing next to them, "I expect you to speak to your sister." And she walked away.

Monica and Imani walked toward Celeste, who was introducing Mama Byrd, Buttah, and Roxanne to Myles. "You into the family thang?" Mama Byrd asked.

"Excuse me?" Myles was confused.

"Do you date a bitch's cousin, her mother, her stepfather's mother, her sister?"

"No." Myles felt a little embarrassed, but Celeste had already explained to him that Mama Byrd was senile. "I don't do things like that."

"Oh." Mama Byrd winked at Celeste. "Don't believe the hype. He'll be the one to get with Imani."

"Mama Byrd, hush," Buttah said.

"Don't tell me to hush, bitch! I don't care what you say, De-aunt and De-uncle ain't Jimmy's kids."

"It's De-niece and De-nephew, and they is his kids!" Buttah screamed.

"Whatever they name is, they ain't Jimmy's."

"If you don't mind me interrupting," Monica said, "I just wanted to say hi, Celeste."

"Awwl shit," Mama Byrd laughed, "it's on."

"Mama Byrd!" Roxanne said. "Don't start no trouble."

"Shut up, chicken wing!" Mama Byrd saw Sharief walk in the door. "There go y'all's baby daddy." She pointed. "He look good than a ma'fucker too."

Kai, Kayla, and Kori spotted Sharief as he walked in. "Daddy, Daddy." They hugged him tightly.

"Mommy said she got a gift for you, Daddy," Kai whispered.

"Yeah, Daddy," Kori said, "I saw her wrap it this morning while Myles was driving."

"Myles?" Sharief said.

"Yup, that's her new boo. He's really nice," Kayla insisted. "But Mommy said that he will not be living with us because she has to get life right for the four of us, without a man."

"Yeah, Daddy," Kai said, "Mommy said the only man she wants in our house all the time is Jesus and the one who delivers your child-support checks."

"Is that so?" Sharief looked up and spotted Celeste. "Daddy will be right back." Walking toward Celeste, he couldn't help but notice Myles. He nodded and extended a hand. "Sharief."

"Myles."

"Nice to meet you. My daughters were just telling me some good things about you," Sharief said.

"Oh yeah," Myles said reluctantly, "they're good kids."

"Thank you."

"Sharief," Celeste said, excited, "I have something for you.

Something I should've given you awhile back. Myles, sweetie, hand me that red box in my bag, please."

Myles handed Celeste the box, and she and Sharief stepped away from the small crowd that surrounded them.

"Look, Celeste, before you go off, I need you to hear this," Sharief said.

"What is it?" she snapped.

"Please, just hear me out. I know you don't want my apologies but I owe you a thousand. You don't have to accept them, you don't even have to own them, but I owe them to you. I know that I hurt you and I need you to know that I always loved you. And what I did wasn't right, I know it wasn't. And all I can simply say is that I wish I had done things differently."

Celeste blinked. "You fucked me over and you think because you lay some sappy-ass apology on me, I should jump up and down and feel wonderful? All those sleepless nights I begged and I asked you if were you cheating on me."

"Celeste—"

"Don't *Celeste* me. You cheated on me with a mistress that will never go away and now, after you've lived with your mistress, had the son you've always wanted, and the shit didn't work out, you want to apologize to me? When did you feel apologetic? Before or after the shit fell apart? You can't do shit for my pain but get the fuck out of my face. I had feelings and you spat on 'em. And you know what, I'm not exactly over that. And I don't have to be. So this is it, I wanna end this. There's no restrictions on you seeing your children or the time that you spend with them, but when you do come or you call for them, make it your business not to say shit to me."

"Damn, it's like that?" Sharief couldn't believe it.

"Pretty much . . . now take this." She shoved the red box in his hand.

As he took the lid off, she lit a cigarette.

"What are these?" he asked.

"You've officially been served." Celeste took a drag. She called Myles and the girls over. "It's time na roll!" As they prepared to walk out the door, she turned again to Sharief and said, "Just so you know, I've highlighted the dotted line for you to sign."

[Starr]

"WELL, I REALLY don't know how I made it this far," Starr said, sipping on a glass of Chardonnay. It was her fifty-fifth birthday and it had been a year since she and her daughters were all together, so she told them that since fifty-five was the new thirty-five, she was giving herself a party in celebration of her youth— and she expected the three of them to attend.

"You don't know how you made it this far?" Mama Byrd said, looking confused. "Didn't you walk down the stairs and flop ya fat ass to the table? Didn't you just get finished eatin'? Oh, now I get it, since all the food is gone you can't remember shit? Ain't this 'bout a bitch and they say I'm senile."

"Be quiet," Buttah said, "just hush."

"You be quiet." Mama Byrd squinted. "And I don't give a damn what you say, them is not Jimmy kids."

"They is Jimmy kids! De-niece and De-nephew is Jimmy kids!"

"Shut up lyin'! You worked roots on Jimmy."

"I did not, Jimmy loved me!" Buttah screamed.

"I swear," Mama Byrd said, pulling her bottom lip down and packing it with snuff, "you gon' bust hell wide open. You know them ain't Jimmy kids. Not De-niece, De-aunt, De-uncle, De-mama, or De-daddy! Ain't none of them cockeyed bitches kin to Jimmy."

"Buttah, don't say nothin' else, please," Starr said, placing her glass of wine on the table and slicing a piece of her birthday cake. "Just give it up. If she don't wanna claim De-niece and De-nephew, just fuck it, give it up."

"But them is Jimmy kids, Starr," Buttah said. "You know they is."

"I know, but it's my birthday." Starr wiped a string of chocolate icing from the knife and sucked it off her fingertip. "So let's not argue tonight." She turned to her daughters, who all sat quietly at her dining room table amid the multicolored streamers, confetti, and red and white balloons. "Y'all just gon' sit here all night staring at me, huh?"

"Truth be told," Mama Byrd said, "they can't help but stare at you. You big as a bear sittin' in that chair. And I don't know about them but you is all in my eyesight. Hell, anybody that step in this room can't help but stare at you."

"We gon' ignore her," Starr said.

Imani looked down at her left hand and stared at the blue streaks running through her pear-shaped diamond engagement ring. She cleared her throat. "Damn," she said, "this *is* Mommy's birthday, and y'all act like we're in recovery. *Hello my name is Imani . . . and I'm sick of y'all shit.*" She pointed at Monica and Celeste.

"Welcome, Imani." Starr stuffed a piece of cake in her mouth. "My name is Starr and I'm sick of their shit too."

"Welcome, Starr." Imani nodded. "Keep coming back, Starr. They gon' either go hard or go home."

"Don't say that," Celeste said, taking a pull off her cigarette. She crossed her legs, stroked the short curls in her hair, and folded her arms across her chest. She'd lost close to fifty pounds, and her breasts were no longer as voluptuous as they'd once been. But her thighs were still thick, which was the way she wanted them. "The last time I heard 'go hard or go home' was from Kayla's triflin'-ass daddy."

"I would've cussed him out," Monica said, almost in a whisper, feeling unsure if she should speak about any of Celeste's men or not. She took a sip of wine and blew the Shirley Temple curls that fell in her face away from her eyes.

"Men can say some shit," Imani said, "that can rock the pit of your belly and have you feeling like you about to die."

"Yeah," Mama Byrd said, "reminds me of the way milk hits the bottom of my stomach. I'm tellin' you, it gets in there and it gets to churnin' and to bubblin' and then it starts to boilin'. And the next thing I know I'm fartin' my ass off."

"Oh my Jesus!" Buttah said. "What does that have to do with men?"

"Buttah," Starr snapped, "what did I tell you? Anyway, what I was going to say was, when men cuss us out and treat us like shit our biggest problem, as women, is that we take it." She took a sip of wine. "Now, say we don't. All of us here know we done been cussed out a time or two."

"Humph," Celeste said, taking a long drag off her cigarette. "And on top of it all, the niggah do us wrong and we don't want him to leave, so we fake forgiveness."

"Uhmm-hmm," Monica agreed.

"And they still," Celeste went on, "run right to the next bitch."

"Or ya sister," Mama Byrd interrupted. "It ain't been that long ago, don't forget that."

Celeste ignored her. "And we sit at home crying, confused, and fucking ourselves with a beaver dildo, sucking our own titties and shit."

"I will kick yo' ass discussin' my business!" Mama Byrd yelled, standing up. "All in my damn sex life. I gotta good mind to tear yo' damn mouth out! Tell somebody else that I be suckin' my own titties."

"That's why they sag like that?" Buttah asked. "That's some nasty shit."

"Oh, now you wanna come for me?" Mama Byrd said, reaching for Buttah.

"Sit down, Mama Byrd!" Starr yelled. "Right now!"

"Why you yellin', baby?" Mama Byrd asked, looking around. "You mind if I sit down? I just got out of church and figured I would stop by."

"Oh Lord." Imani sighed. "Now, Celeste, what did you say about faking forgiveness?" Imani batted her eyes. "I'm surprised that you even know how to do that. I have never known you to act like you forgave anybody."

"Excuse you?" Celeste said. "Everybody can't be as talented as you in the fake-forgiveness-of-a-dirty-niggah-department. 'Cause we all know that you ride or die, or better yet, ride and crash. Walik has been doggin' yo ass just about the entire time I've been knowing you and I'm your sister. And every time Walik goes to jail he begs you to take him back. And you do, so it seems you fake forgiveness very well. As a matter of fact, isn't Walik in jail? So I guess you'll be giving Kree his engagement ring back?"

"Oh I know you ain't talking to me, trick. I'm the one who felt sorry for yo' ass but in a minute I'ma rethink my sympathy."

"Whatever." Celeste frowned.

"Whatever?" Imani couldn't believe it. "You just one bitter bitch."

"You know what," Monica said, getting out of her chair, "I think this is my cue to leave."

"Why?" Celeste asked. "Who are you running from, me? I live in Atlanta, honey. I'm only here on a miserable-ass visit, you don't have to leave." She mashed her cigarette in the ashtray. "But before you do, I just have one thing to ask you."

"What?" Monica threw her shawl over her shoulders.

"Are you still fucking him?"

"Boom—chaka-laka-boom! Duck, the bomb just went off."
Mama Byrd laughed.

"Didn't no bomb just go off," Monica said, grabbing her purse.
" 'Cause I'm leaving."

"No, I need to know," Celeste said. "Are you still fucking him?
And don't lie, and don't dress it up. And don't try to be concerned
about my feelings. Just answer the question."

"I'm not answering that." Monica shook her head. "I'm not re-
hashing it."

"I don't want to rehash it, I want to get over it, but I need to
know, are you still fucking him?"

Monica was silent.

"Answer me, dammit!" Celeste screamed, pounding her fist
into the table. "Answer me!"

"Sit down, Monica," Starr said. "Celeste put the shit out there,
answer the question, you owe her that much."

Monica stood still.

"You fucked my husband, had a baby with him, and a year later
you still can't look at me and speak to me like a woman!" Celeste
screamed. "This shit is real, it happened, and I want to know if
you're still fucking him! Did you know that my anniversary has
been replaced by your son's birthday? Do you know that it's taking everything in me to not jump up and beat yo' ass? Everything
inside of me is playing referee and you can't sit down and answer
my question? So I'ma ask you again. Are you fucking him?"

"You want the truth?" Monica turned to face Celeste.

"Every bit of it."

Monica flopped down in the chair. "I promised myself that I
wouldn't fuck him."

"But you did."

"I almost did. I got *this* close to letting my confusion and hard-
to-let-go-of love for this man take me to a whole 'nother place."

"And what happened?" Celeste pressed.

"Jeremiah started crying and I looked at his father's face and remembered that I didn't want my belly to be in knots anymore, I didn't want to always feel like I wore a sign that read, FUCKED MY SISTER'S HUSBAND SO DON'T TRUST ME WITH YOUR MAN. And what's so fucked up is that just when I was getting ready to forgive myself for what I did to you, just when I was ready to let it all go, he kissed me . . . and feeling his skin against mine made me want to try, just once, with him again."

"So why didn't you?"

"Because I can't. I can't revisit that pain, that confusion, the not knowing. I don't want to be in a relationship where I have to pretend that the bad memories don't exist. And more than that, I don't want to spend the rest of my life being separated from you. I know I messed up . . . but I need you to be my sister and whatever I feel for him doesn't measure up to the pain that I have caused you."

"Damn, your speeches are good, girl." Celeste lit a cigarette, took a drag, and flicked the ashes. "Almost good enough to make me want to forgive, well scratch that, make me want to think about forgiving you."

"I can't believe you said that to me!" Monica started to cry.

"What the fuck do you keep crying for?" Imani said. "I am so sick of this shit. You know what, Celeste? Monica keeps trying and trying, but quite frankly I don't want to hear no more apologies. Fuck it. Now I'ma put the shit out there. The truth of the matter is you are nasty and have always been nasty. You say mean and hurtful things and then you think because you are fat and fuckin' miserable that people should take shit from you. Well guess what? It doesn't work that way. So you were her sister, my sister, our sister, but you have always treated us like shit."

"I have not always treated you like shit!"

"Yes you have!" Monica dried her eyes. "You have never treated us like your sisters, so get off your high horse and kill it! 'Let's see if ya rotten-ass womb makes you a baby.' Remember that shit?"

"Yeah, and?" Celeste said. "Did it?"

"You tell me. It seemed you learned the lesson the hard way."

"Monica—" Starr said, attempting to interrupt.

"Oh please," Monica continued, "don't *Monica* me. 'Cause it's not just me, it's you too!" She pointed to Starr. "You created this ex-factor bullshit. You taught us how *not* to let go. When we were kids, every time we turned around, it was man after man after man. Never once did we have anybody stay around. And the ones we liked—seemed like they left the fastest. So when we grew up and got a man of our own, we struggled to hold on to him! And now look at us. Look at us!"

"Wait a minute now," Starr said, surprised. "You can't sit back and say that I'm responsible for every fucked-up decision that you've made because I've had a lot of boyfriends."

"Ma," Celeste said, "as much as I hate to agree with Monica, we each have different fathers that we don't even know."

"Okay," Starr said, not sure how else to respond.

"Ma," Imani said, "what do you mean okay? I'm not really the one to talk . . . but how do you stop making the same mistakes? Don't get me wrong, I love Kree and I want to be with him for the rest of my life, but I'm scared. I'm scared of this love that feels right, one day feeling wrong, and how will I know when that has happened? And what will I do? I mean, how many times did I go through love feeling right with Walik and then some kind of way it turned out to be wrong."

"Then it was never love," Starr said. "You have to understand that although the way Walik treated you was messed up, you always had the choice to walk away."

"Yeah, but you have to be taught different to know different. And what I learned from you was that I needed to find a man to hold on to. That's what I learned, which is why I always chose Walik—"

"And Sharief," Celeste added.

"No matter the cost," Monica said.

"Okay." Starr swallowed hard. "I will agree that I've made some bad choices. But your problems are not all my fault."

"No, Ma," Monica responded, "they're not all your fault. We are grown now, but you damn sure laid the foundation for us not being able to tell the difference between one bad ex and the next."

"Now look, I will take responsibility for what I've created, but don't blame all of your broken hearts on me. We are women and we have to accept the past and move on. I know that I have had plenty of men, some of them I regret and some of them I don't. The truth is that every time I was with one of your fathers, I loved him. Period. There is no analyzing why, when, and how much, just know that I did. But when I left them it was because it was no longer working. That's what I was taught: if the shit doesn't work leave it alone."

"But did you think about us?" Celeste asked.

"No." Starr bit her bottom lip. "I didn't. I never thought of you as being a part of your fathers. I always thought of you, each of you, as being mine. And where I went you went and if your fathers didn't follow then so be it. And maybe that was wrong, or maybe I was running from something, I don't know. But now that I'm married and have been in the same relationship for six years I've learned that love starts with me loving me. And it's not dictated by how big my man's dick is, how great he can lick and stick, if he takes me home to meet his mother, or even how well he treats my children."

"Ma—" Celeste said.

"Let me finish. This pains me because you are my children and I see the emptiness that used to be me inside of each of you, and that's not what I want for you. I want you to know that love is not abuse, it's not cheating or having to settle. Love is unselfish, understanding, and compromising. It doesn't beat your ass because you want something different. It doesn't come to you because the one it's married to can't screw like you, and it doesn't turn away from you because you've gained a pound or two.

"Love doesn't hurt; it's what we do and the craziness we accept in the name of love that causes us pain. Now." Starr cleared her throat. "I want every woman in this room to take her past and put it in perspective. Don't let it run your life. It's a lesson in everything. So you need to figure out what your lesson is, apply it, and keep it movin'."

"That's something we may try, Ma. It may not happen all at once." Celeste glanced at Monica. "But somehow we don't have a choice."

Starr did everything she could not to cry. She sniffed and poured herself another glass of wine. She handed the bottle to Imani, who poured herself a glass, with everyone else following suit. After filling their glasses, they each held them in the air. "Here's to the abundance of shit ex-factors left us to deal with."

"Amen." They all laughed. "Amen."

"Look, I don't mean to break up ya moment," Mama Byrd said, "but speakin' of shit, anybody seen my portable toilet?"

THE EX FACTOR

Tu-Shonda L. Whitaker

A Reader's Guide

Reading Group Questions and Topics for Discussion

1. Do you think it would have made a difference to Celeste's, Monica's, and Imani's stories if the three sisters' fathers had been involved in their daughters' lives, or if the sisters had had the same father? How does the presence or absence of a father affect a woman's life?

2. Each sister had her father's last name. Do you think it was wise for Starr to give her daughters different last names? What part, if any, do you think that played in their family dynamics? If a mother has children by more than one man, whose last name should they have?

3. What responsibility, if any, do you think the sisters should take for the state of their lives? Did you have sympathy for them? How much of a factor is our parenting in terms of the adults we become?

4. Celeste and Sharief did not have a happy marriage. Would Celeste have forgiven Sharief for cheating if he had been having an affair with someone other than her sister? Is cheating ever acceptable?

5. Monica thought she couldn't have children, but then found out she was pregnant by Sharief. What are your feelings about Monica's pregnancy? What would you have done in a similar circumstance?

6. Should Starr have been more involved once she found out about Monica's affair with Sharief? How involved should a mother be in her adult children's lives?

7. Do you agree with Celeste's leaving her children with Monica and Sharief? Was this an act of revenge, or did she need to leave her children for her sanity? If you were the "other woman," would you have taken the children in?

8. Why do you think Imani kept going back to Walik? Are there reasons, other than love, for staying in a relationship?

9. Which of the characters had the greatest impact upon you?

10. Which character made the biggest change by the end of the novel?

11. Starr, Imani, Monica, and Celeste all had their ups and downs involving the men in their lives. Do you think that any of the characters in the novel were truly in love? Did anyone in the novel know or understand love? How would you define a loving relationship?

About the Author

Award-winning author TU-SHONDA L. WHITAKER has emerged on the fiction literary scene with her highly acclaimed novels *Flip Side of the Game* and *Game Over* and has contributed to the short-story collections *Cream* and *Kiss the Year Good-bye*. She received the Ella Baker and W.E.B. Du Bois International Award for Fiction Writing while serving as the editor in chief of Kean University's literary magazine. She is a social worker and lives in New Jersey with her husband and two daughters. Visit her website at www.tushonda.com.